CATCH ME TWICE

CHARMAINE PAULS

Published by Charmaine Pauls

Montpellier, 34090, France

www.charmainepauls.com

Published in France

Cover design by Simply Defined Art

(www.simplydefinedart.com)

ISBN: 978-2956103196 (eBook)

ISBN: 978-1690927884 (Print)

❀ Created with Vellum

PART I

CHAPTER 1

Kristi

The one minute, I'm enjoying my first legal drink at Roxy's Bar, and the next, my stomach drops like the Tower of Terror. Goosebumps contract my skin. My heartbeat and breathing accelerate even as trepidation paralyzes my limbs and brain. It's a strange thrill, a mixture of anxiety and anticipation.

I've frozen with the bottle tipped to my lips. Shaking off the immobile spell, I take a swallow of the bitter beer and try to blend in with the other grade twelve students. A part of me wants to run. Another, pitiful part hopes the guy who's just entered the bar will notice me.

What am I thinking? Jake Basson has never even glanced in my direction. Just because I'm clutching my first beer in my clammy hand in Rensburg's shadiest bar doesn't mean the fact will change. It doesn't make me cool, all of a sudden. I'm still the redhead with the freckles, the kid who lives with her mother in the trailer park.

He's dark and beautiful, and his father owns the brick factory that provides the rest of us with a means of living. Unlike me, Jake doesn't need a scholarship to further his education or work as a cashier at OK Bazaars to pay for his books. He has enough money and the grades to not worry about his future, but he seems like a fallen angel constantly tormented with unwanted temptation. He's broody, a genius, a god, and my secret crush since first grade.

"Kristi!" My best friend, Nancy pouts. "You're not listening to me."

"Sorry." I wipe my mouth with the back of my hand. When I pull away, a streak of lip-gloss shines on my skin. "I better go fix my face."

"Why?" She slurps her vodka and orange juice through her straw. "It's not as if you want to hook up with anyone."

Reflexively, I search Denis out in the crowd. He's lanky and his movements are awkward, as if his arms and legs are too long for his trunk, but he's stable and kind. Reliable. Good husband material, as my mom likes to remind me. He's asked me out every year since high school, and I've rejected him every time. Niceties aside, I simply can't imagine myself tangling tongues with Denis Davies.

I look back at Jake. It's wrong to compare, but I can't help it. When I think about Jake's tongue in my mouth, all the parts below my bellybutton heat. The forbidden fantasies in which he always plays the leading role pop into my head. The lustful acts are dark. I don't get turned on by gentle kisses. It's the rough against a wall, a strong hand around a fragile neck, and bold acts of dominance that work me up. I won't admit it to Nancy, who's a hardcore feminist, but I love masculine power. I admire male strength. Maybe it's because I never had a father and suffer from daddy issues. Whatever the case, sweet, obedient Denis, who'd be shocked by my sexual fantasies, can never do it for me. It's Jake's brand of maleness I crave. Britney batting her eyelashes at Jake as he strides inside is a kick back to reality. A girl like me will never have a chance with a guy like Jake. He's destined for the popular Britneys.

Witnessing him go straight for the dark-haired girl with the pretty green eyes leaves a yeasty burn in my throat. His dark jeans hugging his ass, he walks toward her with purpose and leans a palm on either side of her on the counter. The stance is a challenge. Britney doesn't shy away. She leans her elbows back on the bar, opening herself, or rather her breasts, to him. I have a good view of her face in the mirror. She's offering her own kind of challenge.

Enthralled by a game I haven't yet played, I can't tear my attention away from the scene unfolding a short distance away. Jake's gaze strays to Britney's cleavage. My cheeks burn for her sake. My reaction isn't only from self-consciousness, but also from terrifying arousal. It's that Tower of Terror reaction. You're excited to get on but scared of the ride. Jake makes me want him and afraid of wanting him at the same time. How can Britney stand there so casually while he appears to be seconds away from grabbing her?

His gaze trails up to her lips, which she licks. I've seen Jake shirtless in his rugby shorts after a match, the star of the team, and I've seen droplets roll down his happy trail at the public pool, but I've never seen him kiss a girl. Will he take his time or be rough and demanding? I've got my money on the latter, but I have to know for sure. I can add the visual to the stock of fantasies I save for touching myself in bed at night.

I'm holding my breath, biting my lip, but he doesn't lean forward and press their mouths together. He lifts his gaze higher, over the top of her head, to collide straight with mine.

The blood drops from my head to my feet. I can't read the look in his eyes, because it's the same as always—scornful—but I can guess what he must be thinking. I've been staring like a peeping tom. He must think I'm a creep. Nancy says something, but I can't hear over the buzz in my ears. I'm aware of nothing but the smirk pulling at the corner of Jake's mouth.

Hopping from the barstool, I stammer, "I'll be right back."

Nancy gestures at our drinks. "I'll guard these so no one spikes them."

I grab my bag from the counter and rush down the corridor, escaping to the ladies' room. I almost make it to the door before a tall figure cuts me off.

"Going somewhere, Kristi?"

The rough timbre of Jake's voice sends ripples of physical awareness through my body. My belly heats at how he says my name, that he actually said it. There's only one school in Rensburg. We've been in the same class for twelve years, but he's never said my name.

I try to move around him, but he blocks my path. "You haven't answered my question."

His presence is overwhelming. He's so much taller than me. He's also two years older than the rest of us in our class. Well, three years older than me, because my mom sent me to school a year too early. Jake's parents sent him one year too late. My mom says he was a clever child, but they kept him back because he had difficulty adapting socially. Then he flunked grade eight, a stupid grade to fail because the subjects aren't that complicated, but Jake was at the peak of his rebellion. He disagreed with the educational program, our teachers, and just about everything and everyone else. After he realized he wouldn't be accepted into any university with bad grades, he pulled up his socks.

That smirk again. "Kitty caught your tongue?"

The goddess of composure grants me enough use of my brain cells to give him an answer. "Ladies' room."

He glances over his shoulder at the door, as if he doubts there's a toilet. When he looks back at me, it's with too much intensity. He crosses his arms and widens his stance, taking up the entire width of the narrow corridor. It makes me nervous, but something deep inside me responds with a pang of excitement. It's the part of me that fantasizes about being held down and ravished, for a lack of a better, more modern word. Yep, I just had a mental image of being held down and fucked in a dark corridor with a dirty floor. Only Jake can do that to me.

He moves his jaw left and right as he studies me, seeming to weigh his words. "Let me buy you a drink."

I blink. "What?"

"Beer, right?"

"Excuse me?"

He gives a patient, almost-smile. "That's what you're drinking."

"Uh, yeah. I mean, no."

He seems amused. "No?"

"I don't like it very much."

"I can fix that." He takes a step forward, compressing the air between us. "Still want to use the bathroom?"

My cheeks heat. He knows the answer, that I was only using the excuse to escape. "I'm good."

"Let's go then."

His heat folds around me like a blanket of static electricity. Every hair on my body stands erect when he places his hands on my shoulders. His palms are branding irons. They scorch the naked skin under my tank top. I only recover from my stupor as he turns me toward the bar.

"Wait." I dig in my heels. Jake wants to buy me a drink? "Why?"

"We're all here to celebrate. I assume that includes you."

The last day of school, yes, but, "You're with Britney."

He lowers his head, pressing our cheeks together. His stubble pricks my jaw. His voice is low and smooth and deep and dangerous and every other delicious thing I can dream up. "I'm with no one, ginger."

"Ginger?"

"It's a compliment."

He mumbles something about fucking loving ginger as he takes my hand and pulls me back to the main room, but his words are lost in the loud flapping of wings in my chest and the noise from the partygoers.

Nancy's eyes bulge when Jake approaches with me in tow. Her gaze drops to our intertwined fingers before settling questioningly on my face. I wish I had an answer.

Jake clasps his hands around my middle and lifts me onto the bar stool. I utter a shriek when my bum collides with the seat. He grips my knees and turns me toward the counter so he can throw an arm around my back and rest a hand next to my waist on the countertop. Normally, I wouldn't tolerate being posed like a Barbie doll. It just so happens that his bossiness ignites a warm glow in my chest. He can play doll as much as he likes.

A queue of people wait to be served, but Jake intercepts Snake, the barman. "Three vodka tonics."

Snake gives us a demeaning look. "Why is it always the first thing youngsters do when they turn of legal age?"

Snake works in a drunk yard, but he acts like the holiest person alive. In his defense, he doesn't drink a drop of alcohol, and he's never missed a Sunday church service.

Jake takes a two hundred rand note from his pocket and pushes it over the counter. "Good question. Let me see. Because we can?"

"Don't be a wisecrack, Basson."

"Just do your job, Snake."

The way the barman looks at me makes me feel dirty.

"You're doing nothing wrong," Jake says in my ear.

His lips are a hairbreadth from my skin, and the air that escapes them is warm. A shiver runs down my arm. I can't believe this is happening. I can't believe Jake is buying me a drink. It helps that I feel pretty tonight in my short denim skirt, Cowboy boots, and pink top. The color goes nicely with my skin, and it softens my freckles. My hair is tied in a high ponytail, and I'm wearing only mascara and lip-gloss for a natural look. Scrap that. I wiped off the gloss. I guess I only have my eyelashes to my aesthetic advantage. Maybe I should try to bat them like Britney.

Snake places our drinks in front of us, not bothering to hide his condescending expression.

"Cheers." Jake clinks his glass against mine and takes a sip.

I pick up my glass but hesitate. I've tried a little wine before, but never strong liquor. I'm not sure the vodka is a good idea. Nancy doesn't mind. She finishes the drink she's been nursing and reaches for the cold one.

"What's wrong?" Jake asks, brushing the end of my ponytail over my shoulder. "Don't you like vodka?" The fleeting caress of his fingertips sends a ripple down my spine.

"I've never tried."

He leans closer, pressing his leg against my thigh. "Don't you like to try new things?"

My heartbeat quickens at the nuance of his seductive tone. "I'm not sure it's a good idea."

Actually, it's not. I'm ten seconds away from losing my heart, and Jake is going to some fancy financial school in Dubai at the end of the year.

I slide off my seat. The act pushes our bodies flush together. Oh, my gosh. He's hard. For a moment, I'm too shocked and stunned to move. I want to both reach out and trace the outline of his erection pressing against my stomach and flee. Fantasizing about something is one thing. Reality is quite different, and in real life my traitorous nerve fails me.

"I, um, have to go."

He wraps an arm around my waist. "Just one drink."

Pushing on his shoulders, I try to gain much-needed distance. "It's late."

"I'll walk you home before midnight."

Nancy shoots me a what's-wrong-with-you look.

"Nothing is going to happen, Kristi Pretorius." Only Jake can make my full name sound hot. "I'll take care of you." He holds me a little too tightly. "Promise."

Maybe it's those daddy issues or how badly I like the way that sounds, but I suddenly want him to take care of me. The sincere way in which he says it makes me believe him. Just like that, I fall for him. Hard. My stupid crush unfurls in my chest where the seed has been hibernating for too long, blooming into a delicate flower of one-sided love.

Crap. No, no, no. I've been keeping my infatuation under control for twelve long years, and I let it get out of hand for one drink and a sweet promise.

"Drink up, ginger."

The knowledge that nothing can come of this sobers me slightly. I may as well enjoy the moment. Taking a sip, I make a face. I can't say I'm an instant fan of vodka.

A soft laugh rumbles in his chest. "You're cute when you do that nose thing."

"What nose thing?"

His russet-colored eyes, a color Shakespeare poetically used to describe sorrow, haven't lost their broody edge, but there's a smile in them. "That thing when you wiggle your nose."

"I don't wiggle my nose."

"You do too."

"When?"

"When you can't figure out a math formula, or when Haley challenges your interpretation of a poem."

As if he's said too much, he clamps his lips together.

I'm at a loss for words that he noticed something so trivial. About *me*. Not wanting him to feel uncomfortable about a private disclosure he obviously had no intention of making, I try to lighten the moment. "Well, you have awkward habits too."

He lets go of me slightly, giving me breathing space. "Yeah?"

"You scratch your chest just here," I tap his breastbone, "when you get angry."

He lifts a brow. "Is that so?"

I turn to my friend. "Isn't it, Nancy?"

She shrugs. "I wouldn't know. I've never paid attention that closely."

No. She didn't just insinuate I pay Jake special attention. I make big eyes at her, but she only giggles.

Jake raises his glass. "To habits."

I take another sip of my drink so I can hide my embarrassment behind my glass.

"Oh, that's my song." Nancy hops off her stool and grabs our arms. "Let's go dance."

She pulls us onto the small dance floor and immediately loses herself in the music. Nancy is a great dancer. I suck at it, which is why I'm just standing watching Jake while he's watching me. We're caught in a stare-off, only it's charged with attraction instead of animosity. It's confusing and unsettling. Why talk to me tonight when he's always ignored me? Is it because I stared? Was my interest that obvious? He closes the distance until the tips of our shoes touch.

"Dance with me," he says, making it sound like an order.

My hips start to sway of their own accord as he places a hand on my waist.

His fingers tighten on my skin. "That's better."

I melt at the approval in his tone. Boy, those daddy issues are worse than I thought.

"Now drink."

I take another sip.

"Better?" he asks almost gently, his eyes glued to my lips.

"I'm getting used to the taste."

"Glad I could initiate you."

The song ends, and a slower one comes on. Denis asks Nancy to dance, his puppy eyes resting on Jake and me. Leaning my cheek against Jake's chest, I escape that sad look. I know what unrequited love feels like. I hate being the reason for Denis's pain. He'll outgrow his crush and find a good girl to marry, someone who'll return his feelings. The reasoning makes me feel better. So does the steady beat of Jake's heart under my ear. His maleness and smell envelope me. It's a smell of cheap cologne and fallen angels. His masculinity locks me in a safe bubble where everything else vanishes, even time.

At the end of the second song, my glass is empty. A sudden bout of dizziness makes me stumble as we aim for our seats. I must've drunk too fast.

Jake puts his arm around my shoulder to steady me. "Whoa. Are you all right?"

"My head's turning."

"Want to get some air?"

I nod.

He changes direction, going for the exit, but I hold him back. "I have to tell Nancy."

We find her on the dance floor, which is packed by now.

"Kristi's not feeling well," he says over the music. "I'm walking her home."

"Sure thing," she yells back, winking at me.

"Are you sure?" I ask her.

"I'll get a ride with Denis." Hugging me, she whisper-screams in my ear, "Have fun."

I cup my ear in a pointless effort to soothe my bruised eardrum. Jake takes my hand and leads me toward the back. As we reach the far side of the room, Britney steps in front of us. She looks me up and down before glaring at Jake.

"What's going on?" she asks him.

"I'm taking Kristi home, not that it's any of your business."

"Asshole."

She turns on her heel, but Jake grabs her arm.

His voice is stern, but not unkind. "I don't owe you anything."

Her kohl-rimmed eyes flare. "You asked me to the matric dance."

"I'm not your boyfriend, Britney."

"Are you dumping me for the dance?"

He glances at me. "We'll talk about that later."

"I want to know now." She stamps her foot. "Are we still going together or not?"

"Later."

The world spins a little as he drags me toward the exit. I don't resist for fear of falling on my ass.

"I'm keeping you to your promise, Jake," she calls to our backs as Jake pushes the door open with a palm and cool air rushes over me.

After the heat inside, the fresh night air is welcome, but instead of clearing my head, it makes the turning worse.

I bump against Jake. "Oops."

"Shit." He fastens his fingers on my hip. "I didn't think that drink would hit you so hard."

"I'm just a little tipsy," I say defensively, snuggling closer to him.

We're in the dark alley, next to the trashcans. Uninvited, the fantasy of earlier erupts in my mind. Maybe it's the alcohol, but my inhibitions vanish, and my nerve returns with a flare of self-confidence. I'm with the guy I've been dreaming about for twelve years, and he's finally paying me attention. He's also leaving in three months, most probably for good, but all I can focus on are the tingling of my nipples and the way my lower region pulses with need. It's an opportunity I can't waste, even if I'll regret this later when I'm alone with my unrequited love and broken heart.

Slipping out from under his hold, I walk a few steps ahead and lean against the wall.

"What are you doing?" he asks, watching me from hooded eyes.

Gathering all the courage I possess, I tell him. "Kiss me."

CHAPTER 2

*J*ake remains plastered to the spot. His tone is surprised, shocked even. "What?"

"Kiss me."

I won't live down the humiliation if he rejects me. A long moment passes before he moves in my direction, doing so slowly as if he's not sure he wants me to be his destination. A heavy dose of nervousness mixes with my excitement, but I cling to my newfound courage.

Stopping short of me, he looks down at my face. I have to crane my neck to hold his gaze, which seems serious and broodier in the streetlight. I wait, my heart about to pop like a balloon, but he doesn't act. My chest tightens until the air in my lungs is a painful bubble.

"Don't you want to?" I whisper.

"How can you even ask me that?"

"I'm not sure if that means yes or no."

"Fuck, Kristi. Of course I want to kiss you. I just didn't expect this."

"Why not?"

Again, that almost-smile. "You're a good girl."

"I'm shy, not good."

His smile vanishes. Heat darkens his eyes. My words excite him. He likes shy girls who aren't good.

Pressing a finger on my lips, he says, "Now's a good time to stop talking."

My lips rub over the calloused skin of his digit when I part them to ask, "Why?"

"It's the alcohol talking."

I have an effect on him. It's evident from his hard-on. I'm determined to get what I want. I'm also curious to explore my feminine power. Parting my lips, I suck his finger into my mouth. I've never done *the deed*, but I've watched enough porn to simulate what my teeth and tongue would do to his cock. He sucks in a breath as I work my lips around his digit. His body goes rigid and his breathing comes quicker. A stunning wildness replaces the usual broodiness in his eyes. Our gazes remain locked as I nip and suck his finger, the suggestive act making me wetter than what I already was. He lets me tease him for a while before he snaps out of it, blinking and yanking his finger from my mouth.

"Fuck," he mumbles, looking at me as if I've just arrived on Earth in a UFO.

My tone is confident and demanding, a far cry from the real me. "Hold me down and kiss me."

His nostrils flare. "What did you say?"

"I like to be restrained." In my fantasies, at least. When there's no choice, there's no guilt. "I want you to take charge."

Those are the magic words that coax him into action. He does what I request. He charges. Grabbing my wrists, he pins them next to my face against the wall. I utter a content little sigh as the backs of my hands collide with the bricks.

"Like this?" he all but growls, squeezing a little too hard.

If he's hoping to discourage me, his roughness has the opposite effect. I moan my appreciation at the pressure of his fingers around my wrists.

"Fuck, Kristi," he groans. "Fuck, fuck."

Ah, I found Jake's fetish. He likes to be bossy, and I like to be bossed around. Only by him. Only like this, when we're touching.

"Kiss me, Jake. Please."

"Do you know what you're doing? 'Cause I'm not cruel enough to let you beg again."

"I want this."

He crashes his mouth on mine, bruising my lips with his teeth. I open eagerly for more. He takes what I offer, giving me the roughness I crave in return. When the metallic taste of blood fills my mouth, we both still. I take a moment to digest the sensation and swipe my tongue over a cut on my lower lip. The simple idea that he bit me makes me crazy with want. Lifting my hips, I grind against him, silently begging for more. It's as if a thinly stretched elastic band snaps between us. The non-verbal permission makes him wilder, but he's much better at controlling his lust than me. His kiss turns tender even as his touch becomes more urgent. He lets go of my wrists to knead my breasts while planting a trail of kisses down my neck. I moan at the way he nips my shoulder, but it quickly turns into a cry when he pinches my nipples through the layers of my clothes. Despite the pain, I arch into the touch.

"Keep your hands up." He abandons my nipples to slide down my body. Crouching down, he lifts my skirt over my hips.

We're moving too fast, but I want this so much I can't even muster embarrassment when he buries his nose between my legs and inhales deeply.

Staring up at my face, he asks in a deep, low voice, "Are you wet?"

I bite my lip and nod.

His fingers dig into my hips. "I'm going to taste you."

It was a statement, not a request, but I nod my agreement again.

Despite his verbal warning, I give a little start when he yanks my panties down to my knees. I don't have time to widen my stance. He's already licking my slit from the bottom to the top. His hot, wet tongue is unlike anything I've felt. I can't prevent a tremulous mewl from escaping. When he teases my clit with the tip of his tongue, I shudder. His kisses are soft on my folds as he impatiently moves my underwear down farther, but it gets stuck on my boots.

"Fuck it," he mumbles, and then there's a tearing sound.

Oh, my gosh. He ripped off my underwear. I must be depraved for finding it hot.

"Open your legs."

He leans back, studying my exposed parts as I do so. A gush of cool air washes over my wet skin. Should I have trimmed? Never in a million years would I have expected to be in this situation tonight.

"I'm, uh, a little unprepared."

He threads his fingers through my curls and pulls gently. "You mean this?"

"I should've shaved."

"I like you fine how you are."

He drags a finger along my slit, gathering my wetness, and then he traces that same path with his tongue. This time, he applies more pressure. The onslaught of sensations has me going on tiptoes. Gripping my ass firmly, he holds me in place without interrupting his assault. His caresses are too soft to get me off, but I'm enjoying his slow exploration. I don't want to rush him. He nips and licks until I'm a sagging ragdoll against the wall, crazy with need. I want to see him naked.

"I want to taste you too."

My words are scarcely spoken when the backdoor bangs against the wall.

In a flash, he's on his feet, pulling down my skirt and covering my body with his. He presses our foreheads together, giving me a reassuring smile even as he warns me to be quiet with a soft, "Shh."

Shit. It's impossible not to see us in the streetlight. There's nothing to hide behind. I tense as I look over his shoulder. Double shit. Denis walks out, an unlit cigarette dangling from his lips. He stops short of the exit, takes a lighter from his pocket, and looks left and right as he brings a flame to the cigarette. When he spots us, he jerks a little. I suck in a breath.

"It's all right," Jake whispers, his thumbs drawing soothing circles on my hips under the skirt.

The slouch of Denis's shoulders as he recognizes us makes me cringe. Without a word, he pockets the lighter and goes back inside. The door closes quietly behind him.

"Hey." Jake's voice pulls my gaze back to his. "You're not doing anything wrong."

As if to drive his point home, he reaches between my legs and dips a finger inside. The pleasure is instant. Just like that, I'm hurled back into the moment with him. Fresh flames consume me. I reach for his pants. I want this. Who better than Jake to be my first?

I manage to release the button of his waistband through the buttonhole without fumbling. When I reach for his fly, he grabs my wrist.

"Hands above your head, ginger."

I obey immediately. My head reels as Jake finishes the task of unzipping his jeans and pulling out his cock. I still want to taste him, but he spears his hardness between my thighs, dragging the head through my wetness. I only had a second to look, but I can feel how big he is. Our naked lower bodies pressed together are enough to make me crazy with want. Lust takes over my reason. I shiver with need. From the way he rubs his cock faster between my legs, we're both out of control. I need him inside me. All of him. It feels as if I'd die if he doesn't fill me.

He grinds his groin against mine. "Show me your tits."

It's a command, but I don't lower my arms. I know instinctively he'll execute it. Lifting my top over my breasts, he flips down the cups of my bra. My nipples extend to aching tips in the cooler temperature of the night.

He inhales sharply. "You're perfect. Even more than I imagined."

I moan, feeling decadently wicked so exposed and spread against the wall. "I want you."

"You'll get it," he says, cupping my cheek. "I'm going to come all over these pretty tits."

"Inside me."

He stills. After a short hesitation, he says, "I don't have a condom."

That hesitation meant he considered it. It was just for a moment, but he thought about it. He wants it as much as I do.

I roll my hips, rubbing my clit over his erection. "I'm clean."

"I don't doubt that." The hesitation stretches longer this time. "Are you on the pill?"

"No, but I've had my period not so long ago."

"How long?"

"A week." Or was it two? "Just over a week."

"How long, Kristi?"

I'm irregular. I can't remember exactly. It was just after our first exam. That must make it almost two weeks. "Ten days."

He puts our foreheads together while he covers my breasts with his hands and asks in a gruff voice, "Do you know what you're asking me?"

"To fuck me bareback."

His fingers clench on my curves at my words. His grip isn't painful, but the firm touch sends more moisture to my slit.

He hisses as his cock slides through the lubrication. "Are you sure?"

This isn't a decision we should be making in a back alley, and certainly not with our bodies full of vodka, but I only have this one shot with Jake. If I don't take it, I'll regret it for the rest of my life. I'll always wonder what it would've been like to have hot, forbidden alley sex with my secret crush.

It takes a second to make up my mind. "Do it."

The corner of his mouth lifts. "Giving me orders?"

"Scared to obey?"

"You have no fucking idea."

"If you need me to push you against the wall and call the shots, I could."

He narrows his eyes. I crossed a line. I feel the consequences on my nipple as he flicks it with his nail.

"Ouch," I cry out, covering my breast, but I like the bite of pain. Maybe too much.

"Hands above your head."

Abandoning my sore nipple, I raise my arms.

"Who's in control?" he asks.

"You are."

A sharp bolt of pain shoots through my other nipple. He flicked me again. "Ow! What was that for?"

"Just making sure you understand how this is going to work."

He lowers his head and sucks my aching nipple into his mouth. The hotness of his tongue soothes away the hurt as he laps gently, but it also makes the need between my legs unbearable.

"I need—" I break off the sentence as he bites down softly.

He lifts his head and gazes deep into my eyes. "I know what you need." Folding his fingers around my wrists, he pins them to the wall.

"Oh, my gosh. Yes."

His stubble grates over my skin as he drags his lips to the arch of my shoulder. "You need it rough, don't you?"

"Yes," I say on a sigh, shocking myself. It's the first time I'm admitting it out loud.

The broad head of his cock nudges my entrance. It feels so good, my eyes drift closed. We're both sleek from my arousal. A shift of his hips, and he'll slide in easily. Yet, he keeps still. I tilt my pelvis forward, trying to take him inside, but he pulls beyond my reach.

"Please, Jake."

"If you want to back out, now's the time."

"I don't."

"Do you know what you're doing?"

"Yes," I whisper.

"Look at me."

Opening my eyes, I find his sober gaze staring down at me.

"Tell me," he insists, "so I know you understand."

"You're going to push your cock into me as deep as it'll go and come inside."

He pinches his eyes shut for a second as a tremor runs over him. When he looks back at me, his expression is conflicted. "The way you say things. Kristi, I—"

"Shut up and do it," I say before he can deny me.

"Fuck it."

With a single, hard thrust, he tears into me, taking all of me in one go. The stretch is not what I expected. It burns. My breath catches in my throat. A silent gasp turns into a loud whimper as he pulls almost all the way out and impales me again. It feels as if he's splitting me in two with the thick invasion between my legs. The pain is exquisite. I can't help the scream that tears from my chest as he repeats the grueling action. My wrists burn where his nails bite into my skin. Instead of dampening my arousal, the pain makes me want more.

He pulls out to hover at my entrance, teasing me with cruel anticipation. When he slams up, using his hips to aid the action, I let out a wail. Gripping both wrists in one hand, he clamps the other over my mouth, muffling my sounds, and makes use of my forced silence to pummel me hard with his hips. Rough is what I asked for. Hard is what I wanted, but this is almost too much. My naked back scrapes over the raw bricks as his thrusting forces my body up and down the wall while I scream into his hand. I need to touch my clit. I try to pull a hand free, but his grasp becomes like a vice. He fucks me without reprieve until his face shines with perspiration, and then he suddenly stops.

"Too tight," he says through clenched teeth, giving his head a small shake. Droplets of sweat fall like glass splinters around his face in the streetlight. "Need a moment."

Comprehension dawns. He doesn't want to come yet. Neither do I, but I'm not sure for how long I'll be able to endure his punishing strokes. I want to tell him to finish, and at the same time, I'm not ready to be left empty.

Laughter suddenly sounds from behind the closed door. The voices turn louder. People are on their way to the exit. Shit. Jake is buried balls-deep in my body with his jeans around his ankles, seconds away from ejaculating.

His cock jerks inside me as he gives a start. "Fuck."

At the same time his hand closes more firmly over my mouth, he takes me harder and faster, racing toward the finish line while the talking gets nearer. Letting go of my wrists, he pushes a hand between our bodies to rub my clit. It's what I need to finish with him, but I can't get off with those voices just on the other side of the door, sounding as if their owners are about to exit.

"Come, Kristi."

I try, but the moment is gone. I can't focus on anything other than when that door is going to open. A grimace contorts Jake's face. He clenches his jaw. His whole body pulls tight. Warmth fills my channel. It's comforting until the burn sets in, which tells me he tore me inside. He shoves twice more before he stills. His reprieve only lasts a second. In the next, he pulls out and drags my skirt over my hips to cover my naked lower body. A gush of slick runs between my legs. Perversely, I mourn the loss. Squeezing my thighs together, I try to stop the spillage, but there's too much. It dribbles down my inner thighs as Jake adjusts my bra and top. I'm a quivering mess, needier than before we've started, but unable to move as he pulls up his jeans and shoves his softening cock back into his briefs. He's still zipping up his jeans when Snake and one of the cleaners exit, carrying trash bags.

They're deep in conversation, not noticing us until they reach the trashcans, and then Snake stops in his tracks. "Kristi, is that you?"

"Fuck," Jake mumbles under his breath, still sheltering me with his body.

"You all right?" Snake asks.

"Uh, yes." I clear my throat, forcing myself to stand on my wobbly legs. "Perfect."

Snake takes a step toward us. "You sure?"

"She said she's fine," Jake snaps. He puts an arm around me and pulls me to his side. "We're leaving."

"You take her straight home now, you hear?" Snake says.

Jake leads me from the alley into the main street. At this hour, it's thankfully deserted. I don't need a mirror to know in what state I am. Anyone who looks at me will know what we've done. Despite his wealthy father, Jake doesn't have a car. Hendrik Basson keeps a tight fist on his money when it comes to luxuries. He told Nancy's mom he doesn't mind paying for Jake's education, but he believes Jake has to earn everything else by himself. Jake delivered newspapers from eighth grade to buy himself a bicycle.

"You all right?" Jake asks.

"Yes."

It's a half-truth. My body feels battered, and the ache between my legs won't stop. I'm sticky and sore, but need still throbs in my core despite the fact that Snake's untimely appearance killed our lust-filled craze.

The temperature must've dropped more. I shiver against Jake's side, but it's more from the aftereffect of the sex than the cold. Rubbing my arm, he pulls me closer. We don't talk on the long walk back to the trailer park. Jake has gone from bossy and hot to tense and withdrawn, and I'm too strung out to make sense of the

23

warring emotions in my chest. I'm both proud that I did it, with Jake no less, and sad knowing nothing can come of tonight. It doesn't help that I still feel out of sorts from the alcoholic buzz in my veins.

In front of our trailer, he turns me to face him. "Want me to come inside?"

With my mom there? "I'm good."

"Okay." He looks at me for a long moment. "It was great."

I'm not sure I agree. It started out good, but it went kind of wrong in the end with Snake and his colleague barging in on us.

His eyes widen slightly. "You're not regretting it, are you?"

"Of course not." Never. I go on tiptoes to kiss his lips. "Thank you."

He hovers, seeming uncertain, which is a new look on Jake Basson.

"Do you *want* to come in? It's not that I don't want to invite you, but it's late and, well..." I have an open relationship with my mom, but this will be too awkward.

He glances over my shoulder at the trailer. "I understand."

There are many things I want to ask, but all of them will scare Jake away. Will I see him again? Will he remember me when he leaves for Dubai? Will he visit me when he comes home for the holidays? Instead of expressing what's on my mind, I give him the easy way out by getting the key from its hiding place in the bird feeder.

He walks to the end of the pathway that marks our small patch of garden but waits until I've closed the door behind me before taking off.

Inside, I lean against the door. I don't know if it's the physical exertion or if all first times are like this, but my body starts shaking in earnest. My mother snores softly on her single bed. Tiptoeing to my side of the trailer, I grab my toilet bag and pajamas and head for the ablution building. Under the stark glare of the tungsten light, I strip naked in front of the mirror. My body looks like a battlefield. Bruises bloom on my wrists. I'm bleeding in half-moon marks where Jake's nails cut my skin. There's a hickey on my shoulder, and my nipples are an angry red. My back is scraped from the bricks. Blood mixed with semen have dried on my thighs. I better not let my mom see the marks I bear from our sexual adventure. It looks as if I've been assaulted. It will give anyone the wrong impression.

For a fleeting moment, I consider touching my clit to make myself come and finish what Jake and I started, but it feels wrong. I don't want to spoil what we shared by coming alone. Adjusting the water in the shower stall, I quickly rinse my body and hair, wincing at the burn not only on the surface but also much deeper. For an inexplicable reason, my tears start to flow. Why am I so damn emotional? From where comes this sudden need for Jake to hold me?

After toweling myself dry, I pull on my pajamas and a sweatshirt. I can't use a hairdryer for fear of waking my mom, so I sneak back to the trailer and slip into my bed with wet hair. Turning on my side, I clutch my pillow against my chest. It's easy to relive the moment in the alley. Jake's smell, aftershave mixed with cotton and soap, is burned into my memory. The way in which he filled me makes my folds throb and swell. For the time it lasted, Jake was mine. He was my first, and no one can ever take that away from me. With that secret held close to my heart, I drift into a content, dreamless sleep.

WHEN I WAKE UP, my mother's bed is made. The blinds are open and sunlight filters through the window. I stretch like a lazy cat. I don't have to be up early for school. It's finished. I'm free. I feel like a kid on the first morning of a holiday. The feeling is tied with a pretty bow, the beautiful secret I carry in my heart. I jackknife into a sitting position as a disconcerting thought hits me. What if Jake tells everyone? What if I'm nothing but a notch on his list of alley fucks? Oh, my gosh. I hope he hasn't fucked many girls like that. I'm sure he's done it at least a couple of times before. He was too sure of what he was doing to have been a virgin.

The door opens on my smiling mom. "You're awake. Finally. How was last night?"

Pulling the long sleeves of my sweater over my wrists, I smile. "Great."

"No headache?"

"I only had a beer and vodka."

"Vodka?" She puts her toilet bag on the counter and fluffs her hair in the mirror. "You didn't have enough money for vodka."

"Jake was buying."

She turns to face me. "Jake?"

"It's doesn't mean anything."

"That boy is trouble."

"It was just a drink, Mom."

"All right," she says slowly. "There's muffins for breakfast." She straightens her uniform and grabs her bag. On the way to the door, she kisses my forehead. "See you later."

When she's gone, I dress and go to the ablution building for my grooming before having breakfast and doing my morning chores. I clean the trailer and take minced meat from the freezer compartment of our mini-fridge for dinner.

After a quick sandwich for lunch, my duties are done, and I'm surprisingly bored. The race toward the end of the school year kept me so occupied, I never thought about what I was going to do with myself once school was out forever. I call Nancy, but her phone goes straight to voicemail. She's probably sleeping off last night. I leave a message, telling her I'll be at the lake.

Taking my bicycle, I peddle down the dirt road to the small lake at the foot of the hill, not far from the brick factory. I feel my bruises in the saddle. Every time I hit a hole in the road, I wince. The lake is deserted when I get there, a nice treat. Usually, the place is packed on holidays or weekends with families having picnics and fishing. Finding a spot in the shade, I sit down on the shore and dangle my legs over the mud wall. Not far away, a sparrow is building its nest in the branches of a willow tree overhanging the water. As kids, we used to hunt the ground under the trees for their speckled eggshells that dropped from the nests when their chicks hatched. The memory puts a smile on my face. My childhood days were carefree and happy. Those days are over. Legally, I'm an adult. I have to start earning a living and leave the nest. My thoughts turn to the future and the university applications I've yet to complete when a branch snaps behind me with an ominous crack.

CHAPTER 3

Turning quickly, I survey the surroundings. I jerk when Jake appears from a dense cluster of trees. My heart starts thrumming as my head fills with vivid images of last night. I don't want to be the dork who blushes, but I can already feel the heat seeping into my cheeks.

"Hi," he says when he reaches me, searching my face.

I can't look away from those russet-brown eyes. They're brilliant in their torment, shining as if they're illuminated from the inside. "Hi."

He motions at the spot next to me. "Can I?"

I shrug. "The lake doesn't belong to me."

He sits down with one leg bent and his elbow resting on his knee. He's wearing his ripped jeans and a white T-shirt that stretches over his lean muscles. The fabric hints at the flat disks of his nipples and the contours of his abs. I look toward the lake before he notices I'm staring again. A fish breaks the surface to catch an insect, causing ripples to circle out over the brown water. It's soothingly familiar and so very unfamiliar with Jake's overbearing presence. I'm back on that Tower ride, waiting for the chair to drop and my stomach to climb up in my throat.

Hugging my knees, I keep my gaze trained on the distance. "We both had the same idea, huh?"

His head turns toward me. "What idea?"

"To come here."

"Actually, I came here looking for you. Nancy said you'd be here."

"Oh?"

Afraid of what I'd find, I don't want to look into his eyes, but I can't help their pull. When our gazes connect, I almost cower under the intensity in his. He's a mixture of sexual virility and wildness, way out of my league. Underneath the animalistic prowess flow darkness and hunger, but the most powerful undercurrent is pain. It's also the most confusing. Jake Basson has no reason to be pained. He's the most privileged kid in town. The suffering is there though, just like the danger, and the trouble my mom warned me about.

He pins me with his signature broody stare. "I came to see if you're all right."

The smile I force stretches my lips. The effort hurts my face. "Why wouldn't I be?"

His tone turns stern, angry, almost. "You didn't tell me it was your first time."

Oh, goddess of shame. From the state my body was in, I can only imagine how he knows.

Instead of sounding light like I intend, my voice comes out like a squeal. "It's no big deal."

"I disagree."

I mold my embarrassment into anger, using it like a shield to protect my feelings. "Do you have a problem with virgins?"

Eyes widening slightly, he continues to stare at me. When he finally speaks, his words are measured. "I would've done it differently."

"Differently how?"

The single word he utters is soft, infused with its meaning. "Gently."

Just like that, the anger that masks my shame dissolves. "I was the one who asked for it rough, remember?"

"Doesn't matter. You shouldn't have kept it from me."

"You didn't ask."

"I thought—" He bites his lip.

"You thought what?"

The thick layers of his dark hair ripple into a new messy pattern as he moves his head in denial. "Nothing."

Nothing, the most loaded answer in the universe. I'm not letting him get away with it. "You thought what, Jake?" When he still denies me an answer, I grab his arm and give a shake. "You thought what?"

He scans my face. "That you had experience."

"What gave you that idea?" Oh. "I suppose I acted rather boldly."

He smirks. "It wasn't that, although it's damn hot when you're so honest about what you want."

My cheeks heat again. "What, then?"

"Let it go, Kristi."

There's only one possibility left. "Who?"

"No one."

"Someone lied about fucking me. If you know, I can only assume the whole school knows, or think they know. I deserve to know who the asshole is."

He sighs. "What are you going to do about it?"

"That's for me to decide. Spill the beans, or are you on his side? What is this? Some kind of fellow fraternity where you guys protect each other so you can pretend your fuck-me-another-notch fantasies are true?"

"Calm down. I'm not on his side. On the contrary, I'm seriously considering giving him a shiner."

I make to get up. "Forget it. I don't care, anyway."

He pushes on my shoulder, forcing me to stay. "You care, or you wouldn't be upset."

"Just tell me or let me go home."

"Fucking hell, Kristi." Interlacing his fingers, he drags his hands over his head. "Denis said he popped your cherry."

"You believed him?" I exclaim.

"How was I supposed to know? The guy's had a crush on you like forever."

Unlike Jake, who only noticed me for the first time last night. I shrivel just a little under his touch. The heat of his palm on my shoulder stirs the secret memories I've locked in my heart. I don't want to let them out. It would hurt so much more if I nurture my one-sided love.

Shaking off his hand, I say, "If it makes you feel better, I'm sorry I didn't tell you."

"It doesn't."

"Are you regretting it?" I ask with my heart in my throat.

His eyes soften. "I only regret that I didn't get you off. I'll never regret that it happened."

The knot in my throat eases up a little. "Good."

"I'm going to do a number on Denis. Want to kick him in the balls? I can hold him down for you."

"No," I say quickly. "I don't want you to do anything to Denis."

"Know what will make me feel even better? Breaking a few of his ribs."

The scary part is Jake isn't joking. He means every word. I can see it in the firm set of his unsmiling lips.

"It's for me to decide how I'm going to handle it."

"Fair enough. If you change your mind, I'm at your disposal."

"I can fight my own fights."

"I don't doubt that. I still remember how Werner howled when you kicked him on the shin."

"That was in second grade, and he stole my apple."

He grins. "Yeah, well, it kind of left a mark."

Wait. He remembers that? Before I can comment, he lifts my wrist and pulls back the sleeve. The marks he left have matured. The fingerprint bruises are a deep purple, and the half-moon cuts puffy and weepy red.

"Fuck," he says under his breath.

I pull away self-consciously. "It looks worse than it feels."

"Kristi, I—"

"Don't say you're sorry." I beseech him with my eyes. "Please, Jake."

"That's the really fucking frightening thing. I'm not."

He looks at me for a long moment. We're both trapped in the truth, unable to move away from the blinding headlights speeding at us. He's right. It's dead frightening, but it's also liberating. It's beautiful in its stark, naked truth. I've never been as honest with anyone as I'm being with Jake, and I have a feeling it's mutual.

"I hurt you," he continues, hurling us farther onto a path of no return, "and I liked it. What the fuck does that say about me?"

The broody, tormented look I've always found sexy on Jake turns into something deeper. He looks nothing short of being haunted.

The need to comfort him is overpowering. The pain in his eyes isn't only melancholic in an arty, slash, alternative, slash, adolescent kind of way. It's real, and he's right. It's fucking scary.

I squeeze his hand. "There's nothing wrong with you. I like it too."

"The blood." A small shiver wracks his body. "I don't even want to think about how you must be feeling inside."

Seeing him suffering with remorse dumps a bucket of guilt on my conscience. He's right about that too. I should've told him. I lied on purpose. I didn't tell him because I didn't want him to stop. I never considered how withholding the fact that I was a virgin would affect him. In my vodka-infused haze, I never stopped to ask myself how Jake would feel at disrobing his bloodstained cock.

I dare a glance at him. He has a far-off look in his eyes, seeming to be stuck at the time when he undressed the lie of my silence.

"Jake." I nudge his shoulder to catch his attention. "I'm sorry."

"I'm a bastard."

"You're not. You gave what I asked."

He grabs me so fast, I yelp. His hand folds around my chin, his fingers digging into my cheeks, but there's no malice in his eyes. He doesn't realize the force of his touch.

"I'm not a good person." I open my mouth to contest, but he doesn't give me a chance. "You're better off staying away from me."

"Jake." I try to shake my head but he holds fast.

"You don't know the kind of thoughts that are running through my head." His gaze trails over my face, coming to a halt on my lips. They're pouted in his hold. He goes from tortured to heated in a second, all that dark pain suddenly transferred into something sexual. "You don't know half of what I want."

That's when I get scared. It's not the thrilling kind of scared from last night. It's not a fantasy of being held down or tied up. It's no longer a game. It's real and cold like the blade of a knife, parting my ribcage and cutting out everything inside. The real threat Jake holds is not physical. It's far worse. He'll cut me open and suck me dry. He'll take everything I have, and then he'll be gone.

Our gazes remain locked when he pushes me down into the dirt. The nasty, naked truth is that I want this. My fear makes me wet. This is what makes it beautiful when he yanks my sweatshirt over my head. There's no pretense. Our secret is sublime in its deviance. His roughness makes my body heat, coming alive with a pulse that beats only for him. He straddles my hips and strips my T-shirt. When my upper body is bared in nothing but my bra, he inhales sharply as he takes in the mark he left on my shoulder.

His tone is a mixture of remorse and pride. "I ruined you."

He has no idea.

Lowering his face to mine, he whispers in my ear, "And I'm going to do it again."

I turn even wetter despite the fact that it still hurts after last night. I exhale a shaky breath as he lifts himself and unties the drawstring of my sweatpants. He wastes no time in undressing me. When I'm naked, he lifts my hands above my head and spreads my legs. Then he steps back to study the way he arranged my body on the ground.

It's not Jake who cuts a path over my nakedness with a satisfied, starving gaze. It's the person he warned me about. It's the person he warned me about who unzips his jeans and takes out his cock, pumping it in his fist as he kneels between my legs. It's the person he warned me about that I welcome inside my body as he positions the head at my entrance and greedily plunges inside. With a single sweep, he owns me. The air leaves my lungs. My back arches off the ground as the dormant pain in my sensitive channel blooms to life.

"Am I hurting you?" he asks, sliding up and down over my body, his cock stroking new pain and pleasure as his shaft rubs over my clit.

The metal of his zipper scratches my inner legs, making a stark contrast with the soft cotton of his T-shirt that brushes over my chest and stomach.

"Yes," I moan.

He pulls out and plants a sweet kiss in my neck. "I'll make it better."

Pebbles and tufts of grass dig into my back and buttocks, but I can only focus on the wet heat of his mouth as he drags his lips from my collarbone down to my navel where he tickles me with his tongue before moving to my clit. I whimper when he sucks the most sensitive part of me into his mouth, flicking his tongue over the nub. His pace is unhurried. There's no backdoor that can open or people who can interrupt. I melt into the dirt with the knowledge, giving over to his wicked ministrations.

"That's it," he says against my folds, sensing the exact moment I relax.

I drift in the pleasure he gives, letting the discomfort of sharp sticks and thistle thorns add to it. In no time, my orgasm starts to build. My body bows for him, pulling into a tight arch as he drags his teeth over my clit. I dig my nails into the dirt, not bothering to lower the volume of my moan.

My arousal glistens on his chin as he lifts his head to look at me. "Are you coming?"

"Almost."

I sound as if I'm in pain, which I am if you could consider the need to come painful. He stretches out over my body, his jean-clad thighs spreading my legs wider. "I don't have a condom."

Darn it. "Seriously?"

He cocks a brow. "Contrary to what you may think, I don't walk around with a wad of rubbers in my back pocket."

It's tough buying condoms in Rensburg when premarital sex is considered the biggest sin of all, and everyone knows everyone, and the pharmacist is your father's best friend. Same goes for getting the pill. You need a doctor's prescription, and he won't give it without your parents' consent. Of course, now that I'm of legal age, I won't need my mom's consent, but I'd still have to find the money to pay for the doctor's visit. We have limited medical coverage.

"I'll pull out," he says.

As much as I want this, hovering on an orgasm I've been craving since last night, alcohol isn't dulling my reason this time. "We can't."

"Just a few strokes to get you off."

He presses his hardness against my opening, giving me a taste of how good it would feel if he penetrates me, but he doesn't push deeper. He only drags his erection over my folds and clit, up and down until I'm squirming with need.

The way in which he pets my folds with the head of his cock makes me whimper. "It's not safe."

"You said it was last night."

"Jake."

He nudges my pussy lips apart and slips in an inch. "You feel so good. I'm just going to fuck you a little."

I bite back another moan as he shoves in all the way, sending a shiver of pleasurable agony over my whole body when he hits too deep. I should push him away, but I'm too close to the release I so desperately need. Instead, I wrap my legs around him and rock my hips, inviting him deeper and harder while letting him know how much I want this with my moans.

He answers with a growling sound, reacting instantly by picking up his pace. Lifting on his arms, he stares down at my face as he keeps a perfect rhythm with his hips, slicing his cock in and out of me as if he's keeping time to a melody. His face is contorted with concentration, maybe not to come or to make me come. There are many things I can read into his expression, but tenderness isn't one of them. He reminds me of a wild animal or, right now, while he's working so hard for my climax, a sweet bad person. It's sweet of him to want to get me off first.

A drop of sweat runs down his nose and drips between my breasts. "You're so tight." He grunts but doesn't break his pace or our eye contact. "Who broke this pussy in?"

I know instinctively what he wants. The part of me that wants that too answers, "You."

"Do you know what that makes you?"

"Yours?"

Satisfaction mars his features. The broodiness, the hollowness, the pain, all of it vanishes. What's left is an animalistic desire. "Mine."

For this moment, as long as our mutual dark desire binds us in the biggest sin, as long as he's pushing me higher to a crescendo I no longer crave but need like air and water, I let it be. I become his. The blue sky with its single fuzzy cloud and the chirping of the sparrows from my childhood vanish as I become a woman in Jake's arms. Nothing else matters. If someone were to walk in on us this very instant, carrying a trash bag because trash bags belong in dirty allies, I wouldn't care. I wouldn't care that I'm lying on a bed of stones and thorns, naked with my soul exposed. I wouldn't care that they hear my screams. I'd let Jake finish me off right in front of any witness. My abandon is so huge, I disobey Jake by lifting my hands to his face. I need to hold on to him. I need to touch him when he makes me fall apart. I cup his cheeks, leaving streaks of dirt that mix with his sweat. The tender act earns me a slap on the thigh that stings my skin. I jerk in his hold at the rebuke.

"Do you make yourself come?"

"Yes," I admit. "Why?"

"I want you to come with me," he says, pivoting his hips harder. "Now."

He's close, or he wouldn't be rushing me. "I don't think I can."

He rewards my honesty with a straightforwardness that doesn't feel awkward, not with him. "How do you normally get yourself off? Tell me what you need."

"I touch my clit."

He slides a hand between our bodies and rubs a finger over the nub. "Like this?"

"Faster." I grip his wrist and move his hand to show him. "You don't have to be gentle."

Instead of massaging my clit like I expect, he pinches it hard between two fingers and pulls.

A groan tears from my chest when he starts rolling the sensitive bundle of nerves with cruel pressure.

"Like this?" he asks again.

Yes! The climax knocks my world off its axis. I'm floating. Flying. I open my mouth on a silent scream. My channel clamps down on his cock, the unrelenting spams pulling him deeper.

Tossing his head back, he grits his teeth and closes his eyes. "Ah, fuck."

The arm that keeps his weight up starts shaking. He's fighting hard not to come so I can finish my orgasm on his cock. It's heaven to be so full, to be filled with the guy of my dreams when release wracks my body, and even as I don't mean to make it harder on him, I can't help the way my body clenches around him.

"Shit." He jerks his cock free. Lifting himself higher, he points the tip toward my breasts.

I'm still dazed, riding the aftershocks of my orgasm, but the smooth, bulbous head and thick streams of cum that erupt from the slit mesmerize me. The jets land on the upper curves of my breasts. Another marks my collarbone. He groans as more warm, sticky liquid follows, and manages to aim those at my nipples. They react to the wetness, turning into hard pebbles. A shudder runs over him as he continues to empty his cock on every accessible surface of my upper body. His climax seems to last forever. I expected one or two spurts, not the unending supply of semen he milks aggressively from his shaft with a fist. Yes, I've seen porn, but Jake's cock is real, and I've never seen one looking manlier. Veins protrude on his tightly stretched skin. He's thick and long, his shaft capped by a velvety mushroom-shaped head.

Only when he's ejaculated dry, does he still. We're both battling to catch our breaths. Jake finds his first. He moves up my body to straddle my shoulders. Shit. He's still hard.

Touching his cock to my lower lip, he says, "You wanted a taste. Suck."

I open without preamble. The minute my lips part, he sinks deep. He tastes salty and tangy, a mixture of our arousals. When I gag, he pulls back a little.

"You're going to suck me off," he says. "You know why?" I can't speak with his cock shoved down my throat, but he gives me the answer. "I'm your first, Kristi. Get that? Curl your tongue. Just like that. Fuck, yeah." He moves up and down, taking my mouth with steady strokes. "I'm your first in everything."

My heart agrees. My sated body obeys gladly. My not-lucid mind is high on ecstasy. Leaning over my body, he catches his weight on his arms, using his hips to pump faster. His happy trail tickles my nose. He smells of clean sweat and dust and sex and cheap aftershave. He goes deep once more, pushing all the way to the back of my throat, and then he gives me breathing space.

"Touch my balls," he grits out.

I have to push his jeans and briefs down farther to oblige. Once I have his balls in my palm, I'm glad he told me to fondle him this way. I like how they sway when he moves, and how they contract when I drag my teeth over the head of his cock.

"Fuck, yes," he says, "Just like that."

When I scrape my teeth over the underside of his shaft, his balls draw up higher.

"Coming," he grunts.

Warm, salty liquid bursts over my tongue. It's a lot less than he spilled during the first round. It doesn't take much to swallow. Nancy says it makes her want to vomit, but I like to think I carry a part of Jake inside me now.

Pulling his flaccid cock from my lips, he presses a kiss to my mouth and flops down next to me. "That was…" He drapes an arm over his face. "Fucking amazing."

He's my first. My first in everything. I lay a palm on the cum on my chest, rubbing the slick over my heart where a disconcerting thought aches.

I shouldn't ask, but I can't help myself. "Have you done that before?"

Rolling onto his side, he faces me with a stern look. "You know the answer."

Jake doesn't belong to me. I have no reason to sulk. It doesn't mean thinking about Britney, and whoever else he's been with, hurts less.

He leans in and kisses me, a slow exploration of his tongue in my mouth that makes me taste myself on him and get lost in the moment all over again. Tomorrow is a distant concept, a faraway horizon for another day. His hands glide over my body, making a sticky mess from my breasts to my pubic bone, but that's where he stops. I guess he doesn't want to risk getting any of that sperm close to the baby factory.

While he draws lazy circles through the cum on my belly, I ask, "How many?"

He turns me roughly on my side, our noses touching. "I'm not a whore."

"I just want to know."

"Trust me, you don't."

"How do you know?"

"Because I wouldn't have wanted to if the roles were reversed."

"Why not?"

"It would make me want to kill."

I give a strained laugh. I'm only half-certain it's a joke. "Are you going to tell everyone?"

"Tell what?"

"About us."

"Is that what you think about me?"

"I don't know what to think. Until last night, you never spoke to me."

He looks up at the sky. "Storm's coming. We better get going."

He gets up, but instead of tugging his cock back into his pants, he undresses.

"What are you doing?" I ask, skimming my eyes over his naked form. He's lean and hard in all the right places.

"Get up." He offers me a hand.

I squeal when he sweeps me off my feet, lifting me into his arms. Realization only hits when he's already charging toward the lake.

"Jake, no!"

My protest is ignored as we fly through the air and tumble over the side. The cold water is a shock. Gasping, I swallow a mouthful of dirty, brown water. It feels as if I'm coughing up my insides. I push on Jake's chest for enough distance to drag air into my lungs, but he won't let me down.

"Wrap your legs around my waist," he instructs. "I'll keep you up."

"It's not deep." The water only reaches his chest. "I can stand."

"The bottom is muddy."

I continue to fight for my freedom, coughing and squirming in his arms. After another second, he lets me go. I immediately regret my decision. Yucky, slushy mud pushes between my toes. Something slimy drifts against my leg.

Yelping, I grab his shoulders and lift my legs around his waist.

His laugh is deep. "It's always better to listen to me."

"There's a reason no one swims here, you know."

"Just because no one does it doesn't mean we shouldn't."

"It's dirty. There are catfish the size of men in here."

He chuckles. "Who told you that?"

"Snake."

"Like all fishermen who never catch anything, he's a liar."

"We'll catch diseases in this water."

"I have to wash my cum off your body."

"Really?"

"Why look so surprised?"

"You acted kind of caveman back there, like you were marking me or something. I expected you'd want me to keep the souvenir."

"Yeah, I prefer you never take a bath again, but we have to be careful."

His meaning sinks in as he starts washing gently between my legs. "Oh."

Holding me up with an arm around my waist, he rinses the slick from my breasts and stomach. "What are your plans?"

My heart lurches. Is he asking me out? "I'm going home to cook dinner, and maybe I'll meet Nancy at the bar afterward."

"I meant for the future, and you're not going back to that bar."

"I'm going to apply for a scholarship to study literature at RAU, and you can't tell me what to do."

"I thought your mom told Snake they don't offer full

scholarships for literature, and you don't want to know what will happen if I find out you went back to that bar."

Jeez, for someone who never conversed a word with me before yesterday he sure listens to a lot of town gossip concerning me. "It's a partial scholarship. I'll have to supplement it with a loan. You can boss me around when we have sex, but that's where it ends, Jake Basson."

I'm flipped around so fast, I don't realize what's happening until my ass hits the soft cushion of Jake's groin and the hard length of his erection.

"You don't want to test me, Kristi."

Grabbing his wrists, I try to pull him off me, but my struggling only leads to a lot of water splashing. "What's wrong with the bar?" He goes there, for crying out loud. What is this? Double standards?

"It's not a safe place for a pretty girl. The dump is swarming with creeps. I should know."

"You're not a creep."

"Promise me."

"I'm not going to make a promise I can't keep."

His palm comes down hard on the wet flesh of my globe. It stings like a bitch. "Ow!"

"Promise me."

"Let me go."

"Say yes, and I will."

"That's blackmail," I exclaim.

"Call it what you will, Pretorius. I'm counting to three. One. Two."

Stubbornly, I keep my mouth shut.

"Three."

I'm clenching my ass, anticipating another slap, but I'm not ready for what follows. A stinging, burning pain penetrates my asshole. It comes so unexpectedly, I don't have time to scream. I only have a second to suck in a gasp of air before the sting leaves, only to be repeated. Crying out, I strain my neck to look behind me, and then I cringe in shame and shock. Jake has his finger plunged all the way to the knuckle into my ass. Oh, goddess of deviant devils. He didn't joke when he said I had no idea what he was capable of.

"Jake." His name sounds more like a mewl than a coherent word. "It hurts."

"Promise and I'll take the hurt away."

"You can't do this. It's wrong."

"Two fingers, and then you take my cock."

I'm not nearly ready for that. I'm not sure I'll ever be. "Jake, stop it."

He pulls out his forefinger and pairs it with his index digit. When he sinks both into my backside, light pops in my vision. I'm too proud to scream, but I can't stop the tears that fill my eyes or the shameful arousal that makes my folds slick all over again.

"What will it be, Kristi?"

"Yes," I say on a rush of air. "Yes, Jake."

"Yes, what?"

"I won't go back to the bar." Just make the pain stop.

"This ass is going to be mine, just like all your other firsts. Promise me."

"I–I don't know if I'll—"

"There are two choices here, ginger. Either you promise and we take it nice and slow, or I pop your anal cherry now. It'll be a first for me too. We can enjoy it together."

His fingers in my forbidden entrance hurt worse than being fucked raw for the first time with his big cock. I'll never be able to take him in my backside, but I say what he wants to make the agony stop. "I promise."

When he pulls out, I twirl in the water to face him, my chest rising and falling with indignation. I want to hurt and humiliate him just like he did to me. Without thinking, I raise my arm, but he catches my wrist before my fingers can connect with his cheek.

"Told you," he says, taunting me by holding on to my arm no matter how hard I yank to free myself.

"Told me what?" I snap.

"I'm a bastard. I'm rotten to my core."

I still at that. No matter how badass he makes himself out to be, I'm seeing a side of Jake I never knew. There's something vulnerable in the way he says it. He truly cares what I think of him.

"You behaved like a bastard. You're not rotten."

His smile is slow to come. Letting go of me, he brings his forefinger and thumb together. "I was this close from claiming your ass, and the thought is still tempting. Now tell me again I'm not rotten."

I have nothing to say to that.

He wades through the water to the side and pushes himself out, no longer considerate about my feet on the yucky bottom of the lake. At least he offers me a hand. I allow him to pull me out, suddenly shy about my naked body now that he's angry with me for something I don't understand. My body breaks out in goosebumps in the breeze. Using his T-shirt, he dries me off quickly and dresses me. All the while, I stand there like a doll. When he's pulled on his clothes, he takes my hand and leads me to where I left my bike against a tree. He holds it up for me to climb on, but I shake my head.

"I don't think I can sit in the saddle, at least not for a while."

"Can you walk?"

"Of course I can walk."

"I'll push your bike then."

"You don't have to."

He steers my bike onto the dirt track, not giving me a choice but to follow.

A little way down the road, he says, "Will you go to the matric dance with me?"

Taken aback, I stop. "I thought you asked Britney."

"I did."

"Then you should honor your promise."

"Should I?"

"It's four weeks before the dance. You can't dump her now."

"That's the difference between us, ginger. You're a good person."

"Stop insinuating you're so bad. You're acting like a victim."

A laugh rumbles from his chest as he shakes his head at me.

"What?" I ask.

"Just keep walking, Pretorius. The rain's catching up."

I look up at the sky. Thick clouds are rolling in. He picks up his pace, and I have to stretch my legs to keep up.

At my gate, he hands me the bike.

As if not knowing what to do with his empty hands, he shoves them into his back pockets. "Say you'll at least think about going to the dance with me."

"I'm not going to be the reason you drop Britney at the last minute. That'll be cruel."

"As cruel as me thinking about someone else when I'm with her?"

"Don't do that, Jake. You're leaving in three months."

"Right." He stares over my shoulder into the distance. "Will you be there, at least?"

"Of course." Without a partner. Denis asked, but it would've been equally cruel to give him hope when there's no chance of anything happening between us. With the girls outnumbering the boys with a staggering majority in our class, I'll be going without a date.

"Right," he says again. "I guess I'll see you there."

"We could, um, meet up before." Hastily, I add, "If you like."

He gives me a crooked smile. "I like, but I'm working at the factory for the next few weeks."

"Ah."

Holding out his hand, he says, "Give me your phone."

45

I fish my phone from my pocket, unlock the screen, and hand it over.

He goes to my contact list and punches in a number. "There. My number." He taps the button to dial himself. "And now I have yours," he says with a satisfied smirk, dropping the phone back into my pocket.

Turning on his heel, he saunters down the road in his tight jeans and wet T-shirt, not in the slightest concerned about the lashing thunder or imminent rain.

CHAPTER 4

$\mathcal{N}$ostalgia hits me hard in the four weeks that follow. I didn't think I'd miss school, but it'll be better once I'm at university, keeping busy with studies and making new friends. I'm torn about leaving Rensburg. A part of me is excited about exploring a big city like Johannesburg with nightclubs and restaurants, while another part is sad to leave. I love the quiet serenity and the freedom of venturing to the woods or lake. I'll miss my mom and Nancy like crazy. Nancy already got a job as a receptionist at the factory. I won't see her except for holidays.

I already miss Jake. After seeing him every day for the past twelve years, the separation feels violent, as if he's been ripped from my life by force. The sentiment only adds to my weird state of nostalgia. It leaves me feeling out of sorts, unanchored in a strange way, but I don't dare to look him up. I'm not going to run after him. If he wanted to speak to me, he would've called. Anyway, he's leaving the country. That's what I keep reminding myself. He'll be somewhere foreign with new adventures and exotic girls. I'd be naïve to think he'll remember my good old nerdish self back in a town most people don't even know exists.

For as long as I remember, Jake wanted to get away from Rensburg. Most of us are content with our lives, but Jake has always had a fire burning inside him, a restlessness that seems to drive him. While the majority of our class calls the perimeters between school and the lake home, Jake wants to explore farther borders. He's always said he wants to see the world. He's like a shooting star. The fire that drives him is so intense it makes me worry he'll burn out too fast and all that wild beauty will be gone. I suppose it's the very intensity that makes him so beautiful. It's exactly the kind of tragic-romantic sublimity that attracts a dreamer like me. Sometimes, I get the notion his is a self-destructive beauty, a comet that feeds on its tail until it extinguishes into the dark sky, until all I'll have to look back on is a cold, scientific calculation of a pinpoint location in a black night. But I don't want to think of Jake as a star. Everyone knows stars are dead or dying.

My mom finds the softest, prettiest pink fabric at the local store and makes me a strapless dress with a flowing skirt for the matric dance. It's perfect. She should've been a seamstress instead of a cleaner at the brick factory. We decide to make an outing by going to Johannesburg for the shoes, taking Nancy along. I find a pair of nude pink sandals with heels, and my mom buys me a dainty white silk lily for my hair. She works damn hard to make ends meet. The shoes are setting her back quite a bit. The fact that she pays for them so joyfully to give me a memorable evening makes me appreciate the sacrifice all the more.

Since Nancy's house is bigger, we get dressed there for the dance while my mom is having a glass of wine with Daphne and Will, Nancy's parents. My pink dress is laid out on Nancy's bed, next to her faux leather dress. It's purple and molds to her body like spandex. On anyone else, it would've looked like a cat woman costume, but with Nancy's figure and self-confidence, she pulls the look off perfectly.

I'm applying make-up in the bathroom mirror and Nancy is curling her hair when my phone pings from the bedroom with an incoming message.

"I bet that's Jake," Nancy says.

"I bet not."

"Who else would send you a text?"

"I don't want to know."

Dumping the curling thongs on the vanity, she dashes from the room.

"Don't you dare," I cry, running after her.

I try to squeeze past her through the doorframe of the bedroom, but she makes it ahead of me.

"Our dresses," I shriek as she dives for the bed.

She lands neatly in the middle, grabs my phone, and punches in my secret code.

Stopping next to the bed, I extend a hand. "Give it to me."

She rolls out of reach, her eyes fixed on the screen. "Jake says he can't wait to see what you're wearing. He wants to see it before everyone else. He wants you to send him a photo."

"He didn't say that."

She shows me the screen. "Did too."

My body answers with a flush of heat that rises from my toes to my neck as I scan over the text. Yep, what Nancy said.

Scrutinizing my pink strapless bra and matching thong, she points the phone at me. "Maybe you should send one *before* the dress."

I jump for my phone. "Don't you dare."

She giggles and scoots back. A click sounds. Oh my, gosh. She took my photo.

"Nancy, I'm serious. Give me my phone."

I chase after her around the bed, but she hops off the other side and runs out of the door before I can cut her off.

"If you send that you're dead," I cry at her back, almost

bumping into my mom who comes out of the kitchen with a glass of wine in her hand.

"What's with all the shouting and running?" my mom asks.

"Nothing," I mumble, sprinting for the bathroom, but the door shuts in my face and the lock clicks in place. Grabbing the handle, I twist it frantically. "If you send him a semi-naked photo, I'll never speak to you again."

More giggling comes from inside.

"Come on, Nancy. Open the door. We're going to be late."

"This will take just a sec," she calls.

"Nancy!"

My mom stops next to me, her expression concerned. "What's up with you girls?"

A sudden bout of dizziness overtakes me. It's so intense, I feel weak. My stomach churns and acid pushes up in my throat. Leaning against the door, I place a hand over my abdomen.

"Kristi," my mom exclaims. "What's wrong?"

"I don't feel so well." Sweat breaks out over my body and saliva pools on my tongue. "I think I'm going to be sick."

My mom pushes the back of her hand against my forehead. "Are you coming down with something?"

I drag in a breath. "It's the pizza." Daphne treated us to lunch at Pinky's. I shouldn't have had the shrimps. Nausea makes me heave. "Open the door, Nancy. I'm going to be sick. I swear, I'm not joking."

"Nancy," my mom says, her voice calm but urgent, "unlock the door, honey."

The key turns, and Nancy's face appears in the crack. She stares at me with big eyes. "Are you serious?"

I barely have time to push her away and make it to the toilet before my lunch comes up. Folding double, I empty my stomach. Acid burns my throat. Wave after wave wracks my body until I don't have the strength to stand any longer. I fall down on my knees in front of the toilet while my mom holds my hair and rubs my back, mumbling over and over, "Oh, honey, I'm sorry."

Daphne appears in the door. "What's wrong?"

"Kristi's sick," my mom says. "She thinks it's the pizza."

"Oh, no." Daphne grabs a box of tissues and hands it to me. "It must be a bug. We shared the same pizza, and Nancy and I are fine."

"You done, honey?" my mom asks.

"I think so."

I'm too weak to get up. I just want to curl up on the tiles and lie here. Taking my arm, my mom helps me to my feet and to the basin. Nancy stands to the side, looking on wide-eyed with my phone in her hand. When I've rinsed my mouth, I grip the basin for support, my shoulders turned inward. My face is a mess. Black mascara rings mar my eyes. My eye shadow is ruined and my lipstick smudged. My curls are tangled and wisps of hair stick to my sweat-drenched skin. I look like I feel. Horrible.

"Oh, no," Nancy says pitifully as she takes in my reflection.

My mom is doing what she knows best, flushing the toilet and cleaning the rim with a disinfectant wipe.

There's no way I can fix my face in time. I'll be late for the dance. I'm about to say so when another wave of nausea attacks. Rushing back to the toilet, I ruin my mom's cleaning by throwing up again. There's only bile left, but the dry heaves keep on torturing me until I'm back on my knees.

"I don't think going to the dance is a good idea," my mom says apologetically.

Everything inside me protests, not because I have the perfect dress or I've been looking forward to the end-of-school dance for twelve, long grades, but because it was my last chance to see Jake. I admit it to myself in a puddle of misery on the floor, just as I admit my mom is right when I vomit three drops of bile again.

"Shall I call the doctor?" Daphne asks.

"She doesn't have a fever," my mom says. "I'll wait it out for a couple of hours. If she doesn't get better, I'll call."

No point in calling. We can't afford the call-out fee. There's another possibility though, a possibility I can't utter until we're in the privacy of our home, a possibility that doesn't need a doctor. A possibility that terrifies me.

"I'll drive you," Daphne says.

"I'm sorry for ruining it," I say to Nancy as she hands me my phone. Since neither of us has partners, we were going to go together.

"Don't be silly. You can't help you're sick."

The worry in her eyes says she's thinking what I am. Please, goddess of mercy, let it be a bug. I'll vomit my guts out for a whole month, and I'll never eat pizza again. Anything, just don't let it be *that*.

My mother helps me into my clothes and bundles me into the back of the car while Daphne takes the wheel. She'll have just enough time to drop us before driving Nancy to the dance.

Nancy comes outside, dressed in her robe. "What about your dress?"

"We'll get it later," my mom says. "Bye, honey. I hope you enjoy the dance."

As Daphne pulls off, I type a text and send it to Nancy.

Please don't tell him.

It could be nothing. It could be a bug. Maybe the one, past sell-by date shrimp was on my slice of pizza.

At home, my mom steers me to my bed and sits down next to me with her legs folded underneath her. "Oh, Kristi." She wipes the hair from my face. "I know how disappointed you are. How about we watch a couple of movies in bed? Are you up for it, or do you just want to rest?"

Looking at my hands, I hold back the tears stinging my eyes. "I'm sorry about the dress, Mom, and the shoes."

She nudges my shoulder. "That's nothing, honey. The only thing of importance is getting better."

"Mom." My voice breaks, and I have to stop.

My mom sits up straight. "Kristi?"

I sniff. "There's something I have to tell you."

She grips my hands hard the way she does when mentally preparing herself for bad news.

Lifting my head, I finally dare to look her in the eyes. "I may not be sick as in *sick*."

She frowns, and then her face evens out with comprehension. "Do you think you're pregnant?"

My lip starts to tremble. No matter how hard I bite down, I can't stop it. "I may be."

"Oh, Kristi." She lets go of my hands to pull me into a hug.

For a long moment, she just holds me. I love her so much right now for not getting angry. I didn't know how much I needed to get the worry that's been gnawing at me off my chest.

Putting me at arm's length, she asks, "You're having sex?"

"It happened only twice."

"Unprotected?"

Fiddling with the frayed ends of my bedspread, I nod.

"I wish you told me. I would've gotten you the pill."

"We didn't exactly plan it. Plus, I was ashamed."

"You had sex. There's nothing to be ashamed about."

"I thought you'd be angry."

"Just because we live in a judgmental town doesn't mean everyone's the same. I'll never judge your actions." Her face contorts with something like guilt. "I thought you trusted me. Maybe I haven't been open enough with you."

"This isn't about you," I say gently. "I do trust you. I just didn't want to put you in a position to ask Dr. Santoni for the pill and have everyone wonder who you're sleeping with."

She sighs sympathetically. It's a heavy gesture that's meant for her as much as me. No one better than my mom can understand how I feel. She had a fling with a boy during a summer holiday and fell pregnant. The boy went home, and she had me, the usual story.

"How long ago did it happen?" she asks.

"Four weeks."

She shifts her gaze to the ceiling as she seems to do a mental calculation. "We're not going to get ahead of ourselves without knowing for sure." She gets up and pulls out the drawer under her mattress.

"What are you doing?"

Taking something from the drawer, she lifts it for me to see. A pregnancy test.

"Mom!"

"I'm a mature woman, Kristi. I have needs."

"Unprotected?" I croak. Another illegitimate child would ruin my mom. She's barely managing as it is. I can't wait to get a degree that will secure a good job. I need something that pays more than manual labor wages to help ease her burden. "Please don't tell me—"

"Only a donkey hits itself twice against the same stone," my mom says. "We're taking precautions. My period was late once, that's all."

"I was going to say please don't tell me who you're sleeping with."

"I wasn't going to."

"Your period was late once so you got two tests?"

"The double packet was on special, and you can stop putting me in front of the firing squad for something you did yourself."

"I'm not judging you. I'm just worried."

"I know." My mom holds out her hand. "Shall we find out?"

I tremble slightly as I take the comfort she offers. I want to know, but I'm scared. The short walk to the toilet has my chest heaving with anxiety. My mom explains how the test works and sends me into the toilet stall to pee on the stick.

It's the longest five minutes of my life while we wait for the verdict. Neither of us speaks. My mom only holds my hand where I sit on the counter between two basins.

She checks her watch and hands me the stick when it's time.

I shake my head. "Do you mind?"

Offering me a smile meant to encourage, she pulls off the cap. From her grim expression, I know the answer before she holds the two lines up to my face. I go colder than the tiles under my bottom. Frost creeps over my body from my toes to my ears. My heart freezes, and for a moment I'm numb.

CHAPTER 5

My mom's arms are comforting around my shoulders. She rocks me gently, just like when I sat here on the same spot with a cut on my knee from falling off my bike. I fold into myself, letting the familiar scent of her Blue Jeans deodorant soothe me into the false security of a childhood I can never have back. I've not only outgrown it, I've lost it irrevocably. The truth has my whole body shaking. I'm facing it in a cold bathroom with chipped tiles while the rest of my class is sipping punch in their evening gowns and talking about their after-school plans.

My brain races toward the implications and how they impact my future. I won't go to university. I'll get a job at the factory. I'll be a single mom, despised by the whole gossiping town. I'll have to raise a child alone and live in a trailer for the rest of my life.

Holding me at a little distance to catch my gaze, my mom asks softly, "Do you want it?"

"No." I don't want this, not for me, not for my mom, and certainly not for Jake who's about to venture into the world that exists beyond the borders of Rensburg.

"Then there's only one option."

"You mean an abortion?"

"I love you, Kristi, and I'll never, ever wish you away, but I don't want you to suffer the way I did." She brushes a strand of hair from my face. "You're a clever girl. You have too much potential."

"We can't afford it." Medical aid doesn't cover abortions, and clinics are expensive.

She squeezes my shoulder. "Who's the boy?"

The hinted meaning hits me like a physical blow in the chest. "No," I groan. "Please, Mom. I can't do that. I can't ask them for money."

"It's Jake, isn't it?"

"Yes," I say on a defeated whisper.

"You're not going to ask them for money. You're going to speak to Jake, and he'll ask them for the money. It's small change for Hendrik Basson."

She's right, but my body shrivels in shame when I think about asking Jake for money to terminate my pregnancy.

Gripping the counter until my nails turn white, I fight to hold in my tears. I don't deserve to shed them. How could I have been so stupid? Did I conceive the night in the alley, when I all but jumped Jake's bones, or did it happen by the lake when he didn't pull out quite as fast as he'd thought? If only I had a way of knowing, I'd have a time and place on which to pin the blame. I could blame it on the vodka. I could say it was the blue sky and sad loss of speckled sparrow eggs.

"Come on." My mom takes my hands to help me down. "You'll get bladder infection sitting on that cold counter. Let's go make some black tea and toast."

Black tea and toast have always been my mom's solution for stomach bugs. I wish there was something that could help with what I have.

~

"Aren't you hot in that sweatshirt?" my mom asks at the picnic table where we're having breakfast.

Shiny trots past with his towel and toothbrush. He waves in greeting and ducks into the ablution building. Besides us, he's the only other permanent resident in the trailer park. A few people pull their trailers here for the holidays, but they are mostly poor people like us who can't afford better. The men like to fish in the river cutting through the park, which is just another excuse for drinking beer all day while the women scrape pots in the communal kitchen and run after toddlers in diapers.

"Kristi?"

"Sorry, Mom. What did you say?"

"I asked if you're not too hot in that sweatshirt."

Despite the sun, the chill won't leave my body. "I'm good."

"How's your stomach?"

"A little queasy, but at least I'm keeping breakfast down."

She pushes her bowl with half-eaten cereal away. "Are you sure you don't want me to come with you?"

"It's best I break this to Jake alone."

"Okay, but take your phone and call me if you need me."

"I will."

She cups my hand over the table. "We're going to get through this."

"Thanks," I whisper, hiding my face in my bowl. "Thanks for not being angry."

"I'm your mother. It's my job to support you."

She tries to make light, but I only feel heavy. Forcing a smile, I gather our bowls and escape to the room with the big sink and metal table that serves as the trailer park's kitchen. After doing the dishes, I find a private spot next to the river and dial Jake's number. I lean my head against a tree as I wait for him to take the call, my stomach squeezed tight.

The phone rings for so long, I give a start when he finally answers.

He sounds tired. "Pretorius."

"Did I wake you?" He may be sleeping off the big party night.

He chuckles. "I've been up since sunrise, ginger."

I can't hide my surprise. "Doing what?"

"Working."

"Working?"

"At the factory."

"On a Sunday?"

His tone is wry. "Saturdays too. My father believes I need to work twice as hard as everyone else to prove I'm worthy of the peanuts he pays me and that I'm not privy to any special treatment because I inherited his surname."

"Oh."

"Why?"

"I was hoping I could see you."

"I wanted to see you too."

"When?"

"Now."

"At work?"

"I have a tea break in an hour."

"I can wait for tonight."

"I'm working late shifts, and I'll be back again at the crack of dawn."

"For how long?"

"Until I leave this godforsaken, pimple-on-the-ass-of-the-world town."

My breath catches as Jake brings up his future and the rest of us commoners' dead-end existence.

"You all right, ginger?"

"Um, yeah."

"Come over. Please? You can have half of my sandwich."

That makes me smile. "Your sandwich isn't going to do it for me, Jake Basson."

His voice lowers an octave. "Want something else? 'Cause I can do better than a sandwich."

I snap out of my entrancement with his humor. One drink, a sweet promise, and a hickey on my shoulder got us into this mess. "I'll be there."

"I'm looking forward to it."

I hang up and pinch the bridge of my nose. He's not going to be so eager when I tell him the reason for my visit. I didn't want to mislead him, but my news isn't something I can share on the phone.

I go back to the trailer to tell my mom I'm on my way. She kisses me on the cheek, watching me with a heartbreaking expression that only adds to my guilt when I walk down the path to the road.

Nancy calls on the way. "How are you feeling?"

"Better," I lie. "How was the dance?"

"You didn't miss much."

I adore her for lying to make me feel better about missing out. "How come?"

"The punch didn't even have alcohol and the meatballs were stale. Henley was DJ, so of course, the music was crap. The first dance I danced, Denis stepped on my toe and ruined my shoe. I swear he took the purple right off. I walked around with a big, white mark on my Lady Di vintage all night. No one told me they'd put Cheddar in the breadsticks, so I got a rash. Oh, and my photo is horrendous. My smile looks like a grimace. You'd say I was giving birth to a ten-pound—" She sucks in a breath. "I didn't mean to say that."

"It's okay."

"You sound out of breath. Are you walking?"

"Yes."

"Are you coming over?"

"No."

A short silence follows.

"You're going to see Jake," she cries. "Oh, my gosh. Does that mean what I think it does? You're sure, then?"

"Don't tell anyone, okay? We haven't decided what to do yet."

"You mean... You mean you're going to get an abortion?"

"I first have to tell Jake."

"I'm so sorry, Kristi."

"It's not your fault. Look, I have to go. I'll call you later."

"Do you need my mom to give you a lift? I mean, should you walk? Last night, I thought you were dying."

"I'm actually a lot better this morning. Anyway, I'm almost there. I'll speak to you later."

I hang up when the black iron gates of the factory come into view. Supported by two redbrick columns, they guard Hendrik Basson's empire. Until those imposing gates with the spikes on the top locked us out, we dug clay from the big pit for *kleilat*, a game where you attach a ball of wet clay to the end of a green willow branch and swing it like a catapult. The objective was making the ball fly through the air to hit one of the running targets. Whoever got hit was out. The last one standing was the winner. Our parents complained about the red mud stains on our clothes, and the clay stuck in our hair, but we loved that game. Coming to think of it, Jake always won, and he always seemed to target me.

Squaring my shoulders, I sign in at the guardhouse and walk down the tarred road to the office building. I feel the door, but it's locked. The place looks deserted. I hesitate, suddenly uncertain. Maybe Jake is working at one of the other locations. His dad has several factories in the area, but this is the only one in Rensburg.

Going around the back to where clay mixed with straw are shaped into bricks and baked in a trench kiln, I stop in my tracks. Jake is hauling a long pole from the kiln. He's shirtless, wearing gloves and faded jeans. His lean torso is covered in dust and sweat. His biceps bunch and his abs contract as he loads a row of sundried bricks on the paddle before pushing them into the kiln. If this is how he spends his weekends, no wonder he's so ripped.

Wiping an arm over his forehead, he stands back to inspect his work.

I approach hesitantly, my heart beating harder with every step.

The movement attracts his attention. His lips twitch into a semi-smile when he spots me. Dumping the pole carelessly on the ground, he pulls off the gloves, drops them, and stalks toward me. The way in which he walks, too fast and too urgent, makes me pause. He grabs his T-shirt from a small pyramid of bricks and wipes his face.

"Pretorius," he says, coming to a halt in front of me. "You came."

I look around. "You're the only one working."

The half-mast smile masks whatever other emotion is running under the surface. "Paying overtime will hurt the great Hendrik Basson more than he'd ever admit. Lucky for me, family don't qualify for overtime." He walks ahead to where a red cooler box stands under a tree. "Come," he says with a cocky wink from over his shoulder.

I trail behind, trying to get my words in order. Shit. How do I break the news to him?

He fishes his phone from his back pocket and chucks it in a rugby cap that lies to the side. Sitting down next to the cooler box, he spreads out his T-shirt on the ground and pats it.

I lower myself onto his dirty T-shirt awkwardly. I can't help but inhale the masculine scent of his sweat. Being so close to him sends electric shocks to my stomach, which doesn't help my nerves. I'm so beyond saving.

He opens the box and offers me a beer.

"No thanks."

"It's cold."

I wet my lips, which are suddenly dry. "I just had breakfast."

His eyes scrunch up as he studies me. "We're legal, Pretorius. You can have a beer if you want. I already know you're not a good girl. You don't have to be shy with me."

"It's not that." I have every intention to terminate this

pregnancy, but it doesn't feel right to drink knowing there's something growing inside me.

He cracks the can, still watching me through the slits of his eyes. "Where were you last night?"

"At home."

"I gathered. I mean why? I was going to fetch you to that damn dance myself, but Nancy said she'd cut off my balls and feed them to me raw if I left the party, so what's going on?"

"Um, that's what I want to talk to you about."

"I'd really like to hear it, especially after you sent me this." He picks up his phone, scrolls over the screen, and holds it up to me.

It's me in my pink underwear. A gasp catches in my throat. "I'm going to kill Nancy."

"Pity. I was hoping you sent it."

"Jake, I…"

He lowers the beer and watches me intently.

"I came here to tell you something."

The color drains from his face. He goes as still as the pyramid of bricks. "You're pregnant."

I didn't come here to cry, but I seem to be incapable of doing anything else since last night. I cried myself to sleep. I cried in the shower. I just don't want to cry anymore. Pressing my heels on my eyes, I rub hard. It takes a moment to find my composure. He's kind enough to give me time, waiting until I have enough of a handle on myself to lower my hands before he speaks.

"When did you find out?"

"Last night."

He puts the beer and phone down and rests his elbows on his bent knees. "That's why you didn't come?"

"I was throwing up."

A wry smirk pulls at his lips as his gaze drops to my stomach.

"It's not funny, Jake."

"I was just thinking I'm so rotten, even my sperm makes you sick."

"Don't say that. Morning sickness is a common symptom for many women."

"It's my fault. If I didn't fuck you at the lake—"

"You don't know that. It could've happened at the bar. I don't want to throw guilt around. That's not going to help."

"Do you want to keep my ... the baby?"

"No."

He nods and looks into the distance. "What do you want to do?"

"I can't afford to pay for an abortion."

"Is your mom okay with that?"

"Yeah. She's supportive."

"Cool mom."

"She is."

He brushes a strand of hair over my shoulder. "Don't worry about it, okay? My dad will pay."

"I'm sorry—"

"Don't apologize. My dad has more money than what he knows to do with. We'll fix this."

Lowering my head in my hands, I whisper, "Okay."

"Hey." He puts his arm around my shoulder and pulls me to his body. "It's going to be all right. I promise."

"Yeah." I let out a tremulous breath.

"I'll be there. I won't let you go through it alone."

That means so darn much to me. I can't explain it, but I need him for this in a way my mom can never fulfill. "When are you going to talk to your dad?"

"Today, still. I guess the sooner it gets done, the better for you."

"How do you think he'll take it?"

He tenses. "Not good. We can take you to a clinic in Joburg. No one needs to know."

"I shouldn't let you face him alone. It's not right."

"I can handle my old man."

I don't doubt that, but he's so rigid just talking about

confronting Hendrik Basson, I feel bad all over again. What must it be like to be in Jake's shoes? Judging from how involved Jake's parents are in the church, they're religious. It's not going to go down well for him. I can't let him face the judgment alone.

"I'll come with you."

He looks at me quickly. "Why would you want to do that?"

"It's not fair to let you get grilled alone."

"That's so fucking cute. Told you you're way too good for me."

"Stop saying that. It's not true."

"Your offer is very honorable, and I'm touched, but I'll face my own music."

"I have a right, Jake. It's my body."

He sighs deeply. "You're not going to budge on this, are you?"

"No."

"I suppose my father won't be as hard on me as he can be if you're there."

"It's settled then. Shall I meet you at your house?"

"I'll pick you up after work, around six, before I have to be back at eight."

"Until what time do you normally stay?"

"Around eleven."

"Why so late?"

"I have a quota of bricks to make if I want to get paid."

"What do you need money for?"

"Airfare. I need a one-way ticket to Dubai." At *one-way*, he seems to catch himself. "Wouldn't mind being able to buy a car, either."

"Why is your dad driving you so hard?" It doesn't seem kind or fair.

"To make a man out of me," he says with poorly disguised bitterness. "To teach me money doesn't grow on trees."

He turns the can over and empties the beer in the sand. "Want me to get you a soda? I think there are some in the office bar."

"I have to get home." And he has a quota of bricks to make.

What's the big deal with buying Jake a car? Even if his dad is against giving his son expensive gifts, he could've let him pay it back. Denis's dad is a brickmaker at this very factory, and he bought Denis a truck when he turned eighteen.

Jake gets up and offers me a hand. When I'm on my feet, he doesn't let go immediately. "You're sure about this?"

"Yes. Why?"

"Just wanted to double-check."

"Are you...? Do you...?" I can't ask if he's having doubts.

He squeezes my fingers and drops my hand. After searching my face for another moment, he turns and strides back to his workstation, saying from over his shoulder, "I'm keeping the photo."

It takes me a second to catch on. "You have to delete it."

"See you tonight, ginger."

When he shovels the raw bricks on the paddle, no longer paying me attention, I don't have a choice but to go home.

WHEN I TELL my mom I'm going to see Jake's parents, she insists on coming with. It takes a lot of arguing to persuade her to let me handle this on my own. At six sharp, I wait at the gate of the trailer park. A minute later, Jake pulls up in Hendrik's brand-new Toyota truck.

"Your dad lent you his truck?" I ask as I climb inside.

"It's a long way. I wasn't going to make you walk."

He's wearing a clean T-shirt and pair of jeans, and he smells like soap and the cheap brand of aftershave from the supermarket. My cheeks heat as I recall how I sniffed every bottle on the shelf until I found the one that smelled like him. I bought one I'm hiding in my underwear drawer. Whenever I unscrew the lid and bring the blue liquid to my nose, the reconstruction of his physique is so vivid in my mind's eye, I can pretend he's standing right next to me.

He shoots me a sidelong glance. "How are you feeling?"

"I'm all right."

"No more puking?"

I laugh. "Only like ten more times today."

"Fuck. I'm sorry."

I motion at his clean clothes. "You showered."

"I went home a little earlier for the truck."

He did that just so he could fetch me. "Thank you."

"Are you kidding?"

The truck wobbles over the potholes, making me bounce in my seat. "You're going to a school in Dubai, right?"

"My father has some contacts. He managed to secure an intern position for me with a company specializing in restaurant management. I'll work there part-time, and go to school to get my degree in finance."

"Don't you have to speak Arabic?"

He gives a rare full-blown smile. My ignorance amuses him. "The school I'm going to offers their classes in English. It's an international school."

"With a fancy reputation, no doubt."

"Something like that."

"Is that what you want to do? Restaurant management?"

"I want to open a restaurant specializing in South African dishes abroad and develop it into a chain."

"Dreaming big, huh?"

"You've got to. Life's too short to be mediocre."

"It depends on what you perceive as mediocre."

He glances at me. "Explain what you mean."

"I think we're all different, and that's okay. We have different ambitions. For some, it's to work at your dad's factory. I don't think it's mediocre."

"That's not what I meant."

"I know what you mean. You want to fly higher than the rest of us. You want to go all the way to the moon and find out if it's really just a big old, fat chunk of cheese."

He laughs. "You and your words, Pretorius. You sure have a way with them. What about you? What's your ambition?"

"To be happy."

"Happy? That's it?"

"Isn't that the ultimate goal?" I ask a little defensively.

"Let me rephrase that. What are your ambitions for being happy?"

"To get a degree so I can get a decent job and earn enough money to move into a real house."

After a short silence, he asks, "How is it to live in a trailer?"

"Cramped."

"Seriously. I really want to know."

"Haven't you ever taken a holiday in one?"

"My mom hates camping. We usually book a hotel."

"I've never stayed in a hotel."

"You haven't?"

"Nope. In fact, we've never been away on holiday. The farthest I've traveled is Johannesburg."

"Jeez." He drags a hand over his head, shooting me another look.

"What's the nicest hotel you've stayed in?"

He's quiet for a while, seeming to consider his answer. "The Mount Nelson in Cape Town. There was this lobby boy who taught me card tricks."

"You're choosing Mount Nelson because of the lobby boy?"

"What's wrong with that?"

"Not because of Table Mountain or the V&A Waterfront or Robben Island or high tea or any of those things?"

How lonely is Jake Basson really? He's an only child, like me, but I never feel lonely. My mom has always been there for me, and I've been friends with Nancy since kindergarten. Now that I think of it, Jake doesn't have any close friends. He's always been the most popular boy with the girls, and he was always surrounded by groups of boys, but I've never seen him single out anyone. Despite being the center of every group he's been part of, he's remained on the outside. He has everything going for him—money, good looks, talent, and plenty of intelligence. It never occurred to me that he could be lonely.

He dismisses my question with a shrug. "You didn't answer my question about the trailer."

"Besides the stigma, it's actually not that bad. One, there's a lot less to clean than when you have a big house. Two, we get to eat outside all the time. Three, I'm never scared to go to bed after watching a horror movie because my mom is only an arm-length away."

He chuckles. "You have a nice way of looking at things."

When iron gates similar to the ones at the factory come into view, my stomach contracts. My mouth is suddenly too dry to swallow when he parks in front of a two-story house with stone walls and a broekie lace veranda.

Turning off the engine, he faces me. "Ready?"

I nod, even if I want to run straight back home. The house sitting in the middle of the huge lawn is intimidating. The lights inside the pool make the blue water look like liquid turquoise. The fragrance of the rambling roses that cover the gazebo drifts on the early evening air. Everything is so huge and pretty and out of my league.

I've never spoken to Jake's parents except for a polite greeting whenever I ran into them in town. I was right there in the kitchen with Nancy when Jake's mom, Elizabeth, told Nancy's mom, Daphne, that my mom is an atheist who has no respect for her body or else she wouldn't be so *easy*.

Jake hops out and comes around to open my door. In our town, gentlemanly behavior is drilled into boys from the age they can walk. It's considered as big a sin as blasphemy if a man doesn't get up when a woman enters a room.

He holds the front door and motions for me to enter ahead of him. I stop in a huge entrance hall with a terracotta tile floor and a mural of what looks like a Tuscan village framed by vineyards.

"This way," he says, going down the hallway.

We stop in front of a solid wooden door at the end. He knocks twice and waits.

"Enter," a deep voice calls from inside.

I don't miss the way sweat breaks out on his forehead as he pushes open the door and pulls me inside by my hand. We're standing in a room the size of our school library. Shelves filled with books line the walls on one side, and a sitting area with stuffy couches take up the other. The books all have burgundy spines with gold lettering. A huge desk stands on a Persian carpet in the middle of the floor. Hendrik Basson sits behind it, his glasses pinched on the tip of his nose. He doesn't look up from the big ledger in which he's writing but finishes his sentence before raising his head. His gaze falls on me. The way in which he examines me with unmasked disapproval makes me fidget. I pull on the hem of my sweatshirt, stretching the sides that are already out of proportion.

"Yes?" he says, directing the question at me.

Hendrik is a huge man and not the friendliest in the world. He makes me feel like an annoyance, as if I'm here to sell girl scout cookies he doesn't want.

"Sir," Jake says, "we'd like to talk to you."

Hendrik turns his attention to his son. "Close the door and try again."

A red flush moves up Jake's neck. He balls his hands into fists but walks back to the door and shuts it. Then he approaches again and says, "Good evening, sir."

Hendrik leans back in his chair, folding his hands over his stomach. "That's better." He turns his head to me.

Oh. "Good evening, sir."

He nods stiffly. "What can I do for you, Jake? I'm busy."

"I need your help."

"Excuse me?"

"I need your help, sir."

"I'm sorry, Jake. I don't hear you."

"I need your help, please, sir."

He sighs. "Manners. You'd think we didn't do our job as parents."

Oh, my, gosh. What a jerk. My mom would never humiliate me in front of my friends. If she had a problem with my manners, she'd tell me in private.

"I assume whatever you need help with involves Miss..." He looks at me pointedly.

"Kristi Pretorius," I say.

As if he doesn't know who I am. My mom cleans his offices and scrubs his toilets, for crying out loud. He must walk past her at least ten times a day. Plus, this is Rensburg where staying anonymous is as impossible as turning a frog into a prince with a kiss.

"Well? I don't have all night. What do you and Miss Pretorius want?"

I hate to ask this man for money. If there were any other way of getting the cash, I'd walk out of here right now.

Jake glances at me before clearing his throat. "Kristi is pregnant. We need money to terminate it."

Hendrik crosses his arms. "Who's the father?"

My soundless gasp catches in my throat at the crude insinuation. Jake's nostrils flare. His chest rises and falls twice before he says, "I am, sir."

Hendrik drags his gaze over me again. "Are you sure, son?"

"Yes, sir," Jake grits out.

"In that case, you're both in a sad predicament."

"Which is why we're here, sir," Jake says.

"What you do suggest, son?"

"We can take Kristi to a private clinic in Joburg. If we keep it quiet, we won't ruin her reputation."

Hendrik leans back farther, making the back of his chair squeak. "No."

Jake blinks. "Excuse me?"

"Abortion isn't an option. We taught you better values than to come here and ask for this."

Jake's mouth drops open. "We can't have a baby now. Our lives will be ruined."

"You should've thought about that before you took your dick out of your pants."

"Look, I made a mistake, and I'll be damned if Kristi is going to pay for it."

"Watch your language, son. I won't allow you to disrespect me in my own house."

I turn my head between Jake and his dad, my anxiety with how the conversation is going growing by the second. I just want to get out of here.

"Jake." I touch his hand.

He jerks away and takes a step closer to the desk. "It's not like you can't afford it. It won't even make a dent in your bank account."

"It's not about money, Jake. It's about principles, and if you can't figure that out you're a bigger disappointment than I thought."

I try to catch Jake's attention again, but I may as well not exist.

"What do you suggest she does?" Jake exclaims, pointing at me. "Her mother can't afford it. Knowing how well you pay your staff, I doubt she can afford to pay for the birth."

Hendrik turns to me. "Does your mother have medical aid?"

I'm trembling with anger and humiliation. He pays his staff a gross salary exempt from fringe benefits because he's too stingy to contribute the required company portion of a medical or pension fund. His employees are forced to take out private medical aid plans, which, in a country crippled by a low life expectancy, doesn't come cheap. He knows darn well what my mother has.

Forcing myself to speak, I say, "She has a limited medical aid fund, sir."

"Ah." He removes his glasses and places them squarely on the ledger. "In that case, birth won't be covered. You'll have to go to the public hospital in Heidelberg and try your luck there."

Jake's voice climbs in anger. "I can't believe you said that. Don't you watch the news? Last month, twelve babies died in that hospital due to negligence. Everyone knows in what state the public hospital is."

Hendrik raises his hands. "What do you expect me to do? Clean up your mess? Sorry, son. You made the bed."

Jake stabs his fingers in his hair, clutching the dark locks. "What do you want from me, Dad? What else must I do to win your approval? Work harder? Longer hours? Wait, I already work seven days a week. I guess breaking my back isn't going to do it. Better grades? Oh, I got straight A's. I guess not. Tell me. What will it take?"

I clutch the chair back in front of me, my head spinning from the animosity flying through the room.

"Man up, Jake. Face your responsibilities. Nothing in life is free. I worked for every cent I have. No one gave me a dime." He turns his palms to Jake. "I earned what I own with these two hands. That's the biggest gift my father gave me—nothing. It taught me the value of things."

"What do you suggest we do?" Jake cries, shaking with rage.

"Jake." I take his arm. "Let's go. Please."

"You'll be employed by January," Hendrik says. "Your contract comes with medical aid."

Jake shakes me off again. "What are you saying?"

Oh, no. "Jake, no."

"If you're the father, as you claim, you're going to do right by the girl and marry her. Your medical aid is comprehensive. It'll cover her medical expenses for the birth and healthcare for the baby."

"Wait. You're saying I should marry her, go to Dubai, and leave her here to have a baby alone?"

"I've always told you not to stick your dick in a woman you're not willing to marry, son."

I can't listen to this conversation any longer. "Jake, I'm leaving."

"You're a fucking hypocrite," Jake sneers.

Hendrik turns white. Pressing his knuckles on the desk, he pushes himself to his feet. "What did you say to me?"

"I know you fucked Dollie Brown for years. The whole town knows. They laughed behind your holy back while Mom sobbed herself to sleep every weekend you were away for *work*."

The chair hits the floor as Hendrik pushes away from the desk. I jump. Jake is tall and lean, but Hendrik is a giant of a bulky man.

The look on Hendrik's face is murderous. "You're never too old to be put back in your place."

When he stalks around the desk, unbuckling his belt, I stifle a scream.

"Jake, please!" I pull on his arm with all my might, but he's like a block of granite.

"Come on," Jake says. "Want to take your failure to be a decent husband and father out on me? Do your fucking best."

The belt zips through the loops in Hendrik's waistband. He folds it double and grips it in one hand, his knuckles clenched around the leather. When he charges, nostrils flaring and arm lifted, Jake doesn't cower or budge.

"Jake!" His dad is going to hit him. "Mr. Basson, no!"

Without thinking, I throw myself between the two men, trying to stop an assault in which Jake stands no chance. I try to catch Hendrik's arm before he brings the belt down on Jake, but the force of his momentum is too big. The leather cuts through the air with an angry hiss. Pain explodes on my cheekbone. I stumble, crashing into Jake's body. He catches me under my armpits before

I hit the floor. The pain blooming on the side of my face is so intense, black spots pop in my eye.

"Kristi!" Jake twirls me around. "Oh, fuck." His eyes turn cold and hateful as he lifts them to his father, who stands frozen to the spot. "It wouldn't have been the first time, but this was the last time you raised your hand at me."

My cheek throbs with heat. Something warm trickles over my skin. I press my fingers to the spot. When I pull them away, they're covered with blood.

Jake takes my arm and pulls me to the door. It opens just before we reach it. Elizabeth Basson rushes through the frame.

She covers her mouth with a hand when she sees me. "Oh, my goodness. What happened? Jake?"

He pushes past his mother, dragging me along.

"Hendrik?" Elizabeth runs after us down the hallway, her voice hysterical. "Someone, please tell me what's going on."

Jake doesn't stop until we're outside. He opens the truck door and lifts me into the seat. He jerks off his T-shirt and pushes it against my face. "Hold this. It may need stitches."

I've never experienced domestic violence. I'm shaking uncontrollably as Jake starts the engine and spins the wheels on the gravel.

"Fuck, Kristi. I'm taking you to the clinic."

"No," I say quickly. "We can't afford the clinic. Just take me home."

CHAPTER 6

*J*ake stands awkwardly to the side while my mom cleans the cut on my cheek with a wet facecloth in the ablution block. The bleeding has stopped, but there's a five-centimeter-long gash on my cheek. The metal buckle must've caught my skin. Kudos to my mom for not freaking out after Jake told her his father hit me in the face with a belt by accident.

Watching my mom work, Jake chews his bottom lip. He's pale and quiet.

My mom clicks her tongue. "It needs stitches."

"Can't you just put on a plaster?" I ask.

"It's too deep." She turns to Jake. "Can you drive us?"

"Yes, ma'am."

"Take Kristi to the truck. I'll go grab my bag."

The nearest emergency unit is in Heidelberg. It takes twenty minutes to drive to our neighboring town. When we fill out the paperwork, the receptionist asks for payment upfront.

"I want to pay for it," Jake says.

My mom takes her credit card from her bag. "It's all right, Jake."

"I only have fifty bucks on me, but I'll pay you back."

"Forget about it."

"I'm serious, Mrs. Pretorius."

"Stop calling me Mrs. Pretorius. You're only making me more nervous with all the formality. It's Gina."

"Fine, Gina, but I'm still getting the bill."

My mom is proud that way. She hands over her card without arguing further. She'll never let him pay.

We wait two hours before a doctor can see me. After injecting me with a local anesthetic and stitching me up, he asks if I want to lay charges for assault. I decline. Hendrik is a bastard and a sorry excuse for a father, but he didn't attack me on purpose. Besides, the gossip will be humiliating for Jake. Not to mention that he'd have to testify against his father. I'm not putting him in such a position.

Jake's phone rings again. It's rang at least ten times since we've been here.

"You better get that," my mom says. "Your parents must be worried."

"They deserve to be," he says bitterly.

"Your mom too?"

He clenches his teeth. "Excuse me." Getting to his feet, he walks a far enough distance away to be out of earshot and presses the phone against his ear.

The doctor gives me a prescription for antibiotics and explains how to disinfect the wound. When he's secured a gauze with a plaster to my cheek, Jake comes back, even more tense and withdrawn.

"It's late," my mom says. "We better get you kids home."

At the trailer, Jake follows us to the door and hovers on the threshold. It's clear he's not ready to go back to his place.

"You better come inside for a cup of tea, Jake," my mom says. "You're both in shock."

Jake gives her a grateful nod. He looks around the interior of our small home, taking in every detail while I shift onto the bench by the foldable table and my mom heats water on the portable gas stove.

"Are you hungry?" she asks. "There are left-over meatballs and spaghetti."

"Yes, ma'am."

I've always thought my mom is a great person, but my opinion of her rises tenfold as she makes tea and heats up food in the microwave without asking what we're going to do about our dilemma or what happened at Jake's place. My mom is meticulous about solving problems. First things first. Food and strong tea always take priority. Only when our physical needs have been taken care of will she tackle the emotional issues.

Jake accepts seconds and cleans his plate. "That was good. Thank you, Gina."

"You're welcome."

"Do you mind if I stay the night?"

My mom gives a little start at his straightforwardness.

"I can't face my parents yet," he adds apologetically.

She thinks for a couple of seconds. "All right, but only if you let your parents know where you are."

"I'll send them a message." He punches out a text and hits send.

They refuse to let me help tidy up. My mom clears the table, and Jake carries our dishes to the kitchen. When he comes back with everything cleaned, my mom excuses herself to have a shower while we lie down on my single bed, fully clothed minus our shoes. I'm sandwiched on my side between the wall and Jake's warm body, a rather nice place to be. It feels safe, much like when I crouched under my towel as a kid and reveled in the cozy feeling of my makeshift tent.

He brushes a strand of hair from my face. "I'm sorry about tonight."

"Is he always like that?"

"Mostly."

His evasive answer says a lot. When I accused him of acting like a victim, I never thought he was a victim.

He cups my injured cheek, his fingers resting just underneath the plaster. "I'm sorry for the things he said, and I'm really fucking sorry about your face."

Placing my hand over his, I let the heat of his palm soak into my skin. "You don't have to apologize. You're not responsible for his behavior."

He shuts his eyes and blows out a heavy sigh.

"What is it, Jake?"

"He's right, you know. If he doesn't help us out with money, the only solution is to get married."

The clinical way in which he says it makes me stiffen. "You can't possibly want that."

"Neither can you, but I'm afraid what we want is no longer a freedom we have." His lips pull into a crooked grin. "It won't be all that bad marrying you."

"I'm eighteen. You're twenty-one. Besides, you're moving at the end of the year."

He opens his eyes and turns his head to look at me. "Or I could stay if that's what you want."

"No," I say quickly. I won't be responsible for ruining his dreams. I don't want to become the person Jake resents.

"Adoption?"

"I don't think I can deal with that. I won't be able to live knowing I have a child somewhere, and not knowing how he or she is, if he's being treated well or suffering."

"Same for me." Folding his arms under his head, he stares at the fluorescent stars on the ceiling above my bed. "Tell me what to do, and I'll do it."

"Oh, no. You're not doing this."

"Doing what?"

"Making the decision my responsibility. That's not fair."

"I'm just saying I'll do whatever you want. I'm the one who screwed up."

"*We* screwed up, and we'll make the decision together."

"What do you want to do, then?"

"I have to think about it."

"Understandably."

I'm strung out, and I don't see a solution. "Can we talk tomorrow?"

Slipping an arm around me, he pulls me close. "It's been a rough day. Rest."

I snuggle against him and close my eyes. I'm asleep even before my mom gets back from the bathroom.

I WAKE WITH A LANGUOROUS FEELING. I try to stretch, but a big body that occupies most of my bed restricts my movement.

Jake.

My eyes fly open. Jake's lips are slightly parted, and stubble darkens his jaw. His lashes are so long they brush his cheeks. His leg is thrown over my thighs and his arm over my stomach. I'm anchored to him by limbs and a very tangible life growing inside me, a life my body apparently has a hard time adjusting to, because I'm nauseous again. I peek at my mom's side. Her bed is empty. The time on the alarm clock is six. She must be in the bathroom. If I weren't so damn queasy, I would've tried to sneak in a kiss. I'm dying to feel the abrasive grating of Jake's unshaved jaw on my lips and neck.

"Morning, ginger," he says, eyes still closed.

"How did you sleep?"

"Awful."

"Yeah?"

He blinks his eyes open, staring at me with those dark, intense pools. "I'm as stiff as a stick."

"My apology for the single bed. Small trailers don't allow for the luxury of doubles."

"That's not what I meant." He takes my hand and places it over the bulge in his jeans. "It was agony sleeping next to you and not being able to fuck—"

"Jake!" I jerk my hand from his crotch and cover his mouth. "My mom can walk in any minute."

He kisses my palm and moves my hand away. "That was the only thing that saved you."

With his light-hearted banter, I almost forget about yesterday and circumstances, but my body is eager to remind me.

Untangling our limbs, I climb over him. "I think I'm going to be sick."

He jumps to his feet, his hair wild and his eyes wide. "What can I do?"

"Stay here." It'll be too humiliating if he witnesses me barfing up digested meatballs.

I don't take the time to fit my shoes. I run barefoot to the bathroom but only make it halfway. Bending over, I puke into a flowerbed.

"Fuck," a male voice says.

I fling around. A broody, shirtless Jake is stalking toward me.

Rolling my eyes, I breathe through a dry heave. When the urge to throw up again passes, I give him an accusing stare. "I asked you to stay in the trailer for a purpose."

"Damn, Kristi."

I wipe my mouth with the back of my hand. "What?" Please don't tell me I have puke on my lips.

He frames my head between his palms. "Your face."

"What's wrong with my face?"

"Outside here, in the sunlight..." His Adam's apple bobs. "It looks like you've been in an accident."

I swat his hands away and press my fingers around my injury. My cheek feels like a spongy ball, and it's the size of one too.

Tilting his head, he gently grips the plaster. "May I?"

When I nod, he slowly peels it away. I grit my teeth at the sting. If this is what pulling off a small plaster feels like, I'm never having my private parts waxed.

"Am I ugly?" I ask when the gauze comes free.

"Never." He flinches. "But the cut isn't pretty."

I escape to the bathroom, slipping into the ladies' toilets, but Jake is not to be deterred. He follows short on my heels. My mother must be on the side with the showers. I stop in front of a mirror and suck in a breath. My hair is tangled, my make-up smudged, and my cheek the size of a golf ball. A bruise has spread to a dark ring under my eye. To round it all off, I have puke breath.

Jake stares at my reflection in the mirror. "Can I get you anything? Ice? Anti-vomit pills?"

"You can give me a moment."

He hesitates.

"Please, Jake." I hate for him to see me like this.

"Are you done puking?"

"Yes."

"I guess I have to be on my way, anyway." His smile is strained. "Work."

"You're going back there after what he tried to do to you?"

"I don't have a choice. I need money for my plane ticket." He adds too quickly, "If I'm still going to Dubai."

My head hurts, my cheek throbs, and I feel like puking again. I can't talk about this right now. "We'll talk later, okay?"

"When you're ready."

I need a shower and to brush my teeth. "I'll call you."

"I'll hold you to it."

After pressing a quick kiss to the top of my head, he leaves.

When I get back to the trailer for my toilet bag and a change of clothes, Jake's T-shirt my mom rinsed and hung out to dry as well as his dad's truck are gone. My mom stands in front of the gas stove, boiling water for her morning coffee. She's not dressed in her uniform, but in a T-shirt and jeans.

"Aren't you going to work?" I ask.

"I took the day off."

She never takes time off. We need the money too badly. "Why?"

"Has Jake gone?"

"Yes. He has to be at work by seven."

She pours boiling water into two mugs and puts a cup of Rooibos tea in front of me. "Tell me what happened last night."

No more caffeine or tannin for me, at least not for as long as I'm pregnant. Sipping the tea, which helps a little to settle my nausea, I tell my mom what Hendrik had said when Jake confronted him. The longer I talk, the harder my mom's clenches her mug. When I'm done with my grim tale, the lines of her face are tense with anger.

She doesn't say anything. She gets up calmly and rinses our cups in a dish of soapy water. Too calmly. She's not going to just let this go.

"What are you going to do, Mom?"

"I'm going to have a word with his parents."

"Mom! You can't do that."

"I should've gone with you last night, then this whole debacle wouldn't have happened." At *debacle*, she waves a hand at my face.

"Please don't do it. I beg you."

She grabs her bag. "I'm not letting Hendrik Basson or anyone treat you like this."

Desperate, I search my mind for reasons why she can't go. "You can't walk all the way there."

"Daphne is giving me a lift."

Now she's dragging Daphne into this. "Mom."

"Enough, Kristi. Jake's parents and I are going to talk about how to best handle the situation."

"The situation? You mean the fact that I'm pregnant?"

"What else? And I'm going to give him a piece of my mind about his violence."

"He's your boss."

"This has nothing to do with work. It's a private matter."

"He'll fire you."

"Then I'll sue him for unfair dismissal."

A car pulls up outside. She's out of the door before I can find my bearings.

"Wait!"

Grabbing my backpack, I run after her. I barely have time to jump into the back before Daphne pulls off.

She stares at my face in the rearview mirror. "What in the sweet heck happened to your face?"

"Hendrik hit her," my mom says.

"What?" Daphne shrieks.

"It was an accident," I say.

"Yes," my mom replies wryly. "Apparently the blow was meant for Jake."

"What's going on, girls?"

My mom clutches her bag to her chest. "That's what I'm going to find out."

Daphne catches my eyes in the mirror again. "I didn't know you and Jake were dating."

"We're not," I say miserably.

Daphne must've sensed the tension, because she doesn't ask more questions. I find a hairbrush and elastic band as well as breath mints in my backpack. Tying my hair into a ponytail, I make myself as presentable as I can. Too soon, the big property with the pristine lawn the size of the entire trailer park comes into view. My stomach turns over.

"Do you mind waiting?" my mom asks Daphne when we pull up at the gates.

"Not at all. Take your time."

Daphne rolls down her window to press the intercom button, but a gardener opens the gates.

I try again to discourage my mom. "Maybe we should call first."

My mom gets out and walks with determined steps to the front of the house. I try to jump out, but the kiddies' lock is on. By the time Daphne has unlocked my door and I've caught up with my mom, she's already ringing the bell.

The door swings open. Elizabeth Basson stands on the step, dressed in a cashmere top and matching cardigan with strings of pearls draped around her neck. Her eyes tighten as she takes in my mom.

"Good morning, Elizabeth."

"Gina, right?"

"We need to talk. May I come in?"

"I'm sorry," Elizabeth says sweetly. "I don't know who let you in, but I don't entertain uninvited guests."

"Then we'll just have to talk out here." My mom crosses her arms. "Kristi tells me you won't help with the cost of terminating her pregnancy."

"Kill our own grandchild? No, we definitely won't pay for that."

"Do you understand the implication this will have on their lives?"

Elizabeth looks my mom up and down. "Nobody will understand better than you. Unfortunately, the apple doesn't fall far from the tree."

I can't believe my ears. It's last night all over, only this time Jake's mom is dishing out the punches.

"Kristi is a good person," my mom says, "better than anyone I know."

Elizabeth snorts. "She's a lazy little slut trying to catch herself a rich husband. This may come as a surprise, but Jake won't be wealthy until he's earned it." She searches me out over my mom's shoulder. "Sorry, darling, but if you thought you found a way out of having to work for your money by using the oldest method in the book, you're going to be sadly disappointed."

"How dare you insinuate this is all Kristi's fault."

"What better example do we set for our children than with our behavior? Promiscuity obviously runs in your family."

"Like violence runs in yours?"

"How my husband disciplines our son is none of your business."

My mom motions at my face. "This is how he disciplines Jake?"

"Kristi got in the way. It was a stupid thing to do."

"That's all you have to say?"

"I'm afraid so. Just because we're going to share a grandchild doesn't mean we're going to drink tea together at Rosie's or have Sunday family lunches."

"You're going to do nothing to help them," my mother says with disbelief.

"If Jake is old enough to have sex, he's old enough to solve his own problems. Good day, Ms. Pretorius. I have a Bible group meeting to attend."

"I'm not done—"

Before my mom can finish the sentence, the door shuts in her face. Hands balled into fists, she stands on the step and stares incredulously at the door. I hate seeing her like this, discarded and humiliated, like she's not worth the dirt under Elizabeth Basson's shoes.

I take her hand. "Come on, Mom."

She lets me lead her back to the car, her shoulders square and her spirit far from defeated.

"Always remember one thing, Kristi. What matters is what's in your heart, not in your bank account."

Chin lifted, she climbs into the car and says to Daphne, "Drive."

. . .

BACK HOME, my mom doesn't invite Daphne in. She walks to the river and stands on the grassy bank, looking into the distance. By the time I've showered and changed, she's still standing there.

"Mom?" I say quietly as I approach.

She turns to me with a sigh. "I've thought about it from every angle, but it seems you only have one choice. You're going to have to marry Jake."

"I'm not ready for this. Not for marriage. We'll find a way. I'll have the baby at the public hospital."

"It's not just the birth. Babies cost a lot of money, more than you can ever imagine. They need regular checkups and vaccinations. What if your baby gets sick? How will we afford the medicine?"

"How did you manage when I was born?"

"My parents helped me, bless their souls."

"I'll go to the free clinic, like the minimum wage workers."

"There's no medicine for the poor. The government health fund is bankrupt. At least Jake's private medical aid will cover whatever costs you and the baby may incur."

"I can't use him like that."

"What happens if there are complications during the birth? What if you need an emergency cesarean? I'm not trying to spook you, but all kinds of things can go wrong."

"I'll work."

"Who's going to employ a pregnant woman? No one in this town. You'll battle even in Johannesburg. The unemployment rate is too high for any company to take a risk on a future mom who may decide to not go back to work after the birth, or who'll need to take off many hours. As a single mom, you have no one else to take care of your child when he's sick. Of course, I'll always be there for you. You know that, but companies don't think that way. They make employment decisions based on what's in their best financial interest."

I sink down in the muddy grass, not caring that my jeans are getting soiled and soaked. "What if I borrow the money?"

"No bank is going to grant you a loan without a credit history. If I could've taken a loan myself, I would've done so without thinking twice, but I'm in overdraft as it is. My repayments are way overdue." Her face softens. "I'm so sorry, Kristi. I wish there was another way."

"Jake is going to hate me," I whisper.

"He has a fifty percent part in this," she reminds me gently.

I hug my knees tightly. "Are you disappointed in me?"

Going down on her haunches, she wipes my hair from my face. "Never. You surprised me, that's all. You're normally so level-headed."

Except where Jake is concerned. "We got carried away."

"I know, honey. The heart is so passionate at your age, and the body its slave."

Does she have any idea how much I appreciate her not saying, I told you so? I look toward the reeds on the other side of the shore. "I guess I'm not going to university."

"That may be a bit difficult. Childcare is expensive, and I won't find another job elsewhere. I'm lucky to have one in Rensburg as it is. It doesn't mean your life is ruined. Your path is altered, but what you make of it is in your hands." She straightens. "Explain your decision to Jake. Be upfront about marrying him for financial reasons. You can always get divorced later if things don't work out."

She makes it sound easy and uncomplicated, a gift my mom has for taking the drama out of emotional situations.

"Come on." She puts on a bright face. "I'll make milk tart for teatime."

I don't have the heart to tell her the sound of that only makes me want to puke.

. . .

It's cruel to let Jake stew in worry when I've already come to a conclusion, but it's something I have to tell him in person. I call and ask him to come over before his night shift. I'm a mess the whole day. When six o'clock arrives and he cycles up the road to the trailer park gate, I'm worn out from anxiety. He leans the bike against the trailer and walks to where I sit on a picnic bench under the trees.

"Feeling better?" he asks when he stops next to me.

His pale face and strained features give away his own stress. Dark patches mark the armpits and front of his T-shirt. His jeans are dirty with the red dust of clay soil. He must've come here straight from work.

I motion at the bench facing me. "Maybe you want to sit."

He glances to where I indicate but takes a seat next to me. He moves so close our legs touch. The warmth of his hard thigh pressing against mine does things to me it shouldn't, especially since we're already knee-deep in our predicament. I suppose I can't get more pregnant. Kissing and doing more than innocent fondling aren't what I should be thinking about, but it's difficult to ignore his body when his signature scent invades my senses and reminds me of twelve years of infatuation with a boy who grew up into a man. Closing my eyes for a second, I try not to inhale too deeply or stare at the dark, masculine hair on his forearms.

Did his mom tell him about our visit? The fact that he doesn't bring it up makes me think not. I'm not going to tell him his mother called me a lazy slut and shut the door in our faces. Jake doesn't need that on top of everything else.

He tilts his head left and right as he studies my face with those intense, brooding eyes. "Does it still hurt?"

"Only when I smile."

His expression darkens. "I hate to be the reason you don't smile."

"It's not you." I don't want to talk about last night anymore. "Thanks for coming over."

"You said you thought about a solution."

"It's for you to decide if you agree."

His voice is calm, but the way he starts bouncing his knee gives away his nervousness. "Let's hear it."

"I think it's best we..." I bite my lip. It's tougher to say than I thought. "I can't have this baby without financial support. I think it's best we get married."

He stares at me for a moment that stretches too long. "For financial reasons."

"I'm going to need medical aid. I wouldn't have asked if I could've secured my own somehow, but it'll be tough finding a job being pregnant."

He rubs a palm over his breastbone as if he's trying to massage away an ache. It's a gesture I know well, one he only makes when he gets angry.

"What about us?" he asks carefully.

"You go to Dubai as planned. I have the baby, and then we see."

He intertwines his fingers on the tabletop. "Then we see what?"

"Then we see where we go from there."

"That's all you want from me?" he asks with a tight jaw. "Money for the birth?"

"Of course not. You're a part of this baby as much as me. I want you to be involved if you wish. I'll never take that right away from you. I just don't want you to give up your dream."

"What about your dream, Kristi?"

"Mine was never as big as yours." My laugh is too uncomfortable to sound natural. "I was only going to get a BA degree in Johannesburg. I would've probably ended up working at the town library. It doesn't compete with studying at a posh school in Dubai and launching a chain of restaurants."

"Don't put yourself down."

"I'm only stating the facts."

"You're saying my dream is more important than yours. Didn't you tell me everyone's ambition is important?"

"I'm saying I don't really have a dream, not like you." Except for renting a proper house and giving my mom the break she deserves. "You know what you want. You know how to get there. I'm not even sure if literature would've been the right choice for me."

"I'm offering to stay."

"And I already declined." I rub at my temples where a headache starts building. "Look, let's just get the logistics sorted and take it from there."

"Don't you want me to ask you to marry me the proper way, on one knee with a ring?"

Something deep inside me twists. It hurts more than I could've ever anticipated because I do want that. I want a proper proposal more than anything, but not for the wrong reasons. I don't want it forced or staged.

"I'm just trying to be rational about all of this."

He pushes to his feet. "Whatever you want."

I only come to my senses when he's halfway back to our trailer.

Jumping up, I rush after him. "If this isn't what you want I'll—"

He spins around to face me. "You're asking me to walk away from my responsibility."

"I don't want to destroy your future. I don't want you to end up hating me."

"The only person I'll hate is myself."

"What are you saying?" I shake my head in frustrated confusion. "I thought you'd be happy."

"Don't worry. I'll do what you want."

"Jake, don't be like this. Tell me if you don't agree."

"You made the choice for me. I'm going to Dubai. The rest we'll just have to play as it fucking goes."

Tears burn at the back of my eyes. A knot lodges in my throat. "That's not fair. You do have a choice."

"Let me know when and where," he says as he stalks away. "I'll be there."

CHAPTER 7

The magistrate can't give us a date before the end of December, four days before Jake is due to leave. I only know his departure date because he sent me an impersonal text message with his flight details so I could fix our civil wedding date.

When I try to involve Jake in the planning, he ignores my voice and text messages. People's actions sometimes hurt, but I never thought any non-action could cut so deeply. Why is he so angry with me for trying to salvage his dream? I love him too much to allow circumstances to change him. Living a monotone life in a dead-end town with nothing but red clay and an overwhelming majority of small, box-shaped houses that speak of unsophisticated poverty will definitely change him, and not for the better. I'd lie if I say I'm not devastated about his departure. I'm terrified. I'm scared of facing the future alone, even if I can always count on my mom. There are holes in my heart my mom's love can't fill.

My mom took it upon her shoulders to arrange a wedding lunch. Even if it's a forced marriage, she refuses to let the event go uncelebrated. According to her, ceremonies are sacred and traditions define our roots. We'll have a simple picnic lunch after the morning formalities.

Elizabeth and Hendrik declined the invitation, saying they wouldn't be at the magistrate's office to witness the sad occasion, which left it up to my mom and me to find witnesses. Daphne and Will accepted the *honor*.

Since we haven't announced the wedding like the norm with big, joyous celebrations, the rest of the town is oblivious as to how drastically my status will change in a few days, but there's plenty of gossip about my *condition*, courtesy of how early I'm showing. It didn't take long for Snake, who'd seen Jake and me in suspicious circumstances in the alley, to add two and two together, and now everyone knows Jake knocked me up. The whole town is talking about my condition as if it's a shameful disease.

No longer going to university, I have to continue living with my mom and find a job here. I'm still working weekends at the OK Bazaars as a cashier, but there are no permanent positions available. I applied at the gift store, the hairdresser, and even at Eddie's without declaring my pregnancy on my applications. If I'm lucky enough to get any interviews, I'll be upfront about my *condition*. I put my name on waiting lists at restaurants, the library, the municipality, and every other business as far as Heidelberg. The only place I refuse to try is the brick factory. I'd have to be starving before I work for Hendrik Basson.

The baby seems to be thriving. At the rate I'm eating, being constantly hungry, he'll definitely not be underweight. If I'm not having stomach-growling cravings for fries drenched in vinegar, I'm vomiting. I'm not slender. I have well-rounded hips and ample breasts, but I've always had a flat stomach. My choice in clothes favored tight-fitting jeans and skirts, which doesn't count in my favor for keeping my pregnancy hidden. At three months, I already have a bump, and my pants don't fasten any longer. Under the stretch fabric of my dresses, my rounder stomach is a dead giveaway of my *sin*.

I'm wearing my increasingly tight-fitting maxi-dress, one of the few items in my closet I can still wear, getting groceries at Eddie's on the corner, when Denis walks in. I duck behind a shelf, but he's already seen me. Rounding the pyramid of corned beef tins, he drops his shopping basket to the floor.

"Hey, Kristi." His gaze drops to my stomach, his eyebrows pulling together with disdain. "I see the gossip is true."

I rub a hand over my belly where everything goes tight. "What gossip may that be?"

"You've got a bun in the oven. It's Jake's, isn't it? I saw you that night in the alley."

"Oh, I thought you meant the gossip about how you popped my cherry." Eddie, who's behind the counter, lifts his head. "Because you and I both know that's a lie."

Denis's face turns redder than the packets of chili noodles on the shelf next to him. "You're just like your mom."

He said it softly enough for Eddie not to hear. I should ignore him, but the insult to my mother has me bristling. It takes all my self-control and more not to project packets of ginger cookies at his head. "Oh, good, because I admire her. She doesn't have to lie about having sex, because she's actually getting some." I lift my arms. "I'm the living proof."

"You're disgusting," he spits as he picks up his basket and pushes past me. "I can't believe I wanted to date you."

I raise my voice to his back. "I'm glad you find pregnancy so disgusting because you're not man enough to handle it."

He grabs a bag of flour from the shelf and slams it onto the counter without sparing me another glance.

Great. Why don't I just burn a big A for adultery on my forehead like in The Scarlet Letter? I pretend not to be fazed, but my hands shake as I continue with my shopping. So much for believing Denis to be kind. In the end, he's just like everyone else. I'm not sure if I'm more disappointed in him or myself for being so naïve.

When the chime of the bell announces Denis's exit, I still with my hand on the margarine. It takes a moment to gather myself. Turning my mom's words over in my mind, I take comfort from them. I didn't do anything wrong. I had sex. Agreed, having unprotected sex was not only foolish but also highly irresponsible. I'm paying a heavy price for a few moments of magical lust, but it wasn't filthy like Denis implied.

On second thought, I exchange the margarine for butter, even if the price makes me cringe. The trans-fatty acids in the margarine aren't good for the baby. I put back the ginger ale I was going to buy for the nausea. Adding wholegrain bread and the cheapest brand of tuna to my basket, I go to pay.

"How's the baby?" Eddie asks with his strong Mandarin accent while he's ringing up my items.

I may as well make a public announcement in the local newspaper. "Good."

"You?"

"Better when I'm not being insulted."

"It'll be better when you're married."

"Who says I'm getting married?"

He gives a goofy smile. "You've seen the doctor. He made a test."

"Dr. Santoni told you I'm pregnant?" I exclaim. "That's breaching patient confidentiality."

"No, not the doctor." Seeming to check himself, he takes a six-pack of ginger ale from behind the counter and puts it with my groceries. "For you, on the house."

My mouth drops open. Is this the same Eddie who made me walk all the way home in sixth grade because I was three cents short on the price of the milk my mom had sent me to buy? Is this the Eddie who wouldn't give me a five-cent Wilson toffee in second grade because I only had four cents in my pocket?

"That's kind of you, but not necessary."

"Please. Take it. For the baby."

My cheeks heat. His kindness is touching, but also embarrassing. I don't like that he saw me put back the soda.

He takes my cash and waves me out. "Go on, now. Can you carry this, or must I drop it off?"

Hiding behind the veil of my hair, I pack the items in my reusable shopping bag. "It's not heavy."

"See you soon then," he says, dumping a cereal bar into my bag with great show. "For the road." He throws in another with a wink. "For your mom."

For no explicable reason, my eyes tear up. Maybe it's because he's trying to make me feel better, or because it's the first time he's being kind to me. Or maybe it's just the pregnancy hormones.

"Thank you," I whisper, hurrying to the door.

"You're welcome," he calls after me. "You call when you need a delivery, any time."

Keeping my head low, I walk down the dirt road with my load. I'm not ashamed to be in my own skin, I just need a very thick one to not let the insults get to me. Does Jake suffer the same treatment? Do people look at him as if he's worse than the muck at the bottom of the lake?

Eddie is right. The whispering and sideway looks will calm once we're properly married, but my reputation is stained forever, not that I care. I don't believe in the hypocritical values of the people who judge me. Sometimes, it's just hard to pretend you don't mind being an outcast. For the first time, I have a true taste of what my mom went through.

The noise of a vehicle draws my attention. I stand to the side because the curb is narrow. A truck pulls up in a billow of dust that makes me cough. Jan and Kallie, two boys from my class, hang their arms down their open windows.

"Hey, Kristi," Jan says. "Want a ride?" He winks. "I've got a nice, big backseat."

"Yeah, big enough to do us both," Kallie chimes.

My thinly stretched patience snaps. "Go fuck yourselves on your nice, big backseat."

"Come on now, girl," Jan says. "Don't get your hackles up. Since you're giving it away for free, a man's got to try, right?"

"The problem with that phrase is you're not a man, so sorry, darling." I bat my eyelashes. "No freebies for you."

Kallie whistles long and hard, slapping Jan on the back in a fit of laughter. "Doesn't say much if you can't even get laid by the town slut."

I wasn't going to take the bait. I've learned it's easier to beat them at their game than to show their cruel words have an effect, but my emotions are all over the place today.

"You're such assholes," I hiss. "Good luck finding a virgin to marry you two man-whores. By the way, that prostitute in Johannesburg you paid to teach you how to hit a hole-in-one said it took several tries before you hit the right hole."

It's a low blow. Apparently, in Jan's over-excited and inexperienced state, he stabbed the poor woman twice in the ass before he managed to put it in the right place. Normally, I wouldn't use the information Shiny shared with me, which he heard from Snake, who heard it from Jan's sadly disappointed father, but they need to be put back in their place.

Jan pulls his face into an ugly mask of hatred. "You filthy little slut. Maybe I'll pay you a visit and show you how a *man* hits both holes. Your slut mother can watch, or maybe Kallie can teach her a trick or two."

"Are you threatening me?"

"What are you going to do about it?" Kallie taunts.

"I just want to know if I should file a harassment complaint with Sarel."

Sarel is our local police officer, and he's old-fashioned when it comes to upholding law and order. He'd take the skins off their backsides if I tell him what they said.

The handbrake groans as Jan jerks it up. He's out of the truck and in my face before I have time to blink. The grocery bag drops as he shoves me with a palm against my shoulder. Losing my footing on the lumps of dry mud on the boulder, I stumble backward with flailing arms. The earth disappears from under my feet as I fall back into the ditch. The air leaves my lungs with a humph when my ass hits the ground.

Pain shoots up my coccyx. Lying in the rocky bed between nettles and thistle thorns, my vision goes blurry with anger. I ball my hands into fists. My fingers close around something round and hard. I lift a heavy lump of dry clay and hurl it with all my might at Jan's head. The compacted sand explodes on his temple. Brittle particles fly everywhere. The impact sends him staggering. Dust rain downs on his face and torso. He shakes his head and blinks a couple of times. When the worst of his shock wears off, blind fury replaces his stunned expression. Before he can take a step toward me, I hit him again, this time aiming for his chest. He ducks, trying to escape the blow, and takes it fully in the face.

"Fuck," he hurls, spitting sand and blowing a string of mud-colored snot from his nose.

I've already gathered more ammunition. I pepper his knees and stomach, leaving the last for his crotch. When the clot of clay hits his balls, he folds double. Wheezing, he cups his testicles.

"Kallie, you fucking idiot," Jan yells in a high-pitched voice. "Get the fuck out and help me."

When Kallie jumps out, I'm ready, but he's more agile than Jan. He folds his thin, rubber-like body to the right, neatly ducking the lump meant for his head.

Fear sets in. I can't fight off both. Not moving my eyes away from the men, I claw through the dirt on either side of me in search of a weapon, but there are no more clumps. I grab at stinging nettle and pull out weeds by the roots.

"Fucking cunt," Jan screams, making his way to the ditch.

I'm scrambling backward, trying to get myself out of the bottom, but my feet lose purchase, and I slide down again. Just as Jan jumps down next to me, Eddie comes charging down the road with the pellet gun he uses as protection in the shop.

"You there," he calls as he waves the gun. "Get away from the girl or I shoot you in your sorry asses."

Jan and Kallie pause. Everyone knows Eddie can shoot the dot on the I on a can of Iron Brew.

Eddie skids to a halt a next to us. Aiming the gun at Jan, he says, "You go now, or I shoot."

"Go back to your shop, Chinaman," Jan says. "This isn't your fight."

My heart drops to my stomach when Eddie lifts the barrel, pointing it away from the guys and up in the air. Just when I think he's going to abandon me, a shot goes off. The sound reverberates in my skull and rings with a metallic echo in the air.

"What the fuck?" Jan says, giving Eddie an incredulous look.

Eddie aims again. "Warning shot. Required by law."

"He's bluffing," Kallie says.

Bang. Another shot rings in my ears. It takes me a second to register the aim of the barrel has changed, right before I register Kallie's thin shriek.

Two seconds of silence follows as each of us seemingly tries to get a handle on what happened. Where did the bullet go?

"He shot me," Kallie cries, turning around with his neck strained backward like a dog chasing its tail. "He fucking shot me in the ass."

"You fucking crazy Chinaman," Jan cries, clambering out of the ditch.

"That enough warning for you?" Eddie asks, keeping the gun pointed at Jan.

"He shot me! Ow. Ow, it fucking hurts. Son of a bitch. Ow."

"Shut up," Jan says, grabbing Kallie's elbow and dragging him to the truck. "Get on your stomach in the back. If you get blood on my seats I'll finish you off personally."

Pointing a finger in Eddie's direction, Jan says, "I'm reporting you, you crazy fuck. You're going to jail."

"I'm reporting you first," Eddie says from behind his gun. "This is my property. I have a right to protect myself and my customers. The law says so."

"Ow," Kallie hurls as Jan roughly pushes him into the back and slams the door.

With a last murderous look in our direction, Jan gets behind the wheel. The tires kick up sand and pebbles as he takes off into the direction of town.

When only a dust cloud and tracks are left, Eddie offers me a hand.

"You all right?" he asks, helping me out of the ditch.

I dust my dress, trying not to show how shaken I am. "Thanks for helping me. Wait. Why did you help me?"

"They're assholes," he says, as if that explains everything.

He smells of toffees and incense, of glass soda bottles exchanged for candy and happier days.

Sniffing away my tears, I give him an insufficient, "Thank you." I don't know what I would've done if he hadn't shown up. "I'm really sorry I made fun of your silk shirts with the other kids."

"It's nothing. You were only nine years old. What does a nine-year-old know of style?"

"I can't believe you really shot him."

"It's just a little metal ball. It won't kill him."

"They'll have to make a statement at the hospital. The hospital will notify the police."

"I'm not scared. I'll make a statement with Sarel. He'll back me up. He knows the kind of trouble those no-good boys get into. Just last month, they tried to break into the shop. A security camera caught them. Just in case, you better go make a statement too."

"Sure. Of course."

"You'll be all right now?"

"Yes. Thanks again."

"Good." He throws a thumb over his shoulder. "I have to get back to the shop."

"Don't let me keep you more than I already have." When he walks away, I call after him, "Be careful. They may come back."

He only waves his gun in the air.

A strange silence dawns around me when Eddie is gone. It's surreal, as if none of the drama has ever happened. A bird chirps somewhere in a tree. The sound of the transport truck engines at the brick factory is an ugly but familiar, distant buzz.

Gathering my scattered groceries, I pack the dirty items back in the bag. Hot, unwelcome tears burn their way to my eyes, no matter how hard I try to blink them away. My vision turns too blurry to see where I'm going. I walk on pure instinct, knowing this road and its every pothole and bump like the back of my hand. At the empty plot serving as an illegal garbage dump, I flop down onto a heap of sand. Broken things stick up from the debris—pots missing handles and one-armed dolls. When I was young, this was my treasure hunting ground. I found many discarded toys here. This is what I feel like as I let my tears out for the first time after I told Jake we have to get married. Broken, discarded, garbage. I cry big, fat, ugly tears with loud sobs. I cry until my head hurts and my eyes are puffy.

When I have no more tears left, I feel strangely purged. I wept out all the poison that was trapped in my chest. A newfound calmness invades my senses as I place a hand over my belly. Determination beats in my heart. I have not only myself to live for, but also my baby. Like my mom said, the choice is in my hands. I'm not going to waste my young life. I'm not going to let the Jans and Kallies ruin it.

I choose to be happy, and it starts now. I've been holed up in the trailer ever since I found out I'm pregnant, hiding away in shame. It ends now.

Getting to my feet, I dial Nancy.

"I feel like going out tonight," I say when she answers.

"Really? Wow."

I can't blame her for being surprised. I've refused to go anywhere during the last three months, no matter what she suggested. Tonight, I don't only want to go out, I want to feel pretty again.

"What do you have in mind?" she asks.

"Sugar Loaf." It's Friday night. That's where the action will be.

"Count on me. I'll pick you up."

After a tuna-mayo toasted sandwich, I shower and wash my hair. My skirts and shorts don't fit around the waist, but the black dress I bought last year at the Chinese store has enough stretch to cover my bigger breasts and belly. It reaches my thighs, leaving my legs, which I've always considered my best feature, exposed. My boots add a casual touch. My denim jacket finishes off the outfit.

I consider my clean-scrubbed face in the mirror. The wound from Hendrik Basson's belt has healed, but it has left a small L-shaped scar. My freckles are more pronounced from the time I spent outdoors instead of in a classroom. Applying a coat of foundation, I dab concealer onto the scar to soften it. The one advantage of being pregnant is that I have a natural glow on my cheeks and my unruly hair is, for once, behaving. I add a dusting of bronze eye shadow, mascara, and colored lip-gloss, and then I'm ready.

My mom gives me an approving look when I return from the bathroom. "I'm so glad you're going out. It'll do you good."

My mom doesn't ask why Jake isn't coming around any longer. She knows I'll tell her when I'm ready. I also haven't told her what happened at Eddie's today, because I don't want to worry her, but she'll hear it from someone sooner than later. I'll tell her in the morning when she's had a good night's sleep. Not now when she's just returning home, tired after a grueling day's work.

A horn honks outside.

"That'll be Nancy." I grab my bag and kiss my mom on the cheek. "I won't be back late."

"Have fun, and be safe."

Nancy whistles. "You look nice," she says when I get inside.

"It's kind of your mom to let you use her car."

She pouts. "There's only one snag."

"No drinking and driving?"

"You really have to get your driver's license. Since you're pregnant, you can't drink anyway."

"That's exploitation," I say with a laugh.

"Uh-uh. That's benefitting."

"We have five months left. I guess I better learn quickly."

On the way, I fill her in about what happened the afternoon. When I get to the part where Eddie shot Kallie in the backside, she laughs so hard she has to pull off the road.

"I can't believe Eddie did that," I say. "I never thought he had it in him."

She wipes away tears of laughter. "That'll teach them a lesson, one they're not going to live down for a very long time."

At Sugar Loaf, the field that serves as a parking lot is already packed. Sugar Loaf is a house with a thatched roof on the riverbank with tables under strings of colored lights on the lawn and a covered dance floor on the side. The pub dinners are affordable, and there's live music on a Friday night.

We grab a table outside where we can watch the entertainment. Tonight's performer is a pretty blonde accompanied by a guitarist. When she launches into a popular country song, a group from the bar forms a line on the dance floor.

Nancy squeals. "Let's join them."

"Line dancing isn't my thing."

"Oh, come on. It's easy." She grabs my hand and pulls me to my feet. "Just follow my lead. It'll be fun."

"I don't know."

"It's the first time in months you're coming out, and you're all dressed up." She raises her palm. "All or nothing, what do you say?"

"All," I laugh, high fiving her.

The heaviness that's been pushing me down lifts a fraction. It's good to be out. I haven't realized how badly I needed a change of scenery.

By the time we get to the floor, there are two lines of dancers. I slip into the back in case I make a fool of myself, but it doesn't take long to get the hang of the steps. Nancy was right. This is fun.

The guy in front of us dances like someone with a lot of practice. It's obvious he's enjoying himself. He's dressed up for the occasion, wearing a Stetson, checkered shirt, dark jeans, and boots. He's not from around here. When he turns again, I pay better attention to his face. He's got an open, friendly smile and kind blue eyes. He looks older, maybe late twenties.

Catching my gaze, he tilts his hat with a playful, "Ma'am," before rolling his hips and kicking out his heel.

Nancy elbows me. "Who *is* that man?"

I shrug, trying not to trip over my own feet.

"Well, hello cowboy," she mutters, her gaze glued to his ass.

I elbow her in turn, whispering, "You're staring."

In the middle of laughing me off, she stops abruptly. Grabbing my arm, she points at the bar. I search the crowd until my gaze falls on Jan. He's with a group from our class, throwing back shooters. It's impossible to miss Kallie, who sits on an inflatable pool doughnut. If being shot weren't so serious, I would've burst out laughing.

"Want to go?" she asks.

I'm having fun for the first time in three months. "I'm not running because of them."

"That's my girl." She gives me a thumbs-up.

When the song ends, we go back to our table and order the chicken wing basket with fries and two sodas. The night is heavy with summer. Carefreeness is like a perfume in the air. I inhale it greedily, even if it's only a short-lived illusion.

"Mind if I join you ladies?" a male voice asks next to our table.

The man with the Stetson looks between Nancy and me, but his gaze lingers a little longer on Nancy.

"Oh, sure," she says, shooting me a questioning look as an afterthought.

"Of course," I add for what it's worth.

"Steve." He shakes Nancy's hand, then mine.

"I'm Nancy, and this is Kristi."

She moves up the bench to make space for him. "New in town?"

"Just helping my dad move."

"To Rensburg?" she asks, her voice tinged with disbelief.

"He's a lawyer, and, well, since folks have to travel all the way to Johannesburg for legal consultations, he thought he'd open an office here."

"Here? Sorry," Nancy says, "but I can't imagine anyone from Johannesburg wanting to move to Rensburg."

"My mom died a few months ago. He thinks the change will be good. Plus, getting out of the rat race and all that."

She places a hand on his arm. "I'm so sorry."

"My condolences," I add.

"It was a long illness. We're both relieved her suffering is over."

"For how long are you staying?"

"Until Dad is settled. I'm one of two foremen at a hydroponic farm north of Pretoria, so my time is somewhat flexible. What about you girls? What do you do for a living?" He frowns. "You're not still in school, are you?"

"No," Nancy says quickly. "I'm starting my first job in January at the brick factory."

"Does that mean you're free over Christmas?"

"Yeah." Her cheeks turn bright pink. "Why?"

Oh, my gosh. I can't believe she's blushing. She never blushes.

"I'm planning on spending Christmas here with Dad. Maybe you could recommend some excursions?"

"There are a few hiking trails and a lake that's good for fishing."

"Do you fish?"

"No," she laughs, "but I'm more than happy to show you around."

His smile turns broader. "I'll definitely take you up on the offer." Making an obvious effort to include me in the conversation, he waves a hand at my bump. "How far along are you?"

"Three months."

"I hope you don't think I'm forward for asking."

"It's actually a relief. Most people pretend they don't notice."

"Getting married?"

"Um, yeah." I fiddle with the straw in my glass. "In a few days."

"If this is your hen's night, I shouldn't have gatecrashed." He makes to get up.

"No," I say quickly. "It's just a night out. You're not intruding."

Nancy shoots me a grateful look.

"In that case," he holds a hand out at Nancy, "care for a dance?"

She glances at me again.

"Go on." I wave them off. "I'm still too tired from the first round." Besides, the line dancing has broken up and couples are two-stepping.

With her cheeks still bright pink, Nancy accepts his proffered hand.

He plants his Stetson on my head. "Hang on to that for me. I'm planning on taking your friend for a few fast spins around the floor."

Steve really is a skilled dancer. So is Nancy, but he's giving her a good go. They're both out of breath when they return to the table after dancing three songs back-to-back.

"Sorry for leaving you alone for so long," he says, shifting onto the bench next to me. "I'm getting your bill to make up for it."

"That's kind but not necessary," I say. "I enjoyed the show. You dance well together."

Nancy fans her face with the menu. "I can do with a glass of water."

"I'll wave the waitress over." He turns to me. "What would you like to drink, pretty pregnant lady?"

"I'll have another—" The word ginger ale dies on my lips as Jake walks through the door with Britney on his arm.

CHAPTER 8

*H*umiliation is the first emotion that hits me, and then betrayal. Even as the logical side of my mind argues Jake doesn't belong to me, it doesn't prevent pain from slashing my heart open. It doesn't help that he looks unreasonably hot in skinny jeans, a black T-shirt, and leather jacket, or that Britney looks equally hot—and thin—in stretch pants and a crop top.

Frowning, Nancy follows my gaze. "Shit."

"Anything the matter?" Steve asks.

"Her *future husband* just walked in," she says with frost in her voice.

Can I make it around the back before Jake sees me? Too late. Sensing our stares, he turns his head and stops in his tracks. His gaze goes from me to Steve and back to me. The expression in his dark eyes turns from broody to downright murderous. Dumping Britney on the spot, he makes his way over with long, angry strides.

Questions bombard my mind. Why is he charging at us like a fuming bull? Is Britney the reason he's ignoring me? Are we making an even bigger mess of our situation by getting married?

None of the answers I'd like are meant for other people's ears. Whatever he's going to say when he reaches our table, it's best we take it outside. I open my mouth to say so, but before I get a word out, he swings back his arm and hooks his fist under Steve's jaw with a force that makes Steve fall backward from his seat.

I jump to my feet. "Jake!"

Nancy comes charging around the table, screaming, "What the hell is wrong with you?"

She grabs Jake's arm as he tries to land another punch.

Cracking his neck, Steve gets up slowly. "Whoa." His body is tense, his non-verbal language a warning that he's ready to fight back. "Whatever you're thinking, buddy, you've got it wrong."

Jake turns his attention to me. "Did he touch you?"

A small crowd has gathered around our table, Jan and Kallie included.

I grab my bag. "Steve, I'm so sorry. Jake, we're talking outside."

"Not before you answer my question."

"Back off," Steve snaps. "This is no way to treat your future wife."

Jake charges again, but this time Steve is ready. He lands a blow on Jake's cheekbone before Jake hits him in the stomach.

"Stop it!" I yell, trying to break them up, but they're really going for each other.

Fists fly while the crowd cheers them on.

"Shut up," I scream at the spectators, "and stop them."

Jake kicks Steve's feet from under him, but Steve has his hand fisted in the fabric of Jake's T-shirt and both men go down. They're rolling in the grass, their arms cartwheels as they swing more punches.

"Get the bouncer," Nancy yells, but nobody moves.

Jan pushes from the crowd, taking up a stance in front of me. "Why should we do anything you say?"

Are they all crazy? "Now's not the time."

I try to move around him, but he catches my arm. "We've got unfinished business."

Grunts fill the air as the two men on the ground strangle each other.

"Let her go," Nancy says, trying to shove Jan away.

"My money's on the new guy," someone says.

"Fifty on Jake," someone else calls out.

Between the fighting, the hooting of the crowd, and Jan's fingers that are locked around my arm, my head is spinning.

Nancy grabs a beer bottle from a nearby table and points it at Jan. "Let her go. Jake! Steve! Stop fighting you idiots and help Kristi."

Two bouncers come charging outside. One grabs Jake while the other takes hold of Steve's shirt collar. Pulling them apart, they drag them to their feet. Jake's nose is bleeding, and Steve is sporting a cut on his cheek. Steve's shirttails came free of his jeans and Jake's T-shirt is torn. They're both covered in streaks of mud. Grass sticks to their hair.

"Out front," the bouncer restraining Jake says, pushing him toward the door. "That goes for you ladies too." He points at Jan. "And you."

Jan releases me and lifts his hands. "I didn't do anything."

"Out. Now. Or I'll drag you by your ear."

Jan throws his arms in the air.

"Show's over," the other bouncer says. "Everyone back to their tables."

The crowd slowly disperses as we make our way to the front where Talana, the owner, waits.

"I can't believe you lot," she says when we're lined up in front of her, our heads down. "You're banned from my bar for a month."

"A month!" Jan says. "But that's until January."

"Two months," she says.

Jan purses his lips. "I didn't do anything."

"Three months."

"Fucking hell," he mumbles under his breath.

"I called Sarel," she continues. "You all wait here until he arrives."

"I didn't do anything," Jan says again.

Giving us a disapproving shake of her head, Talana goes back inside and leaves us with the bouncers.

"You're wearing his hat," Jake says, spitting blood on the ground.

I'm so focused on Britney who has just joined us, it takes me a minute to register he spoke to me. "What?"

"I said you're wearing his hat."

"She was keeping it for me," Steve says.

Jake's attention doesn't waver from me. He doesn't even acknowledge Steve. "Give it back to him."

My first reaction is to tell him he can't tell me what to do, but Britney is watching the spectacle with too much interest.

Removing the hat I've forgotten I still have on my head, I hand it back to Steve. "Sorry for ruining your evening."

"You all right?" he asks.

"How she is, is none of your business," Jake says.

Nancy steps between the two men. "Cut it out, Jake. You've caused enough trouble as it is." At *trouble*, she glances at Britney.

Jake only continues to stare at me, the intensity of his gaze so uncomfortable I can't help but look away.

It's a small town. It doesn't take long for, judging by his civilian clothes and safari hat, an off-duty and unhappy Sarel to arrive.

He points at Jake and me. "You and you, get in the van." He turns on Jan. "You too."

"I didn't do anything."

"Get in the van, Jan."

"Want to lay charges?" he asks Steve.

"No, sir."

Sarel nods. "Then we're good here. The rest of you can go home."

"Where are you taking Kristi?" Nancy asks.

"Police station."

"Wait." Nancy grabs his arm. "Why?"

"For something she should've reported this afternoon. Had any alcohol, Nancy?"

"No."

He tips his hat. "Drive safely."

"Call me," Nancy mouths as I turn to follow the guys.

Britney comes running up, trying to take Jake's hand, but he shakes her off. At the rejection, she clenches her jaw and follows two steps behind.

"Not you, Britney," Sarel says as we get to the van.

"I came with Jake. I'm leaving with him."

Sarel plants his hands on his hips and utters a sigh. "Get in. I'll drop you at home." He opens the back but catches my wrist as I make to clamber inside. His gaze drops to my stomach. "You can sit up front."

The divider between the front and back of the van is open, a fact I regret when I have to listen to Britney and Jake's conversation on the way to the police station.

"What's going on with you, Jake?" Britney asks.

"Nothing," he says in a flat voice.

"You still care about her."

"Shut up, Britney."

"Why else would you go after a guy over a hat?"

"That's enough," he grits out.

"I thought you said she was a gold digger."

My ears burn. My cheeks flame. My heart thumps like a pendulum in my chest.

Without taking his eyes from the road, Sarel slams the window partition shut, mercifully saving me, albeit a little late.

After dropping Britney off, he brings us to the station and makes Jake, Jan, and me sit in his office while he stands in front of us with the same disapproving expression Talana had worn.

"You're legal, Pretorius," he says to me, "but considering your condition, I'll call your mom if you'd like her to be present."

"No," I say quickly. "I'm good."

He slams a piece of paper and a pencil down in front of me. "Declaration of this afternoon's events."

Jake turns his head toward me. "What happened this afternoon?"

I'm too upset to even look at him.

Jan jumps to his feet. "I already told you."

"Sit back down, son," Sarel says. "I want to hear it from her."

"What the hell happened, Kristi?" Jake asks again.

Sarel pins Jake with a stare. "You can wait in the cell if you're going to be a problem."

Jake lifts his hands. "Calm like a daisy."

I stare at the blank paper. "Where do I start?"

"From where Jan and Kallie came into the picture," Sarel says, standing over me like a headmaster.

As I press the sharp point of the pencil on the paper, Jan mumbles, "She started it. I told you."

Sarel places the toe of his boot on Jan's chair and leans an arm on one knee. "That's not what Eddie said."

"Eddie's lying," Jan exclaims.

"How can you know he's lying if you don't know what he said?" Sarel asks, twisting his moustache between a thumb and forefinger.

"Eddie attacked us for no reason. We want compensation for what Kallie is suffering."

"Is that so?" Sarel straightens. "According to Eddie, Kristi was lying in a ditch with you raising your fist at her."

At the word *ditch*, Jake is on his feet so fast Sarel doesn't have time to stop him before he jumps for Jan. Both of them crash to the floor as Jake tackles Jan in his chair.

"If you touched her—" Jake growls.

Sarel grabs him by the back of his T-shirt and tears him off Jan. "Be wise and shut your mouth before you utter a threat."

Jake shakes off Sarel's touch. "Did he hurt you, Kristi?"

"Eddie got there on time," Sarel says. "Kallie got a pellet in the ass for his trouble."

Jake balls his fists. "I swear—"

"Threats, Jake," Sarel warns. He doesn't offer Jan a hand when he struggles to his feet. "You're going to do six months of community service," he says to Jan. "Use the time while you collect litter wisely to reflect on why you're picking up other people's trash."

"But—" Jan starts.

"One year," Sarel says.

At that, Jan shuts his mouth.

"You, Jake," Sarel turns on him, "will do voluntary work at the old age home until you leave town." He hands out more notepads and pens. "I'll also need a statement from each of you about tonight's fight. Make it snappy. It's late, and I haven't finished dinner."

We each write down our version of the events, but Sarel has already made up his mind about punishments. Jan and Jake aren't complaining. If Sarel goes the proper route, they'll each end up with a big fine and a record for violent behavior.

When we're done, Sarel drops us off at Sugar Loaf to get our vehicles and asks if I need a lift.

"I'll take her home," Jake says.

"No, thanks. I prefer to go with Sarel."

"We need to talk." He doesn't seem to care that both Jan and Sarel are still present, overhearing our argument.

"We don't," I say.

"I'm going to let you kids fight it out," Sarel says. "You make sure she gets home safely, Jake, or you'll get to deal with me. Just to be on the safe side, I'll follow you home, Jan."

Jan huffs and puffs like a big, bad wolf, but he gets into his truck and pulls away with Sarel following behind.

"You should've told me about this afternoon," Jake says when they're gone.

"Why?"

"You know why."

"Actually, I don't."

"I fucking care, even if you don't."

"Is that what you told your girlfriend, that I only care about your money?"

"She's not my girlfriend."

"Could've fooled me and everyone else at Sugar Loaf."

"It's not how it seems."

"You know what? You're right. I don't care. In fact, I don't want to marry you. I don't want your money. I'll manage on my own." Flinging around, I head toward the road.

Before I make it to the end, Jake's fingers close around my wrist. "Britney is a friend."

"That's not what she believes, not that it's any of my business."

"I can't believe that just came out of your mouth. We're four fucking days away from getting married."

Says the man who brought another woman to the bar. "We're not."

I jerk free and start walking again, but Jake cuts me off.

"I'm marrying you, Kristi. I'll even do it on your terms, just *seeing what happens afterward*. What I'm not going to do is let you carry all the responsibility for a mistake we both made."

Yes, it's a mistake, but deep down I don't want it to be, and that's what hurts the most. It's that he regrets what we've done. "I don't need your money."

"Stop being so fucking proud."

As much as I'm in love with him, I hate him for being right, because I still don't have a job, and there's really no way I'll be able to afford the medical bills on my own.

115

Angry tears blur my vision. "I don't want to be a *gold digger*. Let me go past."

"You know I'll never let you battle it out alone. I'm more than willing to pay for everything. In fact, I insist." He hesitates. His next words sound like an accusation. "My mother told me you and your mom came to the house."

"My mom was upset. Can you blame her? She thought she could talk sense into your parents."

"Did you do it on purpose?"

"Did I do what on purpose?"

"Fall pregnant. Did you try to catch me?"

I can't believe my ears. Is that what his mom told him? He believes her? If I ever regretted having sex with Jake, it's now. "Go to hell, Jake Basson."

I try to slip around him again, but he takes a step to the side, blocking my way. "Tell me."

"If you have to ask me that, you definitely don't know me."

He grips my arms. "Maybe I shouldn't have listened to my mother, but look at it from my side. You claim getting married is only for financial reasons just before you all but chase me away. That hurt. Then I come here tonight and find you with another man. What am I supposed to think? That you need my money but want someone else?"

"Don't be like your father."

"What the fuck is that supposed to mean?"

"Don't be a hypocrite. You came here with Britney."

He holds up his hands. "I didn't."

"Are you saying there's something wrong with my eyes? With everyone's eyes?"

"Are you jealous?"

"What does that have to do with anything?"

"Tell me."

"Why is it so important?"

"I thought you didn't care."

"I never said I didn't care."

"Does that mean you do?"

"Of course I do."

"About what? Us? That guy whose hat you were wearing?"

"For crying out loud, Jake. It's you. I care about you."

"How? Like a good lay? Like a friend? Or just like the accidental father of your child?"

"What do you want from me?" I cry in frustration.

"If you care so much, why did you chase me away?"

"I didn't chase you away."

"You told me to leave. You were very clear about it."

"I told you to go to Dubai. There's a difference."

"Why? Why do you want me gone so badly? And don't give me some bullshit excuse about my dream being better than yours."

I give up. I don't care if it makes me vulnerable or weak. I'm tired of hiding my feelings. I'm tired of playing this game of emotional ping pong.

The words leave my mouth in a rush. "Because I'm in love with you, dammit." There. I said it. It feels scary rather than good, but also liberating. "That's why I'm letting you go, why I want you to chase your dream. If you haven't figured it out by now, you're a fool."

He looks taken aback. "You're in love with me."

"Why does that surprise you?"

"I knew you were kind of physically interested—I saw the way you looked at me in school when you thought I didn't notice—but I never thought a clever girl like you would fall in love with someone like me."

"Oh, come on, Jake. Don't pretend to be humble. Half of the town is in love with you."

"I don't give a fuck about half the town or anyone else. I care about what *you* feel. I thought you didn't want more."

"I never said I didn't want more."

"No," he says gently. "You never said that. You just put my

interests before yours, and I was too blinded by hurt and jealousy to recognize the sacrifice for what it was." He folds his arms around me, dragging me to his chest. "Fuck, Kristi. I'm such a jerk. I don't deserve you."

"You're right. You don't." I push away, flustered by my admission, and still angry and hurt by his behavior. "Why do you even care? You ignored me for the past weeks like you ignored me for all the years we went to school together, and tonight you show up with Britney."

"Have you ever wondered why I stayed so far away from you? I wanted nothing more than to get my fingers in your panties since you turned sweet sixteen in that pink dress with the white flowers. I couldn't think about anything but getting my cock between your legs from the moment you grew breasts. That's why I stayed away from you. You're a good girl, a good *woman*. You're sweet, and honest, and caring. You don't deserve a bastard like me."

His admittance takes my breath. Jake wanted me like that?

"As for ignoring you these past weeks," he continues, "when you told me to leave, I thought you didn't want anything to do with me, so I stayed away. To top it all, my mother told me you and Gina came to the house asking for money."

"What? My mom asked your mother to help us terminate the pregnancy, nothing more. I can't believe you'd think my mom and I would exploit such a situation for money." I wrap my arms around myself. "You want to know what hurts? That hurts."

"I'm sorry." His russet eyes fill with remorse, making them look even more sorrowful than usual. "I said things I didn't mean, things I shouldn't have. I was hurt. I felt used. I shouldn't have listened to my mother, but I wasn't thinking straight."

"You used Britney to get back at me," I say as the insight hits me.

He stares at me with guilt. "Britney was a setup. One of the guys from class sent me a text to tell me you were here with someone else, so I brought Britney to make you jealous, but seeing you with that guy's clothes on your body freaked me out."

"I was wearing his *hat*, and he was making a pass at Nancy, not me." I motion at my stomach. "I'm pregnant, Jake. No one is going to hit on me."

"I would've," he says softly, resting our foreheads together, "even if I weren't the father."

"Oh, Jake." How can I stay angry with him? "This is all so screwed up."

"Did you mean it? Do you want more?"

"I want you to go and do whatever it is you have to do with your life."

"I want to be here for you and our baby."

"What will you do in Rensburg?"

"Work at the factory."

No. Not that. Not now that I know how his father treats him. Hendrik Basson will pay his son peanuts and continue to abuse him, at least emotionally if not physically. It's a worse fate than the one I face going forward on my own.

"What about the medical aid?" I ask. "Without the job in Dubai, you won't have one."

"I'll speak to my father. He has to pay me enough to afford a private fund."

I can already tell him what his dad's answer will be. Staying is simply not an option, not from a financial point of view, and certainly not if I value Jake's wellbeing. There are no jobs here, no future for him.

"What if I came with you?" I ask.

"I hardly have enough money for one plane ticket. I don't even know what the conditions will be like there. Besides, I'll be so busy, you'll never see me. You'll be all alone. At least here you have Gina." He lowers his head to catch my gaze. "We can't have both, ginger."

He's right. We can't. "You have to go to Dubai." I look deep into his troubled eyes. "I don't want you to give up your dream, especially not to work for your father. Besides, you and I both know he's not going to pay you more than the other workers. He'd sooner pay you less. You'll never be able to afford a private medical aid."

"Fuck." He lifts his head to the sky. "This is checkmate, isn't it?"

"Yes," I whisper. "I'm afraid so."

He turns his despondent gaze on me, his wild, broody eyes filling with a spark of hope. "Will you wait for me?"

My heart starts beating furiously, freely, reflecting that same hope. "Do you want me to?"

"Yes, Kristi Pretorius. I want you to."

"Then I'll wait."

Crashing his mouth on mine, he steals whatever breath I have left. He kisses me until I'm dizzy and drowning in the delirious lust only he can provoke. When he takes my hand and leads me to his father's truck, I surrender my heart and body wholly to Jake.

I'll wait as long as it takes.

PART II

CHAPTER 9

Four years later

Jake

Smoke fills the interior of the private club in Bur Dubai, the part where the brothels thrive, adding to the haze in my mind. The area is not called Sodom-sur-Mer for nothing. If everyone turns a blind eye to the sex trade, why shouldn't I? The lights are low and red, a monotone picture in which everyone and everything looks the same. Candy or Cathy or whatever she's called is draped over my lap. I push her off to cut another line. She shoots me an irritated look but doesn't complain.

"Go fetch me a vodka and get under the table when you get back." That's what I pay her for.

My request doesn't faze her. She swings her ass in her tight glitter dress as she saunters off to do as I've said. I roll a hundred and snort, waiting for the high to kick in and dull my thoughts. The whore on the other side of the table looks at the residue powder and licks her lips.

"Go on," I say.

She doesn't let me invite her twice. Licking her pinky finger, she scoops up my scraps and rubs it into her gums.

Candy-Cathy comes back with my drink. She places it in front of me with a sultry look and kneels between my legs. Her red nails walk a trail over my stomach to my belt. She undoes it, unzips my fly, and drags the tablecloth over her head with a grin. Spreading my arms out along the backrest of the bench, I lean my head against the wall. The first swipe of her fingers over my cock is always the best. As soon as her palm squeezes around my girth, my sense of touch is already desensitized. Not even the warmth or wetness of her tongue can bring me back to that first moment. The rest is just a race to shoot as fast and hard as possible. Release is always physical. The aftermath is as empty as fuck. No matter how many whores I pay or how deep I sink into any cunt, my ejaculation is always anti-climatic. I'm left wanting, and fuck if I can say what's missing.

It's not the women. They're all kinds of pretty, whatever flavor I crave for the night. It's me. I'm incapable of feeling. My life is a monotone layer of red. Whatever little there was inside me before, I snuffed out with my own two hands. I once had a shot at something, but I didn't make it. Not professionally, and as sure as hell not personally. My life is one big waste. I'm known as the man who lost Yousef-al-Yasa millions in investment, a failure that still burns bitter in my gut.

"Come, baby," the brunette on the floor mutters.

It's taking too long. My mind isn't on her tongue or her fingers. It's on the disgust in my soul. I need more than a line and a mouth tonight. Shoving her away, I zip myself up and scan the bar until I see the one with the black wig who likes it rough.

C crawls out from under the table. "What's wrong, baby?"

I slap a bill on the table for her effort and down my drink before striding to the bar.

"Private room," I say to the woman with the wig.

She adjusts her bra and strides ahead of me up the stairs. We take the first room with a door that stands open.

"You want it rough?" she asks in her thick accent.

She knows I do. That's what we always do. She lets me spank her pink and hammer her doggy style until her legs cave.

"From where are you?"

"Told you already." She smiles. "You don't want to remember."

I walk her backward to the wall until her body hits it with a thump. Adrenalin surges through my veins. My flaccid cock jumps to life. Something drifts to the surface of my feelings, something within my grasp but so damn untouchable. Every time I reach for it, it shifts a little farther into never. She's pretty, even with her wig. I home in on her slanted eyes as I fold my fingers around her neck.

"Yes," she gasps, lifting her chin to give me better access.

I tighten my grip marginally.

"Yes, baby," she mewls. "Just like that. Do it harder."

I give it to her, allowing her just enough air not to choke, but her eyes don't dilate with anticipation or perverse excitement. Her facial expression is a practiced mask. It's swooning and sugary and over the top. She doesn't really want this. It's a job. It's just a show.

I let her go with a shove.

She takes two steps to the side. "What's wrong?"

"Nothing. I changed my mind."

"That's never happened to me before."

"Sorry to be your first. Don't take it personally."

"You'll still have to pay for the hour. What do you want me to do?"

Unfastening the top two buttons of my shirt, I sit down on the sofa, the only piece of furniture in the room. "Take a break. Hang around here. Do what the hell ever you want."

She's still contemplating my answer when the door opens and Ahmed enters with a box clutched under his arm. He looks from me to the wig.

"Leave us," he says with a tilt of his head toward the door.

The wig doesn't argue. Behind those round, nerdish glasses and slight body lies a lot of power. He's Yousef-al-Yasa heir, one of the wealthiest men in Dubai, and fuck only knows why he still bothers with me. For all the flak I give him, he's the only true friend I have.

He kicks the door shut. "When was the last time you've been home?"

"That depends on which day it is today."

"It's Sunday."

"Then I guess two days."

He turns over the box and dumps a pack of mail the size of an ant heap on my lap. "Try a week."

I stare at the paper littering my softening dick. Mostly junk mail, holiday brochures, and a few bills. It's no secret I have a regular room at the hotel that hosts the private club. I stay here when the colorful multi-layers of my fancy apartment, the one Ahmed pays for that I don't deserve, get too much.

I pull a packet of cigarettes from my jacket pocket. "Thanks for emptying my mailbox."

He swats the packet away. It flies from my hand and hits the floor. He stares at me with an expression I'm well familiar with. Disappointment.

"You're married," he reminds me, his gaze habitually slipping to my naked ring finger.

"It's not a real marriage."

"It's legal. It's real."

I smirk. "It's not wrong if I'm paying for it." I hold up my hands. "No emotions involved."

"Tell yourself that if it makes you feel better, but you don't fool me with your I-don't-care charade."

"Is there a reason you're here, other than delivering my mail?" No one can accuse me of not being self-destructive. I'm being a bastard, biting the hand that feeds me, but I don't know how to stop.

He takes a white envelope from his inside jacket pocket and throws it on top of the pile in my lap. My gaze shifts down. The cursive handwriting makes me pause. Something flickers in my chest. It reminds me of my grandfather fiddling with the rusted wires of one or the other machine, eliciting a spark that never quite ignited. It's been a year since a letter has arrived. I'm amazed she kept them coming for so long, seeing I never replied to one. I'm about to say I'll add this one to the stash when I notice the broken seal. I flip it over. The flap is torn.

Anger is not a new emotion to me, but it's mostly self-directed. The kind flowing through my veins right now makes me want to break the glasses of the last person on earth who gives a shit.

"You opened my fucking letter?"

"You should read it."

"Don't tell me what to do."

"You should read it."

"You obviously did. What the hell gives you the right?"

"Read the letter, Jake. Then go home and get your life in order. If you decide to come back, do it a free man so you can fuck these women without disrespecting another."

Dropping the box on the sofa next to me, he walks from the room, gently closing the door behind him. It's the last part that gets to me. A free man.

Alone, I don't have a choice but to face myself. There's no one to play the jerk for. There's no Ahmed I can use as a punching bag by throwing his kindness back in his face. In the privacy of a fuck room smelling of sex, there's no excuse to not admit the truth. My attempts at sabotaging Ahmed's friendship is a way of avoiding my own disappointment, not his. One day he'll realize like everyone else what a piece of shit I am, and that he's wasting his time.

I flick the pristine envelope over and back, over and back. Alone in a room with only myself and my black soul, I slide out the thin sheet of paper and unfold it. No photo drops out. There's no picture of a boy with strawberry curls and blue eyes. Not that I've ever seen a photo. I only felt the outline of the photograph through the paper, imagining what he looks like in my head. The pinch in the dead cavity of my chest is more than disappointment. It's fear. I scan over the words, each letter neatly shaped like the handwriting of a schoolmistress, but I can't make sense of the meaning. I read it again, and then all the red in my world turns black. Something I didn't know I had, the last anchor tying me to a reason to exist, drifts away.

Kristi wants a divorce.

CHAPTER 10

Jake

A steady beat falls like a hammer in my skull from all the vodka I drank on the plane. I'm bloated and dehydrated. Checking my face in the rearview mirror of the rented car, I see nothing of the symptoms I bear, nothing of the decay from drug, cigarettes, and booze inside. My face is freshly shaven, a business-class luxury paid for by Ahmed.

After four years, this godforsaken town has changed little. The towers of the brick factory still dominate the flat skyline, sending billows of smoke up in the air. The house I've been renting since I got my first paycheck sits on the other side of the lake, as far away as possible from the pollution. I follow the GPS directions and pull up at a raw-brick, flat-roof house that looks exactly like the pictures the estate agent sent. There's a rock garden and a birdbath with a ceramic frog in the front.

Cutting the engine, I clench the wheel. I didn't prepare

anything to say. I have no idea what I'm doing, only that this is the only thing standing between living and putting a gun to my head. I flick the rearview mirror down and use my fingers to comb my hair. There's no time like the present. I quit stalling and get out of the car, ignoring the stammering of my heart. I ring the bell and pull my cuffs straight while I wait. As the seconds tick on, I start to sweat.

At last, an elderly woman opens the door and peers through the security gate. "May I help you?"

The wrinkled face and gray hair stun me. It takes a moment to find my voice. "I'm looking for Kristi Pretorius."

"Who?"

"She lives here."

Her brow scrunches up. "I think you have the wrong address."

"Sixty-eight Brandwag Street?" I stretch my neck to read the number on the wall.

"That's us, but there's no one by that name here. It's just me and my husband."

"Maybe she moved?"

"Wouldn't know, sir. You'll have to check with our landlady."

"Who'll that be?"

"Mrs. Basson." She points with a crooked finger toward the hill. "Lives up there in the big house. I can get you her number."

"I've got it. Thank you."

I'm down the step before she's even closed the door, uneasiness eating into my gut and chasing me along like a dog barking at my heels. I don't have to think about where to go. I head straight to the trailer park.

It's late summer. The day is warm with that tad of melancholy that hangs in the air like a prelude to pending loss as dusk arrives earlier and winter crawls closer. The sun is soft, the light a clean yellow that cuts wedges through the green lawn of the park. My heart jolts when their trailer comes into view. Shattered pieces of memory push to the surface, cutting deeper than bone. This is what I left behind for fame and glory. What I'm returning with is failure and degradation.

Parking at the big gate, I walk down the dirt road. I'm expecting desertedness and a playback of memories, not the woman kneeling in the grass in front of a flowerpot or the boy sitting in the swing. I slow down. Long, strawberry-blonde curls fall in a veil over her face. Her arms and legs are naked, the dusting of freckles like pale stars on her creamy skin. She's wearing a pink T-shirt and frayed denim shorts with green gardening boots. In contrast to the snug T-shirt and shorts, the boots are bulky. The picture forms a beautiful image of vulnerability and innocence, like a little girl dressed up in her mother's shoes. When she stretches her back and throws back her head to wipe a garden-gloved hand over her forehead, the dying sun catches her hair, making it glow like rose gold around her face. Her cheeks are pink with a healthy shine, and the huge, blue eyes that dominate her face glitter with vitality. The whiteness of her eyeballs has always amazed me, how free they are of spidery red veins. She's thinner, but still rounded in all the right places, a vision of wholesome prettiness, of a voluptuous woman and soft heart and all the good things bad, rotten people like me shouldn't admire or crave, not even from a very far distance. She still hasn't noticed me. It's fucking dangerous. She needs better security.

She finishes planting the orange cluster of daisies and sits back on her heels to admire her work. The whole path is lined with pots overflowing with cheerful daisies. The lawn is watered and mowed, complete with a white-picket-fence border. My attention goes back to the boy in the swing. It's impossible to ignore the pull in my soul, the ache that spreads into a bruise that bleeds deep. He looks just like his mother, minus the eyes. The eyes are definitely mine. The swing creaks as one pole lifts off the ground, making my gut twist. I walk faster without thinking, reaching out to steady the pole.

She jerks at my presence, her gaze turning wide as she freezes in her crouched position. Our eyes lock, and recognition slowly sets in. She shoots a worried look between me and our child, her fear blossoming into a stunning, wild panic. Her eyes wordlessly beg me, her clenched jaw saying she'd fight me to protect her child if she has to. She's a good mother.

I give her all the time she needs to get over her shock. It takes the few seconds she trails her gaze over me, pausing on the suit, shirt, and lastly the tie.

When she's finished her evaluation, her lips are slightly parted. "What are you doing here?"

Her voice is a little breathless. It's soft, like her rose gold hair and the picture of her kneeling amongst flowers in the dusk. So is the hint of perfume that reaches my nose. She smells of vanilla and amber. Warm. Clean.

"I got your letter," I say. "What are *you* doing here?"

Her hair whips around her face as she looks over her shoulder at the trailer and back to me. "I live here, as always."

"Why aren't you in the house?"

She rests her gloved hands on her thighs. "What house?"

"You returned the money I sent."

"Jake," she says softly on a sigh.

Everything inside takes notice when she says my name. My dead soul rises like a zombie.

She gets up and dusts her knees, non-verbal language that clearly dismisses me. "It's time for Noah's dinner."

"I need to talk to you."

Her eyes dart between Noah and me. "Not in front of him."

"He's four."

"Children are sensitive to atmosphere. They sense conflict and stress."

"I won't say anything that will upset him. I just want to catch up."

She makes a snorting sound. "Catch up?"

"You know how it works here. If you don't fill me in, someone else will."

She watches me for a couple of seconds with scrunched up eyes as she battles to make a decision. After some obvious mind-wrestling, she says, "You better come inside for a drink."

She sounds so much like her mother did all those years ago when my father hit Kristi with his belt. The scar is still there, a tiny, L-shaped, silver line on the curve of her cheekbone. I itch to reach out and swipe my thumb over the mark, but she's already packing the spade, watering can, and pruning scissors in a wheelbarrow. She lifts Noah from the swing, clutching the kid to her chest. He puts his finger in his mouth and stares at me, drool running over his chubby chin. He's as cute as fuck.

"Noah." She kisses his temple to get his attention. "This is Jake. He's going to come inside for a second."

When she starts walking toward the trailer, I rush ahead to get the door.

She mumbles, "Thank you," and lowers Noah into a toddler's eating chair by the table.

It's the same table and bench I remember. Not much has changed, except for the crib crammed in next to Kristi's bed where the vanity used to be.

The space is too small for the three of us. Leaning on the doorframe, I cross my ankles and watch her move around. It's oddly calming. I've never felt comfortable with being quiet like people do when they claim to get in touch with themselves, but there's a warm humming in my chest as I study Kristi, and for once the tormenting thoughts are absent.

She opens the freezer compartment of the mini-fridge and takes out one of six plastic dishes neatly stacked by twos and lined up in rows of three. Then she removes a pan from a cupboard and puts it on the gas stove.

The little man is still staring at me, something new in his

environment he's not used to. The acknowledgment rips a little part of my heart out, but I don't give the emotion breathing space. It's best not to let such sentiments grow. I wink, and he looks away shyly.

How does one talk to a child? I don't know why I have an urge to make conversation. "What are you having for dinner, little man?"

Kristi quickly looks at me from where she's stirring the frozen contents in the pan. Her expression is a mixture of hurt, disappointment, and accusation.

"He doesn't speak," she says, dragging her hand in a tender gesture obviously meant to reassure over his curls.

I still. Questions run through my mind, none of which I can ask in front of the kid. Why? Has she seen a specialist? At what age do kids start speaking anyway? Of course, if I'd read her letters, I would've known this.

"What would you like to drink?" she asks as I stare at her, dumbfounded, unable to come up with a suitable reply. "I have tea or coffee."

Her hand shakes on the pan handle as she serves what looks like veggie mash on a plate. My presence makes her nervous. Who can blame her? I didn't warn her of my visit. I squeeze past her, open the fridge, and scan the contents. There's a carton of milk, two eggs, and some dinosaur kiddies' brand yogurt. Taking out the jug of water, I fill a glass from the drip tray and turn back to watch her while she puts the plate and a spoon down in front of my son. He utters a happy grunt and attacks his food like a little starving caveman.

"How's your mom?" I ask.

"Good."

I glance over at the bed with the orange bedspread. "She still stays with you?"

"Yes. She's out getting groceries."

She takes a packet of two-minute noodles from the shelf above the stove where two more in the same red flavor are aligned. "Do you mind if I have dinner? There won't be time after Noah's bath."

"What happens after Noah's bath?"

"It's story and bedtime."

I take a gulp of the water, my eyes pinned on her. "Let me buy you dinner."

She stills in the middle of ripping open the packet. "I can't do that."

"We need to talk, and we can't do it in front of Noah."

"You could've just called or sent an email." She rests her hands on the counter. "Why are you here, Jake?"

"Just dinner, nothing more." I'm not going to let her eat a fucking cup of instant noodles.

"The answer is no. Anyway, I have no one to babysit."

The logistics of having a child significantly imposes on a person's freedom, something I've never had to deal with. Fuck, it's never even crossed my mind. My life has always been conveniently free. Selfish. I've fucked up in the biggest way ever, lost millions as well as my professional reputation, but I've never had to eat a cup of noodles for dinner.

"If your mom has nothing planned for tonight, I'm sure she won't mind."

She glances at Noah.

"Has your mom never babysat?"

"Of course she has."

I don't like the statement. It confirms she's been out, maybe with other men, and unjustified as my jealousy is, especially coming from a man who's bought sex as frequently as breakfast, I can't help the darkness spreading in my chest. It festers and burns, churning the rot into something far more ugly than failure. It's so severe I have to press a palm on the aching point between my breastbones.

I force my face to remain blank. "Then what's the problem?"

"I have nothing to say to you."

"I do."

"I don't care about what you want."

"We need to talk about logistics. A divorce has all kinds of implications."

Her eyes flare as she quickly looks at Noah again, who's made a big mess all over the floor. "I need to talk to you outside." She takes a tub of yogurt from the fridge, peels back the lid, and leaves it in the empty plate. "Mommy's just going to step outside for a minute. I'll be right back." She goes out ahead of me.

When I follow, she's standing three steps away from the door with her arms crossed.

"What's up?" I ask, knowing damn well what's bugging her.

"Are you talking about custody? Is that the implication you're referring to?"

"Relax. I'm not here to take Noah away from you." Enough money could do that, especially to single mothers who earn just enough to afford a trailer and noodles for dinner.

"You can't just walk into his life like this. I won't see him hurt or disappointed when you pack up and disappear in a couple of days."

It's going to be a hell of a lot longer than a couple of days. I had no real plan coming here, but the intention springs on me as I'm standing face to face with her, close enough to smell, see, and hear her, close enough to touch her if I reached out.

"Dinner," I say. "We'll talk then. When is Noah's bedtime?"

"Seven," she says, the word hesitant, reluctant.

"Seven-thirty. Will that give you enough time?"

Her tense shoulders and troubled face tell me she doesn't want to agree, but she knows I'm right. Eventually, we'll have to talk.

"Fine," she finally says. Without another word, she enters the trailer and shuts the door in my face.

. . .

WITH AN HOUR and a half to kill, I book into the only hotel in town, have a shower, and dress in a clean pair of slacks and shirt. Then I drive up the hill to the house in which I grew up. At the gates, I sit quietly in the car for a moment. A part of me hoped for change, but the stagnant similarity is sadly familiar. The sight of the pretentious house with its square, stiff walls and the pristine lawn with the crystal blue pool in which no one ever swims still leave me with a sense of detachment. My father died a year ago. Heart attack. I didn't come back for the funeral. What would've been the point of pretending? I felt nothing then. I scour my sentiments carefully, not hard to do when there's so little of them. Dissecting the threads left of my humanity for sadness, loss, or regret, I don't find a shred of compassion or caring. One more thing that hasn't changed.

Winding down the window, I take a wild gamble and punch in the old code. What do you know? The gates swing inward, giving access to the kingdom my father lived and died for. High blood pressure. Too much stress. That's what my mother's telegram said. Who the fuck sends telegrams in a world of modern technology?

I park in the visitor's spot and crunch my way over the gravel to the imposing door. Did my parents make it that size to show the world how important they were or to hide how small they felt? I ring the bell and wait. Inside, heels clack over the floor. The steps are hard and unhurried, indicating they'd let whoever stands in front of the door wait. It opens on the scowling face of my mother. Despite a few wrinkles, she looks the same. It startles me. I don't know why I expected her to be different than my unflattering memory. Her hair is dyed the same yellow shade of blonde, stiffly curled, teased, and plastered in place with hairspray. I can smell the chemicals all the way to the step where I'm standing. Not even her French perfume can mask the odor. Chanel no. 5. A cliché, if there's ever been one. She's wearing a sleeveless dress, stockings, and heels, all black.

No shock registers on her face as she looks me up and down. "I was wondering who got through the gates."

"Aren't you going to invite me in?" The question is mocking, not a request for a scrap of a welcoming.

"What brings you back to town?"

"Who's living in the house?"

"What house?"

"Spare me the games. You know which house I'm talking about."

"Mrs. Coetzee and her husband, I think. I'm not sure if he's still alive."

"Why are you sub-letting a house I'm renting for Kristi?"

"She didn't want it."

"I just saw her. She doesn't even know about the damn house."

Her lips thin. "What did you expect? Your father is dead." She spits *dead* at me like an accusation, as if I killed him. "His life insurance barely covers the bond on this house. It's tough times for the business. How am I supposed to live?"

For four years, she's been pocketing the money for the roof I meant to put over her grandson and Kristi's heads. Judging by the contents of Kristi's food cupboards, my mother has been stealing the monthly allowance too. When Kristi returned my first payment, I've stupidly transferred it to my mother's account with the instruction to use the money to take care of my kid. My mother has always been a status-driven, luxury-hungry bitch, but she's never been selfish, at least not when I was living under her roof. I'm going to do the righteous thing and give her the benefit of the doubt without coming to nasty, premature conclusions.

"Did you ever give Kristi a cent of the money I sent?"

"I'm your mother. I have bills. Have you ever offered me a cent?"

"Have you ever bought the kid a toy, a jersey, food, anything?"

"As I said, I had expenses."

My control is unraveling. I'm doing a shit job of keeping it together. "Have you even seen him? Have you ever visited Noah?"

"Have *you?*" she deadpans.

Guilty as charged. It doesn't prevent anger from whirling in my chest, squeezing until the air in my lungs hurts.

Slamming my fist against the doorframe, I hurl an insult. "Goddamn you."

My mother flinches at the outburst. "You will not use that language with me. Your father may have disowned you, but I'm still your mother."

"A title you don't deserve."

Bunching her fists and stretching to her full height, she hisses, "How dare you?"

"You used my money, the money you clearly knew was meant to take care of my child, to keep up your life of luxury and pay for a monstrosity of a house you live in alone."

"You wanted neither the girl nor the child, or you wouldn't have wiped your hands clean of them. You ignored their existence. I didn't do anything you didn't do first." She points at her chest. "You have a responsibility toward me."

Pain travels through my knuckles up my forearm as the adrenalin from the physical blow starts wearing off, but I welcome the sting. "If you'd asked, I would've given you what I had, but *this* I won't forgive."

I'm done. I can't stand here any longer, breathing the same air as the woman who claims to love me. The problem with that love is that it's always been conditional. Love is only given to kids who behave, who act as they've been taught, adhering to the values of their parents, regardless if they believe in them.

Turning my back on her, I walk back to my car.

"Who took care of you, huh?" she yells, running after me. "Who bought your clothes and paid for your meals?"

She bangs a fist on my window as I close the door and start the engine, staring at me with helpless anger in her ridiculous heels on the gravel as I point the nose of the car to the gates and get the fuck out of there.

I ARRIVE EARLY at Kristi's trailer. Parking at the main entrance, I make a few quick transactions on my phone, canceling the monthly transfer to my mother's account and giving the rental agent notice on the house. It's the quickest way of getting rid of the illegal lessees. I'll find another house for Kristi and Noah.

At five minutes before the agreed time, I knock on Kristi's door.

Gina opens. Her expression isn't hostile. It's something between anxious and disappointed. "Jake."

"Gina. You look well."

She places a palm on her nape. "I don't know what to say."

"I hope babysitting isn't a problem."

"I understand you and Kristi need to talk." She hesitates. "It took Kristi a long time—"

"I'm *right here*, Mom," Kristi says behind Gina, kissing her on the cheek and pushing her aside with a warning look.

"Just don't mess it up for her again, okay?" Gina says.

I look over Kristi's shoulder and find the little man I've been looking for. Dressed in pajamas with an airplane motive, he sits in his crib, quietly playing with a plastic truck. Fuck me if that scene doesn't shred me up inside.

"I won't be late," Kristi says.

She kisses the top of Noah's head and grabs her handbag from the bed. I study her as she walks ahead of me to the car. She's wearing a lilac summer dress with sandals. In the light from the lamppost, the fabric is slightly see-through. The curve of her hips and outline of her thighs are visible. It reminds me of the day we got married when she showed up at the town hall in the pink dress with the white floral print she wore to our last Spring Day at school. It was the only day we were allowed to swap our uniforms for casual clothes. The thin fabric of her dress was translucent in the sun. I couldn't stop staring. I almost gave Jan a shiner for looking for a second too long. There was no sun on our wedding day to highlight the shape of her body under that dress, but I knew those curves by hand and heart. With the passing of time in Dubai, I forgot how her softness fitted in my palms. The memory I religiously revisited in my mind eventually started fading, its potency diminished as the stress of a failing project and flunking grades took the foreground. Being back makes those repressed memories vivid again, as if they happened yesterday. Only, it's not yesterday. A lot of dirty water has run into the sea between then and now, and it's going to take a hell of a lot to fix what I've broken, if I even stand a chance.

I get the door for her, something I haven't done for a woman in a while, four years to be exact. She doesn't ask where we're going, and I don't offer. There seems to be new things in Rensburg after all, one of them the steakhouse I noticed on the drive from the hotel. I didn't make a booking, but it's a weeknight. Few people will be out.

It turns out I'm right. There are plenty of free tables. The night is warm, so I ask for one in a secluded corner on the terrace where we'll have more privacy to talk. The checkered tablecloths and soft lantern light are cozy. It could've even been romantic under different circumstances.

"Have you been here?" I ask as I pull out her chair.

"Once." She doesn't offer more, like with who she came with, for instance.

I don't like it, but I have no grounds for starting an interrogation. "What do you recommend?"

"The ribs were delicious."

I scan the menu for the most nutritious meal I can find. "The steak sounds good. Will that do?" She can do with a healthy portion of protein.

She nods as if to say *whatever*.

The waitress who approaches our table looks vaguely familiar. "Have you decided, sir?"

"We'll have the steak with the salad and a side order of baked potatoes for the lady." After she's taken our cooking preferences, I look at my date. "Wine?"

"Red, please."

"A bottle of Meerlust, Rubicon."

"The house wine will do just fine," Kristi says.

"No, it won't."

"Say, you're Jake Basson, right?" the waitress asks. While I'm wracking my brain for where I know her from, she continues, "I'm Tessa."

I frown. "I'm sorry, but I can't place where we've met."

"My dad worked at the factory. He's retired now."

"I don't recall you from school."

"Oh, no, you won't remember me. My parents sent me to boarding school in Johannesburg. I saw a few of your rugby matches. You were a legend for scoring tries."

I shift on my seat. "That was a long time ago."

"Don't you play any longer?"

"I didn't carry on playing provincially. I moved abroad."

"Dubai, right? Must've been amazing. I hope I'll be able to travel one day. Well, I'll put in your orders straight away." She smiles prettily. "It shouldn't take long. We're not busy tonight."

"Snobbish, much?" Kristi asks when Tessa is gone.

"Because I can't remember a woman I've never met?"

"I'm referring to the wine."

"I suppose I cultivated a taste for the better stuff in the restaurant business."

"No vodka then?"

"Sadly, I'm still a vodka drinker." Especially when I want to dull my senses.

She leans her elbows on the table. "You said you wanted to talk about the settlement. This doesn't have to be a complicated or drawn-out divorce. If you're worried about your finances, you have nothing to fear. I don't want anything from you."

I can't help my dry tone. "You got that point across when you returned the money I sent."

"I'm glad we're clear on that."

"We're not. I rented you a house and made monthly deposits for your expenses."

"What?"

"I found out this afternoon my mother put tenants in the house and never handed over the money I transferred to her account. Apparently, she doesn't have contact with Noah either."

She stares at me as she seems to be processing what I said. After a moment, she utters a soft sigh. "It doesn't matter. I wouldn't have accepted a house or your money."

"Why not?"

"I don't want to give anyone reason to think I *caught* you for financial reasons."

Her words poke at an old piece of guilt, an accusation I once threw at her in the heat of the moment. "Your pride prevented you from giving Noah a proper home?"

Her face tightens. "He has a proper home."

"That's not what I meant."

"We're getting by just fine."

"I don't want to fight about money. I want to know you're comfortable. That's all."

"Thanks for the noble intention, but I'll manage."

Tessa arrives with our food, placing a hotplate with a sizzling steak in front of each of us while a waiter uncorks our wine and fills our glasses.

"You'll take the money," I say when Tessa and the waiter are gone. "I'll make sure it goes into your account."

"You're not listening to me, Jake. I said it's not necessary."

"What's wrong with my money?"

143

"I haven't heard from you in four years," she exclaims softly. "Why would I take your money now?"

"I've always been giving it, ginger. What my mother did is unforgivable. Let me make it up to you."

"Is that why you flew thousands of miles? To offer me money?"

"No."

"What do you want then, Jake?"

Good question. What *do* I want? It takes me all of one second to make up my mind. I want her. I want my kid. "I want to be a part of Noah's life."

"You're kidding, right?"

"Never when my kid is concerned."

"You can't just fly back into town and say, 'Oh, hi, let's pick up where we left off four years ago. Hey, I never kept in touch or answered one of your one hundred and twelve letters, but I want to tell Noah he has a daddy and break his heart when I leave.'"

"I'm not going to leave."

Her lips part. "What are you saying? Are you back for good?"

Just like that, I am. "I'm back for Noah."

Her voice becomes more animated. "He's a sweet kid, and he hasn't had it easy. He—"

That twist I felt in my chest when the swing lifted off its frame hits me again. Harder. "What's wrong? What happened?"

Taking a deep breath, she blinks a couple of times to get rid of the moisture she probably hopes I won't notice. "I'm not going to let you hurt him."

"I understand why you have doubts. You have all the reason in the world. I get that. I'm not asking you to tell him I'm his father and trust me when I haven't earned it yet. Let's just tell him I'm Jake for now. Let me have a little time with him. That's all I'm asking."

She takes a sip of wine and fiddles with the stem of the glass. "If he gets used to you and you leave again—"

"I'm not going to leave, but I won't expect you to trust me on that. I'll prove it. I'm only asking to be around him every now and again."

"Why now, after all this time?"

Because I'm selfish that way. Because if I don't fix this, I'll have nothing left. "I finished the project in Dubai."

"Where are you staying?"

"At the hotel until I find a place to rent." Just figured that out too.

She sighs again. "I won't keep you from seeing him without a reasonable motivation."

"Good. Now eat. The food is getting cold."

She cuts into her steak and takes a bite.

"Why did you call him Noah?" I ask.

"It's my father's name."

Of course it is. All Kristi ever wanted other than her mama is a daddy. "Have you tried to contact him?"

"He said he wasn't interested. He has his own family."

She says it factually like it doesn't matter, but I recognize the hurt in her eyes, the longing. It puts Noah in much of a similar situation, and I'm not surprised she hates me for it.

When she's finished a good portion of her food, I raise the question that's been driving me insane since Ahmed made me read her letter.

"Why do you want a divorce, Kristi?"

She stops eating and gives me a level look. "Do you have to ask?"

Fine. I know damn well what I've done. "Why now?" Why not sooner?

"Does it matter?" she asks, avoiding my eyes.

"It matters. I don't deserve a second chance, but I'm going to ask for it anyway."

"Jake," she implores softly. "Don't."

"What do you want? Tell me and I'll give it to you."

"My freedom."

145

"You've waited four years. Can't you put it off for another few months, give me time to prove myself?"

"No."

"Why not? What do you have to lose?"

She lifts her pretty blue eyes slowly to mine. "The reason I want a divorce is because I want to marry someone else."

CHAPTER 11

Jake

A shockwave travels through me. I expected many reasons, but I didn't foresee this one, a most obvious one, no less, and it hits me straight in the heart. I hate the sympathy in her eyes, the pity she offers as she waits for the blow to settle.

"There's someone else," I say, disbelief like a golf ball stuck in my throat.

She takes a gulp of wine. "Obviously."

I clench my fist under the table, resisting the urge to uplift everything and send the fine crockery shattering to the ground. "Who?"

"That's none of your business."

"Come on, Kristi. You're going to have to tell me eventually."

"You and I haven't spoken in four years," she says as if to justify her decision.

I drag my fingers through my hair, letting the sharp pull ground me. "Are you sleeping with him?"

"Again, not your business."

I'm sick with rage. My brain says my jealous anger is unfounded, but my heart doesn't give a fuck. It feels what it feels. My appetite is gone. "I just want to know who Noah's stepdaddy is going to be."

"I don't want trouble."

"None offered." I swallow down half of the wine in my glass, which tastes like nothing and makes my tongue feel like cotton in my mouth.

"I work for him."

"You're having an affair with your boss?"

"Technically, it's not an affair. You disappeared."

"Technically, we're still married."

"Are you for real?" The neckline of her dress gapes as she leans over the table, unknowingly teasing me with a flash of her cleavage. "Did you expect me to remain faithful to a non-existing husband who married me only to give me a medical aid?"

"So, you *did* sleep with him." I want to smash the jug of water against the wall in a fit of burning jealousy.

"What about you, Jake? Did you sleep with other women?"

Fuck. Here we go. Staring at her, I weigh my options. I can lie, but I don't want to build what I have in mind for us on the foundation of untruths. The ugly part of my life is over. If I'm to start with a new slate, there's only one answer. "Yes."

Something flickers in her eyes, but I can't make out the emotion. She's keeping it too well concealed. "How many?"

"Don't go there, ginger."

"Don't call me that. How many, Jake?"

"A lot."

"Like in five, ten?"

I'm going to come clean, and then I'll make it better. I'll work to make it up to her every day. "Try fifty."

She swallows a gasp. Her pity turns into disgust, and then her face distorts into a mask of incomprehension and hurt she doesn't quite manage to hide.

I watch her as she battles to come to terms with the knowledge. She must despise me, hate me even. Maybe she's realizing everyone who warned her about me was right.

"Tell me what's going through that pretty head of yours."

"I'm tempted to call a cab and walk out on you," she says.

"If you do, it'll mean you care."

Her eyes flash. I'm blackmailing her into a corner. Storming off now will be a declaration that I hurt her, something she doesn't want to admit. I'm using the knowledge to my advantage, to keep her where I want her, which is right here in this very uncomfortable and hurtful moment with me. I'm a bastard, but I can't let her go. Not like this.

She leans back and hugs herself, putting whatever distance she can between us, but she's not reaching for her phone to call a cab. Even if I win, the victory holds no joy.

"God, Jake. How do you even find that many women to sleep with?"

"All of them were prostitutes. None of it meant a thing."

"Why do men always use that excuse?" She drains the rest of her wine. "Not that it matters."

It obviously does.

"I don't even want to think what kind of diseases you have," she continues, grabbing at stones to throw, anything to hurt me as much as I've hurt her.

I know the strategy well. I perfected it with my late father. "I'm clean. I've only gone bareback with you."

She snorts as if it means nothing. "On the up-side, you don't have any more children to neglect."

"I'm sorry I wasn't here for you, for both of you."

"Know what? I'm glad you shared that with me. At least you proved I'm making the right decision."

"What's his name?"

"Luan Steenkamp."

"The lawyer, right? Didn't Nancy get engaged to a Steenkamp?"

"Steve, his son." She pins me with a narrowed gaze. "The guy you attacked at Sugar Loaf."

"Fuck, Kristi. That means he's old enough to be your father."

"Luckily, you don't have a say in who I choose to share my life with."

Like hell. "Do you love him?"

"He's a good person, and he's great with Noah."

That says it all. Kristi has huge daddy issues. On top of that, I fucked up her life. She needs stability, but I'd put my head under a guillotine if she loves him.

"I have a right to move on," she says. "I want to build a new life."

"Agreed."

"Then there's no problem."

"You can build a new life with me."

"Too little, too late, Jake."

"I'm going to fight for you, ginger."

"Spare yourself the effort. You'll lose."

We'll fucking see about that. "Dessert?"

"No, thank you. I want to go home."

AFTER DROPPING HER OFF, I go to my hotel and type the name of the scumbag Kristi wants to marry into the internet search field on my smartphone. He used to be a lawyer at a mediocre firm in Johannesburg. Moved to Rensburg the year I left. It's as if worms crawl over my skin when I think about his hands on Kristi, and how many times he could've laid those hands on her in four years.

I shouldn't have left to chase my selfish, pretentious dream. I wanted to be bigger. Better. Maybe the deep-cutting need to earn my father's approval never worked itself out of my system, and I just wanted to impress my old man. Well, what do you know? I didn't come back better or bigger. I came back with an ugly trail of destruction, a very good reason to continue staying away from my wife and child, but when I look at the old lawyer's face on my smartphone screen, I can't harvest enough selflessness in what's left of my soul to let him have Kristi. I can't because she's mine. I may have left her, but that didn't change the notion that she belongs to me. Fucking every whore in Dubai didn't change that sentiment. I'm not an idiot. I know I'm scum. Kristi deserves better. I fucked up, and I want another chance. Screw everything. New boyfriend or not, I'm going to take that chance, even if I don't deserve it.

Damn. I need a smoke. At this hour, the only gas station selling cigarettes is closed. I won't mind a drink either, but there's no mini bar in the room.

A lukewarm shower later, I crawl into bed. Stretching out on my back, I fold my hands under my head and stare at the green light from the pharmacy across the road reflecting on the ceiling. A bedspring stabs my kidney. I shift closer to the hollow in the middle of the mattress. The sheets smell like dry cleaning chemicals and the pillow is humid.

Closing my eyes, I hope for rest, but like the many nights in a foreign country, the sweet oblivion of sleep evades me. In Dubai, when I couldn't sleep, I snorted drugs and fucked like an animal, and I can't say I enjoyed it. It was a coping mechanism. Something to pass the time.

I throw the scratchy sheets aside and stride across the floor to grab the bottle of water I left on the desk. After a long drink, I go back to bed, but the hours stretch on, each one marked by the toll of the church bell tower on the town square. I switch on the television mounted on the wall. A grainy image flickers to life. The sound is tinny. I flick to a news channel, not that I register much of the broadcast. My mind is elsewhere, at a trailer with a haphazard swing.

Despite the air conditioner, I sweat on top of the sheets. When daylight breaks, I give up. I pull on a T-shirt and pair of shorts and go down into the quiet street. I used to hate this street and its cheap clothing, fabric, low-quality electronics, and pawn shops. I never stood in the middle of the main crossing at daybreak and saw the way the rays fanned out behind the stone church or smelled the scent of the Eucalyptus trees wafting on the breeze. My restlessness and a quest for something better chased me hard, never allowing me to stand still for one second and take it all in. It's like seeing my hometown for the first time.

Regarding everything through new eyes is more than a little disconcerting. The drive is gone. The belief that I was born to be someone, a man better than my father, has dissolved into the bitter realization that I'm nothing special after all. I'm tired and washed out. This is what all the chasing after things I can't name has gotten me. A disillusioned morning on a deserted sidewalk. Despite my loathing of this town, there's a measure of peace in homecoming, something about the familiarity that's like a salve on my soul. A bittersweet hint of nostalgia haunts me, a longing for happier years long gone, and at the forefront of my sentiments lingers the sour regret of the biggest mistake of my life, leaving Kristi.

What's done is done. I can't take it back. I can only try to be a better man and be what she needs.

Filling my lungs with the fresh air, I turn the corner and jog south. My feet find a rhythm and my muscles adapt. Before long, I'm enjoying the strain. In no time, I'm drenched with sweat and out of breath, but it beats the crap out of tossing in an uncomfortable bed.

At the end of the neighborhood, I stop on the hill. The factory with its smoke-producing towers is a jagged line on the horizon, a choppy reminder of edgy days and sharp-cutting moments. In the midst of all those tainted memories something soft grows, something luminous emerging from a hazy cloud of dirty gray, a memory of a girl with strawberry blonde hair and an innocent face walking toward me in an over-sized sweater to tell me she was going to have my baby.

Brushing an arm over my sweaty face, I turn away from the black towers on the red soil and make my way back. After shaving and showering, I stop at the deli on the corner to buy three coffees and bran muffins before driving to the trailer park. It's barely seven when I park. As I get the breakfast from the passenger side, a Volvo pulls up. The car rolls past me and stops at Kristi's gate. Flicking my sunglasses up over my head, I watch.

The trailer's door open at the same time as the driver gets out of the car. Kristi exits the trailer with Noah in her arms. Her hair hangs loose down her back. She's dried it straight. The sun catches the long strands, making them glow like translucent copper fibers. She's wearing a pink T-shirt and tight-fitting jeans, the epitome of shining, wholesome beauty. She shifts the strap of a tote bag on her shoulder and transfers Noah to the other hip. He's chewing on a plastic toy. Like those quiet people who are often overlooked but who observes everything, his eyes find mine before Kristi notices me. When I give a little wave, he pauses in the middle of sucking a dent in what looks like a yellow giraffe. Curious, he watches me with drool running down his chin. The small hesitation catches Kristi's attention. She turns her head my way. A small frown disturbs her pretty features.

I straighten and saunter over. The dude freezes.

"Morning." I resist the urge to ruffle Noah's curls or pinch his cheeks. I detested both of those things being done to me as a child.

Her gaze flitters to her would-be fiancé and back to me. "What are you doing, Jake?"

I hold out the cardboard tray. "Breakfast."

"Um, Luan, this is Jake."

The guy sizes me up like an opponent, which he should, but he's polite enough to offer a hand. "Kristi told me about your unexpected visit."

My handshake is unnecessarily hard. "Dinner."

He scrunches up his eyes. "What?"

"It was dinner, not a visit."

Kristi gives me a narrowed look. "We needed to talk." She's telling Luan it wasn't a date, or maybe the message is aimed at me.

Luan takes her arm and steers her toward his old-man Volvo. "Excuse us. We have to go or we'll be late for dropping Noah off at the crèche."

Ignoring him, I address Kristi. "I was thinking I could drive you, get to know Noah a little better."

She fiddles with the strap of the bag. "It's too much too soon. I don't want to disrupt his routine. This is what he's used to."

Meaning he's used to Luan. Fuck that. "Tomorrow?"

At the car, she hands Noah over to Luan, who straps him into a car seat in the back.

"Look, Jake," she starts, shifting her weight, "let's talk about this later, okay?"

"What about lunchtime?"

"Luan and I don't take lunch."

"You're entitled to a lunch break, aren't you?" I look at Luan as I pose the question.

"Just…" She closes her eyes and holds up a palm. "Not now."

The look Luan shoots me is one of those mature, good mannered, if-you-fuck-with-me-I'll-put-my-lawyer-on-your-ass kinds. He opens her door and bundles her inside before almost running around the car to get behind the wheel.

I lean through her open window. "Want to take your breakfast to go? It's healthy. Bran."

"Sorry, Jake," she says with a small shake of her head.

Luan gives a pathetic little wave to indicate he's about to pull off and I should remove my body from his car. When I don't move, he hits the gas, and I don't have a choice but to straighten or be ripped off my feet. Clutching the tray in my hand, I watch as the car passes through the gates and turns onto the gravel road. As the only two people I truly care about in the world move farther away, the three of them cozily together and I alone, I have an odd attack of loneliness. Unjustified betrayal burns like a fire in my chest. Abandonment settles over me. It's a godawful feeling, and I fucking hate it. For the first time, I get a taste of what Kristi must've felt when I left.

"Jake," a voice says behind me.

I turn around.

Gina comes down the step, dressed in her uniform. "What are you doing here?"

"I brought breakfast, but it seems I arrived too late."

"Kristi is finally getting back on her feet. You can't simply come around and disrupt her life. Noah needs stability."

"Can I give you a lift?"

"Luan would've dropped me," she says defensively. "I like to take the bike. It keeps me fit."

"I have three coffees that'll go to waste."

After a short hesitation, she sighs. "Okay, then. Can you fit my bike in the boot?"

"Hop in. I'll bring you home after work."

"I don't want to make work for you."

"What else do I have to do?"

I get the door and wait until she's fastened her seatbelt before handing her the tray. While I drive, she stirs sugar into our coffee and places one in the cup holder for me.

I steal a glance at her. Except for a few laugh lines, her skin is smooth. Her cheeks have the same natural glow as Kristi's, and her eyes are bright. "You look good."

She peels back the wrapper of a muffin and breaks it in two. "You don't."

I chuckle. "Thanks for your honesty."

She puts a paper napkin on my knee and hands me half of the muffin. "You look like you can do with a holiday."

I lift a brow. "Yeah?"

"You have dark rings under your eyes, and your skin has an

ash-colored undertone." She bites into her muffin. "Signs of over-working, too little sleep, and unhealthy eating habits. Am I right?"

"Not on the over-working."

"Ha. You'll die an early death if you don't take care of yourself." Watching me from over the rim of her cup, she says, "I'm sorry about your father."

"Yeah."

"Why didn't you come to the funeral?"

"Are you always this straightforward?"

"Only where my daughter is concerned."

"This is about Kristi?"

"This is about you, but you're the father of my grandchild, therefore it concerns Kristi."

I hand my untouched half of the muffin back to her and wipe a hand over my face. "I don't think he would've wanted me there."

She turns in her seat. "I guessed things were bad between you, but you're entitled to your closure. That's what funerals are for."

My laugh is wry. "I called him once." When I was at my lowest, just after the deal I'd made behind my mentor's back had folded. "Want to know what he told me? He said it was best I didn't come back."

Stay away, Jake. We're all better off without you.

"I'm sorry to hear that, Jake."

The question she really wants to ask, why I didn't come back for Kristi or Noah, hangs between us like a bad whiff in the air, but she doesn't voice it. Gina is the kind of person who knows when to give a little space.

"How are things at the factory?" I ask.

I'm genuinely interested in how Gina is doing. My father wasn't a good employer. He had no interest in his employees other than the money they made for him. He left everything to my mother, and I learned via the grapevine she employed a manager from out of town.

"Working conditions improved a bit. We had a bonus in December," she shrugs, "so, yeah."

"Tell me about Noah's speech problem."

"It's not a *problem*. He's just late at talking."

"Has Kristi seen a specialist?"

"If you'd read her letters, you would've known."

Blowing air through my nose, I stop in front of the factory gates. "I'm sorry I didn't read the letters."

"Why didn't you?"

"It's not something I can explain in one sentence."

She checks her watch. "I have five minutes." Her lips curve on one end. "You drove fast."

How do I explain something I haven't dissected myself? I'm not going to beat around the bush with Gina. I like her too much. I'll give her whatever honesty I'm capable of finding in the mash of my confusing emotions.

"At first, it was too hard. If I'd read one letter, I would've given up on Dubai and come back. Then I started feeling guilty about not reading them, and like I didn't deserve to read them. I fucked up. Big time." The truth hits me with startling clarity. "In the end, it was a way of punishing myself." For failing at everything I've ever attempted, including relationships, studies, and my profession. Failing at life.

She brushes crumbs from her skirt. "You don't deserve them, Jake."

"I know."

"Good." She gives me a level look. "Go fix your life. Do what you have to, but leave Kristi to live hers. She's finally happy."

"Want me to sign in? I can drive you to the entrance."

"No," her smile turns broader, "but you can get my door."

"Yes, ma'am."

Taking the tray from her, I dump it on the backseat before going around to let her out of the car.

"Thanks for breakfast." With a wave, she's off.

Hands in my pockets, I stand in front of the gates as my mother-in-law walks with no-nonsense strides to the redbrick building. She exudes strength and compassion. I admire the Crocs off her feet for her fighting spirit, for raising Kristi alone and never allowing the dirty gossip and ugly attitudes of the small-minded people in this town to break her pride or good nature.

Tossing the cold coffee that was meant for Kristi, I dump the trash in a nearby can and set out to start my first task of the day, finding my family a new home.

CHAPTER 12

Kristi

"Ow." I curse under my breath and cradle the finger I caught in the filing cabinet drawer against my chest.

First, I burned my wrist when I heated up our lunch in the oven, then I punched a staple into my thumb, and this is going to leave me with a blue nail.

"Everything all right?" Luan asks behind me.

His voice doesn't rise in volume or panic at the way I suck air between my teeth and try not to cry as I wait for the pain to pass. It's one of the things I appreciate most about him. He's always soft-spoken, even in a crisis. Slamming your finger in a drawer isn't a crisis, and I'm guessing not all of the tears are inspired by pain. My emotions are all over the place since last night.

Taking a deep breath, I glance over my shoulder. He's standing in the doorframe, arms folded. We work from his home. He converted one of the spare bedrooms into an office for me when I came to work for him four years ago. Knowing how badly I needed money, Steve arranged the job for me after Noah was born.

I look away from his serious expression. "I'm just a bit clumsy today."

"It's not like you," he says from closer behind me. "You're upset that Jake is back."

"Of course I am," I snap. Closing my eyes, I blow out a sigh that doesn't relieve the tightness in my chest. "I'm sorry. I didn't mean to raise my voice."

His hands fall on my shoulders, kneading gently. "He's no good for you."

I don't know why his words make me so defensive. "You don't know him."

"I know what he did to you."

I pull away from his touch and turn to face him. "He married me for medical benefits because I asked him. He had no real obligation to me as a husband." But he asked me to wait, and I did. Far too long.

"He had an obligation to his child."

I can't argue that fact, not that I'm in the mood for arguing anything. "I'm going to make tea. Want some?"

"He left you to your own devices and never once asked about his child. Did he even know it was a boy?"

Pushing past him, I make for the hallway. "You don't have to remind me of what he did."

He catches my arm and carries on in his gentle, monotone voice. "I watched you suffer. I know what you went through. I don't want to see you hurt again."

My resistance melts a little. Guilt for trying to avoid Luan in favor of solitude makes me feel bad. "Thanks for looking out for me."

"Don't let him put ideas into your head."

"Like what?"

"Like not going through with the divorce. I'd like to marry you before Christmas."

"That soon?"

"I know we haven't discussed a date, but we made the decision. Why wait? I want you to move in with me."

I want to ask why rush, but I don't want him to think I suddenly have doubts because Jake is back in town.

"I want to announce it," he says in his reasonable voice. "We need to make arrangements."

"You said not before the divorce is through."

"All the more reason to get him to sign those papers."

"I will."

"What about Noah?"

"I'm not going to keep him away from his child without good reason, but we agreed not to tell Noah until Jake has proven Noah can count on him."

"He'll first have to prove he's going to hang around."

There's that, yes, and that's the part where I have difficulty believing Jake. "I'm not an impulsive person. I won't do anything that could hurt Noah."

"I know. That's one of the things I like so much about you."

I don't want to talk about Jake any longer. "Tea?" I throw back over my shoulder as I eventually denounce my guilt and escape to the kitchen.

"I wouldn't say no." He calls after me, "Don't forget to prepare the spare bedroom. Steve will be here tomorrow."

AFTER BALANCING the cheque book and capturing invoices, I have thirty minutes to spare before I have to pick up Noah. I use the time to air the spare room and make the bed with clean linen from the lavender-lined cupboard. I'm fluffing out a pillow when my phone rings. Nancy's name appears on the screen.

"Jake's in town," she blurts out when I answer.

161

News travels fast in this town. "I know."

"Why didn't you tell me?"

"I was going to call you later tonight."

"I can't believe you didn't call the minute he arrived."

"It was late, and then I got caught up with work this morning."

"Is it the divorce? Is that why he's back?"

"I'll tell you tomorrow at the barbecue."

"Are we still on?"

"Why wouldn't we be?"

"I thought maybe you and Jake—"

"I moved on. Nothing is changing."

"You're okay with that?"

"With what?"

"Seeing him after all this time."

"I'm not the nerd from high school who had a crush on the bad boy in town."

"You sure chose well."

"Done and dusted. I'm cleverer now."

"Good. Got to go. I have to shave my legs and paint my nails before Steve sees me looking like a chipped painting with cactus thorn legs." She blows a kiss and hangs up.

Luan enters as I slip the phone back in my pocket.

"That was Nancy," I say.

"Again? Didn't she call yesterday?"

"She wanted to know if we're still on for tomorrow night." He doesn't reply for long enough that I have to ask, "We are, aren't we?"

"I have a lot of work. If I burn a little midnight oil tonight I suppose I could take a small breather on the weekend."

It's not about work. It's about my friendship with his future daughter-in-law. "If you avoid Nancy, it's only going to make the situation weirder."

"She's engaged to my son."

"A fact of which I'm well aware."

"My son's wife will be the same age as mine. I'm not comfortable socializing with them as a couple."

"What's your solution? To see them without me? How is that going to work for the rest of our lives?"

"You're an adult. You need to cut the high school ties. A little distance from Nancy can only do you good."

"Are you asking me to give up my friend?"

"No, but put yourself in my position. Can you imagine what people are going to say? All I'm asking is that you don't rub the fact that father and son date two girls of the same age under their noses."

"I'm not ashamed of our age difference."

"When Nancy marries Steve, she's going to move to Pretoria. You won't see her nearly as often. It's not a bad idea to start weaning off each other."

"This is your problem, not mine. I suggest you find a way of dealing with it before we tell the world we're getting married."

"You *are* married."

"What's going on? You're never this combative."

"You're right." He raises his hands. "I'm sorry. I wanted to tell Steve this weekend about our plans and until you're divorced, I can't tell a damn soul, not even my son. Hell, I can't even start dating you until you're divorced."

"I can't help the way things are."

"Of course you can't. Maybe..." He sighs and shoves his hands in his pockets.

"Maybe what?"

"Maybe we should tell Steve. I'd feel a hell of a lot better not pretending around him. I don't like lying to my son."

"I never asked you to lie to Steve. You're the one who didn't want to tell anyone about our plans until I'm legally free."

"Getting together with a married woman will ruin my reputation, and in my profession—"

"Reputation is everything. Yes, I know."

"It doesn't help that your husband is in town, prolonging the process."

Ah. The crux of the matter seems to be Jake's refusal to sign the divorce papers. "I can't go into a court battle with Jake. You know the financial implications and risks better than anyone."

"I do." He paces to the window and back. "We can file a case of neglect."

"Jake rented a house for Noah and me. Apparently, he sent a monthly allowance via his mother too, but Elizabeth kept the money."

"Damn. That will be traceable."

"I don't want to get into a name smearing campaign with Jake. It's not what I want for Noah, not if he has a chance to get to know his father."

"This is coming from here." He presses a finger on my heart. "From the part of you who grew up without a daddy."

"Yes, and I know what it's like. I don't want that for Noah, not if it's avoidable."

"He'll have me."

"It won't prevent him from having questions about his father when he grows up."

"What if his father isn't a good man?"

"Just because Jake chose a different future over us doesn't make him bad. It happens to lots of people. I prefer that to tying him down with something he didn't want."

"We're talking in circles."

"And we're going to be late for Noah."

He lifts his face to the ceiling, reflecting for a second. When he looks back at me, his expression is decided. "Let's wait until you're legally free to make a public announcement, but I'd like to tell Steve tomorrow."

"You realize if you tell Steve he's going to tell Nancy."

"Yes," he says regretfully. "I only hope she'll keep it to herself."

"She's my friend. She will."

"If you say so." He checks his watch. "If we catch all the traffic lights green, we'll only be one minute and thirty-five seconds late."

~

Jake

AFTER DROPPING OFF GINA, I browse a property site on my phone for houses to rent and come up with a list in the area on which one agency has a mandate. A guy named Basie answers the phone and agrees to meet me in an hour. Rentals are slow in small towns.

We drive from Rensburg to Heidelberg's side, visiting flat-roof houses with sad little gardens more depressing than Gina's trailer. I almost give up until we park at a stone house with an A-line roof on the outskirts of Heidelberg. It's old but newly renovated. The wooden floors have been sanded down and varnished, and the pressed ceilings repaired and painted. Basie tells me the fireplace is in working condition. The bathroom has a clawfoot tub and a nice mosaic of black and white tiles. The kitchen is redone, too, with wooden cupboards and brass fittings. The property is big with lots of apricot, peach, apple, and fig trees. The vast lawn is green. Perfect for a little boy. The only problem is that the house is for sale, not for rent. I take the details and drive back to the hotel where I order room service.

While devouring a tough steak and stale fries on the dusty sofa, I log into my bank account and check my balance. Ahmed pays me a salary to run a small part of his holiday resort franchise. The money is a lot more than the labor is worth, but what's left of it won't last for six months. If I'm staying, I'll need a job, and soon, a commodity in Rensburg that's tougher to come by than turtle teeth.

I give up on the cold fries and dial Ahmed on video chat. The least I owe him is letting him know I arrived in one piece. From the sport club towel draped around his neck and the sheen of sweat on his face, he's at the gym.

"I was expecting you," he says. "How's your wife and kid?"

"He's cute as fuck. She's still pretty."

He wipes his face on the towel. "Do you need a return ticket to Dubai?"

"No."

"She took you back?" he asks with disbelief, going down a staircase.

"I'm working on it."

"Do you have a job lined up?"

"Working on that too."

"I guess then you're calling to resign."

"You don't really need me. You've been charitable for long enough."

"I'll be sad to see you go, but happy if things work out. I can have your flat packed up and your belongings shipped to you."

"I'll appreciate that." There isn't much other than clothes. "I'll text you the address."

"Anything else you want from Dubai? A souvenir? A keepsake?"

"The letters."

"You threw them in the trash."

"I know you kept them."

He stops in the change room. "Do you remember that day on the yacht?"

"You said one day I'd regret throwing them away. Fine, you told me so. I want them back."

"I read them."

"I know."

"She's a good girl, Jake."

"Yeah. I know that too."

"If she wasn't taken I'd—"

"Don't fucking say it."

"I'll send your letters."

"You're a good friend."

"We all deserve one. Keep in touch, Jake."

The line goes dead.

I HAVE a coffee in the bar downstairs where they no longer sell cigarettes. The barman tells me it's a new law. I'm craving a smoke but am in too much of a rush to make a detour to the gas station. I want to stock up with groceries and swing by the hardware store before they close at five.

A couple of hours later, my purchases in the trunk, I drive to Kristi's place. It's a little after five. They're not home yet. While I wait, I hammer the pegs I got at the hardware store into the feet of the four swing poles. Happy that the frame is stable enough to hold an elephant, I carry the boxes from my car and wait. Then it hits me like a brick on the head. Gina. Fuck.

Jumping back into the car, I race down the gravel road to the factory. I make out her figure in the dirt road near Eddie's corner café from a distance. When I reach her, I pull over and get out of the car.

"Fuck. Gina, I'm sorry. I got busy."

She regards me with her hands on her hips. "Not being good for your word doesn't set a great example. Neither does forgetting your commitments."

"I apologize profoundly. I mean it. I swear. It won't happen again."

"What were you so busy with?"

"House hunting. Grocery shopping."

"Where are you moving to?"

"It's for you, Kristi, and Noah."

"Mm." She walks around the car and waits.

I dive around, getting her door before she changes her mind. When we pull off, I study her a little closer. Her face is red from the walk, but she doesn't complain. Reaching behind me, I grab a bottle of water from one of the shopping bags and hand it to her.

"Thank you," she says, chin lifted like a proper lady and not like someone who's just walked far enough to earn a blister.

"You're cool, Gina."

"You're not."

"Okay, I deserve that."

She glances over her shoulder at the bags. "That's a lot of food for one person."

"It's for you. I already left the big boxes at the trailer."

She lifts an eyebrow. "What's the occasion?"

I shrug. "Nothing."

"Can you cook?"

"Not really."

"Hmpf. If you stick around, I could teach you a few basic recipes, stuff you need to know if you're going to battle it out on your own."

"Sounds like a deal."

"We'll see."

Meaning she's not taking my word for sticking around yet. Fair enough.

At the trailer, I carry the rest of the bags inside while she takes off her shoes and massages her feet. I appreciate that she doesn't tell me where to pack the stuff, but lets me find my own way around the cupboards. My mother has a place for every item. The pasta can never take the spot meant for the rice.

Through the window, I see Luan's Volvo pull up. Kristi gets out and takes Noah from his car seat. Luan doesn't accompany them to the door. He must've seen my rental. That's where we're different. If I were in his shoes, I'd be stuck to Kristi's side, making sure the unwelcome rival in her trailer leaves before me.

She looks tired when she pushes the door open. Her shoulders are slumped and her face drawn. Automatically, I reach for Noah to ease her heavy burden, but she clings to him with a small shake of her head.

"What are you doing here?"

"He brought food," Gina says.

Kristi's proud face hardens. "We don't need your food. We're getting by just fine."

"I know." I place the last packet of pasta in the cupboard and close the door. "Just sparing you the trip to the supermarket."

She drops her tote bag on her bed and puts Noah in his highchair. "It's Noah's dinner and bath time."

"Mind if I hang around?"

She gives me a startled look. "You want to watch me feed and bathe him?"

"Yes."

She ponders the request for a moment, then shrugs. "Suit yourself."

"I'll throw something together for dinner," Gina says.

While Kristi grabs what she needs for Noah's bath, I take a seat at the table. Cheeks puffed out, he makes a *brrrr* sound as he pushes a red truck over the tray part of his chair. If he can make sounds, there's nothing wrong with his vocal cords.

I grab a yellow cab from the toy basket on the floor and add it to Noah's truck. "Have you had hearing tests done?"

Kristi takes a towel from the shelf that holds a stack of toddler clothes and spreads it out on the bed. "Of course."

"His hearing tested normal," Gina says.

Kristi puts a plastic tub on the bed while Gina fills a pot with water and places it on the portable gas stove. When the water is warm, Kristi reaches for the pot, but I'm on my feet before she can lift it. I empty the water into the tub and refill the pot to heat more water. Soon, they'll have a proper damn bathroom.

Kristi undresses Noah while Gina starts dinner and I heat up two more pots of water. Before she puts Noah in the tub, she tests the temperature with her elbow. I memorize every detail, putting the information away for future use. The little guy loves the water, splashing it everywhere with a big grin, getting the front of Kristi's T-shirt soaked. She laughs at his antics, unaware of how the wet fabric defines her curves under the lace of her bra. I barely manage to tear my gaze away lest she catches me staring.

"Please pass me the shampoo," Kristi says.

I check the label and memorize the brand too, which claims to not burn kids' eyes.

She squirts a drop on his copper-blond hair and lathers it into foam, which she also uses to wash his body. The bathing ritual mesmerizes me. Noah gurgles happily, and Kristi chuckles every time he slams a little palm on the surface to make more water slosh over the rim of the tub onto the towel. She lets him play for a short while with a plastic duck before lifting him out, much to his protest. When he's dry and dressed in his pajamas, she puts him back in his chair while Gina serves his dinner in a bowl. It looks like more of the homemade veggies from last night.

Gina regards me with her hands on her hips. "Want to feed him?"

I don't miss the quick turn of Kristi's head.

"Stop spoiling him," Kristi says. "He has to eat by himself."

Gina hands me a spoon. "Once won't make a difference."

"Tell you what." I take another spoon from the drip tray. "We'll make it a team effort. What do you say, Noah?"

"Let me tie his bib first," Kristi says.

"Why don't you bathe him after dinner, let him get the messy part over with first?"

"He tends to throw up in the bath if his tummy is full."

Ah. "That makes sense."

When a bib the size of a dishcloth protects his clothes, I hand him one of the spoons. "One time you. One time me. Get it? Here goes. I'll start."

He quickly gets the hang of it. I'm not sure who enjoys the game more. It may just be me. It's cute as hell how he concentrates on sticking the spoon in his mouth and not in his nose. I can't help the laugh that shakes my shoulders every time he takes aim. A nagging notion at the back of my mind says he has to be better at this kind of motor skill for his age, but I dismiss the worry. Every child has his own rhythm. I've never been a big fan of *norms*.

I manage to get through his dinner without making a mess. By the time we're done, his pajamas are still clean, and I only have to wipe his face.

"Did I pass the test?" I ask as Kristi lifts him from the chair.

She doesn't smile, but her expression isn't unfriendly. "Maybe."

I'll take maybe. I'll take anything. Maybe is more than I deserve.

"Want to stay for dinner?" Gina asks.

"I don't think—" Kristi starts, but Gina cuts her off.

"Since you bought the food."

I grab the opportunity with both hands. "I appreciate the invitation."

While Gina fries the steaks I got, Kristi tucks Noah in and reads him a story. I'm sitting at the table, glued to the scene. It's soft and loving and something I never had, something I suddenly ache to be a part of with all my soul. I'm so engrossed in watching how good Kristi is with Noah, Gina has to nudge me to get my attention.

"Can you make a salad?"

I glance at the ingredients she's put on the table, making it easy for me without being obvious. "Of course."

My salad is a lopsided affair of unequally sliced tomatoes and chunks of cucumber on humps of lettuce, but both women are too polite to say anything. I open a bottle of wine, the one thing I'm good at, and serve us. Noah sleeps soundly through our dinner noises.

"He's used to it," Kristi says when I ask her about it.

In such a cramped space, he doesn't have a choice.

After clearing the table, I do the dishes in a bucket of soapy water while Gina goes for a shower and Kristi folds the laundry.

Drying my hands on a dishcloth, I turn to face Kristi. She's folding a T-shirt, ironing out the creases with a palm. Our bodies are close in the small space. Mine comes alive for her like I've never reacted to another woman. It takes every ounce of self-control and more not to touch her.

"I'd like you to look at a house," I say softly, mindful not to wake Noah.

She adds the T-shirt to the pile of folded ones. "What will be the point? I'm going to move in with Luan."

Clenching my fists, I let it slide. "There's still now until then."

"Don't."

"Don't what?"

"We're not going to be a family, so don't pretend we are."

"Just look at the place. If not for you, do it for Noah."

She bites her lip.

"Is Gina moving in with you and Luan?"

"No," she says, but adds hastily, "I'm going to rent her a flat."

My guess is Luan doesn't want Gina to move in with them, or Kristi wouldn't look so guilty. "Tomorrow, after work?"

"Jake." She sighs. "Please."

"Please what?"

"Stop pushing so hard. I appreciate the groceries, but I don't want your money."

"We've established that. Have a look at the place. No strings. I promise."

She sighs again. "I don't—"

"Five. I'll pick you up."

Before she can argue, I plant a kiss on my finger and press it gently on Noah's forehead. "Tell Gina I say goodnight," I say as I see myself out.

～

I'm disappointed when I pick Kristi up at five the next day and find her alone.

"Noah?" I ask as I get the car door for her.

"He's staying with my mom."

"I don't mind bringing him."

"He'll get hungry soon. You don't want to hear him bawl when his tummy is empty."

Actually, I do, but I say nothing. It's enough that I get to spend the next hour with Kristi.

She's quiet during the drive and gives my questions about her day short yes and no answers. Getting the message, I keep my mouth shut until we arrive. When we walk up the garden path to the front door, I watch her face carefully.

Her expression is reserved while I take her on a tour of the house, but her eyes light up when we exit into the small fruit orchard at the back. Running a hand over the petals of the roses, she stops and looks at me in a way that tells me she's got lots on her mind.

"What are you doing, Jake?"

"What do you mean?"

"I already told you. If you're doing this for us, you're wasting your time."

Fine. Time to change tactics. "It's for me."

"You? The house is enormous."

"I can't stay in the hotel indefinitely."

"Your mom's place is big enough for both of you."

"Not nearly."

She clears her throat. "I know things were difficult between you and your father, but shouldn't you try to sort out your differences with your mom?"

"Not your business."

"Sorry, you're right." She turns and walks back toward the car.

Catching up with her, I grab her elbow. "I didn't mean it like that."

"I can't do this with you."

"Do what?"

She looks at where I'm gripping her arm. "Whatever game you're playing."

It's no game, not where she's concerned. When she pulls a little, I let go, giving her space. "Would you let Noah visit here if I stay? I mean, is the house childproof enough for you?"

"There's nothing wrong with the safety here."

"That's all I wanted to know," I lie blatantly.

"Really?"

"Yes. Why? What did you expect?"

She gives a small shake of her head. "I better get back. My mom will need a hand."

"I'm happy to help with Noah's bath, or dinner, or cooking." I'm sure she can do with a little downtime.

"Thanks, but Luan is coming over for dinner."

I hate the sound of that, but there's nothing I can do but drive her home, see her to her door, and tell her goodbye. She can have her dinner with Luan, but I'm not done fighting. Not even close.

Kristi

I'm still not myself when I get ready for the barbeque on Saturday evening. It's a weekly event in town and normally a lot of fun, but I feel disorientated. Luan picks up my mom, Noah, and me. He doesn't talk much, perhaps contemplating how to break the news of us getting together to Steve, and I'm grateful for the silence.

Portable tables are set up on the shore of the lake, and the barbecue fires are already lit when we arrive. Nancy hurries over when she sees us, taking Noah from my arms.

"Hey there, champ." She plants a kiss on his forehead.

174

Steve saunters over. "Good to see you, Kristi." He nods at my mom. "Gina." After exchanging small talk about our week, Steve pulls Luan away to get a beer from the stash in the ice-filled tub. Nancy sits down next to Noah on the picnic blanket I spread out while Gina wanders off in the direction of the food table to ask if the women need help.

"He's getting so big," Nancy says, pulling Noah's red cap over his curls. "I can't wait to have my own."

"My advice is to do all that traveling you want before starting a family."

"Nah." She makes a face. "Steve doesn't like to travel." Her gaze moves to where Steve and Luan are standing at the edge of the water, a small distance away from the other men. "They sure seem to be having a serious discussion."

"About that." It's best I prepare her. Besides, I don't want my best friend to hear the news from Steve. "There's something Luan and I are meaning to tell you."

She looks back at me with a happy smile. "He's giving you a pay rise?"

"Not exactly."

"A promotion? A holiday? Business shares?"

"We're together."

Her smile vanishes. "I'm sure my ears just fooled me into hearing you're with him, as in *with* him."

"Noah needs stability. Luan will be good for us."

"That's convenience, not love."

"Love comes in many forms."

"Oh, come on, Kristi. You don't have to bullshit me. I'm your best friend, remember?"

"Aren't you happy for us?"

"I want *you* to be happy."

"I will be. I mean, I am."

"When did this happen?"

"A couple of weeks ago."

"I don't get it. Your behavior toward him hasn't changed. I mean, you're not acting like lovers."

"We're not. We decided to do things properly, to wait until I'm divorced."

"Forgive me for saying this, but there's no spark between the two of you."

"Our relationship isn't like that. We grew close working together over the years. Luan brought it up one day during lunch. He's lonely, and I'm tired of being alone. We're not blind to our age difference, but we want the same things. Luan wants a companion, and I want stability. Battling it out on my own is exhausting, both emotionally and financially. It will be nice to have a partner for a change.

"We talked about my situation with a non-existing husband and him being a widower for four years. We're both at a point in our lives where we're ready to move on. It's important to him that we remain respectable. That's why I asked for a divorce. We decided to wait until I'm legally separated."

"Wow. Then it's serious."

"We're getting married as soon as my divorce goes through."

"Fuck." She covers her mouth with a hand. "Sorry, Noah."

Steve's face turns toward me, his forehead scrunched up. "It doesn't look like he's taking it well."

"You do realize if you marry Luan, that will make you my mother-in-law?"

I smack her arm. "It's not funny."

She giggles. "Yes, Mom."

"I'm serious, Nancy. Cut it out. It's hard enough as it as."

"How's Gina taking it?"

I search the crowd and find my mother sitting on the edge of the mud wall, her legs dangling over the side with her feet in the water. Eddie approaches with a soft drink, asking something. She smiles and takes the can when he pops it. Eddie's been nice to us ever since I fell pregnant, giving us freebies and dropping off our groceries.

"My mom is happy for us. You know it's not in her blood to be judgmental."

"Neither am I—" Nancy starts, and then bites off her words with a mumbled, "Shit."

I follow her gaze and freeze.

Jake is crossing the lawn, looking dark, dangerous, and broody in a pair of well-worn jeans and a faded T-shirt. His gaze roams over the crowd until he spots us. He gives me a half-smile and a nod but doesn't approach. He cuts away in the opposite direction. I'm unable to move or look away. It's yesterday reincarnated, when he pinned me down in the mud on this very shore before the municipality covered the memory with grass and flowers. My body reacts to the picture in my mind as if it's never forgotten. Dormant parts of my anatomy begin to tingle. There's a buzzing noise in my ears.

"You all right?" Nancy asks softly.

My effort at uttering a carefree laugh fails miserably. "Why wouldn't I be?"

"You're whiter than icing sugar."

"Blood sugar. I need to eat."

"I'll get you something," she says, but before she can push to her feet, Luan and Steve appear next to us.

"It's done," Luan says, dusting his hands as if he's just dug a grave.

Steve's smile is no less warm than usual. "Congrats, you guys. I'm glad for you. You both deserve someone. The only line I'm going to draw is calling you Mom, Kristi."

Nancy bursts out laughing. "That's what I said."

"It's no joking matter," Luan says, his face tight.

Someone opens a trunk, exposing two monster car speakers, and a popular song starts to play.

Steve pulls Nancy into his arms. "Dance with me?"

They walk off with their arms around one another's waists toward a group already moving their bodies to the rhythm of the music.

Luan takes a seat next to me on the blanket. "That went well."

"I'm glad."

"Shall we say hi to Mozie? I want to chat with him about a business contract he asked me to look at."

"You go. I'll stay with Noah."

"It's Tessa's turn to watch the kids. Let him play with the other children. It'll do him good."

At the edge of the water, kids are throwing breadcrumbs at the ducks. "I don't know." Noah won't be the youngest in the group. Maddy is two months younger, but Noah can't express himself. My mom and I are the only ones who understand his non-verbal language.

"You've got to cut the ties a little." Luan gets up and waits. "Let him mix with kids of his own age. It may even help him with his speech impairment."

"It's not an impairment."

"Delay," he corrects with his ever-present patience.

When I look toward the kids again, my heart skips a beat. Jake stands to the side, talking to none other than Britney, his matric dance date. She's married now with two kids, but that doesn't stop her from twisting a lock of hair around her finger and giving him a sultry smile. Her husband is too focused on putting bait on the hook of his fishing rod to notice. Jake seems absorbed in their conversation, laughing at whatever she said.

Tearing my gaze away, I push to my feet and pick Noah up. "Fine."

It shouldn't hurt, but I can't help the little twist of rejection that lances into my heart as I stride past Britney and Jake with Jake's son in my arms. Not trusting my face to hide my feelings, I avoid a greeting by pretending not to notice them. Is it wrong of me to feel like this when I'm walking next to the man I intend to spend my future with?

I leave Noah with the other kids in Tessa's care and follow Luan to the beer table where he quickly gets into a deep discussion with Mozie, our butcher, about the legal implications of a contract. I do my best to follow the conversation, but after a while, my mind wanders.

Is Jake serious about the house? A house means he's truly planning on staying. How difficult will it be to see him every day and not think about our past? I don't want to look at him, but I can't help it. When I sneak in a glance, he's still chatting to Britney. Hovering between a confusing mix of relief and shameful disappointment that he didn't even come over to talk to us, I interrupt Luan to tell him I'm getting something to drink. I take a beer from the ice tub and unscrew the cap. The brew is bitter and refreshing. It goes down a lot easier than vodka, not that I've had any since the night Jake and I—

Nope. Not going to go there. I look around for a diversion. Nancy is still dancing. I could join one of the groups, but I'm not in the mood for small talk. I walk toward the mud wall, but my mom is no longer there.

Strolling along the edge of the water, I seek out some privacy. The late afternoon is warm. A breeze plays in the air, lifting the leaves on the willow branches. It's soothing weather, the kind that holds the gentle promise of an Indian summer. The music and voices are pleasant background noise with laughter piercing the banter from time to time. As these events go, the ambience is cheerful, but something inside me refuses to settle. Bittersweet nostalgia lingers in my chest. Damn Jake. I finally have my life on track. I didn't need him to come back and stir these memories.

I watch the sun as it sinks below the horizon. At the picnic site, the lanterns come on. By the time the golden hues of the sun turn to deep purple, my beer is finished, and I'm buzzing a little. Not ready to go back yet, I enter a canopy of willow branches reaching all the way to the ground that forms a clever hiding place. In the deepening dusk, I'm sheltered from view, but I can see the lantern lights through the veil of leaves. The smell of grilled beef sausage and smoke from the wood fires drift on the breeze, a familiar and welcoming fragrance. The party is in full swing. I better go back to see if Noah is hungry.

As I turn, I bump into a hard chest. Gasping, I take a step back. I would've taken several steps, but a pair of strong hands catch my arms.

"Easy."

Jake.

There's nothing easy about this, not when his hands burn my skin and there's not enough space between us to take a breath or hide from disregarded memories.

His piercing stare drills into mine. "You all right?"

"Of course."

"What are you doing out here alone?"

"Nothing."

"It's dangerous. Someone could attack you."

"This is Rensburg. No one is going to attack me."

"You never know."

"Thanks for your concern, but I just needed some air."

His harsh stare softens. He slides a hand up my arm, all the way to my shoulder. "If I didn't know better, I'd say you look sad."

"I have to get back." I try to pull away again, but he doesn't let go. He keeps me in place with one hand on my shoulder while he lifts the other to my face. "What are *you* doing?" I flinch as he wipes a thumb over the scar on my cheek, sending a bolt of awareness through my body.

He pulls me closer at the same time as he lowers his head. It's not a fast action that allows no room for escape. It's slow and intentional. I know where it's going even before his lips feather over mine, but I can't move. I can't flee. My heart is pumping with a rhythm I haven't felt in four years. It's as if I'm waking from a coma.

He molds his lips carefully around mine, meticulously, letting me feel the full impact of their heat and pressure. For a moment, it's all he does, savoring the shape of my mouth, but it's enough to make my knees weak. He smells of cheap aftershave and cotton, a scent that infiltrates my nostrils and makes me want to weep with the promise of belonging. My common sense screams at me to run. Warnings of imminent regret go off in my brain, but my starving senses greedily suck up the sudden overload. It's pathetic how needy I am. It's dangerous. It makes everything that came after Jake seem like mere reflections of emotions.

Whatever little reason I have left flies from my mind when he supports my head in his big palm and curls an arm around my waist, pulling me impossibly tight against his body. I gasp into his mouth. He answers with a hungry groan. I steal his oxygen and drag it deep into my lungs. We're living on the same air. Time falls away, and I'm back in his arms as if I've never left them, as if fifty women haven't since been pressed up against the dizzying masculinity of his chest or the hardness of his arousal. It's the bitter to the sweet, a reminder of what Jake is and why I've been walking the shore alone like someone who misses what she's never had.

The thought pierces through the haze of my lust. I place my palms on his chest to push him away, but he dips his knees and presses harder on my lower back, encouraging me to ride his erection. For a crazy moment, I almost do. For a crazy moment, I almost ignore who he is and why we are here. I almost lose all control when he moves his palm lower, gripping my ass and pulling me into the cradle of his groin.

I'm high on his kiss, panting into his mouth, and lost in his maleness. I'm barely hanging on to the threads of my pride, whimpering when he growls deep in his throat as he parts my legs with a thigh. At the sound of my moan, he threads his fingers through my hair and deepens the kiss. The pull at my roots and the scrape of his teeth over my bottom lip are my undoing. I sag against him, like clay in his thorough hands. God, how I missed this. How I craved the depraved foreplay no gentleman would ever give.

His grip on my hair tightens as his free hand searches for the button of my jeans. He pops it with a skilled flick, a sad reminder of how well versed he is in women's clothing. The notion punctures my heart, but it's not enough to break the powerful spell of lust he holds over me, not when his hand dips down the front of my jeans and into my panties. I hang onto him for life, my arms snaked around his neck as he rests three fingers over my folds, the middle digit lightly covering my slit, gently exploring, testing. When he curls that finger up to tease my clit, I arch into the touch. I'm a wanton woman possessed by a demon. I'm beyond logical thought, beyond caring.

"Kristi," he whispers against my lips, sounding as if he's in pain.

I understand what he's asking. He's asking me to take away the unbearable need, and there's only one answer. I'm about to give him that answer when giggling comes from nearby. Cruelly, the sound pulls me back to reality. My body stiffens in shock. Shame heats my face. Jake jerks his hand from my jeans, but there's not enough time to put distance between us before the owners of the voices round the wall of willow branches.

Hand in hand, Gina and Eddie come to an abrupt halt. We stare at each other, four sets of wide eyes.

Jake comes to his senses first. "We were just getting some air."

My mom and Eddie? "Mom?"

Tugging on my hand, Jake pulls me out from under the canopy. "We'll catch you later."

Gina's gaze follows us, a mixture of worry and shock etched on her face.

"Let go," I say when we're a short distance away, pulling on Jake's hold. I'm angry and confused. Betrayed. By myself.

He stops to look at me. "You're not going to pretend that kiss didn't happen."

I open my mouth to tell him that's exactly what I'm going to do when someone screams.

"Noah," Tessa yells from farther up the shore. "Noah's in the water!"

CHAPTER 13

Kristi

*S*weat breaks out over my skin and a sick feeling settles in my stomach. My brain screams run but my feet are stuck to the ground. In the second it takes for my body to move, Jake is already sprinting up the shore. I'm faintly aware of my mom calling my name, but I don't stop to acknowledge her. When a red cap floating on the water comes into view, everything else cuts out. Seconds have lapsed, too many seconds, and a horrific fear stabs into my gut as Jake dives into the water even before he's at the beer table.

With a few powerful strokes, he reaches the ripples circling out from around my baby's cap. He sucks in air and dives under the water. Breathless, I reach the shore as the other adults get there and dive in after Jake. Tessa is on her knees, hugging her stomach, crying and muttering she can't swim. I don't think. I dive in after the others, using every ounce of strength I possess to propel myself through the water.

Dragging in a hasty breath, I duck below the surface. I barely feel the sting on my eyes as I open them. The water is murky, and it's dark. Grass and dislodged mud from the bed of the lake obscure my view. I feel around frantically, trying hard not to give in to the sobs and pull water into my lungs.

I come up for air and am about to dive again when Jake's voice rings out.

"I've got him."

My breath catches. The three men who went in after Jake move out of the way. In the midst of their circle, Jake clutches Noah to his chest. Using one arm, he swims to the shore with backstrokes while everyone offers hands and advice.

I rush after them, adrenaline giving me an extra spurt of strength. Jake hands Noah to Gina. Dr. Santoni is already there. There's a blur of bodies as someone offers a blanket, and someone else asks if he should call an ambulance. Jake pushes himself out of the water and drops to his knees next to the doctor and Noah.

Someone offers me a hand as I pull myself up the muddy wall to the embankment. There's a cough and a cry. Noah's cry. My legs sag. Falling down next to Jake, warm wetness mixes with the cold water on my cheeks.

"He's fine," Dr. Santoni says. "Swallowed water and had a mighty fright, but there's no need for an ambulance."

Picking a crying Noah up gently, I hug him to my chest and make sure I keep the blanket around him. My tears are from joy and fright, from acknowledging everything I could've lost in brown ripples of muddy water.

My gaze locks with Jake's. His face is ashen, his cheeks smeared with mud. Pieces of underwater grass stick to his wet T-shirt. His chest rises and falls rapidly. Sitting back on his heels, he rests his palms on his thighs while his shoulders sag in a gesture of exhaustion and relief. I know, because I suffer the same symptoms.

"Thank you," I mouth, pressing my lips to the top of my baby's head.

The moment stretches, words unnecessary as our gazes communicate what no one else can understand. The only person in the world who can truly share my devastation with the same intensity is Jake. No one, no matter how much they care, can feel what we do. For a bizarre instant, the knowledge brings a measure of relief. I'm not alone. As long as Noah is a part of both of us, I'll never be alone, no matter the distance or differences between us.

Someone throws a blanket over my shoulders. I'm shivering. More picnic blankets are handed out for Jake and the other men who dived in. Jake thanks the men before he gets herded away to warm himself by the fire. His gaze searches mine from over his shoulder, but the circle of people around Noah and me forms a buffer between us.

Nancy drops down on her knees in front of me. "My God, Kristi." Tears run down her cheeks as she hugs me with Noah sandwiched between us. "Are you all right?"

Gina puts a mug in my hand. "Tea to warm you."

I take a sip. It's laced with alcohol.

"Let's give them some space," Dr. Santoni says, ushering the crowd away.

Luan touches my shoulder. "We better get you home."

"I'll drive," Steve offers.

"Thanks," Luan says, "but I've got this."

He steers me to his car while people ask if we need anything. As I'm about to get inside, Tessa runs up.

"I'm sorry," she sobs. "It happened so fast. He was feeding the ducks and leaned over too far. He just fell in." She wipes her nose. "He just fell in."

"You called for help straight away," I say. "You did the right thing."

"I can't swim," she says through violent weeping.

I squeeze her arm. "Everyone is okay."

"Someone needs to drive Tessa home," my mom says, throwing an arm around the hysterical girl's shoulders.

"I'll take her," Jake says.

"You'll have to stay with her for a while." My mom gives him a meaningful look. "Make sure she drinks something warm that'll relax her."

Jake turns to me. "Will you be all right?" He looks at Noah, his brows pulled together. "Will he be okay?"

"Yes," I whisper. "Thank you, Jake. Thank you for what you did back there."

"No thanks needed."

Luan extends a hand. "Kristi and I are most thankful to you."

Jake accepts the handshake wordlessly, although a little reluctantly.

"I was going to jump in," Luan continues, "but you were already in the water, and I'm not a powerful swimmer like you obviously are." He takes his wallet from his back pocket. "I'd like to reward you for your trouble. Any amount you want. Five hundred?"

I nearly choke on my saliva.

Jake's eyes tighten. "I don't need a reward, especially not for helping my own son."

"Biological," Luan says.

Jake takes a step toward Luan, his fists clenched at his sides. "Come again?"

"Since you haven't made contact until now, Noah is little else than a stranger to you."

What's wrong with Luan? Before he can say more, which will undoubtedly earn him a broken nose, I push him toward the car. "I need to get Noah out of these wet clothes before he catches a cold."

The two men stare at each other like rams about to lock horns. Jake is massaging his breastbone in a way that tells me he's past annoyance. He's furious.

"Luan, now," my mom says, opening the door on the driver's side.

I get into the back with Noah while my mom takes the passenger seat in the front. As Luan pulls off, I look back. Jake stands in the middle of the road, staring after the car. My chest squeezes with an inexplicable emotion. I came close to losing Noah, but so did Jake. Maybe I should've invited Jake home so he could be there for his son like I know he wants. I glimpsed the longing in his eyes. No. Jake is wet. He needs a warm shower and a change of clothes. Or so I tell myself. Besides, Noah's needs come first, and right now I need to reassure and settle him.

I glance at the child in my lap, my precious child. He stopped crying and is resting his cheek on my chest, sucking his thumb.

"Maybe you should stay over at the house tonight," Luan says, catching my gaze in the rearview mirror.

"Noah needs his familiar space, his own bed." So do I. Plus, I'm upset with Luan for how he behaved and what he said to Jake.

He gives me a guilty smile. "The offer stands."

WHEN WE GET HOME, I don't bathe Noah in the tub, but take a warm shower holding him tightly in my arms. After we're both dressed in our flannel pajamas, way too warm for summer but not enough to warm the chill in my bones, I go through the habitual motions of feeding him dinner and reading him a story. After the traumatic experience, he needs the reassuring routine of his everyday life. Instead of putting him down in his crib, I crawl into bed with him. It doesn't take long for him to doze off, probably an aftereffect of the fright.

My mom sits down on the edge of the bed, a tender smile warming her face as she looks down at Noah. "He was very brave."

Pinching my eyes close for a second, I take a tremulous breath. "I still feel sick."

"Can I get you anything?"

"It's more of an emotional sickness." Which I feel in my insides and every bone of my body.

She regards me quietly for a while. I know what's coming even before she asks, "Are you going to tell me what happened with Jake tonight?"

My stomach twists with guilt but showing it will only make her believe she's got a reason to worry. "When were you going to tell me about Eddie?"

"It's not serious." She blinks when she says it, a telltale sign she's lying.

"How long have you been sleeping together?"

She waves a hand. "Four or five years."

I gasp. "And you're only telling me now?"

She scratches the back of her neck. "I didn't know how you'd take it. Besides, as I said, it's nothing serious."

Taking her hand, I squeeze her fingers. "If you were trying to protect me, you needn't have bothered."

She gives me a startled look. "Why?"

"Eddie's been too nice to me for a while now. I should've guessed. Plus, I don't care who you date. You're an adult, Mom. I respect your choices."

"Well," she smooths a crease from the bedspread with a palm, "he does own the corner store, and he is Chinese."

There's a stigma to corner store owners in our town, especially the small stores that sell toffees and chewing gum by the unit, and even more so if the owners are foreigners. Around here, foreignness is a fear all on its own.

"Just because other people look down on who he is and what he does for a living doesn't mean I will."

"You're right." She gives me a hesitant smile. "I should've had more faith in you."

Her words sting, because they boomerang right back at me, throwing an unwelcome spotlight on what happened with Jake behind the curtain of willow branches.

"It's late," I mumble. "After what happened, I'm really tired."

"Of course." She pats my hand. "Wake me if you need anything in the night."

"Mom," I groan. "I'm twenty-two, not five."

"A mother is always a mother, no matter the age of her spawn."

She says spawn jokingly, as if the word is evil, which I most probably am, seeing that I cheated on Luan with my husband. Urgh. I'm not going to even try to analyze that, at least not until morning and only after two cups of coffee.

"Love you, Mom."

She kisses my forehead. "Love you more."

Jake

ALL THE WAY back to the hotel, I can't get the image of Noah's red cap on the brown water out of my head or that kiss. That kiss that could've led to the truth if Gina and Eddie—fuck me—hadn't shown up or Noah hadn't fallen into the lake.

I'm rattled to my bones, more than I'd like to admit. I saw the fear in Kristi's wide blue eyes tonight and felt the thread that binds us as sure as it's a livewire. It's more than a legal contract claiming marriage. I've always felt our bond. I just chose to ignore it, doing my best to keep my toxic self away from a woman who deserves so much more, but double fuck it, she deserves more than that loser, Luan. What a prick.

If I'm dishing out insults, I have to be honest enough to take them. Call me a dick. I shouldn't have ignored Kristi all night in a hopeless effort to make her jealous. I shouldn't have kissed her either, but I'm not going to regret it. Fuck that. At the next chance I get, my hand will be in her pants again.

My trainers slosh dirty water over the floor of the hotel reception where a box with my name on it waits on the counter. I check the sender address. Ahmed. With the box clutched under my arm, I climb the one level up to my room and scare a couple of cockroaches away before I get into the shower. After washing the mud and rancid-reeking water from my body, I dress in exercise pants and a clean T-shirt and sit down on the armchair by the bed with the box poised on the edge of the mattress.

I need a drink and a smoke like never before, but the bar is closed, and I drove past the gas station again, too shaken to give anything other than Noah and Kristi a thought. I stare at the box for several long seconds before tearing off the masking tape that seals it. A whiff rises from inside, a smell of vanilla and amber that still clings to the stash after all these years. It smells like Kristi. And regret. Underneath the stack of letters, which is neatly tied with a ribbon, are two parcels, a big one with Noah's name and a smaller one with Kristi's. Ahmed, that damn dandy. A warm feeling heats my chest. Ahmed has always been a gentleman to the tee. I take out the pile of letters and flip it over before pulling the ends of the ribbon. The refined bastard even steamed the envelopes open. None of them are torn, except for the last one, the one in which Kristi demanded a divorce. Typical perfectionistic Ahmed, they're organized by date.

Leaning back in the stuffy chair, I start with the first one. I don't even get to the third one before I'm bawling like a fucking baby.

Kristi

THANK GOODNESS IT'S SUNDAY, and I don't have to be up early for work or rush Noah through his breakfast to get him to the crèche on time. When he's done eating, I take him for a walk to the river and give him a gentle lecture about the dangers of water, trying my best not to install fear. I don't want to traumatize him, but he needs to understand the implications of falling into water. If he understands, I don't know. He listens quietly until my lecture is finished. Not even a moment later, he pushes his toy truck through a dirt track he carved with a stick around the roots of a tree. Sitting down on one of the roots, I watch him. I'm reveling in the marvel of him when Jake's rental pulls up.

Immediately, my stomach draws tight. Even more so when he gets out wearing a tight pair of jeans that hugs his hips and thighs, and a T-shirt that strains to accommodate his big arms and broad shoulders. In each hand, he carries a gift-wrapped parcel. The heat of his tongue as he explored my lips is seared into my memory. The path of his fingers as he boldly stuck them down my underwear makes me heat in places I'd rather ignore, but it's difficult to deny the effect he has on me when he stalks toward us with tiger strides, his gait sure and determined. He knows exactly where he's heading and what he's doing. It's only when he's closer that I notice how red-rimmed his eyes are and how dark the circles underneath.

"Sleep much?" I ask when he stops next to me.

"Nope." He crouches down next to Noah, who stops playing to look with interest at the parcels. "This is for you," he says, placing the bigger of the two in front of Noah. Then he straightens and holds the smaller one out to me. "And for you."

I take the gift because my mom taught me it's rude to not accept the kindness of the gesture. "For us?"

He shoves his hands in the front pockets of his jeans and says with an embarrassed smile, "They're not from me."

I shoot him a questioning look as Noah starts tearing enthusiastically at the paper.

"They're from a friend in Dubai."

I stiffen at the mention of that place, the place where he entertained countless women, but brush the untimely pinch of hurt away. I'm being unfair. Jake never said he'd love Noah and me. We made a mistake, Jake and I. We made our choices, and we're living with them. Which brings the mistake of yesterday to mind, not that it hasn't been tormenting me all night and morning. I have to be honest with Luan about what happened, and I'm not sure how he'll take it. To say I'm tense is an understatement.

It takes a little help from Jake before the paper finally comes off Noah's gift. Noah holds up a fire truck with a long ladder and big horn. When Jake presses the horn, a siren blares. Noah grins from ear to ear. As if a thought suddenly hits him, he looks at me for approval. Jake is still a stranger to him, and Noah is not yet certain how he should react toward him. I give a small nod. It's all it takes for Noah to discard the old truck and start playing with the new one.

I remind him gently of his manners. "What do we say?"

Noah gets to his feet and gives Jake a quick hug before going back on all fours to chase an imaginary fire.

Jake doesn't say anything, but his throat moves as he swallows. I try hard not to make too much of the emotions squeezing my heart at how Noah's little arms looked around his father's neck. We watch our son play until I sense Jake staring at me and turn my head. Our gazes collide. The heat in his eyes is a reminder of last night, a reminder that I can pretend all I want, but it doesn't make what happened or how I reacted to him go away.

He motions at the parcel I clutch in my hands. "Aren't you going to open it?"

Thankful for the distraction, I tear the paper away and remove a silk scarf in pastel colors.

"That was very thoughtful of your friend," I say. "You'll have to thank her for us."

"Him. Ahmed. I worked for him." Strain creeps into his voice. "Well, technically, I worked for his father."

The way in which he says the last part makes me look at him more closely. His expression is veiled. He's hiding something. Something about that job or the man he worked for didn't turn out well.

"Did you enjoy the job?" I ask carefully.

"Does anyone ever enjoy everything about a job?"

"If you like most of it, the smaller, less pleasurable tasks shouldn't matter."

"Do you like your job?"

Do I? It's always been a means to an end. I'm not passionate about bookkeeping, but I can't say I hate it. "It's not that bad."

"If Luan is planning on marrying you, why doesn't he take care of you?"

I give a start at the abrupt turn of the conversation. "He can't let me move in until we're married."

"Can't or won't?"

"What's that supposed to mean?"

"You've been working for him for four years, and he still lets you live in a trailer."

"It's only been a couple of weeks since we decided to get together," I say defensively.

"Doesn't make a difference. If he cared, he could've put you up in a house a long time ago."

"Don't you dare judge Luan, not when you can't be blamed for the same accusation just because you weren't around."

"I got you a house. That fact that my mother selfishly leased it to pocket the money is no excuse for my ignorance, but I'm going to rectify that."

"I never expected anything other than help to cover the medical costs of the birth from you."

"I admire your pride and independence, but it still doesn't change the fact that for someone who claims to love you he barely pays you enough to eat."

Heat flares in my cheeks, knowing Jake saw the state of our food cupboards before he so generously filled them up. "He pays me what the job is worth. I'm no one's charity case."

"I never would've allowed that."

Jumping to my feet, I cry, "You weren't here."

We both still. Shit. I swore I'd never lay the blame at Jake's feet, and I hate him for making me do it, for making me appear weak.

"I'm sorry, Kristi." He takes a step toward me.

Pulling away, I draw the edges of my jersey together as if the thin wool can keep the coldness spreading to my heart at bay. "No, *I'm* sorry. I shouldn't have said that."

"Thank you for saying it. Thank you for giving me an opportunity to apologize."

"There's nothing to apologize about."

"There's plenty." He searches my face, imploring me with his eyes. "You may not realize it, but I need to say it as much as you need to hear it. I'm sorry I wasn't here for you and Noah." He grips my shoulders gently. "I needed to say that because I need healing too."

The admittance that he may also be suffering throws me off balance. I want to disregard the notion, but it was there in his eyes when he looked at Noah and when he spoke about his job. It was there last night when both of us could've lost our child.

His arms fold around me, warm and strong. There's compassion and understanding in the hug. The embrace offers comfort without demanding anything in return. For the first time, Jake holds me in a non-sexual way, in a way I desperately need. As he gives me his apology with no drama but sincere regret, something heavy lifts off my chest. The strain of carrying all the blame for our mistake falls away as he takes his share of the burden and allows me to face the feelings I've repressed for far too long. He allows me to acknowledge the disappointment of my shattered dreams and unrequited love. I'm far from trusting or forgiving him, but I can let a little of my guard down in the safety of his arms, letting his apology soothe a deep-seated hurt that has never quite vanished.

"I'll make it up to you," he whispers in my hair, planting a soft kiss on my crown. "For as long as I live."

The words are unwelcome. Pushing on his chest, I put distance between us. "I appreciate your apology, but we're over. We both moved on. This doesn't change anything."

He closes his eyes and inhales deeply. When he opens them again, his expression is pained. "I'll be patient."

"Jake, please."

"You can't deny our chemistry."

"It's physical. It's always been physical."

"I disagree. I've been in love with you since first grade. I still am."

I take a step away. "Don't say that."

"Why? Because it's what you don't want to hear? Because you're afraid of the truth?"

"You can't be in love with me." Tears blur my vision. An old wound reopens even as he offered me comfort not a second ago. "Not if you've fucked fifty other women."

He winces as if I slapped him. "They didn't mean a thing. I swear it to you."

I can't think about it. I can't let him see how it affects me, because that will mean I care. "It doesn't matter."

"So you said, but it obviously does."

I turn for Noah, but he grabs my arm.

"I don't even know their names."

"Let me go. I don't want to hear it."

"Yes, you do. Every single time I fucked one of those nameless, faceless women, it was *you* I thought about, *you* who crowded my head."

This is as much as I can take. Jerking free, I turn my back on him and walk to Noah, battling to get my emotions under control.

To Jake's credit, he gives me a moment. He doesn't approach me until I've blinked away my tears.

"I didn't mean to upset you," he says to my back. "That's not why I came."

Flinging around, I ask, "Why did you?"

"To ask if I may take Noah swimming."

"What?"

"I guess now is as good a time as any to teach him how to swim."

"After what happened yesterday?" I exclaim.

Crossing his arms, he gives me a determined look. "You know what they say about getting back on the horse."

"I'm not sure—"

"If he hates it, we'll stop."

"We?"

"I assume you're not going to let me visit with him alone." He adds softly, hopefully, "Not just yet."

"You're right. It's too early."

"Go on then. Get your bathing suits. I'll wait."

"Now?"

"You also know what they say about there being no time like the present."

Can I dare it alone with Jake? What if the same happens as yesterday? "Let me check if my mom can come."

He gives me a knowing smirk. "Afraid you'll jump my bones?"

"Jake! Not in front of Noah."

"Sorry." He lifts a brow, giving me a look that's meant to be humorous but that turns out devastatingly sexy. "Afraid you won't be able to resist me?"

"Not by a long shot," I lie.

"Then hurry. I remember something about Noah bawling when he gets hungry, and we barely have an hour before lunchtime."

He all but steamrollers us to the trailer, watching me with his piercing gaze while I hastily bundle a towel and floaties for Noah into a bag, as well as water and snacks. Despite my unease to be alone with Jake, I do agree with him. I do believe it's important that Noah learns to swim. I've never been a good swimmer myself. How can I forget Jake is excellent at it?

Gina says she has a date with Eddie to celebrate coming out of the closet about their secret affair and gives me a speculative look when I tell her out of Jake's earshot that our outing is only about teaching Noah to swim and nothing else. She waits with Jake and Noah in the trailer while I pull on my bikini, a T-shirt, and a pair of shorts in the bathroom. I appreciate the fact that Jake has gotten a car seat for the rental, as mine is in Luan's car.

Jake turns on the music for the drive. A nursery rhyme starts playing.

"You're maybe taking things a little too far," I say, smothering a laugh.

He gives me a mock-innocent look. "I read up about kids who speak late. Music can be very helpful."

"Indeed."

Noah seems to be enjoying the song, swinging his feet to the beat.

At the lake, I almost regret my decision when Jake strips down to his boxer briefs. He's bulkier than before, the muscles of his chest and back cut deeper. His tall body is perfectly proportioned, down to the bulge in the boxers. He's sinfully beautiful, the unfair kind that will always make a woman feel insecure about rival female attention. His adolescent broodiness has ripened into a very mature, very male darkness, an underlying current of socially unacceptable sexuality, and it both attracts and frightens me.

"What happened to bathing suits?" I barely make the accusation pass for humor.

"Didn't pack one." He grins. "Look at it this way. I could've swum naked."

Biting my lip, I busy myself by fixing Noah's floaties so I don't have to look at Jake's near-naked, all-perfect body.

After yesterday's incident, Noah is apprehensive, but he loves water enough to allow Jake to carry him into the shallow end. For a while, they play, splashing water and chasing dragonflies until Noah is completely comfortable. Jake only lets go of him for a second or two, until Noah understands the floaties will prevent him from sinking. He's only ever been in the public pool with me twice, and even if he wore his floaties then, I never let go of him. As soon as he gets the notion, his confidence increases considerably. It doesn't take long before Jake can let Noah kick and splash on his own.

I sit on the shore, watching them, the view warming as well as tightening my chest. My heart is a mixture of pinches and gentle caresses, of hurt and something so profound I can't call it happiness, because it exceeds happiness to border on pain.

"Come on in," Jake calls, brushing back the wet locks of his dark hair. "I can do with a hand."

Jake never needs a hand. He's got everything under control. Besides, I'm not showing off my imperfections in the shadow of his god-like body.

"You've got this," I call back.

He stops to look at me but holds on to Noah's hand as he takes his eyes momentarily off our son. "It's a defining moment. You don't want to miss out."

Shit. He's right. My son is learning to swim, and I'm worried about my flab. What a dork. Getting to my feet, I strip down to my bikini quickly. Screw this. I don't care what Jake thinks about my after-baby body, because he's not the man whose opinion matters. It's Luan's. When I step up to the shore, getting ready to dive, who matters and who doesn't disappear from the equation. What I see in Jake's troubled eyes matters. It matters too much to ignore. Slowly, he drags his gaze over my body, from my toes to my breasts. His attention pauses there for a moment, and when he finally meets my eyes, I'm scorched by the heat that sizzles in his russet depths.

No man has ever looked at me like this, as if he's in pain, as if he's dying and the remedy lies between my legs. I'm not strong enough to deal with this. I'm not confident enough to stand under his scrutiny and face the flames of a fire for which I'm way too inexperienced.

Breaking the spell, I jump. It's clumsy. There's nothing sexy or smooth about me as I come up, spitting water. At least the cold shock is exactly what I need. What I don't need is the strong arm coming around my waist, dragging me against a warm, hard body, and the deep voice that presses soft words to my ear, words full of feeling and overflowing with meaning.

"You all right, ginger?"

I cough. "Yes."

He chuckles. "That was a mighty water bomb."

"You can let go now. I found my balance."

Another rumble vibrates in his chest, but he obliges, allowing me to put distance between us. Noah splashes happily, excited that I've joined the party.

Taking his hands, Jake pulls him to his chest before turning him around. "Let's see if you can swim to Mommy."

It becomes a new game, Noah swimming to and fro between us. When his lips turn blue, I call it a day. Jake gives me a push to help me out before lifting Noah onto the side. After drying and dressing Noah, I give him water and apple slices, which he chews on hungrily while Jake and I dress.

Noah falls asleep in the car on the way home. Somehow, Jake manages to lift him from the car seat and lay him down in his crib without waking him, something I've never managed. When I comment on it, he says Noah is probably just exhausted from the exercise, but I can't help but notice how his chest swells with pride.

After the trouble Jake has gone to for Noah, I feel obliged to invite him for lunch. It's not the holiday season. There's no one staying in the trailer park except for Shiny and us, but a few people are lighting fires at the barbecue area next to the river. It's not uncommon for people to come here on the weekends for a picnic, but my guess is they're mostly here out of curiosity about what happened at the lake and Jake's sudden return to town.

Jake offers to build a fire and grill pork chops while Noah naps. I agree to make a potato salad. It's not until Jake is outside that I check my phone. Crap. I have three missed calls from Luan. With the tense conversation Jake and I had, and then the swimming adventure, I've shamefully pushed Luan from my mind. Or maybe I selfishly held onto the stolen time with Jake and Noah, reluctant to let the outside world in. Unable to ignore the rest of the world any longer, I dial Luan.

"I was worried about you," he says after a polite greeting.

The bubble in which only Jake, Noah, and I existed bursts, and a fresh spell of guilt brings me back to the harshness of reality. "Jake showed up. We took Noah swimming."

There's the tiniest of cracks in Luan's habitual patience. "You could've called."

My defensiveness rises. "You could've come over."

"You know I can't do that. Giving you a lift as a concerned employer is one thing, but visiting you blatantly on a Sunday—"

"Yes, I know. You're worried about what people will think."

"What will people think if Jake starts to visit?"

"He's coming to see Noah."

There's a lie to that, and the silence that follows tells me Luan knows.

"I hate that I can't see you," he says, adding an extra dose of guilt to my conscience as I stare out the window to where Jake is stacking coals for a fire.

"You can," I say softly, hoping Luan will for once throw caution to the wind and save me from the treacherous feelings growing in the dark corners of my heart. I pray he'll defy his reputation, if only for today, and give me a speck of imperfection, a speck of dare, a speck of the darkness I crave, but my hope shrivels when he replies.

"It's not proper."

To hell with proper. Why can't he behave improper, only this once?

"What are you doing, Kristi?"

"What do you mean?"

"Why are you giving people reason for gossip?"

"I don't give a damn about gossip. This is about Noah."

"Is it?"

"Yes!"

Another short silence. "I'm going to give you the benefit of the doubt, but we'll talk about this tomorrow."

Sometimes, Luan drives me crazy with his righteous behavior. "Yes, we have to talk." I'll have to tell him I kissed Jake. "We also have to talk about what you said to Jake."

"I didn't say anything wrong."

"You owe him an apology."

"I disagree."

"I'm not going to argue about this on the phone."

"If Jake signed the divorce papers, we wouldn't be having the argument over the phone, because I'd be able to see you on the weekend like any normal boyfriend."

Taking a deep breath, I blow it out slowly. "I can't do this right now."

"You're right. We're talking in circles again. We'll talk tomorrow after work."

After work. It's a subtle way of saying work is more important. Always. "If you can wait that long."

"What does that mean?"

"Nothing." I rub a hand over my forehead. "I just have a lot to handle at the moment."

He asks about Noah in the fleeting way politeness requires, and when we say goodbye I'm agitated with Luan in a way I've never been.

Jake

THERE WAS a time I despised this town. There was a time I pitied the people who live here, believing them small-minded with no ambition or drive, but as I put the meat on the grill and watch folks mingle around their own fires and picnic tables, I begin to suspect I'm the loser. They're happy. They're settled. They have normal families. They have fathers who care and mothers who didn't have to raise them alone. They work in the brick factory, but they come home to their kids and play rugby with them on a Sunday. The only outsider without ambition or purpose is me. Whatever I was chasing seems like the wind while their roots, belonging, love, and stability are the true things, the only things, that matter.

I look away from the curious stares, pretending to turn the meat. Pretending not to envy them. Pretending I don't give a fuck is tough when Kristi's letters shred me to pieces. She wrote every week. Every month, she sent a photo. She held onto my promise that I'd be back for her and our baby. Every month, that hope faded. The beauty of her letters was slowly scraped away, a new layer coming off between Christmas and January until it was nothing but impersonal reporting by Easter. Then that final one that said so little and yet so much, telling me with a single sentence she was going to stop writing. What that one line on a white piece of paper couldn't hide was the mountains of heartache underneath. Like an iceberg, she gave me the tip but kept the biggest part to herself. I have more than regret and guilt in my heart. I have admiration. I appreciate her so fucking much for the woman she is. Just like her mother. She's a fighter, a survivor, and a man like me can only hope she'd give me the time of day. I can't take four years and one sentence scribbled on a white piece of paper away, but I can try to make it right.

"Back for good?" a voice asks behind me.

I turn. Jan stands on the riverbank, a bottle of beer in his hand. He holds the bottle out to me. I look from the beer to his face. Remembering what he did to Kristi, I want to break that bottle on his nose.

He lifts a palm. "Peace? We were all young and stupid."

"Is that your way of apologizing?"

"I've already apologized many times over." He shrugs. "Kristi is a good woman."

Tell me something I don't know.

"Come on, Jake. It's not as if you never fucked up."

No, innocence is a label I'll never have the honor of wearing.

"Take the beer, man," he says. "Everyone's looking. Don't make me stand here like an idiot."

After another beat's hesitation, I take the beer.

He nods toward one of the picnic tables where a woman and three kids are sitting. "That's mine. Hooked up with Sally straight after school."

"Congratulations."

"Yeah. They're great kids."

"Good for you."

"So, what brought you back to town?"

My gaze drifts to Kristi's trailer. I take a swig of the beer while contemplating my answer. Kristi won't appreciate my honesty. Small town, gossip, and all that. "Kid."

"Guess you were busy in Dubai, huh?"

Too busy to visit in four years. "Something like that."

"A word of warning, bro." His eyes crinkle as he glances toward the trailer. "A lot of *okes* have tried their luck with Kristi."

I clench the bottle so hard my knuckles crack. "Anyone I need to kill?" I'm not even half-joking.

He chuckles. "No one's hit the jackpot, but if you're planning on sticking around, you better make this marriage of yours real. A lot of guys still have their aims set on Kristi."

"Not going to happen," I say, taking another drink and giving him a look that says I'll fucking kill anyone who brings his dick near my wife.

"There's talk about her boss, Luan Steenkamp. He drives her and Noah around all the time."

The only reason Luan isn't dead yet is because he's a pussy and a ten commandments abider who won't commit adultery. I can't deny the allegation of Luan and Kristi being an item yet. I'm not sure enough of myself. Kristi is still too set on kicking my ass straight back to Dubai.

He takes a packet of cigarettes from his shirt pocket, flips the lid, and holds it out. "Smoke?"

I'm so blinded by jealousy, I don't register the offer. I only realize he's standing there with his outstretched arm, clutching a packet of Winston, when Kristi exits the trailer with a bowl in her arms.

Not taking my gaze off her, I say, "I'm good."

He flips a cigarette between his lips and says from the corner of his mouth, "You're fucked, Basson. Good luck on winning her back." Then more jovially as Kristi comes within earshot, "Hey, Pretorius. How's Noah?"

She gives him a cool smile. "Good. Thanks for asking."

He salutes her. "I'll let you folks get back to your lunch."

She watches his back as he saunters off to his family. "What did he want?"

"Wanted to know what I was doing here."

She looks at me quickly. "What did you say?"

"Don't worry. I didn't tell him I'm back for you."

She dumps the bowl on the picnic table. "You're *not* back for me."

Before she can move, I grab her nape and pull her flush against my body. Her eyes go wide as she stares up at me with a startled expression.

"Then tell me why I'm here." The words are a challenge, a dare.

"To sign the divorce papers," she whispers, her gaze flittering beyond my back, no doubt to the people who are watching, even as she pushes with futile effort on my chest.

I lower my head to hers. "Wrong answer." The words ghost over her lips a second before I bring down my mouth, kissing her right there for everyone to see. Staking my fucking claim.

I don't part her lips, but the kiss lasts longer than the acceptable peck in public. When I let go, she gasps, indignity sparking in her eyes.

"You don't want to make a scene," I warn, not resisting the urge to press my erection against her soft belly. "It'll only make it worse."

"You're a bastard," she says through clenched teeth.

Sadly, yes. Slapping her ass, I let the nuance of my words slip into my tone as I say softly enough for only her to hear, "A hungry one," and loud enough for everyone else, "Where's that potato salad you bragged about?"

Her nostrils flare as she regards me like a steaming little devil with narrowed eyes. "How dare you treat me like this?"

To everyone looking on, I've just treated her like a wife. That's code for loving husband behavior, at least around here.

Yeah, ginger, you better bet your curvy little ass I'm staking my claim.

"Sip?" I tip the beer toward her lips. If anyone still has any doubts, letting her drink from my bottle will definitely seal the deal.

Snatching the bottle from me, she props a hand on her hip. "Just a sip?" Her voice is mocking but there's nothing mocking about the anger in her eyes. "That's not very generous, Jake."

Right there, in front of everyone, she downs my beer. She gulps it down in a few long swallows, lowers her head, and wipes her delectable mouth with the back of her hand.

Stunned, I can only stare at her as she chirps, "How far is that meat you bragged about, cowboy? Noah is awake, and he's hungry."

As she flings around and walks back to the trailer with sashaying hips, a few envious chuckles and a wolf-whistle sound from behind, but I'm too busy gawking to pay them any attention.

What I want has never been in Dubai. It has always been right here, between belonging and what truly matters, wearing tight shorts and way too much sass.

Kristi

AFTER BEHAVING LIKE A TERRITORIAL, macho caveman, Jake pulls another stunner on me by acting the hands-on daddy as he feeds Noah outside and plays on the grass with him. My mom returns after teatime, her cheeks glowing as she joins us for coffee but refuses to say anything about her date with Eddie.

By the time Jake comes back from the kitchen after washing the dishes, the other picnic makers are long gone, and Noah starts sniffling.

"I think he caught a cold," my mom says.

"What?" Jake picks him up, studying his face. "Shall I take him to Dr. Santoni?"

"It's just a cold." I take Noah from his arms. "Nothing vitamin C and a good night's rest won't fix."

"Do you think it's the swimming?" Jake asks miserably as he follows me to the trailer.

"Most probably falling into the cold water last night."

He stops to pull a hand through his hair. "Damn. I feel really bad now."

"Jake." I sigh. "You didn't give him a cold."

"I should've thought about it before taking him into the water today."

"Relax. Kids are stronger than you think."

"Wait." He holds me back with a hand on my arm. "You mean he's been sick before?"

My mom laughs softly. "Don't be an idiot, Jake."

"What?" He rests his hands on his hips, looking genuinely shell-shocked. "When? What did he have?"

"The flu," my mom says. "Measles. A tummy bug. Oh, and there was that terrible time he had his little stomach pumped."

Jake stares at her in horror. "What the hell from?"

"He ate the ants Shiny sprayed with poison."

"What the fu—" Looking at Noah, he catches himself. "Can I get something? Medicine?"

"It's Sunday," I say. "The pharmacy is closed."

"Not the emergency ones in Johannesburg."

"You're overreacting."

"Tell me what to do."

"Give us a little space. He needs to rest."

He lifts his hands and starts to backtrack. "Space. Got it. All right. You sure? I can stay. I'd love to."

"Go, Jake."

"What if you need me later?"

I roll my eyes. "Jake."

"Fine, but call me the minute he gets worse."

"Men," my mom says on a chuckle. "They all turn into babies around illness."

It takes a bit more coaxing to finally get Jake to leave.

DURING THE NIGHT, Noah gets worse. We give him a steam bath, but his nose remains blocked, making it difficult for him to breathe. When morning comes, neither of us slept a wink. He's cranky and tired, and I'm exhausted. I don't know how my poor mom manages to get up early and prepare for work. We kept her up too. I manage to get a bit of breakfast into Noah's tummy, and by the time my mom is gone and Luan comes by, Noah is a little better, but not well enough to drop him at the crèche.

"I'm sorry," I say to Luan. "I know it's going to be a busy week at work, but I have to keep Noah at home."

"I understand."

"Thank you."

"Just remember to fill out a sick leave form tomorrow."

"If Noah is better."

"Let's hope so."

Just then, Noah starts to whine again.

"That's what swimming after near drowning gets you," Luan mumbles.

"Do you have a moment? I–I have to tell you something."

He checks his watch. "I have a lot of work today."

"You work for yourself."

"Doesn't mean I can take liberties with my time."

"I only meant your time is more flexible. You can work five minutes later, can't you?" I have to get this off my chest. I can't live with the guilt for a minute longer.

"Fine."

I usher him outside, out of Noah's earshot, leaving Noah in his crib with his toys, but keeping the door open so I can keep an eye on him. "About Saturday night, something happened."

"What?"

I take a deep breath. "I kissed Jake."

"You did what?"

"I wanted a little time alone so I took a walk. Jake was worried. He came looking for me, and it just happened."

"It just happened?"

"I'm sorry. Really, I am. I needed to come clean. It won't happen again."

"I didn't take you for a stupid girl."

I'm in the wrong, but my spine stiffens at the insult. "Don't call me stupid."

"What would you call making the same mistake twice? Clever?"

"Don't see more into it than what there is."

"How am I supposed to see it? We've never even kissed."

"Because we both agreed it's wrong."

"What you did with Jake isn't wrong?"

"I know it is. That's why I'm apologizing."

"I don't know what to say." He turns in a semi-circle, then back to me. "I need to think."

I hug myself, a chill that has nothing to do with the morning air creeping up on me. "What's that supposed to mean?"

"Exactly what the words imply. I need time. I can't talk about this now."

"Luan." I take his arm when he starts walking toward his car. "Don't act hastily. Please. I want us to work." I need us to work. I need the stability, not the uncertain, crazy, lust that burns out and leaves me alone in cold ashes.

Shaking me off gently, he says without looking at me, "I'll check on you later."

Disappointment drops like a lump of clay in my stomach. I'm angry with myself. The last thing I wanted was to hurt Luan.

THE DAY GETS PROGRESSIVELY WORSE, and by the time my mom comes home, Noah is napping restlessly.

"Poor baby," she says, kissing Noah's brow.

"Why don't you sleep over at Eddie's tonight? I'm sure you can do with a night of uninterrupted sleep."

"I'm not leaving you to deal with this alone."

"Mom." I give her a chastising look. "I'm an adult, for crying out loud. If I can't handle it, I'll call."

"Do you want me gone?"

"What? No! Why would you say that?"

She gives me a level stare. "Is Jake coming over?"

"No! If anyone is coming over it's Luan."

"I see." She says it in her I-know-everything voice, which means she's making assumptions.

"Just go and sleep with Eddie."

"Never thought I'd see the day my daughter orders me to have sex."

"I said *sleep*. Oh, whatever. Just use protection."

My mom gasps as if she's capable of being shocked.

"Go on." I hand her the overnight bag from the shelf. "Need help packing?"

She turns up her nose. "I think I can manage."

Inwardly, I smile. My mom has taken care of me and later of both Noah and me for as long as I'm old. She deserves a night of proper rest. She deserves happiness. I'm happy for her and Eddie. Once you get to know him, he's a nice guy.

She's scarcely gone when Noah wakes, more fidgety than before. No matter what I try, he won't stop crying. I'm contemplating calling Dr. Santoni when Luan arrives with a big paper bag.

"Brought you Chinese takeout," he says, unpacking the containers on the table.

I give him a grateful smile. "Does that mean I'm forgiven?"

"As long as it doesn't happen again."

"Thank you, Luan."

"Don't mention it."

I pull Noah into my lap, trying to eat a bit of noodles with one hand, but he won't stop fussing. "I think I should call the doctor."

"Does he have a fever?"

"No."

"Then maybe wait it out." He sits down at the small table. "Are you coming to work tomorrow?"

"Depending on how tonight goes. I'm sorry for dropping you like this just before the audit."

"I said I understand. Don't worry about it." He folds his hands together. "I want you to sue for full custody. I want to adopt Noah."

My mouth drops open. "What? Why? Noah is only starting to get to know Jake."

"You have to cut him out of your life."

Suddenly, I understand why he forgave me so easily. "This is your condition, isn't it?"

He regards me unflinchingly. "Yes."

"You can't ask me to keep Noah away from his father. Jake is good with him."

"No more Jake, Kristi. It's non-negotiable. I spoke to a lawyer friend who specializes in divorce. He reckons despite the money Jake sent, we have a good case based on emotional negligence."

Noah starts to complain again. I bounce him on my knee, a reflective reaction that stuck from his baby days. "No. Banning Jake from our lives is what's best for you, not for Noah, and I prefer to talk about this when Noah isn't present."

"That's my decision. Take it or leave it."

The words are not yet cold when the door opens and none other than Jake fills the frame, making the trailer looks smaller than what it already is.

At the sight of Luan, he stills. The two men glare at each other. Great. This is all I need.

"What are you doing here?" Luan asks.

Jake clenches his jaw. "Came to see how my *kid* is doing. You?"

Luan lifts his chin. "I came to see how my *girlfriend* is."

Stepping into the room, Jake crosses his arms. "Last time I checked, she was still married to me."

"Only in name," Luan says.

I shift Noah to the other knee. "Cut it out, both of you."

"Come on, Jake," Luan continues. "Admit it. If she didn't ask for a divorce, you never would've come back. You don't want her, but you don't want anyone else to have her either."

Jake's nostrils flare. "Why I came back isn't important. What you should be asking is why I'm staying."

"Jake, Luan, please."

"You didn't stick around the first time," Luan says with a haughty smile. "Maybe I should ask instead what's so different about this time."

Jake advances a step. "You're too old for her."

"Jake!"

Luan pushes to his feet. "You're no good for her."

"That's enough," I say as Noah starts crying. "If this is going to turn into a fight, you better take it outside."

Jake continues as if he didn't hear me. "She deserves better than a man old enough to be her father."

Noah bawls in all earnest.

"She deserves better than a deserter," Luan says above the noise.

Unable to force calm any longer, I jump up, Noah clutched to my chest. "I deserve better than both of you. Out. Now. I want you both to leave."

Luan gives me an incredulous look. "Are you throwing me out?"

"Just go. Both of you."

Luan stares at me for a second, some of the old patience filtering back into his voice. "You owe me an answer. When Noah is better, we'll talk." With that, he stomps past Jake, making the floor of the trailer tremble, and pushes through the door.

"Go, Jake," I say, too tired to deal with this.

He looks between Noah and me. "You look shattered."

"It was a long night."

"Where's Gina?"

"At Eddie's."

Holding out his arms, he reaches for Noah. "Give him here."

"I asked you to go."

"You're dead tired. Let me take him off your hands while you get some rest."

"I don't need—"

"I know. You don't need my help. Look, I'm here now, so you may as well take what I offer." Before I can protest, he takes Noah from my arms. "Go lie down. Have a nap. Just rest for an hour."

To my surprise, Noah stops crying.

"You can't go twenty-four hours without sleep," Jake says.

It's tempting, but can I trust Jake?

"I'm not going anywhere," he says. "We'll be right here when you wake up."

"Promise?"

He gives me a warm smile. "Promise. Go on."

At his encouraging nod, I lie down on the bed and pull the throw over my legs. I'll just close my eyes for a little while. I can still keep an eye on them while I rest. That's the last thought I remember. When I open my eyes again, it's dark outside and the lights are on. I jerk upright.

Jake is sitting at the table with his back to me, and Noah is strapped into his feeding chair. He's banging a spoon on the tray while Jake brings one to his mouth.

"The thing about tackling," Jake says, "is that you can't go into it scared. You've got to go in blindly, trusting your strength. If you doubt, even for a second, that's when your opponent gets the upper hand and you twist an ankle or tear a ligament."

I wipe sleep from my eyes. "Jake?"

He looks over his shoulder at me. "We're just talking rugby."

"Rugby?"

"Isn't that right, buddy?"

Swinging my legs from the bed, I lean around Jake for a better view. Noah's made a huge mess of his dinner. He's covered in food, but at least he's eating. I sniff. There's a delicious smell in the air. Something is bubbling in a pot on the stove, and the rest of the small space is spotless.

"Hungry?" Jake wipes Noah's mouth with a napkin. "I'm heating up some soup."

Mm. Chicken soup. My stomach rumbles.

I push to my feet and stretch. I do feel a whole lot better after my long nap. "I better prepare Noah's bath."

"Uh-uh." Jake waves a finger at me. "Sit. Food." Leaving Noah for a moment, he fills a bowl with soup and places it on my side of the table. "Eat. Noah's already had a bath."

"He did?"

Jake winks. "I paid attention."

I can't help but smile. "You almost passed the test."

He lifts a brow in challenge. "Almost?"

"Looks like he needs another bath."

"A little food has never killed anyone."

"I didn't mean to interrupt your discussion about rugby. It seems like a serious subject."

"Oh, yes. Huh, Noah?"

Noah makes a gurgling sound.

"He looks so much better."

"No fever." Jake touches his forehead. "I think the worst is over."

Cupping the bowl, I let the warmth sink into my palms. "Thank you."

"No thanks needed. It's what anyone would do."

But it's not. It's what he did.

~

Jake

THE PLAN STARTED COOKING in my head ever since that scumbag Luan left. As long as he's around, Kristi will never give me another chance. She's too loyal. She pledged herself to Luan, and she'll keep her word, even at the cost of her own happiness.

She lets me feed her dinner and clean up the trailer, but she won't let me stay the night to make sure she gets more sleep. Understandably. I leave only when she promises to call if Noah starts crying again, but I don't go back to the hotel. I drive to the estate agent's house and put in an offer for the house in Heidelberg. He's grumpy as fuck that I bothered him in the middle of dinner, but an agent doesn't say no to a sale, not in this town where property rarely sells. I have enough to put down a deposit. No bank is going to grant me a loan if I don't have a job, but that's tomorrow's worry. I'll figure out something. Then I drive around, looking in shop windows for help wanted signs. After an unsuccessful full round of both Rensburg and Heidelberg, I wind up at the steakhouse where Tessa works.

I go to the bar and order a beer. Tessa falls over herself to serve me, apologizing again for what happened at the lake, but I don't want to be reminded of that. I still get sick from the thought.

"If I can ever do anything, anything at all," she says, "don't hesitate to tell me. No favor is too big."

"You don't have to worry about favors."

"Are you sure there's nothing I can do?"

I tip the bottle back and take a sip. "As a matter of fact, I do need a job. Think you can put the word out?"

"Oh, my God. I can do better than that." She jumps up and down. "Our manager is leaving. She's getting married. I'll put in a word for you with the owner right now. He's here from Joburg to sort out the logistics of Sonja's departure. He's a family friend. That's how I got this job. Hold on. Let me see if he's available."

Before I can say more, she storms to the back and disappears through the office door. A short while later, a chubby man in grey pants and a white shirt exits.

He walks straight to me and extends a hand. "Jake Basson, I believe. I hear you're looking for a job."

I put the beer aside and sit up straighter. "Yes, sir."

"Your mother told me about that fancy school you attended in Dubai. Restaurant management, right?"

"I didn't finish the degree."

"I'm not fazed about degrees. What I need is experience. We're not talking about running a gourmet restaurant with a top-rated chef. This is a steakhouse. I need good food in quantity, the kind of portions folks from around here are used to. I need the place to run smoothly, and to adhere to safety and health standards. That's it. Think you can handle it?"

"Yes, sir."

"Good." He pats me on the shoulder. "You're hired."

We talk a bit more about the salary and when I can start. Sonja is leaving at the end of the month, so he doesn't need me before then. He promises to have a contract for me by tomorrow, as he's in a hurry to get back to his other businesses in Joburg.

BACK AT THE HOTEL, I email the estate agent to inform him about my job and that he'll have a copy of the contract soon. Then I file an online application for a home loan at the bank, supplying the required documents. When that task is done, I lie on the bed and think about my plan. I think about it the next morning and all day, until I park outside the factory, waiting for Gina to clear the gates.

"Jake," she says, leaning into the open passenger window. "What are you doing here?"

"I have a favor to ask."

"I better get in then." She gets inside and buckles up.

I pull away, gaining a good distance from the factory before I tell her what I want. "Can you take care of Noah for a few days?"

She turns sideways in her seat. "Why?"

"I want to take Kristi away."

"Jake." There's pity in her voice. "She's with Luan."

I rub a hand over my brow. "I don't think she is."

"What do you mean?"

"You saw how she kissed me."

"Jake," she says again.

"Gina, please. Kristi needs time away from her job, and responsibilities, and Luan, even from Noah, to make up her mind. Give us a chance. I know she doesn't love Luan. Think about her happiness."

"Looking after Noah isn't the issue. You know I'll do it with pleasure."

"But?"

"I don't see how you're going to convince Kristi to go away with you."

Giving her a level stare, I say, "I'm not."

"You're not going to what?"

"I'm not going to convince her."

"Oh, my God," she exclaims, watching me with big eyes. Then she laughs as if whatever she's thinking is hilarious. "You want to kidnap her?"

My voice is steady. My mind is made up. "It's not kidnapping if she's your wife."

CHAPTER 14

Jake

"You're serious," Gina exclaims.

"I care about Kristi."

"You have a strange way of showing it."

"I fucked up. All I'm asking is for a chance to make it right."

"By kidnapping her?"

"Kind of." Meeting Gina's no-nonsense gaze, I admit, "Yes."

"She won't survive it if you hurt her again."

"I'm not going to hurt her again. I swear."

"Do you love her?"

"Yes."

She crosses her arms. "What about Luan?"

"If he loves her as much as he claims, he'll grant her an opportunity to choose." Between us. I swallow at the thought.

"What would you have done if the roles were reversed? What would your reaction be if Luan kidnaps Kristi?"

Not an easy notion to stomach. I clench the wheel hard at the thought. "I'd probably hunt the bastard down and steal her back."

She grins.

I shoot her a contemplative look. "Is that a yes?"

"Kristi will kill me."

"You want what's best for her, don't you? Look, if my plan fails and she stills wants Luan, I'll respect her decision."

She narrows her eyes. She doesn't believe me. I'm not sure I believe myself.

"How long?" she asks.

"Three weeks," I reply, hopeful.

"Three weeks is a long time for Noah to be separated from his mom."

"We'll come back if he misses her too much."

"Where are you taking her?"

"Can't say."

"Damn." She shakes her head and says with dry humor, "I've always thought to be kidnapped to an unknown location was romantic."

"It could be."

"How exactly are you going to manage this so-called kidnapping?"

"Let me worry about the logistics. Just say yes. Please, Gina."

She bites her lip and looks straight ahead through the windscreen.

"I'm asking you because I know Noah will be in good hands. If it's too much to ask, I don't mind bringing him with us."

"No, you're right. Kristi has never had a proper holiday, and she's never had time to herself since Noah has been born."

"You *are* saying yes?"

"Ah, hell. I suppose there is something sexy about a surprise kidnapping."

~

IT TAKES a day to find a hideaway and rent a car for Gina. I don't want her to be stuck without wheels while we're gone. Gina has to come with me to collect the rental, thus having no choice but to take a day off so we can do it while Kristi is at work. We park the rental at the back of Shiny's trailer to prevent Kristi from getting suspicious. Then Gina packs a bag for Kristi while I do some shopping for our trip. I make sure to be back at the trailer with enough time to put Kristi's bag in the trunk before she gets home.

"All set?" Gina asks, her smile a little nervous as she leans against the car.

"Don't worry. It'll be fine."

"You better hope so, or I'll have to castrate you. You still won't tell me where you're going?"

"No, but you can get hold of us on our phones. We're not immigrating to another country."

"I don't even know why I'm doing this."

"Because a repressed side of you thinks kidnapping is romantic, remember?"

"Kristi deserves to be happy." She says it like a warning.

"Agreed."

"Call me when you get there."

Placing a palm on my heart, I say, "Promise."

She slaps my arm. "Don't patronize me. I could've been your mother-in-law."

"You are."

"Well, you know what I mean."

"Yeah," I say with a pinch of regret for what could've been. Taking the piece of paper with the address of the house in Heidelberg from my pocket, I hand it to her.

She takes the scrap of paper hesitantly. "What's this?"

"A house for Kristi, you, and Noah."

She stares at the address for a while before lifting her eyes back to mine. "You're mighty sure of yourself."

"I'm not."

The corners of her eyes crinkle in understanding. The house is theirs, regardless. It has nothing to do with Kristi's decision to be or not to be with me. The only difference her decision will make is that I'd be the lucky bastard to live there with them.

"If Kristi still decides to marry Luan," God forbid, "the house is yours."

"I can never accept—"

"Just go check it out."

"Fine," she says just as Luan's Volvo takes the turn at the top of the road.

We watch the car in silence, both of us tense for our own reasons. Kristi gets Noah from the back, but Luan doesn't budge. Other than a tight nod in our direction, he doesn't acknowledge me. Just as well. I'm not dying to say hello either.

Kristi waves him off and stands in the road until his car disappears around the bend before she approaches us.

A grin splits Noah's face when he looks at me. Something inside me gives. The tight control I keep on my feelings shifts, and everything loosens. Vulnerability hits me in the chest. For the first time, I understand the price that comes with parental love. It's a deep-seated fear that anything should ever happen to him.

Reaching for him, I ask in a voice that's suddenly hoarse, "May I?"

Kristi's eyebrows pinch together in an unspoken question as she hands him over.

I plant a kiss on the top of his head and hug his solid little body. "Did you have fun at school today?"

"They saw a silk moth break out of his cocoon," Kristi says.

This, right here, is the irreplaceable value of life I've been missing. "We'll have to get you some silkworms. They spin shapes if you put them on cardboard circles and squares. If you want pink silk, you have to feed them mulberry leaves. I had a box full of worms under my bed when I was a kid."

A visible shudder runs over Kristi's body. "Not in the trailer."

Winking, I mouth, "In the new house."

"What was that?" Kristi asks.

"Nothing," I reply, which makes Noah laugh as if he understands. Does he? My heart beats painfully, my newly discovered vulnerability already having a field day.

"What's going on?" Kristi looks between Gina and me. "Why are you standing out here in the driveway as if you're going somewhere?"

"We are," I say.

Kristi's fingers tighten on the strap of her bag. "What?"

"I'm taking you out to dinner."

"I don't want to—"

Before she can finish her sentence, I put Noah back in her arms. "Give him a goodbye kiss."

"I said—"

"Nothing you say is going to change our plans."

"*Our* plans?" She huffs. "You mean your plans."

I kiss Gina's cheek. "Thanks for taking care of him."

"No worries." Gina's look is meaningful. "I hope you'll enjoy yourselves."

"Mom! Did you two scheme behind my back?"

"Honey, trust me, you don't want to know."

Taking Noah from Kristi, I hand him to Gina. It's like a game of musical chairs, and I already know the empty seat where Noah should be will hit me hard during the next few days.

"Get in, Pretorius," I say, opening the passenger door. Did she have a premonition I was going to bail on her when she decided to keep her maiden name and not take mine?

"I'm not going anywhere if I don't know where we're going."

"Steakhouse."

"What's the occasion?"

"Dinner."

"I can have dinner here."

"Stop bickering." I all but shove her into the car.

With a last wave at Gina and Noah, we're finally off. Kristi does have to eat, which is why I drive to the steakhouse where we had dinner the first night. She's quiet on the way there and mostly throughout dinner. I drag out of her that the town folks decided to have at least three people taking care of the kids during the weekend gatherings at the lake. The idea is to give all the parents a chance to relax. It has a neighborly ring to it, a kind of communal belonging, and I never would've guessed how badly I'd long to be a part of it. Small towns have their drawbacks, but they also have plenty of good.

After dessert and coffee, I ask for the bill and insist she visits the bathroom. We have a long road ahead. She mumbles something about me being bossy but obliges. Lucky for me, she leaves her bag on the table. While she's in the ladies' room, I fish her phone from her bag and pocket it.

Just after ten, we're finally on our way. When I don't take the exit to the trailer park but continue south toward Bloemfontein, she stiffens with her arms plastered at her sides.

"Where are we going, Jake?"

Not easy to answer.

She sits up straighter when we pass the signpost for the highway. A tinge of panic invades her tone. "Jake?"

I cup her hand. "We're not going home. Not just yet."

"I can see that," she snaps. "Where are you taking me?"

"I can't say."

She jerks her hand away and scoots up higher in her seat. "What?"

"Look at it as a surprise."

"What the hell are you talking about?" I reach for her again, trying to calm her as much as driving with one hand allows, but she jerks away. "Answer me."

"We're going away for a few days."

She blinks, then shakes her head as if to rid it from an unpleasant thought. "Did you just say...?"

"Yes, I'm taking you away."

Her eyes flare with full-blown panic in the yellow glow of the overhead streetlights as we take the highway. "Away? Away where? Wait, what?"

"Somewhere quiet." Somewhere away from everything that stands between us. Our past. Our child, as much as I already miss him. Luan.

"Turn around," she says through gritted teeth.

"Sorry, ginger. I can't do that."

She grips the door handle. "Stop the car. Let me out."

I speed up as I cross over to the fast lane. For security reasons, I always activate the lock before I start driving. She fiddles around frantically, searching for the button on the dashboard, no doubt to unlock her door, not that it will do her any good. She won't jump from the car at a hundred and twenty kilometers per hour.

"Kristi," I say in the stern tone that always gets her attention, "calm down. I'm not going to stop, and you're not getting out."

She jerks on the handle. "You can't do this. I'm a mother."

I reach over and close my fingers around her hand to still her movements. "I know that."

"Noah needs me. I need to be there for him when he wakes up."

"Gina is taking care of him."

"My mother is in on this?" she shrieks.

She tries to pull away again, but I tighten my grip and place her hand on my leg. "I didn't really give her a choice, so don't blame her."

She twists her arm in my hold. "Let me go."

"Try to relax, ginger. It's a long ride."

"Don't call me that. How long exactly?"

"Ten hours."

"Ten—" Her breath catches. "I can't be that far away from Noah. If something happens—"

"He's in good hands. I don't want this to be unpleasant for you, so just try to look at it as a holiday that's long overdue."

Her jaw drops. "Do you hear yourself?"

"I'm being nice."

"Nice? You're crazy."

"I could've given you a sleeping pill or tied you up."

If looks could burn, I'd be fried. In contrast, her voice is icy when she asks, "Can I have my hand back?"

"Are you going to try and break off the door handle again?"

"I didn't try to break it off."

"Will you relax?"

"What choice do I have?"

Her reaction isn't pleasant for me either. I much prefer to keep a point of contact that will soothe her, but I release her hand. The minute she's free, she grabs her bag and buries her head inside, rummaging through the contents.

When she can't find her phone, she gives me a seething look. "Where's my phone?"

"Somewhere safe."

"Give it back."

"You can have it when we get there."

"Now or then, it doesn't make a difference. You know I'll call the cops the minute you give me my phone, so you may as well turn around now."

"Tsk. After that confession, maybe I should keep it for the whole three weeks."

"Three weeks?" she cries. "You're out of your mind. I have a job. I have responsibilities."

"Not for the next three weeks, you don't."

She crosses her arms and turns away from me. "I can't believe you're doing this."

"We need time together."

"Stop saying that!"

"Cold?"

"No," she snaps.

I turn up the heater. There's a bite in the air tonight. It's nothing compared to the frostiness in the car, not that I expected Kristi to embrace my plan with enthusiasm. It will take some warming up to my idea, but there's still a hell of a lot more than a spark between us. If she won't admit it, I'll just have to prove it.

"I hate you," she whispers into the darkness.

"Put back your seat and try to catch a few hours of sleep."

"Is that an order?"

"No."

When a strained silence prevails, I switch on the radio. Reaching behind me, I grab the blanket from the backseat and drape it over her lap. "There's a pillow too."

She stubbornly refuses the comforts I offer, but when we reach Kroonstad, she flings around, takes the pillow, and shoves it between her head and the window before pulling the blanket up to her shoulders. She keeps her body turned away from me, her shoulders pulled into herself, but it doesn't take long for her soft snores to fill the space.

Turning up the volume on the radio, I push down on the gas. The road is straight and mid-week quiet, and the expanse flat and deserted. A freedom I haven't felt since leaving the stuffy, angry confines of my parents' house makes my shoulders drop. A band of tension snaps, and my muscles relax. The ever-present strain evaporates, and there's only Kristi, me, a stretching night, and endless possibilities. Hope. Maybe, just this once, I'll do something right.

CHAPTER 15

Kristi

The sun is out when I wake up. The light penetrates my closed eyelids, but I don't open them. I'm groggy and angry all over again when I remember why my neck is aching from the awkward position in which I've fallen asleep. A restless, unconsolidated sleep. It's because I'm in a car with Jake, heading to God only knows where.

Jake's deep voice reverberates through the car. "Morning."

No use pretending I'm asleep. Opening my eyes, I stretch my neck and take in the scenery. We're crossing a dry stretch of land dotted with small bushes.

"The Karoo," Jake says. "We passed Beaufort West a while ago."

Despite my anger, I can't help but be curious. I've never traveled farther than Johannesburg.

"Hungry?" he asks. "There are snacks in the cooler bag on the backseat."

I consider ignoring his damn snacks, but starving like a martyr won't change where I am or that Jake isn't taking me back. I may as well eat his food. Grabbing the cooler box, I open it to find sandwiches, juice, and apples.

As I'm biting into a cheese and ham sandwich, Jake asks, "Can I have one?"

I shoot him a hostile look, about to say no, but there are rings under his eyes and dark stubble on his jaw. I check my watch. He's been driving for nine hours straight. He must be hammered, not that I feel sorry for him.

Grudgingly removing the cling wrap from a sandwich, I hand it to him. As an afterthought, I place a paper napkin on his thigh.

"Thanks," he mumbles with a full mouth, giving me a wink.

I snort before taking another bite. Ew. There's at least an inch of butter between the slices. How much mayonnaise did he use? The whole jar?

"Like it?" he asks. "Made them myself."

"No."

"We can stop at the next gas station. There should be a diner where I can find you a more appetizing breakfast."

I chew and swallow. "Forget it." I hate wasting food.

"Want to stretch your legs?"

Spitefully, I don't answer.

"Need a bathroom break?"

Wait. If he stops at the gas station, I can ask someone for a phone. Who am I going to call? My mom is in on this. There will be hell to pay when I get back. I don't really want the police to charge Jake with kidnapping. That will only strengthen Luan's case in not granting Jake shared custody of Noah. Luan said some things yesterday, but he was upset. He must see reason. He must understand why someone like me, who grew up without a father, doesn't want the same for my child. Luan has a logical mind. He's patient and reasonable. He'd keep a cool head. If I call him, he'd help me.

"Yes," I say, finishing off the last of the bread with an unladylike bite.

At the next picnic area, Jake pulls off on the side of the road. I stare at the single concrete table and bench standing under a threadbare thorn tree. "Here?"

He switches off the engine and leans over me to open the glove compartment. "Here's a *bog roll*."

I gape at the roll of toilet paper he places on my palm. "Seriously?"

"It's biodegradable."

"You know very well I'm referring to going in the middle of nowhere and not to polluting the earth."

"I can't imagine you being scared of doing it camping style."

"Just because I live in a trailer doesn't mean I'm used to roughing it up."

"Better get going if you're serious about that bathroom break. I want to be back on the road in ten minutes."

I glance at the sparse, small bushes. "There's nowhere *private*."

He grins. "At least it's open, so you don't risk stumbling upon a snake."

"A snake?" I screech.

Laughing softly, he gets out and comes around to open my door. Unfortunately, he took the keys. I would've been very tempted to hop over the console and drive off, leaving him and his biodegradable *bog roll* behind.

When I don't budge, he takes my arm, pulls me out of the car, and leads me to a cluster of bushes a small distance away. After scouting the ground, he says, "No snakes or scorpions that will bite your ass. Go ahead."

Snakes and scorpions scare me, but I'm also tempted to refuse going in the open just to make his life difficult. Although, with how full my bladder is, I'd only spite myself.

"Go away," I say on a scoff.

He turns his back on me and crosses his arms.

"Which part of go away don't you understand, Jake Basson?"

"I'm being a gentleman, Pretorius. Just pee, already."

"You're being a gentleman by crowding my space?"

"By blocking the view from the road, in case a car comes by."

I see his point. Without a choice, I do my business and stash the biodegradable paper under a rock. I've barely adjusted my clothes before he turns back and scrutinizes me with a gaze that runs from the top of my head to my trainers.

"Done?" he asks with a glint in his eyes.

"Obviously." Accusingly, I add, "I need to wash my hands. I hope you have a clever plan for that too."

Without bothering to reply, he unzips his fly and takes out his cock. Just like that. Not caring that I'm staring. Flinging around, I fix my gaze on the single hill that disturbs the flat horizon while heat warms my cheeks. I listen to Jake relieving himself, flustered, embarrassed, and all kinds of furious.

"Ready," he announces.

I wait until I hear the sound of his zipper before I face him again, but he's already making his way back to the car. With a glance around, just to be certain there really are no snakes, I follow. He takes gel sanitizer from the door compartment and motions at my hands. When I hold out my palms, he squirts a blob onto each before dumping the bottle on the seat and taking my hands between his, rubbing gently.

"What are you doing?"

"Implementing my clever plan."

I'm not going to comment on that. I watch him while he works, ignoring the fluttering in my stomach as he meticulously covers the whole surface of my hands. "I have to call Luan."

He stills, and then drops my hands. "I'm sure Gina spoke to him."

"It's *my* job to speak to him." I add in a biting tone, "I have to explain why I won't be at work today."

He looks up and down the road as if the answer lies there.

Finally, he dips his hand into the front pocket of his jeans and pulls out my phone.

I all but grab it from him. Oh, thank God. I have a signal. I can't dial Luan fast enough. Please, please, please. Let him come save me. I can't do this. I can't be alone with Jake. Not for three weeks. Not for a day.

"Do you mind?" I say when the ringtone starts and he's still standing toe to toe with me.

He shrugs. "What?"

"Privacy? Duh."

Taking my arm, he manhandles me into the car. "You can talk while I drive."

"What? No, wait."

The door slams in my face. I'm about to protest again when Luan answers.

"Morning, Kristi. Is Noah sick again?"

Jake is all teeth while he starts the engine and throws the car into gear. Obstinate bastard.

"Not exactly." I give Jake another angry look.

"Then what's up?" A car door slams. "I'm just leaving to fetch you."

"You don't have to."

"Why not?"

"I, um, won't be coming in to work today."

"What happened?"

"I have a situation."

Jake is staring straight ahead. At least his expression is serious and no longer mocking. Turning away from him, I lower my voice. "Jake tricked me into going away with him."

Two seconds pass. "Can you repeat that?"

"Jake bundled me into his car last night, and now we're nine hours away in some godforsaken place with snakes and scorpions and nothing but sand."

"And bushes," Jake adds.

I fling around and narrow my eyes before leaning toward the limited privacy close to the door. "He took my phone, or I would've called you last night."

Silence.

"Luan? Are you there?"

"For how long is this *forced* trip supposed to last?" Luan asks.

"I'm getting home the minute I figure out a way."

"I'm calling the cops."

"No," I say quickly. "I don't want to go that route."

"Then you're not serious about getting home."

"How can you say that? How can you even think that? I had no control over what happened."

"Kristi..."

I wait, hoping he'll say he's going to come to rescue me, but I'm not prepared for the words he utters.

"You're fired."

"What?" I cry softly.

"It's over between us."

"You don't mean that."

"I can't accept this kind of behavior."

"It's not my fault."

"You're staying away from work without having filed a leave application. That's serious. If you're innocent, call the cops, get Jake arrested, and come back to work. It's that simple."

"No," I whisper, "you know it's not."

"Well, then you have your answer, and I have mine. Goodbye, Kristi. Enjoy your unemployment."

The line goes dead.

I stare at the phone.

He hung up on me. He fired me. He *broke up* with me.

Before I can come to my senses, Jake takes my phone from my hand and shoves it back into his pocket. "I take it he didn't handle the news well."

Angry tears well up in my eyes. When the first one slips free, I feel like slapping the compassionate look from Jake's face, because it's a gorgeous face that's unfairly sexy for someone who hasn't slept, showered, or shaved.

"Hey." He wipes a tear from my cheek with his thumb. "It's going to be all right."

I slap his hand away. "It's not going to be all right. I lost my job. My *job*, Jake."

"We'll work it out."

"I needed that job." I throw my hands in the air. "How are Noah and I supposed to live?"

"I'll take care of you."

"If you're planning on staying in Rensburg like you claim, you don't have a job. Even if you had one, I don't want you to take care of us."

"It's all right to give up a little of that control you're holding onto so tightly. You don't have to do it all by yourself."

"A little?" I turn away, staring out of the side window. "You're talking about our livelihoods."

"I didn't have time to tell you, but I have a job."

"Oh, yeah?" I cross my arms. "Doing what?"

"Tessa put in a good word for me at the steakhouse. You're looking at their new manager. I start next month."

"Congratulations," I say flatly.

"Kristi, look at me." When I don't oblige, he repeats in a gentle tone, "Look at me."

It's hard to look at him when I'm simmering with helpless anger, but he grips my chin and turns my head toward him, giving me no choice.

"We're going to work it out. I promise. For now, all I want you to do is relax."

"It's a little hard to relax when you're screwing up my life."

He drops his hand and focuses on the road, but not before I've glimpsed a spark of vulnerability in his eyes. Why must I feel guilty? If Jake didn't kidnap me, I'd still have a job and a future with a stable, well-established man. Security. Given, my relationship with Luan wasn't the most romantic in the world, but that's not what I'm looking for. I'm looking for someone I can rely on, someone I can trust.

I'm ashamed to admit I'm more shocked about having lost my job than my boyfriend. I'm disappointed in Luan. I expected more support from him. Am I being unfair? Can any man support you if your almost-ex is taking you against your will on an unwanted holiday? Logic says no, but my heart wanted Luan to fight for me. At least a little harder. I wanted him to get into his car and come rescue me, but now I'm stuck with Jake in the middle of nowhere.

"Everything all right?" Jake asks.

"How can you even ask me that?"

"You're upset."

"How do you expect me to feel? Happy?"

"Not exactly, but I didn't want to make you cry."

I swipe at my cheeks angrily. They're wet, but my tears are more from frustration than the end of my first stable relationship.

His fingers clench around the wheel. "What did Luan say to make you cry?"

"None of your business."

"I'll call and ask him myself."

I scoff.

"Don't test me. You know I'll do it."

"He broke up with me."

"That son of a bitch."

I look at Jake quickly to see if he's mocking me, but he appears genuinely upset. "I thought you'd be happy with the turn of events."

"He could've waited for you to make your decision, or at the very least until you got back."

He seems so truly agitated, I believe him. "Luan doesn't operate like that. He's a black and white kind of guy who does things by the book."

"Boring, in other words."

"That's not fair. You don't know him, and he's not here to defend himself."

"You're right. I'm sorry. I didn't expect him to bail on you for something that's out of your control."

"He's a guy, Jake. How did you expect him to behave? Tell me he'd wait for me and to have fun?"

"I would've."

"Really?"

"Well, not the fun part."

There's something truthful in his eyes as he speaks. All the layers of broody, bullshitting Jake have been peeled away, and what he's showing me is the true essence of his feelings. The seriousness with which he stares at me finally makes me look away again.

"I need to call my mom to ask how Noah is doing." I stare with non-seeing eyes through the window, missing my baby like crazy. We've never been separated.

"You can call when we get there."

"I want to speak to her *now*."

"Not up for discussion."

"You're a jerk."

"I know."

I huff in frustration. "Where are we going, anyway?"

"You'll see soon enough. It's not much farther."

In the silence that follows, we drink the juice and eat the apples. We pass a gas station with the diner Jake mentioned, but he doesn't stop. After another ten minutes, he takes a dirt road that cuts through the terrain and leads to a cluster of trees in the distance. A wind pump towers above the treetops. Judging by the rest of the barren landscape, the tall, leafy trees didn't grow here naturally. They must've been planted a long time ago, and someone must be watering them.

Jake parks under one of the trees and leans forward to squint through the windscreen. A farmhouse with whitewashed walls and a thatch roof stands in the circle of what I make out to be oak trees. When he opens his door, the loud hum of sun beetles greets us. I get out before he has a chance to come around and get my door. Turning in a slow circle, I study the surroundings. It's flat and dry, deserted as far as the eye can see. A depressing shudder runs over me. We're out in the sticks. Unless I manage to steal the car, there's no way of escaping, which is probably why Jake chose this sad location.

"What do you think?" he asks behind me.

I'm about to tell him how ugly and forlorn the place is, but when I turn, I see something very different in his expression. Adoration. Nostalgia. He loves it here. He knows the place.

"You've been here before," I say.

"We used to come here on holiday."

I can't help myself from asking, "Whatever for?"

"My father loved the Karoo." His laugh is wry. "It's probably the only thing we had in common."

I crane my neck to see beyond the trees. There's a concrete dam. A pipe leading from the wind pump feeds it water. Borehole. That explains how whoever lives here keeps the trees green.

"Who's the owner?"

"He lives in Oudtshoorn."

"No one stays here permanently?"

"No."

"Why would anyone rent a house in the middle of nowhere?"

Grabbing two bags from the trunk, he says, "It has its charm. You'll see."

I doubt that very much, but it's hot, even this early and in the shade, so I follow him when he makes his way to the house.

After retrieving the key from a hollow in one of the tree trunks, he lets us inside. It's cool, and it smells like floor polish. Someone must've prepared the house for our unexpected *holiday*. I pad behind Jake over the wooden floor of a spacious lounge with a bay window overlooking the front yard.

We pass through a kitchen with log cupboards and terracotta countertops into a short hallway.

Jake enters through the first door and dumps one of the bags on the bed. "This is you."

"Me?"

"I'll be next door."

That comes as a surprise. I expected him to bully me into sharing a bed. My gaze settles on the familiar green travel bag.

"Gina packed for you." When I don't say anything, he walks to the door. "Make yourself at home while I get the rest of the stuff from the car."

After he's gone, I study the room. It's simple but comfortable. There's a double bed with white linen and lots of scatter pillows. I find a smaller bedroom with a single bed down the hall, next to a bathroom with an old-fashioned tub. Going back to my room, I unzip the bag and check inside. There are some of my clothes, a pair of sandals, and my toilet bag. I can't believe my mom packed my belongings behind my back.

Jake's face appears around the doorframe. "Coffee?"

"Yes." I'm desperate for caffeine, but I refuse to say please.

"With milk and one sugar, coming up."

I hate that he knows how I drink my coffee. "You said I could call my mom."

He takes my phone from his pocket and hands it to me.

I snatch it from his hand and waste no time in dialing my mom.

She answers, "Where are you?"

"Somewhere in the damn Karoo."

"Before you get upset—"

"Too late. How could you do this?"

Jake throws a thumb over his shoulder. "I'll start the coffee."

"Honey, Jake is right. You need time with him to be sure you're not making a mistake."

"Says the woman who always warned me against him."

"My warning is redundant since you never listened to me. Anyway, I think Jake has changed."

"Since when are you a fan of Jake?"

"This isn't about Jake. It's *your* best interest I have at heart. Plus, a few days to yourself can't hurt."

Rubbing my forehead, I walk to the window and stare at the dull landscape. "How's Noah?" My heart clenches as I envision his sweet, little face. "I miss him."

"He's great. Nothing to worry about."

"Will you call me if anything—?"

"I promise."

"I'm not going to forgive you for this." I don't tell her about Luan and my job. There's no point in stressing her about something she'll blame herself for but can't change.

"That's what mothers are for. Got to go. I'm late for work." She blows a kiss into the phone and cuts the call.

How am I going to survive three weeks with Jake in the middle of nowhere? I glance over my shoulder. I'm still alone. Quickly, I pull up Nancy's name from my list of recent calls and press dial.

I interrupt her cheerful greeting with, "I need your help. Jake kidnapped me."

Before she can reply, a big hand folds around mine from over my shoulder. Yelping, I fling around and bump into Jake's chest. Nancy's, "What?" sounds in the space as we fight over the phone, me struggling and Jake tightening his grip. It doesn't take much effort to take the phone from me.

A strangely sympathetic look plays in his eyes as he holds my gaze while pressing the phone against his ear. "Hello, Nancy. It's Jake."

Her voice is so loud I hear every word. "What's going on? What are you doing with Kristi?"

"Kristi is fine. Call Gina. She'll explain."

"But—"

He hangs up. "You've just lost your phone privileges, ginger."

"Give it back," I say through clenched teeth.

"Sorry, but I obviously can't trust you with a phone."

"Can't trust me?" I utter a little hysterically. "Says the man who kidnapped me."

"You need coffee."

Claustrophobia suddenly envelops me. The walls close in, and the vastness is too small a space. "I need to go home."

He grips my shoulders firmly and steers me out of the room and into the hallway. "You need to calm down."

"I am calm!"

I try to dig in my heels, but I'm no match for him. He easily maneuvers me to an island counter and pushes me down onto a stool.

"Stay," he says in an authoritative tone.

"I want to go home."

His touch disappears from my shoulders. It's both a relief and disconcerting. For some crazy reason, I feel less grounded.

A moment later, he puts a steaming mug down in front of me. "Careful. It's hot."

It takes me a couple of seconds to register the smell of the coffee. All I want is out. "I want to go back to Noah."

He grips my shoulders again and starts kneading my aching muscles. "You're full of knots. Don't worry. Tonight, you'll sleep in a comfortable bed."

I try to twist in the stool, but he grips me harder, holding me in place.

"Don't pretend not to hear me," I hiss.

"I hear you fine." He rubs a thumb along the column of my neck, finding another sore muscle. "Here?" he asks, applying gentle pressure.

"You can't massage your way out of this."

"I'm not trying to."

"Then what are you doing?"

"Taking care of you."

His words grind on me. I can't stomach them. They hurt. When I needed his care, he wasn't there. It's too late now. "Stop."

At my harsh tone, he pauses.

"Take your hands off me."

Another second, and he obliges. My shoulders relax only marginally because his body is still pressed against my back.

"Step away." Thump. Thump. My heartbeat falls like an axe on wood, but then his warmth disappears. I breathe easier.

"Drink your coffee," he says.

I sit like a statue, ignoring him as he unpacks groceries from a box and fills the cupboards and fridge.

When he's done stocking the kitchen, he stops in front of me with his hands on his hips. "Feel like having a bath?"

"No."

"There *is* hot water."

"Isn't that good to know?" I say sarcastically.

He rubs the back of his neck. "I'm going for one."

"Do whatever you want. You don't report to me."

He hovers for another moment, staring down at my face, before leaving the kitchen. The minute he's gone, I pick up the mug and fling it at the wall. It breaks into three large pieces, the coffee dripping down the pristine, white plaster. If he heard the tantrum, he doesn't return to the kitchen. In the quiet aftermath of my violence, only the sound of running water comes from the bathroom.

Pushing to my feet, I start searching for my bag and find it in the lounge on the coffee table. It takes me only a second to come to a decision. I snatch up my bag and hurry out the front door. Jake still has the car keys in his pocket, but the gas station can't be farther than ten kilometers. If I walk fast, I can make it there in an hour. I just have to stay away from the road and stick to the outskirts, not that there's much vegetation to hide behind.

I'm about to go down the veranda steps when movement catches my eye. Not far away, an ostrich picks at something on the ground. Judging by the black feathers, it's a male. Three more with gray feathers follow behind. Females. Shit. They're territorial birds and lethally dangerous. They can run much faster than a man and won't hesitate to kick and claw any imposter to death.

"I wouldn't if I were you," a deep voice says behind me.

My back stiffens, but I don't turn around.

"This is an ostrich farm, ginger. They may be the stupidest birds on the planet, but they're deceptively dangerous."

"I know what an ostrich is capable of," I bite out.

"Good," he says, pushing the strap of my bag from my shoulder in an oddly gentle caress before pulling it from under my arm. "I'm glad you understand."

CHAPTER 16

Kristi

*W*hat I understand, is that I'm trapped. My throat closes up. I want to kick and punch something, but another tantrum won't get me anywhere. This is where I'm staying until Jake decides otherwise. Unless I can convince him. The moment the idea drifts into my head, my breathing evens out. Jake is all about the physical. His libido is high. It has to be if he screwed fifty hookers. Ouch. I can't think about it because it hurts. He obviously wants me. I can use that to my advantage. Perhaps, if I give him what he wants, he'll grow tired of this game and take me home.

With the plan settling decisively in my mind, I go back inside and pause in the kitchen doorframe. Jake is cleaning up the mess I've made. I feel bad about the broken mug and that he's doing my dirty work, but I suppress the urge to take over. If not for him, I wouldn't be in this predicament. He lifts his gaze to mine from where he's crouching, wiping up the coffee from the floor, but he doesn't say anything. He doesn't have to. The look in his eyes is back to being broody and intense. Invasive.

I pad over to the coffee maker and pour myself another cup, adding milk and sugar. Watching him work from over the rim, I take a sip. He's shirtless and minus his shoes, dressed in the ripped jeans from earlier. His hair is dry and his face unshaven.

"What happened to having a bath?" I ask, trying to keep my tone normal.

"Feeling better?"

I shrug. "I decided to accept what I can't change."

He scrutinizes me while I blow on the coffee and bravely hold his gaze.

"Go on," I say. "Have your bath." I can't stop myself from adding sarcastically, "You don't have to keep me company around the clock."

"Are you going to try and run again?"

"We've established it's impossible."

He crosses the floor and stops in front of me. The longer he stares down at my face, the harder it becomes not to break eye contact.

"There are books in the lounge," he says. "There isn't cable, but there are DVDs if you feel like watching a movie."

Touching him is going to mess with my head. It will be hard to keep my emotions out of the equation, but I'm not heading down that road again. Not with him. I just have to seduce him into taking me home. Just thinking about it makes my palms sweat. A muscle ticks under my eye. I hope he doesn't notice the nervous reaction. Hiding my face behind the cup, I nod.

He pushes the cup away and drags a thumb over the scar on my cheek. "I'll be quick."

The touch unnerves me further, but not half as much as his piercing stare that seems to miss nothing.

"Call if you need me," he says in an even voice before leaving me alone in the kitchen.

When he's gone, I blow out a breath. I'll need to get my act together if I'm serious about executing my seduction plan, but it's been a while since I've touched a man like that. Since Jake, to be exact. I haven't had sex with anyone since. After Noah's birth, my libido took a dive. My mom blamed it on post-natal hormones and claimed it was normal. Even when my craving for a man's touch eventually returned, I was constantly exhausted during Noah's first year due to breastfeeding every four hours, working around the clock, and a lack of sleep. It's easier now that Noah is older. I can't blame hormones or tiredness any longer. I've been telling myself I wanted to do things morally right by divorcing Jake before tumbling into another man's bed, but the truth is Luan never evoked the same spark as Jake. After the picnic at the lake, it's clear that spark is still there between Jake and me, and it terrifies me. I allowed it to destroy me once. I can't allow it again. Can I play with fire without getting burned? When I consider the alternative, staying here for three weeks and fighting the attraction, I have my answer. I'm just going to have to woman up and be in control of my feelings for once. The newfound resolve gives me a boost of confidence. The earlier despair makes a place for hope. Before Jake knows it, we'll be out of here.

I wander to the lounge and go through the books on the bookshelf, which is an eclectic collection of fiction, before browsing the DVDs, but I'm not relaxed enough to let my mind get lost in a story. Going back to the kitchen, I sit down at the island counter and worry about my jobless status, Noah, and Luan's reaction until Jake returns, dressed in dark jeans and a clean T-shirt.

He smells of soap and that same, cheap cologne from school. The fragrance stirs memories I've banished, touching me far more profoundly than I like. With those memories comes a fresh wave of hurt.

Eager to escape the unwelcome sensation, I hop off the stool. "I'll have a bath after all. I can do with one after the long drive."

Suspicion sparks in his eyes, but he doesn't question my sudden change of mood. I feel his stare on my back as I head for the bathroom where I find the bath surprisingly clean. The wet towel Jake used hangs on a hook behind the door and his dirty clothes are in the hamper.

After running a bath, I soak in the warm water while gathering the courage to go through with my plan. By the time I've convinced myself I can do it, my skin is wrinkled. I pull the plug, drape a towel around my body, brush out my wet hair, and wash the bath. My skin is still wet when I walk down the hallway and pause in the kitchen doorway. Jake sits at the island counter, reading something on his phone.

He looks up and stills. His gaze rakes over me. When he drags his eyes back to mine, he swallows. "What are you doing?"

The question runs much deeper than asking why I'm standing in the door. It's a warning. A pluck of the towel, and I'll stand bare in front of him.

"My neck is sore from that awkward position in which I slept in the car. Does the offer of a massage still stand?"

His jaw tightens. I don't give him time to answer but walk to the stool next to his and plop down in it with my back to him.

His phone makes a clinking sound as he puts it down on the counter. I take a breath and brace myself, but nothing could've prepared me for the heat bursting through my ribcage when he twists my hair around his hand a little too tightly and arranges it over my shoulder with alarming gentleness. His big hands land on my shoulders, his palms warm on my wet skin.

"Breathe," he says when he starts kneading my muscles.

Shit. I've been holding my breath. I drag in some air. My lungs expand, but I blow everything out in a gush when he applies too much pressure.

"Too hard?"

"Mm-mm," I say, biting down on my lip to prevent a moan from escaping as his grip turns gentler.

My back really hurts, and the way he works the knots from my neck and shoulders is amazing.

I drop the towel an inch at the back. "It hurts lower too."

He works his way down my spine to poke at a knot in the middle. "Here?"

"Yes. Ouch."

"Softer?"

"No, that's good."

He needs no prompt when I drop the towel more, clutching the ends together between my breasts. His deft fingers work along my spine until he reaches the top of my globes. He doesn't wait for an invitation to dip his hands inside and smooth them over my skin as far as the stool allows. His touch becomes even lighter, his palms folding around the curve of my hips, but I don't stop him, because this is part of my plan.

When he spans the circumference of my waist, I lean back automatically, seeking the support of his body. Dragging his hands up slowly, he traces every rib before brushing the underside of my breasts. His chest is solid and hot against my back. I ache to push back into the vice of his thighs, but the stools prevent me. The anticipation is unbearable when he runs his fingers up and down my sides. My nipples tighten, and the aching spot between my legs answers with a similar reflex.

He leans in, his weight pushing me forward. His breath moves the air next to my ear. "Do you know what you're doing?"

"Playing with fire," I admit.

He rubs his palms over my breasts, making them turn heavy. "What do you want?"

I gasp when his fingers tighten on my curves while his thumbs flick lazily over my hardened nipples.

His voice is soft, but I don't miss the underlying strain. "Answer me."

"You."

The support at my back disappears. He wheels the stool around so fast I almost topple off. Holding my gaze, he reaches for the towel where I'm clutching the ends together and jerks. I let go, allowing him to pull the towel open and expose my body. His gaze slides over my face and neck down to my breasts and stomach to finally rest on where I have my legs clamped together. Bracing his hands on my knees, he hops from his stool and spreads me in the same movement.

"Fuck." He stares at the apex between my thighs. "I missed you."

Bending down, he lowers his head between my legs. I barely have time to contemplate the move before his tongue enters me. No foreplay. No teasing. He goes straight for the kill. I have to brace myself with my hands on the counter at my back as he hooks my thigh over his shoulder and deepens the penetration.

A mangled moan tears from my chest. I forgot how good he is with his mouth, how he can sear me with branding heat while gently lapping at my clit. He utters a satisfied groan, licking and nipping before going back to fucking me with his tongue. When I squirm to escape the overwhelming onslaught, he grips my hips to hold me in place and doubles his efforts.

"Jake." Panting, I try to find my balance, my control.

He lifts his head and catches my gaze while dragging his chin over my sensitive skin. His dark eyes are feverish, consumed with lust. "I'm going to make you come."

He drops my leg from his shoulder and straightens, towering between my legs. Gripping my face in one hand, he kisses me hard, letting me taste myself on his lips while his free hand slips between my thighs and finds my clit. He knows exactly how to rub to get me off. In an embarrassingly short time, I explode, crying out my pleasure while he catches the sounds in his mouth. He eagerly sucks them from my body and swallows me whole. I expect him to fuck me right here, against the counter, but he brings the kiss to a gentle halt and pulls away.

Confused, I stare up at him. A flush darkens the tanned tone of his skin and wildness reflects in his russet eyes. His hard-on presses against my stomach. He wants this. He wants me. Yet, he's not moving. He watches me come down from the high of my climax as if the sight of my pleasure alone is his reward. I want to ask why he's not fucking me, but I'm too scared of the answer. Maybe I've misjudged his desire for me.

Framing my face between his hands, he says, "I always regretted not making you come that first time." His smile is grim. "Still do. I often think about that night in the alley, and that your first time should've been different."

I don't know what to say.

"Do you know what else I think?" he continues. "I think you're not ready for this."

"What?" I force out on a whisper, my earlier boldness gone.

"I think you're doing this for the wrong reasons."

Unable to deny the accusation, I blink.

"As much as I want to take you up on the offer, I'm not going to." Confirming the verbal affirmation, he drops his hands and steps away from me. "I'm not taking you against a wall or on the muddy ground again. The next time we fuck, it'll be in a bed, for the right reason."

I swallow away the dryness in my throat. "What right reason?"

"The reason any couple take off their clothes."

Dumbfounded, I gape at him as he jerks off his T-shirt and pulls it over my head. It's big enough for the hem to reach my thighs. He puts even more distance between us and picks up his phone.

Beyond embarrassed, I brush a strand of hair behind my ear.

"Spaghetti?" he asks, punching in a four digit-pin.

I drop my gaze to the screen where a recipe for Bolognaise sauce is displayed. "Um, sure."

What the hell just happened? Jake said no to sex? He prefers to cook? What am I supposed to make of this? I watch him quietly, confused, as he puts out ingredients on the counter. I could've offered to help, but I'm a captive, not a guest, and I'm curious about Jake's cooking skills. I'm curious about everything concerning Jake, especially what has passed during the last four years, but I'm not ready to admit that to myself, let alone to him.

It soon becomes clear he sucks at cooking. I bite my lip in order not to smile, and let him battle it out. He's patient. I have to give him that, even when the pasta boils over and the tomato sauce burns. When he finally dishes up, the pasta is soggy and the sauce bitter, but I don't comment.

He takes a bite and makes a face. Waving his fork at my plate, he says, "You don't have to eat that."

"I don't like to waste." I watch him through my lashes. "Never cooked much for yourself in Dubai, did you?"

He twists the spaghetti around his fork. "I preferred restaurants."

"Why?"

He keeps his eyes trained on his plate. "I didn't like being alone with myself."

It's as if a needle drives into my skin. "Is that why you slept with all those women?"

He lifts his gaze slowly to mine. One, two heartbeats pass before he says flatly, "I treated myself like I deserved." The expression in his eyes is naked, vulnerable. He doesn't hide the flash of regret or the self-loathing that replaces it.

My mouth goes a little dry at the revelation of how little he values himself. I want to ask what he's done to harbor such a harsh opinion, but I don't want to give him the impression that I care.

Getting to his feet, he carries our plates to the sink and scrapes what's left of our food into the trashcan. I can't stay in the kitchen as he starts doing the dishes. His proximity is too unsettling, especially after my failed seduction attempt that ended up in oral sex.

I let him clean the kitchen while I go to my room and lie down on the bed. Turning on my side, I fold my hands under the pillow and face the window. There's nothing but those small, olive-green bushes and hard-baked sand outside. How far does this desolate landscape stretch? How can Jake find this place even remotely appealing?

Somewhere between contemplating the answer and listening to the sounds of him rinsing the dishes, I fall asleep. When I wake up, the shadows are long, the sun beetles quiet, and a blanket is draped over my body. I snuggle deeper under the blanket, enjoying the coziness for another while longer before stretching and swinging my legs off the bed. I feel completely refreshed. The last time I had an afternoon nap was when Jake took care of Noah. Before then, it was when I was still in school.

I take a moment to appreciate the freedom of not having any obligations. I don't have to rush to prepare Noah's bath or dinner. Yawning, I stretch and get up to rummage through the bag my mom has packed. After dressing in a T-shirt and denim shorts, I fold Jake's T-shirt neatly and go next door to return it, but his room is empty. A smell of burned baking wafts from the kitchen. I go there. The backdoor stands open. A rhythmic thud-thud comes from the direction of the wind pump.

Following the sound, I find a shirtless Jake chopping wood. He stills for a beat when he sees me, his gaze drifting over my body in a way that tells me he notices every dip and curve, but he doesn't let it linger in an offensive way. He's not perving. He's noticing me, really noticing me, and something warm lights up in my chest.

Perspiration glistens on his skin in the late afternoon sun. He places another piece of wood on the chopping block. The swing of his arms is strong and steady as he keeps an even pace. His biceps bunch and his abdomen ripples with every up and down movement of the axe.

He finishes splitting the stump before wiping a hand over his forehead and giving me his full attention. "Sleep well?"

"Like a baby."

"You needed it. Sleeping in a car isn't quality rest."

"What about you?"

He drops the axe onto the chopping block. "I'll catch up tonight."

After stacking the wood on a small pile next to a circle of bricks, he saunters over to me. "Coffee?" He checks his watch. "It's teatime."

Conditioning wants me to say I'll make it, but I swallow the offer. I'm not here by invitation. "Sounds good."

He tips his head toward the house. "Give me a minute to wash up."

I drag my feet, not particularly wanting to be around him, but the house is small. If we're staying here for three weeks, I can't avoid running into him. By the time I enter the kitchen, he's scooping ground coffee into a percolator. He's pulled on a T-shirt and probably dunked his head under the tap because the spiky strands of his hair are wet. Not sure what to do with myself, I take a stool at the island counter and watch him work. He stacks a plate with cookies and pushes it my way. When he hands me a mug of coffee, the blisters on his hands pull my attention. I push down an untimely bout of sympathy.

Wrinkling my nose, I sniff the air. "What's that smell?"

He throws a thumb in the direction of the counter and gives me a wry smile. "Dinner."

A loaf of bread with a charcoaled crust stands on a wooden board.

I hardly suppress a giggle. "Why didn't you just buy a loaf?"

"Not the same." He wipes a hand over his jaw. "I'm afraid that's going to taste worse than the commercial kind."

I bite into a cookie to hide my smile. "Where did you get the recipe from?"

He taps his front pocket where the shape of his phone is outlined. "Google."

"Mm."

"What?"

"Nothing."

"Are you making fun of me?"

"Me?" I make big eyes. "Never. I'm just thinking you're poorly skilled for a kidnapper. You should've planned better for feeding your captive."

His voice drops an octave. "Careful. Just because I'm a considerate kidnapper doesn't mean I won't pull you over my lap."

His words are playful, but they heat my stomach in a disturbing way. Looking away quickly, I finish my coffee and rinse the mug before escaping to the lounge where I pretend to read a book. The banging of cooking utensils and Jake whistling a song make it impossible to focus on what I'm reading. What is he doing in there? I refuse to give in to the silly urge to keep him company.

When it gets dark, I switch on a lamp and settle back on the couch. Jake steps into the room, his presence overbearing and his cologne once more a too strong reminder of my naivety in the days before he left.

"Why are you wearing that?"

He glances down at his T-shirt. "What do you prefer I wear?"

"Not the clothes. The aftershave."

He walks to the couch and stops in front of me. "Does it bother you?"

"It's what you wore in school. I thought you would've outgrown it."

"I guess old habits stick."

"Ah."

"Want me to get another kind? Tell me the brand and I'll appease you." He winks. "Can't go around with you hating my smell."

"I don't care what you smell like."

His lips tilt in one corner. "Of course not."

When he just stands there without moving, looming over me, I cross my arms over my breasts as if they could form a protective barrier around my heart. "Did you want something?"

He checks his watch. "Gina and Noah should be home. Want to call them?"

I sit up straighter. "Yes."

Flopping down next to me with his arm draped over the back of the couch, he swipes across the screen and dials Gina's number on a video call.

Her face comes onto the screen. "Hey, kids. How are things in the Karoo?"

"How's Noah?" I ask.

"See for yourself." She turns the phone so we can see him. "Say hello to mommy and daddy, Noah."

There's something about that phrase, about using mommy and daddy in the same sentence, that stirs deep-buried longings in my heart, but all thoughts disappear when Noah's face fills the screen. My chest clenches. His smile is bright when he sees me, the purest gesture of genuine joy.

I swallow down the lump in my throat. "Hey, baby. How are you?"

Noah sticks a finger in his mouth. When I bite my lip not to cry, Jake gives my shoulder a squeeze.

"They made water balloons at school," my mom says.

Jake chuckles. "I bet that was fun. You know what? I'm going to buy you a water gun. Best fun ever."

My mom turns her gaze on me. "How are things *really*?"

I'm not going to answer.

"Great," Jake says when the silence stretches.

"How are you getting around?" I'm worried about how my mom is managing to take Noah to the crèche. I doubt Luan will drive them after breaking up with me.

"Jake rented me a car."

I glare at Jake, directing all my annoyance at him even if my mom was an accomplice.

We talk for another few minutes about school and Noah before Jake hangs up. He still has his hand resting loosely on my shoulder. It's a posture that hints at familiarity when we're the furthest thing from it. He watches me quietly as I wiggle out from under his arm and get to my feet. The couch doesn't make a sound as he rises, but the heat from his body brands my naked arms and legs as he comes to a stop behind me. I take a few steps away, pretending to look through the window at the moonlit yard.

"Come outside with me," he says softly. "It's cooler this time of the evening."

Not waiting for my reply, he takes my hand and leads me out the door and around the back. He places two garden chairs next to the circle of bricks and makes sure I'm comfortable before building a fire. When the flames are leaping into the air, he goes back inside and exits with two beers.

For a while, we sit in silence, sipping our beer and staring at the flames. There's something soothing and relaxing about a fire, even more so in the quiet of this vast expanse.

"Look," he says, pointing up at the sky. "The Southern Cross."

I follow the line of his finger. Wow. I've never seen so many stars. The Milky Way is a burst of twinkling lights. In Rensburg, we have street and searchlights that illuminate the night sky, obscuring the stars. I never imagined it could look like this.

"Impressive, huh?" he says, keeping his neck craned. "I used to sit here for hours, trying to spot satellites or shooting stars."

"Did you?"

"Plenty." He turns his head back to me. "I never made a wish though." His gaze caresses my face. "My mistake."

I have to look away from the blatant meaning in his eyes. I'm relieved when he breaks the uncomfortable silence by asking, "Hungry?"

Lunch was a long time ago. My stomach rumbles on cue.

"It's going to take a while for the wood to make coals, but I'm armed with snacks."

He disappears again to return with crisps and a sour cream dip. "Can't let you starve now," he says as he offers me a crisp with a dollop of dip.

"Thanks," I mumble, shoving it into my mouth.

He continues to feed me crisps and dip until my beer is finished and I'm buzzing a little. The night is calm and the air fresh while the warmth of the fire makes me feel cozy. I sink deeper into the chair. The tenseness leaves my muscles, and for the first time in as long as I can remember, I relax. The crackling of the fire and the chirp of crickets form soothing background music.

Later, he grills beef sausages while I salvage the bread by cutting off the burned top and sides, and carry out the potato salad he prepared, which turned out more like mash. Our meal is simple, but I'm hungry, and it goes down well with a bottle of wine. By the time we stretch out on a blanket under the stars, my eyelids are already half-mast. We take a bet on who'll see the most shooting stars, which I win. Or maybe he lets me win, because the loser has to clean the kitchen, and it's clear I'm another half a glass of wine away from falling asleep.

I WAKE up to the smell of bacon and coffee. Yawning, I sit up against the headboard and glance at the clock on the nightstand. It's after eight. A knock falls on the door before it opens.

Jake pops his head around the frame. "You're awake. Good. Breakfast is ready." When I move to swing my legs off the bed, he holds up a finger. "Don't move."

I lean back when he disappears, feeling lazy and set on enjoying the foreign sentiment for once. There's nothing rushing me. I don't have anywhere to be or anything to do.

He returns a little while later with a loaded tray that he props on my lap.

I stare at the bacon, fried egg, buttered toast, and coffee.

There's even a daisy in a vase. "Breakfast in bed? Do you treat all your captives like this?"

"Only the beautiful ones."

I pick up a crunchy strip of bacon. "And it's not even burned."

"You seemed to have forgotten what I said about pulling you over my lap."

Just before blurting out I hope it's a promise, I bite my lip. I don't want to play a teasing game with Jake. He made his intention clear yesterday. Whisking me away isn't about sex. It's a lot more serious than that, and serious isn't where I want to go with him.

"Eat up," he says. "You have ten minutes to get ready."

"Ready for what?"

His smile is secretive. "You'll see."

I don't argue, because I have sleep-breath and bed-hair, and I'll only feel comfortable facing him when I'm groomed. I eat like a starving woman, devouring everything on my plate. The clean, fresh air must be giving me an appetite. After a quick bath, I dress in a T-shirt, shorts, and flip-flops and find Jake in the kitchen where he's loading our laundry into the washing machine. He takes the tray from me and makes quick work of cleaning everything before grabbing a cooler box that stands by the backdoor.

"Let's go."

He drives back to the highway and heads south. After an hour's drive, the scenery changes drastically. We hit a huge mountain range that divides north and south.

"The Outeniqua Mountains," he says with enthusiasm.

I stare up at the iron-gray cliffs. I've never seen anything higher than a mine dump. It's both impressive and scary, but not as scary as when the road starts to climb. In no time, we're halfway up the mountain with lush, green slopes that drop to an abyss at my side. Instinctively, I shift closer to the console. When Jake's hand folds around mine, I don't resist. I grip his fingers hard.

"Relax," he says, glancing my way. "I won't drive us off the cliff."

The sound of that alone makes me tense up more. "Just keep your eyes on the road."

"We're heading down after the next bend."

My ears pop, and then we're on the top of the world. My breath catches. In stark contrast to the dry, brittle world we left behind, everything in front of us stretches out green, and in the far distance glitters the blue water of the ocean.

"Oh, my God," I whisper, excitement and wonder mixing together. I've always wanted to visit the sea. It's like the pictures I've seen, only better. The pretty view suddenly blurs as a multitude of sensations overwhelm me.

"Hey." He nudges me gently. "I thought you'd like it."

I swipe at my eyes with my free hand. "I do. It's just so…" I don't have words. "Beautiful," I declare inadequately. "I wish Noah and my mom could've seen this."

"We'll bring them." When I look at him quickly, he adds, "Whatever happens, Kristi, whatever you decide about us, I want to be in my son's future. I want to bring him here and to all the places that are special to me. Gina too. I like her. She's a cool woman." He lifts my hand to his mouth and brushes his lips over my knuckles. "She raised a damn cool daughter."

Awkwardly, I pull my hand away. He doesn't stop me, but his smile fades a little. I know what he's hoping for, but I can't give him that.

Hopelessness makes me ask, "Why now? What changed? Is it because you finished your contract in Dubai?"

The relaxed set of his shoulders turns rigid. A moment passes before he speaks. "I didn't finish my contract."

"What? I don't understand. That's what you said."

He clenches the wheel. "I lied. I'm sorry."

The steep ascent forgotten, I sit up in my seat. "Why?"

"I didn't want you to know."

"To know what?"

A muscle ticks in his temple. More time passes. "I lost the contract."

"Why?"

"I fucked up."

"What happened?"

"I made the wrong choices, the wrong investments. Lost my mentor millions." His expression is haunted as he glances at me again. "I'm a failure. A scandal. I blew it."

"Why lie to me about it?"

His jaw bunches. "I was ashamed." He utters a wry laugh. "I *am* ashamed."

Insight hits me. "Is that why you didn't come back?"

Again, he stares at me briefly. It's all there in his eyes, the disappointed and bitter disillusionment. Why haven't I recognized it before? There are so many layers of broody intenseness that make up Jake's past, it's sometimes difficult to see the present. He says nothing, but he doesn't have to. His silence is his answer. He couldn't face the shame and humiliation of admitting he didn't make it in the big world, no less to the very people he condemned for living a simple life in a backward town. His pride prevented him from giving us a chance.

I swallow, suddenly emotional for a different reason. "Is that why you didn't read my letters? You didn't want to answer them with the truth?"

He wipes a hand over his face. "It's more complicated than that."

"Explain."

A look of regret filters into his expression as he waves a hand at the view. "I wasn't planning on bringing this up now. I wanted you to enjoy the moment."

"We've put it off for too long already."

The longer the silence stretches, the tighter my guts twist. The air between us is tainted, polluted with hurt and heavy with unsaid words. At the next outlook point, he pulls over and parks. Turning in his seat, he reaches for me.

"What are you doing?"

"I need to hold you when I say what I'm about to say."

He's offering me comfort to ease the pain awaiting. I don't want his consolation. I push on the button to unlock the door and jump from the car. His voice drifts after me as he calls out my name, but I don't stop until I reach the stone wall that stands between high ground and a terrifying drop. Instinctively, I know what he's going to say will dislodge all the old hurt, forcing me to face it, and I can't take that much pain ever again.

CHAPTER 17

Kristi

*T*he car door slams. Gravel crunches behind me. Jake's shadow stretches along the ground, his hand lifting tentatively to my shoulder.

I step to the side. "Don't touch me."

"Kristi," he says, dropping his hand.

Why won't it stop hurting? I both crave and loathe his touch, the belated comfort he's offering, but as much as I need it, I can't bring myself to accept it. He cut me too deep. I'll never make myself that vulnerable again.

Sighing deeply, he sits down on the wall with his elbows on his knees and fingers interlaced, his head hanging low. His words are soft-spoken, a guilty confession wrapped in regret, but I don't look at him. I can't give him even that much.

"I hated Dubai from the word go. All I wanted was to get on a plane and head right back to you, but I needed to prove myself, not

261

just to me, but also to my father." He utters a wry sound. "Too much of my reason for going was for my father and too little for myself. I wanted to return to Rensburg with my own fortune and tell Hendrik Basson he was wrong about me." He laughs softly. "The joke is on me because he was right after all."

He lifts his head, seeking my eyes, but I keep my gaze fixed on the breathtaking view that suddenly, for some reason, cuts through me with its beauty.

"If I'd opened your first letter," he continues, "I would've begged my father on my knees to buy me a ticket back to South Africa. My ass would've been on a plane faster than you could say dropout. I told myself I'd keep your letter as a reward, read it after my first small victory, but I flunked that test. It was a hell of a lot tougher than I thought. That school admitted the best of the best, and I was just an idiot from a small town who believed he knew something but knew nothing.

"I worked harder. It got a little better. Two, three letters arrived. Still, I put off the reward. One more month, I told myself, one more month to have something good to write back about. The longer I waited, the more difficult it became, until I no longer knew how to explain my silence. By then, I used your letters to punish myself. I told myself I didn't deserve to read them.

"It got hectic. Things moved too fast. I started using drugs to cope. The high gave me a sense of bravado. I got cocky. The more I was falling behind the rest of the class, the more I wanted to get myself out of that hole with some fucking giant leap of luck. Yousef al-Yasu, my mentor, gave me an intern position in his business as repayment for a favor he owed my father. For some reason, he took to me. He tried to guide me, let me in on his deals. He liked my franchise idea, thought we had a shot at it, but said it was too early. He said we needed to refine it, even when the opportunity arose.

"I wanted to grab that unexpected opportunity with both hands and take the leap from misery to success. He advised against it, so I went behind his back." He blows out a long breath. "I made a deal. I spoke for Yousef, gave my word on his behalf, and blew it. Ten million dollars. I dishonored him. I was a disgrace. My reputation was ruined."

He glances over his shoulder toward the flat surface of the sea. "I dropped out. I hated myself as much as everyone else who's ever met me in Dubai, except for Ahmed, Yousef's son. God only knows why he still bothered. He gave me a job in his holiday resort business and paid for my flat when Yousef fired me."

He turns his head back to me, and it's only then I gather the courage to look at him, when I'm sure I've got enough of a handle on my emotions not to cry.

"I reckoned you were better off without me," he says, "so I made sure I provided a house and sent money, but I didn't open your letters. And then they stopped. It killed me more than you'll ever know, but I couldn't get out of the hole I dug for myself. I was on a self-destructive path, pushing everyone and everything away until that last letter arrived. If it wasn't for Ahmed, I wouldn't have known."

The pause that follows tells me I'm going to like what comes next even less.

"He read them," he says softly. "Every one of those letters. He's the one who made me read the last one you sent."

Hurt lashes at me from too many directions to keep track. Jake ignored Noah and me because of his pride, but someone else, someone I don't know, were privy to my most intimate feelings and thoughts. Jake threw us away to hurt and punish himself because he believed he deserved nothing better, but he failed to see the repercussion of the selfish act.

"You hurt me," I whisper. "So much."

Remorse fills his eyes. "I know."

"A stranger read my letters."

"I nearly smashed in his face for it. Still want to."

"A stranger read them, but you didn't."

"I did."

"When?"

"When I got back to Rensburg."

"Why now, Jake? Why?"

He looks at me for a long moment, as if contemplating the reason. When he finally speaks, his answer sounds certain. "Because I saw you."

"You saw me?" I exclaim.

"I saw you and knew you were meant to be mine, both you and Noah."

For some reason, the declaration makes the ache in my heart worse. It rubs what could've been in my face, but could haves are futile. Neither of us can go back in time and change the past. It's done. I'll never have it. "Stop it. Don't say things like that."

"It's the truth. I'm not going to lie to myself or you any longer."

"It's too late."

"Don't say that." He grabs his head between his hands. "Goddamn, Kristi, I beg you, please."

It's hard to cling to control. "I can't trust you."

"I broke your trust." He gives me a haunted look. "Believe me, I know what I've done. I'm not asking you to trust me overnight. I'm just asking for a chance."

"What about Luan? Did you ever consider his feelings?"

"We both know Luan isn't a factor in what stands between us. You were using him to make up for the father you never had. Luan was security. I'm pretty damn sure he'll never rock your boat or make you see stars, not like you deserve. Hell, he broke up with you for something he should've taken out on me."

"You and I, we're not getting back together." I'm not getting burned twice. Once was hard enough.

"I'm not asking you to make a decision now."

"Then what are you asking?"

"Three weeks."

Bitterness spills into my tone. "You didn't give me a choice, remember?"

"I made a lot of mistakes, too many to expect anyone to forgive. All I'm asking is that you spend the next twenty days with me trying not to think about the past. It's a hell of a lot to ask, I know, but I just want us to get to know each other. Fuck, Kristi." He drags his hands through his hair. "We never really had a chance to get to know each other. We're not the same people we were in school. Too much has happened, and people change. People grow. If we walk away from here as nothing but friends, so be it."

It's not what I expected. The Jake sitting in front of me isn't the boy I remember. The man who declined sex took me by surprise. So does his emotional turmoil, evident by the deep breaths rattling his chest. I can deny him my heart, but I can't deny him friendship, or at least giving it a shot, not if he's serious about getting involved in Noah's life. God knows, I want nothing more for my baby. I don't want Noah to suffer those father issues I never overcame.

I regard him from under my lashes. "Do you mean that?"

"I'm Noah's dad. I'm a part of your lives. If it's not in a romantic sense, I'll regret it until my dying day, but I won't contest your decision. I'm still going to be the best dad I can and give you the support you never had."

The *never had* part throws me right back into the past, but I ignore the pain that spreads through my chest and seeps into my heart as if the source is infinite, its destructive power unending. This is about Noah, and what's best for him. Not trusting Jake doesn't make it easy for me to trust his intentions.

"Why the sudden turnaround?"

"Without you and Noah, I have nothing left."

Anger sparks. More ache. This is Jake thinking about himself, not about Noah and me. "That's not fair. You can't place the responsibility of giving you a reason to live on our shoulders, and it's not the right reason for wanting to get back together."

His look is level, sure. "You've been my reason since that night in the alley."

I clench my hands so hard my nails cut into my palms. More emotions assault me. Guilt. Regret. His unspoken words are like rocks mauling my heart in my chest. "Are you saying everything that happened is my fault for not asking you to stay?"

"No. You did the right thing. I would've always wondered how it would've turned out if I hadn't gone to Dubai. All I'm saying is I've made some shitty choices. I ignored what was most important to blindly chase my selfish need to prove I'm not worthless. Ironically, I only ended up proving the opposite."

"I can't fix you, Jake." I can barely keep myself together.

"I'm not asking you to."

For a moment we regard each other quietly, a bigger question brewing in my mind. To utter it would acknowledge I wanted to be something more meaningful than a quick fuck in an alley and a dirty roll in the mud, but I can't help myself. "Would you have been here if I didn't ask for a divorce?"

He looks guilty even before he speaks. "Probably not."

His honesty takes the air from my lungs. It's a confirmation I didn't matter. I hold up a hand, not brave enough for the truth after all, but he shakes his head.

"You have to hear this, Kristi. If we're going to get to know each other with no masks or pretenses, however hard it'll be, you have a right to know. If you hadn't asked for a divorce, I would've been well on my way to overdosing or drinking myself to death."

Oh, my God. How naïve can I be? I never considered there could be more than the slush pile of dirt he already disclosed. Paid sex is far from being his only sin. "You can't be around Noah if you do drugs. I don't want you in his life—"

"Haven't touched it since Dubai. Not planning on going near it again."

"Even if we don't happen?"

"Even then. I want to be there for Noah. I swear. Give me a chance to prove it."

"No prostitutes either. It's not the example I want for my son."

He winces. "Our son."

"He won't be yours if you hang around brothels."

"Those days are over. The drugs and whores, they went together. I hated that life. I'm not going back to it."

My body shivers with tremors from the overload of emotions. The information dump from his past is more than I can take. Like a wild rose creeper that has invaded the abandoned mesh of a fence, the feelings strangling my heart are twisted, and warped, and full of thorns with fragile little flowers in between. Even if I don't want to admit it, I still have feelings for Jake. Those feelings are intertwined with the pain, fragile little roses that survive between thorns.

My voice is shaky. "Noah comes first."

"What about you, ginger?"

"What about me?"

"Who takes care of you?"

"I'm a big girl."

"That much you've proven, but there's nothing wrong with letting someone take care of you every once in a while."

The notion has its attraction. I remember how eagerly I responded when Jake promised to take care of me in the bar. Not so long ago, I believed Luan would be the shoulder I could lean on, at least from time to time. How easily Jake has proven that wrong. Still, I'm not letting Jake near my heart again. Allowing someone to take care of you only hurts in the long run.

He gets up and walks to me, his steps slow and careful, his tone apologetic. "This is not how I imagined the day to pan out."

"You said yourself, it's time we're honest. I've been begging for an explanation for four years."

He stretches his arms as if he wants to pull me into a hug. "I'm sorry."

I step away, out of reach.

Dropping his arms, he stares at me with a helpless expression. I wish I knew how to fix this, how to make the hurt vanish, but it's here, in my chest, under my skin, in the rush of my blood through my veins, its thorns embedded with sharp claws in my heart. It's real, and there's no magic wand to make it disappear.

A minivan pulls up. The doors open and four kids tumble out, followed by their parents. As they run yelling and laughing to the wall, Jake and I stand motionless in our bubble, staring wordlessly at each other. The flash of disappointment in his eyes says he resents that our discussion has been cut short. I must be a coward, because I'm relieved.

The woman regards us curiously as she nears. It must be obvious we've been arguing.

Shoving his hands in the front pockets of his jeans, he asks, "Shall we go?"

I turn my back on him and walk to the car. He catches up before I reach it to open my door. We continue in silence down the rest of the scenic road, the atmosphere strained and the past he asked me to ignore hanging like one hundred and twelve unopened letters over our heads.

"Look," he says after a long while, pointing ahead.

We're at the foot of the mountains, crossing a hilly part with the ocean in front of us.

He unwinds his window and sticks out his head. "This is my favorite part."

The air smells of salt and something else he tells me is *fynbos*, the plants growing on the mountain slopes. We drive past a lagoon and turn onto a dirt road that leads to a deserted beach with white sand and dunes topped with wild grass. The sun is shining, but there's a chilly breeze.

He hands me his sweatshirt when he helps me from the car. Grateful, I pull it on while he fetches the cooler box from the trunk. Near the water, he spreads out a picnic blanket and pulls off his clothes. Underneath the jeans, he's wearing swimming trunks. It's an improvement to swimming in briefs. He must've done more than food shopping before the trip.

Holding out his hand, he asks, "Want to test the water?"

I still feel bruised inside, but his outstretched hand is like a peace offering, and I didn't come this far to not dip at least my toes in the sea. Despite the heaviness of earlier, his smile is broad. Knowing how much effort the gesture takes, I accept his hand and shed some of the weight pushing on my chest as I follow him to where the water laps over glittery sand. Angry waves foam not far behind.

Like the mountain, the ocean is both scary and exhilarating. The water is a lot colder than I expected, and I shriek when it flows around my ankles. For a while, we simply stand there, hand in hand. Jake is patient, letting me get my fill of the view. The crash of the waves is a rhythmic build and break, pierced from time to time with the call of a seagull. The smell of salt is stronger here. The sand is soft under my feet, shifting with the ebb and flow of the water. Sunrays bounce off the water, making sparkles on the surface.

"It's beautiful," I whisper.

"Not as beautiful as you."

I turn my head quickly toward him to catch him watching me with that unsettling intensity.

"If I could bottle the moment, I'd carry it in my pocket forever."

My cheeks heat a little. I'm not accustomed to compliments. "Some things aren't meant to be bottled."

"No," he says solemnly, "some things are impossible to capture, even in words."

And some words are too much to handle. Freeing my hand, I head back toward the blanket, away from his words and compliments. My emotions are raw, and I'm fighting not to feel compassion, which is hard. This part of Jake, the unloved boy who turned into an undeserving adult, I understand. I still carry the scar on my cheek to prove it. I know where he comes from, and I know it's not what's in a bank account that matters. In that sense, we're similar. We both have daddy issues. I only hope Jake will make a better father for Noah than Hendrik made for him.

We stretch out on the blanket and eat the sandwiches he prepared for lunch. When the breeze disappears in the afternoon, Jake produces my bikini from the cooler box.

"I didn't want to give it to you at the house and spoil the surprise," he says. "You can change here. If it bothers you, I won't look."

I appreciate that he doesn't bring up yesterday when I tried to seduce him. Flames leak over my neck and up my cheeks when I recall in vivid detail how he rewarded me. He's seen me naked and made me come, but he took us a step back when he declared he wouldn't have sex with me for the wrong reasons. It's a far cry from the old Jake who ravished me at the lake and declared my ass belonged to him. Despite my reservations about letting him into my heart, he has an undeniable effect on my body. Contrary to what I thought yesterday, being naked around him—if sex isn't going to be enough—is too much to handle.

"I'd rather change behind the bushes on the dunes," I say, taking a step in that direction.

He grabs my wrist. "You're not going anywhere near those dunes alone."

I look around. "There's no one but us."

"Sometimes surfers come here, and abalone poachers move along the dunes." He turns his back on me and crosses his arms. "Get undressed."

I know when Jake won't budge. Shedding his sweater, I get naked quickly and pull on my bikini.

"I'm done," I say, tying the strings behind my back.

"Come here." He grips my shoulders and turns me around. "Let me get that."

His fingers brush over my nape as he finishes tying the strings, making goosebumps run over my arms. For a moment, he stills. With a shudder he sets me free.

For the rest of the afternoon, we swim and lie in the sun. Jake insists on covering every inch of my body with sun cream. He tells me about coming here in his youth and shows me the broken snail shells on the top of the highest dune he used for making necklaces. We slide down the dune on our backsides like kids, rinse off in the sea, and dry again in the sun before heading back.

I'm tired and emotionally wrought out, but relaxed. The warmth of the sun still glows on my skin, and my muscles ache in a good way from swimming. On the dry side of the mountain, we stop by a river that cuts through the valley for sundowners. Jake has a virgin cocktail since he's driving.

Energy buzzes in my veins when we arrive at the house, a strange awareness of being alive. Later, after we've rinsed the salt from our bodies and called my mom to speak to her and Noah, we sit down by the fire.

I turn to Jake with something I've been meaning to tell him ever since we arrived. "Thank you."

"I don't deserve any gratitude, especially not from you."

"You're wrong. Thank you for showing me the ocean. For making it special." Despite everything.

"You're welcome."

"Thank you for telling me."

I don't have to spell it out. We both know I'm referring to the letters. Yes, it's hard to deal with the truth, but it brought me a measure of peace.

"You deserved an answer," he says, staring into my eyes as if the flames burn there and not in the fire, "and so much more."

Maybe it's the glass of wine I had in the bath, or I'm simply too tired to keep up my defenses. When I needed comfort as a young girl, I often dreamt about my daddy pulling me into his lap and folding big, strong arms that can fix anything around me. I don't know why, only that my impulse is too big to control when I get up and walk to Jake's chair. He stares up at my face, his dark eyes hopeful and hopeless at the same time.

My control unravels just a bit, enough to let me sit down in his lap and weave my arms around his neck. His skin is warm where my cheek rests on his chest, his heart beating with a steady rhythm. His arms come around my waist. They're strong arms that can chop wood and maneuver a car over a mountain pass. Just for a moment, I pretend they are arms that can fix anything as he holds me in a non-demanding way, giving me something that can't be captured in a bottle or expressed with words until long after the fire has burned out.

Jake

IT TAKES everything I possess and a shitload more to ignore Kristi's body as I lay her down on her bed. She's sleepy, exhausted after a day of sun and sea, but my guess is also from too many revelations crammed into too short a space. She lets me pull off her sandals and pull the blanket up to her waist, but when I turn to leave, she catches my arm.

"Jake."

My name on her lips makes me hard, even if it's not where I want to go. I imagine her saying it under the weight of my naked body and shiver with pure lust. It makes me wish I'd taken her when she offered in the kitchen, but I'll stand fast this time. If I'm lucky enough to have another go at a relationship with her, I'm not fucking it up. This time round, I'll do it right.

"Stay with me," she whispers in a husky voice, reminding me she'd fallen asleep like a kitten in my lap, and how much I liked it.

"Not a good idea, ginger."

"Not for sex. I don't want to be alone."

Kristi has never been alone. Gina has always slept an arm-length away from her. Finding herself stranded in strange surroundings must be more than a little unsettling. Kicking off my shoes, I climb onto the bed next to her.

"Thank you," she says on a content little sigh, cuddling closer.

It reminds me of the night I spent in their trailer, the night my father scarred her face. All she's suffered because of me, I'm going to make better. I can't take the past away any more than I can make her scar disappear, but I can do my damnedest best to make up for it.

I drape my arm around her and pull her tighter. She makes me hyper-aware of my body. As always, I'm the fuse on a stick of dynamite, coming alive at her touch, even at the innocent press of her stomach against my side. It goes deeper though. I feel so much more. I feel pride and affection, worry and care. Concern. It's the inborn male instinct to protect and take care of what's mine, but it's also just Kristi, what she does to me. What she's always done to me. I've always wanted to hit guys with my fists since the day I laid eyes on her in school. It only became worse when she grew breasts, and worse still when she turned into a woman. Catching the other boys staring at her sent me into a murderous rage.

Those rages, furious spells of dangerous jealousy, were the first hints that warned me to stay away from her. When Denis said he popped her cherry, I kicked my model plane collection to pieces, broke three fingers punching the wall, and lost my virginity with Britney. I told myself it was for the best, knowing I was leaving, knowing Kristi deserved better than my fucked-up self, but then she showed up at the bar and locked eyes with me. I saw the way Kallie and Denis were ogling her, knew they were going to hit on her, and my only intention was showing her a good time her first time in a bar, and seeing her home safely. Fucking her against the wall was never part of the plan. Neither was repeating it at the lake. I just couldn't hold back. Not with her.

I've always thought she was the prettiest girl in school with hair the color of ginger and eyes like a summer sky. She was wholesome and glowing. Pure. I fell in love with every freckle on her body. I traced them with my eyes during the lengthy hours of math, literature, and biology. The ones that dusted the hollow of her neck and dipped beneath the collar of her school uniform shirt fascinated me with an unhealthy fixation. I had my first hard-on imagining those freckles on her breasts, in geography class no less. Took me a whole ten minutes before I could get up after the bell had gone. I loved every inch of her creamy skin, but I also admired her. I admired her for how clever she was, but when she kicked our class bully, Werner in the shin, she instantly became my idol. The way she held her head high when the kids teased her about living in a trailer made me wish I were more like her. I admired her for sharing her break-time snacks with the kids who'd forgotten their lunch at home. I admired her for climbing into the highest tree in the schoolyard to rescue a kitten, and for picking up the dove in the road and carrying it in a shoebox to the vet. I admired her for her resilience in getting the math formulas right, her head bowed over her book with a cute little frown while she wrinkled her nose. I admired her for always doing her homework, and for stabbing me with a pencil when I stuck gum in her hair. To me, she was an angel, and I didn't want to ruin her, but I couldn't stand the thought of anyone else having her either. When I boarded that plane four years ago, I had every intention of coming back to her. I had no idea my future was going to get out of hand so fast, so irrevocably. I didn't want my father to be right, but he was, and I have one last shot at proving him wrong.

Rubbing her arm, I listen to her steady breathing. Knowing she's oblivious to my actions, I kiss the top of her head. What I admire her for most is for being the kind of woman who inspires me to be a better man.

Kristi

I WAKE up with my leg thrown over Jake's thigh and my hand on his stomach, our fingers intertwined. It feels right, but it's wrong. I shouldn't have asked him to stay just to fulfill my need of feeling safe, protected. It's not right to give him the wrong idea, or worse, to make him think I'm toying with him.

Yesterday's conversation drifts back to me. Strangely, I feel purged. Lighter. For four years, I tortured myself by imagining reasons why Jake didn't reply to my letters. I no longer have to guess. It's not because he couldn't love me. It's because he couldn't love himself. I could've sent emails or text messages, but letters seemed so much more intimate. Writing them started off as a love declaration and ended as therapy. After no news from Jake, I could've stopped writing a long time before. A part of me instinctively knew he wasn't reading my letters, yet I carried on writing. Not expecting him to read them, I emptied my soul and expressed the feelings I couldn't show anyone else. For the rest of the world, I acted strong. I held my head high. Knowing Jake has read what I so boldly admitted in my weakest moments of longing, hurt, and sadness, makes me cringe, even more so when I think Ahmed read that.

Withdrawing my hand slowly so I don't wake Jake, I try to escape, but his hold tightens on my hip.

"Going somewhere?" he rumbles.

The question reminds me of the night in the bar, when he cornered me in front of the toilets, and it brings back a mixture of bittersweet memories.

I try to push away. "To have a bath."

He kisses the crown of my head. "Stay. I'll run you a bath and make coffee while it fills up."

"Wow. Breakfast in bed, doing dishes and laundry, and running my bath. Is this honeymoon behavior or the norm with you?"

"I don't know. I've never been with anyone like this. All I know is you make me want to take care of you."

The admittance is charged, opening new questions and jabbing at unhealed wounds. "You never spent the night, not even once out of the fifty times?"

"The only time I spent the night was with you, and we didn't even shag." Brushing a finger over the scar on my cheek, he adds teasingly, "Was still worth every painfully hard hour of it."

I push down the relief that threatens to break through the betrayal and hurt I keep like a wall around my heart. I built that wall to remind myself of what Jake is capable. "Careful, Jake Basson. If I didn't know better, I'd say I'm domesticating you."

"You say it like I'm a wild animal."

I swat his chest. "You are. Now get off me, wildling. I need the bathroom."

AFTER BREAKFAST, Jake takes me to visit the curio center of a nearby ostrich farm. We stand on the eggs that don't break under our weight, watch an artist paint them, and eat them scrambled with roast vegetables on the side for lunch. The day is an unexpected surprise, just like yesterday at the beach. When we first arrived, I expected to develop cabin fever, but instead, I'm having fun. I'm beginning to understand why Jake loves it here so much, and I'm beginning to appreciate his efforts. Only two days into this, and it's starting to feel more like a holiday than a kidnapping.

When we've dialed my mom and spoken to Noah, I ask Jake for my phone. I have to check my messages and make sure there's nothing urgent that needs a reply.

"You're still not getting it back," he says, handing it to me where we're sitting on the couch.

"Why not? There's no one left to call who can come rescue me."

"Do you need rescuing?"

I contemplate the question. It doesn't take me long to answer. "Fine, Jake. I'll give you two weeks. Three is too long to be away from Noah. We'll get to know each other, but only for Noah's sake, nothing more."

His smile stretches slowly. "Thank you."

"I keep my phone."

"Deal."

When I switch it on, I have ten missed calls and five messages from Nancy. Nothing from Luan. Jake considerately makes himself scarce while I dial Nancy.

"Where in fuck's name are you?" she shrieks.

"I'm okay. We're on an ostrich farm in the Karoo somewhere."

"I was going out of my mind with worry. I almost called the cops, until your mom explained what was going on."

"I'm sorry. I didn't mean to make you worry."

"What's happening between you and Jake?"

"Nothing. We're taking time to get to know each other. We have a lot to work through. How's Luan?"

"Upset. Naturally."

"How's Steve taking it?"

"You know Steve. He never takes sides. You should know though, there are rumors already."

I groan. "What kind of rumors?"

"That you and Jake are back together. Everyone knows you skipped town with him and got fired for AWOL. Jan says the two of you acted very married on Sunday at the river."

"Oh, God." I place a hand on my forehead. "Just what I need."

"Seriously, though. What's going on between the two of you?"

"Nothing. Jake has a lot to explain."

"He kidnapped you to do it?"

"He kidnapped me hoping I'd give him another chance."

"Are you?"

"Not going there. Never again. We're settling for friendship, for Noah's sake."

"Right."

"Don't say it like you don't believe me."

"I don't."

"You're supposed to be my friend."

277

"Friends are supposed to be honest."

"You're also supposed to have my back."

"I do. I told Luan if he says another bad word about you, I'd break his jaw."

"I don't want to come between you and your future family-in-law."

"He's just being a bitter, old, disgruntled man at the moment."

"He's the one who leaked the rumor, isn't he?"

"He told Mozie he fired you for being absent from work without leave. The rest of the town noticed both you and Jake are gone and put two and two together. Do you need me to fetch you? I swear I will. Just say the word."

"I promised Jake two weeks."

"There will be lots of shit to deal with when you get back."

"I'll deal with it."

"All right, then. Are you going to answer my calls from now on or keep on ignoring them?"

"Jake only gave me back my phone today."

"He's such a jerk, Kristi."

"Not always."

"This is the same guy who left and never wrote back or called once, right?"

"He's making me breakfast and running my bath. He took me to the beach yesterday and an ostrich farm today."

"You're falling for him."

"Of course not. I'm just saying there's a different side to him."

"You've never been able to think straight around him. Don't get infatuated."

"I need to know if I can trust him with Noah."

"Keep on telling yourself that."

"Nancy, please. You're not making this any easier."

She sighs. "Fine. Do whatever you have to do out there in the *bundus*. Just don't let him break your heart again."

"I'm not going to hit my toe against the same rock twice."

"Maybe you should repeat that phrase several times a day. I've got to go. Steve is coming over. Call me. Any time. I mean it."

We say our goodbyes and hang up. Through the window, I watch Jake hose the dust from the car. Dressed only in shorts, he reminds me of the times I watched him strip his sweat-drenched T-shirt after rugby. He's broader now, and more defined. The rings under his eyes are fading and the ashen undertone of his skin is disappearing. The breakaway is doing him good. We've both been dealing with stress in our own ways.

My gaze falls on the coffee table where his phone is lying. With another glance at the window, I pick it up. The day in the kitchen, when he made spaghetti, I memorized the code to unlock the screen, hoping I'd get a chance to use it to get away. Guilt nips at me, but my curiosity wins. With a pounding heart, I punch in the code and swipe over the screen, going straight to his messages. Nothing. I flip to his emails. There's one from an estate agent, confirming his offer on the house we visited has been accepted, and unopened junk mail, but nothing that seems personal, not even from his mother. He didn't lie about not seeing anyone back in Dubai. I switch to his photos. There are several of building sites and logos, and some of the city, but nothing of him. I'm about to switch the screen to dark when I notice an image that looks shockingly familiar. It's the one of me in my pink underwear on the night of the matric dance. He kept it. Something warm and hopeful unfurls in my chest, something too frightening to examine.

"Told you I was going to keep it," a voice says from the door.

CHAPTER 18

Kristi

I jerk my head up. Jake leans in the frame, ankles crossed and one arm above his head. "I didn't mean to snoop."

He shrugs. "Doesn't matter."

I can't believe he's so blasé. "You don't mind that I'm checking your phone?"

"I have nothing to hide."

"Why did you keep it?"

"Because it's you."

"It's a stupid photo."

"It's hot."

"You should delete it."

"It's the only one I have, except for your yearbook photos."

"If it's such a big deal, I'll give you another one."

"I want that one."

"Why?"

"It has special meaning to me."

"Like what?"

"That I got to be your first."

"Is it really such a big deal to guys?"

"To the territorial ones, and believe me, after being in love with you from the first time you walked into grade one with pigtails and a schoolbag twice your size, territorial is a mild word for what I felt." He adds softly, "Still feel."

"You acted like I didn't exist."

"I knew I was going to be bad for you."

"Then why did you corner me that night in the bar?"

"I wanted to make sure I got you out of there safely before one of the pricks ogling you took advantage, but it was your first night out, so I reckoned I'd buy you a drink and let you dance a little first. Fucking you wasn't my intention."

I bite my lip. "No, it was me who initiated the fucking."

"I don't regret it."

The words offer absolution, and I cling to it desperately. "Even if I fell pregnant?"

His gaze holds mine steadily. "Even, yes."

Something inside me gives, a tightness I've been carrying for the past four years. "Thank you."

"It takes two to tango, ginger."

I stare at my hands. "Yes, but I seduced you."

From under my lashes, I watch him straighten and walk to me.

"You didn't hold a gun to my head. If I'd wanted to, I could've said no."

His words are more than an admission that he wanted me as much as I wanted him. They're a proposal to carry half of the guilt for changing the course of our lives. Thank you seems too inadequate for the gratitude in my heart. For the first time since peeing on a stick, I breathe easier. I breathe like I used to when life was carefree, when finding a spotted bird egg was the most eventful part of the day. A layer of hurt lifts, and hope peaks out from underneath.

Pushing to my feet, I wrap my arms around his neck and hug him tightly. For a moment, the gesture is one-sided and awkward, but then he folds his arms around my waist and hugs me back. It's more comforting than anything I've experienced, very different from my mom's embraces. The hardness of his chest reminds me he's a man. The hardness of his erection reminds me I'm a woman. I've been a mother for the past four years, but I haven't been a woman for a very long time.

My voice is breathless, my legs suddenly shaking. "Jake."

He stills with his arms like a vice around me.

Straining my neck, I stare up at his handsome features. "Sleep with me."

His dark eyes search my face. "Why?"

"It's been too long."

Lust smolders in his eyes, a violent storm that can't be hidden by the gentle way in which he answers. "I'm not going to sleep with you for the wrong reasons, but I can take off the edge if you like."

My body is pulsing with desire. I haven't felt anything like it since the day at the lake. The need is so great, I'm willing to take anything, even face the humiliation and shame I'll suffer as a consequence of my weakness.

When he pushes me back down onto the couch, I don't stop him. I don't argue when he grips the elastic of my shorts and pulls them with my underwear over my hips and down my thighs. I lift my feet for him to free me from my clothes. I spread my legs for him when he kneels between my knees, and I lift my arms when he yanks the hem of my T-shirt up. I lean forward so he can unclip my bra and push the straps from my arms. My breasts are heavy. It feels good when they spill from the tight lace into his hands.

He studies my body unabashedly, tracing the lines of my curves with his eyes. Leaning forward, he places a tender kiss on my nipple. His lips fold around the tip, his tongue tracing the hard point. A shudder runs down my spine. My back arches, offering more. I want the darkness we once shared, the forbidden lust, but he doesn't lose control. He draws me deeper, sucking gently while massaging my breasts.

My need climbs, a desperate ache growing between my legs. He drags a palm down my abdomen and over my stomach until he reaches my folds. Like yesterday, I'm wet for him, and he makes a sound of approval from deep in his throat. He moves his lips to my other breast, giving it the same, meticulous treatment, while his fingers part me gently to expose my clit. I gasp when he rubs a finger over the nub. When he lifts his head to look at me, I know from the utter concentration on his face that this is all about me. He's reading my body, tuned to my reactions.

He's not unaffected, because his voice is rough. "How long exactly has it been?"

Telling him I haven't been with anyone else isn't something I want to admit. I don't want to give him that much power. "Long enough."

"How long?"

I moan when he plays with me a little, teasing but not giving. "What does it matter?"

"I don't want to hurt you."

Lifting my hips, I try to take him deeper. "You won't."

"Not going to make the same mistake twice. How long, Kristi?"

I could lie, but not while I'm staring into his eyes. Lies don't belong in the truth playing out between us. They never have. I recall the beauty of my dirty admission, the way I wanted it rough, and how close being truthful made me feel to Jake, even closer than how deep he'd been inside me.

The truth slips out on a breathless whisper. "Not since you."

His eyes flare. They darken with satisfaction and possession. They soften with reward as he finally gathers my wetness and slips his finger inside. My toes curl from the pleasure of his touch. I give over to the sensations he creates, letting desire carry me to a place where I can forget my hurt and the problems I'll face going home, even if just for a little while.

As always, he knows how to get me where I want to be. He knows how to palm and rub and caress until I'm at breaking point. I'm pretty sure I begged, but from the moment he replaces his finger with his wicked tongue, I'm not cognizant of anything but what he makes me feel. I'm also pretty sure I heard him say, "Mine," but everything else vanishes as my orgasm detonates, ripping through me with both a physical and emotional force that ties me a little more to Jake. I didn't foresee the emotional part, didn't want it, but I can't help it. The bond forms automatically, of its own accord, just like it had during our first time, and for all the barriers I put up around myself, I feel closer to him.

Jake

THE WOMAN of my dreams lies naked in front of me, disheveled and sweetly undone. Wiping her arousal from my mouth with the back of my hand, I take perverse pleasure in the chaos I created. I take pleasure in knowing that chaos is mine. She hasn't been with another man. I don't deserve that kind of gift. I don't deserve the woman she is, but I still can't let anyone else have her. If I could, I would've still been in Dubai and given her the divorce she wants.

Some things never change, my feelings for Kristi being on the top of that list. I've always wanted her to have better than me, but I've always wanted to rip out the throat of anyone better than me for just looking her way. Noah added a whole new dimension to the equation. He's ours, and I want to be a better man for both of them. I don't want to be my father's prediction. I want to be me, even if I'm still not sure who that is. It's wrong to wring a relationship out of Kristi when I don't know myself, but we'll figure it out if she gives me the chance.

A small piece of the rottenness I feel about myself evaporates as I look into her eyes. They're hazy with post-orgasmic bliss. It's good to know I put that flush on her cheeks. The way her lips are still slightly parted reminds me of all the sexy noises she made. I'm on my knees in more than just a literal way. I'm aching to take her so much I'm shivering with restraint. Pushing down the need, I get to my feet and gather her in my arms. Her hands lock automatically around my neck, a gesture I find both sweet and painful. It stirs a longing for something she's not ready to give and may never be. I force the *never* down and carry her to the kitchen. Lowering her gently onto a stool, I take the T-shirt I'd removed earlier from the island counter and pull it over her head. Naked, she's a vision, and I'm just a man.

When I move toward the stove, she takes my hand. "Wait."

Her body is all the beauty I've imagined as a horny adolescent, down to the freckles that dust the top of her breasts. I don't want to look at her too much. My control is too thin around her. She wets her lips, the innocent act only making me harder.

"Don't you want me to return the favor?"

Holy goddamn. A vision of her on her knees taunts me. It twists my guts inside-out. I swallow. Hard. "No."

She blinks. "Why not? It seems…" She blushes a little. "It seems unfair."

Brushing my thumb over the scar on her cheek, I try to give her a smile. "Unfair isn't a word I'd use to describe going down on you."

Her blush intensifies. "You know what I mean."

"I don't trust myself, not with that hot little mouth of yours around my cock."

"What can happen?"

"It's not what *can* happen. It's what *will* happen. With your mouth on me? Sex."

"We could just let it be, you know. No strings attached."

The words hit a nerve. They don't just frighten me. They terrify me, especially now that I've tasted her again. "Told you, ginger, no strings isn't what I want."

Sighing softly, she lets go of my hand. "I'll respect that."

She will. I'm not giving her a choice. I'm not demeaning her to a fuck buddy. She's my wife, for God's sake. Maybe not in her mind, but I still want her to be.

I pour her a glass of wine and start cooking dinner. I chose simple dishes when I did the grocery shopping, like chicken and baked potatoes, but even that turns out more than challenging. Padding over to me where I'm trying to skin the chicken, she takes the knife from my hand and wiggles the point under the fatty part on the side.

"Like this." She makes a small cut, and when she pulls, the whole skin comes off.

Patiently, she guides me, teaching me how to spice the chicken pieces and halve the potatoes before drizzling them with olive oil. It's nice. I like it when we do things together. Even cooking takes on a new flavor with her at my side, especially with her wearing my T-shirt and nothing else. My mind wanders a couple of times, my thoughts definitely not leaning toward food. They're about her smell, her taste, the softness of her skin, and all the wonders of her body that gave me an heir and make me a mindless fool. I'll be her fool if that's what she wants. I'll go down on my knees if she asks me to. I'll satisfy her every whim. She only has to flick her fingers.

After dinner, which isn't burned thanks to Kristi, we go to bed with her still wearing my T-shirt and me fully clothed. Like the night before, she falls asleep in my arms, and for another night, it's almost everything I've ever wanted.

. . .

WHEN DAYLIGHT BREAKS, she's still sleeping soundly. Reluctant to disturb her rest, I slip from the bed, shower, change, and leave her a note. I have to pick up fresh supplies at the gas station store.

I wind down the window during the drive, enjoying the hot wind in my hair. I haven't felt this free, this salvaged, since the day Kristi told me she'd wait for me. Everything that happened in between are layers of dirt, but I'm scrubbing them away one by one. Every day with her, I learn something new. I learned that I like to take care of her, and that cooking isn't so bad. I learned that hurting her hurts me more. I learned that putting a smile on her face makes me delirious with happiness. I learned that being away from Noah stings. I'm learning that being away from her, even for an hour, leaves me restless and unsettled. I push down on the gas, needing to get this chore done so I can get back to her.

At the store, I grab fresh fruit, vegetables, and meat. Colorful bunches of flowers are stacked in a bucket at the checkout. The red and orange bouquet is made up of zinnias and daisies. There are purple bunches with carnations and baby's breath wrapped in cellophane. The one that catches my eye is the simplest. Ten pink roses. The color is soft, the pink at the stem lighter than the tips of the petals. The flowers look feminine and delicate, yet strong with their long stems and sturdy thorns. That's the one I choose.

Out of habit, I ask for a packet of Marlboro at the counter. I pack the parcels in the trunk and tear the plastic off the packet of cigarettes. Flipping back the lid, I pause. On second thought, I chuck the packet in the trashcan. I haven't smoked since Dubai. I don't need to now. I definitely don't want to smoke in the air Noah has to breathe.

This time, when I take the road, the feeling of freedom is replaced with urgency, an almost maddening rush to get home.

~

Kristi

THE FIRST SENSATION that grips me when I wake up to Jake's empty side of the bed and a quiet house is panic. Wait. I did *not* just think of the space next to me as Jake's side. Jumping out of bed, I rush to the window. The car is gone. He wouldn't abandon me here. I know it, but it doesn't ease the worry. It's only when I find his note in the kitchen next to a freshly brewed pot of coffee and a muffin neatly laid out on a napkin that I relax.

After a bath, I pull on a pair of shorts and another one of his T-shirts. I tell myself they're loose and comfortable, but I like wearing his clothes. I like that it's big on me, reminding me of his maleness and strength. In a warped way, it makes me feel safe, just like his arms around me.

Jake has been doing all the cooking. Since I agreed to give him two weeks, I'm no longer his captive. It's about time I contribute to the household chores. I find all the ingredients I need to mix pancake batter. I peel and steam a few apples. While flipping the pancakes, I caramelize the apples and whip cream. I'm almost done when I hear the noise of a car. The engine shuts down, and a door slams. My palms turn sweaty. My hands start to shake. I haven't been this nervous and excited since Jake fed me vodka in the bar.

The backdoor opens and Jake walks in, carrying two shopping bags in one hand and a bunch of flowers in the other. He stops when he sees me. His gaze pauses on the T-shirt before slipping down to my bare legs. Heat simmers in his eyes as a slow smile curves his lips. It makes him look simultaneously sexy and dangerous. He turns his head toward the stove and inhales.

"Smells good."

I wipe my clammy hands on the T-shirt. "Pancakes and caramelized apples."

"You made pancakes," he says as he advances, holding my gaze while he drops the parcels on the table.

Suddenly uncertain about my choice of menu, I ask, "You like pancakes, don't you?"

He stops so close I have to crane my neck to look up at him. "I like that you made them."

He likes that I'm playing house. It wasn't my intention. I only wanted to pull my weight, but before I can say so, he puts the flowers in my hand.

"For you."

I stare at the pretty roses. "For me?" I inhale their sweet scent. "What for?"

"Just because."

I'm too touched to find words. No one has ever given me flowers.

Cupping my face, he lets his thumb play over the scar on my cheek. "I hope you like roses. Maybe you prefer carnations?"

"They're beautiful."

"Not as much as you."

Shying away from the compliment, I hastily turn to look for a vase. "I'll put them in water."

He catches my arm and turns me back to him. "You're the most beautiful woman I know, inside and out."

I pull on his hold, but he won't let up. "Jake, please."

"Say it."

"Stop it."

"Say it and I will."

"I can't."

"Then I'll say it again. You're beautiful. Gorgeous. Sexy. Hot as hell."

"I don't believe you."

He considers my answer for a moment before asking, "Why not?"

"There must be a lot of beautiful in fifty women."

He takes the roses from my hand and puts them aside. Gripping my arms, he forces me to meet his eyes. "It doesn't compare. Not even close."

That open wound, the one that refuses to close, flowers to full bloom. "I wondered if you were seeing someone else, if that was why you ignored me, every night while I waited *faithfully* alone in my bed."

His grip tightens. "I'd give my life to take it back."

"When you told me, you killed me fifty times over."

The line of his jaw is tense, his expression remorseful. "I know what I did to you."

"If I told you I wanted to know how it is with someone else, would you let me? Would you still want to be with me if I do it?"

His eyes flare. "What are we talking about here?"

"What do you think, Jake?"

His breaths come quicker. "You mean sex?"

"What else?"

Letting go of me, he drags a hand through his hair. "Fuck, Kristi."

"You did it. Several times. Fifty, to be exact."

He raises his palms. "Enough. I get it. You're right. I can't bear the thought of you with someone else. It makes me want to commit murder."

"It's not the jealousy," I whisper. "It's the betrayal. It's knowing you're not enough."

He turns away. Silence creeps between us. It grows until the air is thick, and the lump in my throat makes it difficult to swallow. I stare at his broad back, at the shaking of his shoulders, unable to reach out or bridge the distance.

When he finally faces me again, his eyes shimmer with wetness. My silence is more born from shock than not knowing where to move from here. I never imagined Jake capable of crying. I want to soothe him, but what I suffered won't let me. We're like chess pieces moved into a chess mate position. Only, nothing about our situation is black and white.

"Yes," he finally says, and from the way he forces out the word while trying to hold back his tears, this is hard for him. "Yes, I'd let you, and I'd still want to be with you."

"How can you make peace with something like that?"

He watches me levelly, pain burning with the tears in his eyes. "Because I love you enough."

His words are like lightning. They crash through the room in a deafening lash. We stare at each other in silence as the enormity of his confession sinks in. Jake loves me. Enough to take me back should I ever stray. He's asking me to love him the same, to strip every single part of my defenses and lay my heart and soul at his feet.

"What will it take for you to forgive me?" His deep voice trembles. "Tell me and I'll do it."

"I don't know," I cry on a whisper.

His expression grows despondent. "If it's a revenge fuck, so be it, but know it's going to happen with me right there. I'll be in the room, watching. I don't want any more lies between us. If that's what you need to get over this, I only ask that you tell me honestly and not do it behind my back."

What he's offering is huge. He's willing to put his possessiveness and jealousy aside to let me sleep with another man if it means he gets to keep me. Not that I'd ever consider anything so destructive. I only wanted him to imagine himself in my shoes, to understand what I'm going through.

I can only stare at him as he walks to the door and pauses in the frame. Turning back to me, he says, "You're enough."

I'm still standing in the same spot long after he's gone, his words echoing in my mind. The revelation that comes to me is sudden and clear. Nothing he can do will make the wrong go away. There's no action he can perform that will ease my pain or make me feel better. Only I can do it. It will take a leap of faith. If we're going to get over this, I will have to open myself up to hurt and give him my trust. I will have to accept the past, however painful, and learn to live with it.

$\sim$

Jake

LEANING with my palms on the windowsill in the lounge, I stare at nothing outside. What if we're beyond fixing? What if the damage I did is too vast, too absolute for us to glue the broken pieces of our lives together? I shake my head, willing the desolate thought away. I want Kristi too much, even more than when I married her. The problem is I didn't realize it in my drug-infused, semi-permanent state of drunkenness. I only realized it when I saw her kneeling in front of a pot of flowers. The accumulated emotions of a lifetime assaulted me at that moment, and I knew with crystal clarity I couldn't let her go. She's the woman of my dreams. She's the mother of my child. If I can't make it with her, I don't want to make it with anyone. It's her or no one. If she rejects me after two weeks, I'll have lost the war for my love. Whatever happens, I won't lose my soul again.

"Jake."

I tense at the way she says my name, full of need. I can't look at her for fear of breaking my own word. The dark part of my lust threatens to erupt, but I suppress it. I want to be gentle with her, not hurt her. My desire for her is driving me insane. It's a constant battle, but I'm willing to fight harder. The prize, if I win, will be worth it.

Her whisper is tremulous. "I need you."

"What do you need, ginger?"

"Take me to bed. Please."

Her request is a powerful temptation. My body breaks out in a sweat. My hands tremble where I clutch the windowsill. I hold on to the ledge as if it's an anchor that will prevent me from being flung into the storm of my waning willpower. It's a battle between body and mind, one my mind barely wins.

"Why?" I direct the question at her reflection in the glass.

"Make me forget."

My shoulders sag. I hate denying her. I hate the disappointment of her answer. Wrong reason. "No."

"Why?" she cries. "Don't you want me?"

I turn to face her. I want to look her in the eyes when I reply to that question. "More than anything."

"Then what's the problem?"

"Forgetting is like hiding."

Her pretty features contort with anger, but I know her well enough to know she only uses it to mask her pain. "You gave it easily enough to other women."

"They didn't ask."

"No, they got paid. Is that what I have to do? Demand money?"

The mere notion sends a bolt of rage through me. "You're not a whore."

"Why can't you give me what you gave them?"

Walking to her, I cup her face. "I value you too much."

I know why she's doing this, why she's demanding sex. She's hurting. She needs a distraction. I knocked her self-image down by making her feel she wasn't enough. She needs an affirmation that she's attractive and desirable, but sex will only be a quick fix for issues that go much deeper, and it will hurt us more than help us in the end.

Pulling her close, I wrap my arms around her. She doesn't resist. She accepts the hug I offer in substitution for sex. We're both aching, our hearts flayed open and our feelings exposed. I knew this holiday was going to hurt, but there's no alternative way of getting to the other side. We're on the top of a steep mountain, and there's no helicopter to offer a quick lift. If we want to get home, we don't have a choice but to battle it down the cliffs.

Rubbing her back, I press a kiss to the top of her head. "Let's start this day over."

"Okay," she says meekly with her face pressed to my chest.

That's the beauty of life. Until it ends, we always get another day, a new start. "What would you like to do today?"

A short silence follows before she replies. "Can we go back to the beach?"

"It's good weather for a picnic."

Pulling away, she wrinkles her nose. "Do you want breakfast, or have you lost your appetite?"

"I can always eat."

She detangles herself from my embrace, suddenly flustered. When she turns for the door, I take her hand.

"If you're embarrassed about propositioning me, you needn't be. I appreciate the offer."

Pulling her hand from mine, she escapes down the hallway. I give it a couple of minutes for her to get herself together before I follow her to the kitchen and take a seat at the table. She puts a plate stacked with pancakes and dripping with applesauce down in front of me. I wait until she's served herself before I cut into the food and take a big bite.

She watches me expectantly as I chew. "Do you like it?"

I hum my appreciation. "Best pancakes I've had."

"Not just mine. I mean in general."

"Sure. I have a sweet tooth."

"Ah." She nods as if she's just solved a daunting puzzle.

WHILE I UNPACK THE GROCERIES, she puts the flowers in water and cleans the kitchen. In just over an hour, we're ready to go. She's quiet during the drive, but I respect the silence. She's got lots to think about.

At the beach, she announces she wants to go for a walk. Alone. I don't like it, but I understand her need for space. To make sure she's safe, I follow at a distance. We walk for almost an hour before she cuts away from the shore to the dunes and sits down on the sand. With her arms around her legs, she stares out at the sea, but she's aware of my presence. She doesn't bat as much as an eyelash when I lower myself next to her, so close our thighs touch.

"I've been thinking," she says.

"What about?"

"Us."

My heart starts pumping in my chest. The thud echoes in my ears, but my voice betrays nothing of my apprehension. "Yeah?"

She shifts until she faces me squarely. "I made my decision."

CHAPTER 19

Kristi

*J*ake holds my eyes, uncertainty flickering in his. "You have?"

He looks more vulnerable than ever, almost as much as I feel with what I'm about to say. I thought about my answer with all the truth I could muster, looking beyond the pain. The part of me that hurts wants to punish Jake and make him suffer as much as me. The part that looks at what lies beyond the hurt knows my feelings for him aren't dead. When he wraps his arms around me, I ache with all my soul to embrace the comfort he offers. My heart begs me to fall into the gentleness of his love, to let him soothe and give me the happiness I crave. My mind begs me to not give up on what we can still have together, the family I so desperately want with him. To punish him by denying what my heart wants most would be repeating the mistake Jake made by staying away out of shame of his failure. I'd let my pride win over the possibilities of what we can be.

He takes my hand, brushing his thumb over my knuckles. "Just say it. Whatever you've decided, I'll deal with it."

Taking a deep breath, I lay down my destructive pride and take the scariest step of my life, opening myself up to unthinkable hurt by taking the biggest emotional risk I'll ever take. "I want to try again with you."

He searches my face. "You do?"

"I'm not saying I forgive you. It will take time. I'm not even sure I'm capable of that kind of forgiveness."

He presses my fingers to his mouth. His hand shakes slightly. "Doesn't matter. I'll live with it."

"It won't be easy."

He brushes his lips over the back of my hand. "I know."

The enormity of the consequences suddenly crashes down on me. "Where do we even begin?"

"By moving into the house in Heidelberg," he says with the certainty I need.

"I'm unemployed."

"I've got a job. Let me take care of you."

"Maybe we should put the house off until I can bring money into the household again."

"I'm putting a roof over our heads. I want you and Noah out of that trailer. End of discussion."

"It's not so bad."

"You deserve better." Cupping my nape, he drags a thumb over my jaw. "If you like, Gina can move in too."

"She's with Eddie now."

"The guy lives in a bachelor flat above the mechanic workshop. Hell, he can come too for all I care."

"Really?"

"The house is big enough, isn't it?"

"Yes, but what if we can no longer afford the rent?"

"Let me worry about that."

"That's not how a partnership works."

He gives me a gentle smile. "Fine. We'll make the decisions together." His gaze is imploring. "We have little over a week left just for ourselves. Let's enjoy the time instead of wasting it with worry. I want to make the most of every minute I have you alone."

Biting my lip, I smile up at his hopeful face. "I suppose I could do that."

The ache still lies shallow under the weight of my feelings, but a little more of the hope I felt earlier pushes through the surface.

Getting to his feet, he offers me his hand. "Shall we head back?"

Clouds are rolling in. A breeze has picked up. Shivering a little, I let him pull me up. With his arm around me, we walk along the shore to our picnic spot at the edge of the water. Our lunch is a little uncomfortable with the tension hanging in the air. The build-up to this moment has been too momentous for us to be casual about it.

There's nothing any longer preventing Jake from touching me as I want, but he still abstains. He lets our fingers brush when he hands me a sandwich and a glass of wine, and he wipes crumbs from the corner of my mouth. He doesn't take it further, which only makes me more nervous. By the time we pack up, every muscle in my body is tense. I wish he'd just kiss me or fuck me and get it over with so we can both relax.

Once everything is loaded into the car and we're about to head back, I can't take it any longer. I go on tiptoes and fold my arms around his neck. The length of my body presses against his, and his hardness tells me the truth. He wants this as much as I do, but when my lips cover his, he doesn't participate in the kiss. He doesn't open for me. His hands wander to my hips, his fingers digging into my flesh, but that's where it ends.

Pulling back, I stare at him. "You're not kissing me back."

"If I do, I'll lose it right here, and I made you a promise."

The mention of a bed flitters into my memory. "The sand is soft."

"You're a tease, know that?"

"For wanting you?"

"Damn." He presses a finger against my lips. "And hard to resist." Grabbing my hand, he leads me around the car and opens my door. "Get in."

My seductive powers must be out of practice more than I thought. Biting my lip, I get inside and try to not think about the only thing my one track-mind brain can seem to focus on.

His banter is easy on the way back, for my benefit, I guess, but it doesn't make me relax. My tension doesn't ease at home when he offloads the car in the setting sun and offers to run me a bath. Trying to ignore my growing apprehension, I sink into the warm water and soak the sticky saltiness from our day at the seaside from my skin. When the water cools, I wrap a towel around my body, go to my room for a change of clothes, and stop dead in the door.

Candlelight basks the room in a soft, golden glow. Some are on the nightstand and others on the windowsill. Pink rose petals are scattered over the bed and floor, making the scene look like a picture from a wedding night.

"Like it?" Jake asks behind me.

I give a little start and turn to stare up at his handsome face. I've had sex with him twice, but I feel like a novice as my body heats with nervous expectation. I fumble for words in my mind.

He takes a step closer, putting our bodies flush together. "Say something."

"This is…"

"Romantic?"

"I was going to say unexpected."

He raises a brow and waits for me to continue.

"You destroyed the roses." Ugh. What a stupid thing to say.

"I'll get you another bouquet."

"I didn't mean it like that. I mean it's, um, sweet."

"Sweet?" His lips tilt in one corner. "Not the ambience I was aiming for. My information must've been poorly verified."

"What information?"

"I had to read up about this stuff."

"About being romantic?"

"The articles claim a guy can't go wrong with flower petals and candles."

"No," I whisper, "you can't go wrong with that, but having you in the picture makes it a winner."

He watches me from hooded eyes. "Is that so?"

"Maybe," I look him up and down, "without the clothes will be even better."

Gripping the towel where I'm clutching it between my breasts, he gives a gentle pull. When I loosen my hold, it falls around my feet. His gaze travels down my body for a slow evaluation. "Definitely better."

Without him laying a finger on me, my breathing quickens, and my skin breaks out in goosebumps. We're caught in the charged stare for another moment before he hooks his arms under my legs, lifts me to his chest, and carries me to the bed. The covers and petals are cool underneath me as he places me carefully in the middle.

"I've been dreaming of this," he says as he strips, first the T-shirt and then his shorts.

Naked, he crawls over me, making every inch of my skin where our bodies touch come alive. He lowers his hips between my thighs and rests his weight on his elbows. "Sometimes, it feels I've been waiting a lifetime for this."

Being in love with Jake since I've been six years old is a lifetime. "I've loved you even before I could ride a bike or before I ate pizza for the first time."

A sensuous smile curves his lips. "You didn't manage to stay on until grade four, so I'm not sure that's a compliment." He chuckles when I swat his arm. "However, Pinky's Pizza opened just after I'd turned seven, so there's that."

Threading my hands through his hair, I pull at the wet strands. "You washed up?"

"While you were having your bath."

"There's only one bathroom."

"I used the outside tap."

I shiver for his sake. "That must've been cold."

"Believe me, I needed it."

"Not any longer."

Framing my face between his palms, he brings his lips down to mine for a kiss that starts out like rose petals but soon deepens with a slow burn. He takes his time to explore the shape of my mouth and the depth of my desire, his hands tracing aching paths over my body as he follows it up with kisses that end between my thighs.

When I come for the first time, it's in his mouth. I'm wet from my arousal and still shivering with aftershocks of pleasure when he grips his cock and positions it at my entrance. It's a moment I embrace with my eyes wide open, watching the ecstasy etched on his face as he lodges the tip inside and waits. Our kiss is languid but our sounds urgent as he slowly sinks deeper. I revel in every step of his possession, in each inch he pulls back to slide two inches deeper. The buildup of my pleasure is unhurried. Rocking a slow rhythm into me, he brings me to another peak, and another, until I beg for no more. Only then does he pull out to fit a condom and allow himself release.

Boneless, I snuggle closer as he turns us on our sides, keeping my back to his chest. He drags his fingers over my arm and brushes the hair from my face before pressing a tender kiss on my neck.

"Love you, Pretorius."

"Love you right back."

. . .

I FALL asleep in the sweetest bliss and wake up in an inferno of desire with Jake pressing into me from behind. We fuck wildly this time, with an animalistic savageness. Our frantic touching borders on the darkness we explored during our first two times, but Jake doesn't cross that line. He remains careful and gentle. Afterward, he strokes my hair as I doze off with my head on his chest.

Twice more during the night, he wakes me, taking me with opposing gentleness and urgency. By morning, I wake with an ache between my legs and every muscle in my body reminding me of the sexual marathon of the night, but a feeling of contentment leaves me peaceful for the first time in four years.

"Good morning," he whispers, kissing the shell of my ear.

"Mm."

He rolls over, bringing me on top of him. "Ride me."

I bite my lip. I'm about to say I'm too sore, but when he looks at me with such desire, his voice hoarse when he admits, "I want to watch you," I can't deny him.

I lift onto my knees and sink down on his hardness, loving the way in which he stretches me. His grip around my waist is firm, his eyes fixed on my face as he starts moving me to his rhythm. Despite the many orgasms from last night, my need builds again, a fire that's meant only for him, a fire that will never go out.

Abandoning my hips, he cups my breasts and squeezes gently. "Show me."

I lean forward to kiss his jaw, rubbing my nipples over his chest as he nips the tender skin of my neck. I grab his shoulders, digging my nails into his skin as he picks up his pace. We're both panting, our chase for release desperate when his phone vibrates on the nightstand.

"Ignore it," he grunts.

I want to say the call must be important, seeing it's early, but he rolls his hips to hit a sensitive spot. I cry out, everything else fading until my ringtone disturbs our moans.

I still. Just like that, passion and desire evaporate. Trepidation fills me. Something happened. I push on Jake's chest to get off him and crawl over the bed to grab my phone from the nightstand. I don't know the number that flashes on the screen. Swinging my legs from the bed, I press the phone to my ear and answer with a breathless greeting.

"Kristi?" a male voice says. "This is Dr. Santoni."

Oh, my God. "Is it Noah? My mom? Did something happen?"

In a flash, Jake is at my side, the warmth of his body a welcome support where it presses against mine.

"I need to speak with Jake. He's not answering his phone. Your mom said you're with him."

I clear my throat. Anguish makes my chest shrink. "He's right here. Hold on, I'm giving him the phone."

Jake frowns as he takes the phone and greets the doctor. He listens quietly, his face growing paler as he continues to listen without speaking. Finally, he says, "Thank you, Doctor. I appreciate the trouble."

He cuts the call and stares at the phone in his hand.

"Jake." I touch his shoulder. "What happened?"

He drags a hand over his face and stares through the window to where the first rays of the sun are breaking over the horizon. "It's my mother. She had a stroke."

I clasp a hand over my mouth. "I'm so sorry. Is she all right?"

His voice is distant, flat. "She didn't make it."

CHAPTER 20

Jake

The honeymoon is over. Kristi and I pack up in a hurry and tackle the long road home. Our marriage is in a delicate place, our new beginning still fragile, and already we're thrown back into the clutches of reality, as cruel as it can get.

I can't stop thinking about how my mother and I parted, about the last things we said to each other. Not wanting to lay the ugly burden on Kristi's shoulders, I keep this part of the grief to myself. Regret has no place at a funeral. Regret is personal. Selfish. A funeral is about the deceased, about paying respect as honestly as one can. I disapprove of what my mother had done to Kristi and Noah. I can't forgive her for that, not even in her grave. There was a time I was close to my mother, but it was long ago. The bits and pieces of what I can remember about those better times constitute my earliest memories, of having toast and tea at the kitchen table on Saturday mornings while she listened to a radio broadcast. Her attention wasn't focused on me, it was on the broadcast, the news followed by recipes she'd scribble down, but she was, for that short period of time, in the same room as me, and it made me feel warm.

As I became older, we drifted apart. A television replaced the radio in the kitchen, and cereal came into fashion. The final blow came when I told my mother Kristi was going to have my baby. After all her preaching and warnings, I'd turned into the son she'd hoped I'd never be. Despite the embarrassment and disappointment I caused, she didn't disown me like my father. She left the factory and all her assets to me. I'm not sure if it was because she reserved some of her maternal love for a son lost to the sins of the world or if she simply didn't have a choice. After all, I'm her only living relative. Who else could inherit the accumulated riches?

Kristi and Gina are amazing, supporting me with the funeral arrangements, the packing up of my mother's house, and the logistics of putting it on the market, while Eddie takes care of feeding us. I never knew he was such a good cook. I have no choice but to resign my job as restaurant manager before I've even started and hastily familiarize myself with a business I swore I'd never run.

The only highlight of this bleak and daunting time is my family and especially our reunion with Noah. Since Kristi is staying at home for the moment, we take him out of the crèche. That little man makes me look forward to coming home after a trying day at the factory. Kristi makes me never want to leave.

The trailer is bursting out of its seams with the four of us—Kristi, Noah, Gina, and me. The minute we're more or less back to normal, I organize the move into the new house on the outskirts of Heidelberg. There's my childhood house, but I don't want to build our memories on the foundation of the bitter disappointment and hurt I suffered there. Kristi and I move into the master bedroom, keeping Noah's crib in our room while we wait for the bed we ordered for him to be delivered, while Gina and Eddie move into the guest quarters.

We get along without being under each other's feet while carving a new routine for ourselves. Everything else is a challenge. Town gossip is in full swing. Everyone knows Kristi lost her job because she ran off with me, which is an undeserved stain on her reputation. She acts like it doesn't bother her, but I don't miss the way her shoulders tense when people whisper behind their hands every time she walks into a room. There are the Jans, Kallies, and Britneys who seem to take pleasure in the sensational scandal, while others like Nancy and Steve give the support that makes me glad we can call them friends. They offer rides and meals and help with our move, all the neighborly stuff I'll never take for granted again.

Those same people judging Kristi have gone from despising me to kissing my ass. The motivation? Money. I've gone from dropout to millionaire overnight. If my father could see me now, he'd cry big, ugly tears of vengeful joy. All he ever wanted was for me to be more like him. He's gotten his wish. I'm overseeing the factory he built up by stepping on others along the lengthy way to success. I'm even sitting in the same chair behind the same desk.

I can't lie.

I hate every minute of it.

~

Kristi

WITH THE FUNERAL BEHIND US, I drive to Luan's house in the brand-new car Jake bought for me and knock on his door. Unannounced. I doubt he'd let me see him if I called, and he needs to hear what I have to say.

He opens the door with a frown that turns into a scowl as he takes me in.

"Hey, Luan."

His voice is cold. "Kristi."

"May I come in?"

"Not a good idea."

"All right." I look around. The curtain in the lounge of the house opposite the street where Mozie lives lifts. "How are you?"

"Do you really want to know?"

"Don't be like this. Please."

"Don't be upset? What do you want me to be?"

"Reasonable."

"You ran off with the man who abandoned you, losing not only your job but also the future I offered. Is *that* reasonable?"

"May I at least have a chance to explain?"

"I'm not interested. Not any longer."

I sigh. "Look, I'm really sorry things didn't work out the way we planned. I know you don't believe me, but I truly didn't know what Jake's plans were. You can ask my mom."

"She knew about it?"

"Yes."

"Then this whole situation is even more screwed up than I thought."

"I came to tell you I'm sorry about us, but also that Jake and I are together." I swallow. "I didn't want you to hear it from someone else."

He crosses his arms and says with sarcasm, "Jake must be happy."

"I realized there's still something between us, and that's the other reason I'm here, to say thank you. If you hadn't broken up with me, I never would've given Jake another chance."

He snorts. "Now you believe he deserves one?"

"I deserve another chance at being happy. I just wanted you to know I wish you the same, and that I'm thankful for the job and help you've given me over the years."

"At least we didn't make our plans public."

"Yeah." Luan wouldn't have lived down the humiliation of being dumped for Jake. I offer a handshake. "Friends?"

He stares at my proffered hand. "I don't believe we can go back to friendship. That ship has sailed."

Dropping my arm, I nod. "I'm sorry you feel that way, but I respect your decision. Goodbye, Luan."

The door slams in my face.

~

Jake

WE HAVE an Indian summer in May. June and July bring a mild winter. My efforts are focused on my family and making our new home comfortable, but there's still much to do. We need beds, sofas, and desks. I didn't want the overly formal furniture from my parents' house to bring the bad memories attached to them into our happy environment. Those material items represent everything I loathe. I want to start with a clean slate.

We buy beds in Johannesburg and have them delivered. Kristi falls in love with a kitchen table and chairs in an antique store. The next day, I load them onto the back of my new truck and drive them home. I'll do anything for her, anything to make her happy.

The hunt for sofas drags into August as I get busier at the factory. I'm a young owner, some say too young, and I have high expectations to live up to. There's always more to learn and more to do. I'll be honest. There's no way I can handle it all by myself, which is why I'm pathetically grateful for the manager my late mother employed. The guy is motivated, but we keep on clashing heads about the vision I foresee for the future. I don't want to be my father. Money isn't everything. I want to give the employees better working conditions, better salaries and fringe benefits, but the CFO disagrees. I appoint a few advisors, people I can trust, and together we go through the painstaking process of mapping out new objectives, a process that isn't exempt from internal conflict.

After another day of playing catch-up with the manager, I go in search of Gina and find her packing the vacuum cleaner in the broom closet.

"What do you say we call it a day?"

She checks her watch. "Give me five. I have to lock the kitchen."

"I'll meet you downstairs."

I go to the parking and lean against the car, watching the other staff members knock off for the day. Gina follows a short while later, her bag in one hand and lunch box in the other. I take the lunch box and throw it in the backseat before getting her door.

"You know you don't have to work any longer," I say as I start the engine. "I have enough money to take care of all of us."

She snorts and crosses her arms. "What about the day you're no longer around?"

"Wishing me dead, already?"

Her forehead pleats into a frown. "You never know what's going to happen."

I know what's going through her head. She may have helped me to escape with Kristi, but she's still not sure of me, not one hundred percent. "I'm not going anywhere."

"Good." She looks me up and down. "It doesn't mean I don't appreciate what you've done, what you're doing, for us."

"Then what's the problem?"

"Just prove to me you're not an ostrich, because an ostrich can't change its feathers."

I smother a laugh. "I'm sure that's not how the saying goes."

"Did you get what I was trying to say?"

"Yeah."

"Then it doesn't matter how the saying goes."

I love this about Gina. As long as the message came through, she doesn't give a rat's ass about semantics. She's right. It's not about the words. It's about the intention.

"If you insist on working until retirement, we can find you something else at the factory."

"Like what?"

"What interests you?"

"I don't want people to say I'm getting special treatment."

"Do you really care about other people's opinions?"

She thinks for a while. "I've always thought it's fun being a tour operator."

"It's a brick factory, not a travel agency."

"Exactly my point. What we want and what we have to do to survive aren't always the same thing."

I ponder that for the rest of the way home. The sudden career I've been flung into isn't what I would've chosen for myself, but I'm not going to be ungrateful for a means of providing for my family.

When we pull up at home, Kristi is playing with Noah in the garden. They come up to greet us, Noah running straight into my outstretched arms. I turn him in a circle, inviting a breathless giggle.

Tickling his tummy, I ask, "What did you do today?"

"We baked cookies," Kristi says.

Holding Noah in one arm, I put the other around my wife's waist and pull her against my side to kiss her lips. I bury my nose in her neck and inhale deeply. "Mm. Smells delicious."

She flushes a little, her gaze going to her mom. "They're chocolate chip."

"I wasn't referring to the cookies."

Gina shakes her head and cuts over the lawn to the front door. "I'm making coffee if anyone wants. I'll be heading over to the shop later to help Eddie count stock. It'll keep us busy until late, so we'll just grab a pizza for dinner."

I press another kiss to Kristi's lips. "Seems I've got you all alone tonight."

"I heard that," Gina calls back. "TMI."

The minute the door shuts behind my mother-in-law, I kiss Kristi like I meant to, until her knees buckle and Noah starts to squirm. Reluctantly breaking our embrace, I take in her beautiful face. Her cheeks are flushed and her eyes shining. She looks happy, and that makes me ecstatic. Being a housewife agrees with Kristi. She loves baking with Noah and potting around in the garden. She's uncomplicated and easy to please, happy in her own skin.

"I love you," I say on a sudden bout of emotion.

Her gaze sharpens. "How was your day?"

"Good."

"Good?"

"Yes."

"Happy?"

"I'm always happy to come home to you."

"Are you happy at work?"

"We don't always have to like everything about a job. Said so yourself." I take Noah's hand. "What do you say we play a game of rugby before dinner?"

He swings around and runs as fast as his short legs can carry him to the crate at the back where we keep the balls and kites, stumbling in his haste. I shoot forward when he goes face down into the grass, but he picks himself up and carries on without as much as a chirp.

Chuckling, I turn to Kristi. "Do we have time for a quick game?"

"Dinner won't be ready before seven. Nancy is coming over in a bit to help me unpack. I still have a few boxes left."

I steal one last chaste kiss before going around the back of the house to where a little person smiles at me as if I'm his whole world.

~

Kristi

NANCY ARRIVES with a wedding catalogue and swatches of fabric samples under her arms just as my mom leaves.

She dumps everything on the kitchen table. "I can really do with your input. It's all so confusing. I can't decide between apricot or lilac."

"Coffee?"

"Wine." She opens the fridge, pulls out a bottle of white, and pours two glasses while I tackle one of the boxes filled with Elizabeth's crockery.

She hands me a glass before picking up one of the plates and studying the hand-painted border. "Doesn't it bother you to keep this stuff, knowing the woman hated you?"

"You shouldn't speak like that about the deceased. I'm sure she didn't hate me. It must've been hard for her to accept that Jake went for someone who wasn't worthy of her son in her opinion. Besides, I think it's important for Jake to keep some of the things he grew up with. He won't miss it now, but he may as he gets older."

"Jake doesn't strike me as the sentimental type."

"It depends." He kept a smooth, white stone I'd given him in exchange for a marble in second grade, and one of my hair elastics. I found them while I was packing up his room in his parents' house.

"How are things going between you?"

"Good. Great, actually. We're still finding our feet after the funeral and with Jake getting involved in the factory."

What I don't mention is the niggling worry at the back of my mind that Jake isn't happy in the job he's inherited. He could let the manager run the business without getting involved, but it's not a feasible option in the long run. As the owner, he needs to understand the business and not only be on top of all changes and situations, but also provide the necessary direction, something Elizabeth hadn't done and that's already showing in last year's losses, at least from what Jake told me.

Nancy waves a finger at me. "You better not get pregnant before my wedding. The maid of honor dress is already cut."

"We're not planning to, at least not for now. Noah has had a lot of adjustments to deal within a short space of time."

"Not to mention, the two of you need time together. Let's face it, you didn't have much between falling pregnant and Jake leaving town."

The ring of the doorbell cuts our conversation short. Strange. It's close to dinnertime. In a small town like ours, it's considered rude to pitch at this hour without calling first.

Nancy glances down the hallway. "Expecting anyone?"

"Could it be Steve?" I ask, leaving my glass on the table and making my way to the door.

"Nope," Nancy says, following in my footsteps. "Said he wouldn't swing by until six-thirty. Unless he's early?"

I open the door and pause. On the step stands a brunette with a baby in her arms. It's not the fact that the tiny bundle can't be more than a month old, or that, with her exotic looks, she's obviously not from here that renders me speechless, but the suitcase standing at her feet.

Glancing over her shoulder at the taxi idling in our driveway, I finally find my voice. "Can I help you?"

She brushes a strand of her perfectly styled bob behind her ear. Her words are soft-spoken, uncertain, as she says with a faint accent, "I was told Jake Basson lives here. Yes?"

I frown and look at Nancy, who's standing like a statue with her wine in her hand. "That's right. I'm Kristi, his wife."

The olive tone of her skin turns darker over her high cheekbones. "I'm Jasmine." She lifts the bundle in her arms toward me. "And this is his baby."

CHAPTER 21

Kristi

She may as well have punched the wind from my stomach. Gasping, I take a step back. Nancy stands frozen, her wide eyes fixed on the strikingly beautiful woman with the slanted eyes and slim frame. The cry of the baby pulls me back to my senses.

Placing a palm on my suddenly sweaty nape, I step aside. "You better come inside."

She picks up the suitcase, balancing the baby in one arm. "Can someone please get the taxi?"

Get the taxi? I blink. Nothing makes sense right now. "What?"

"I don't have enough money," she says, the flush on her face deepening.

"Oh." I look between the woman and her baby. *Jake's* baby. Ignoring the painful twist of my insides, I grapple for words. "Yes. Of course. I, um..."

Nancy's hand on my arm is a calm touch that grounds me, her sympathetic voice a beacon of reason when I can't think. "Shall I get Jake?"

"Yes." I swallow away the dryness of my mouth. "Please."

As she scurries away, the glass still in her hand, I look around the lounge that misses furniture. We haven't had time to buy sofas yet. *We haven't had time*, my mind screams as I battle to come to grips with what's happening.

"I…" I point toward the hallway door. "There are chairs in the kitchen."

Jasmine drops the suitcase. "He's hungry. I have to feed him."

Not knowing what to say, I hurry ahead to the kitchen. If I walk fast enough, can I run away from this? The crying stops abruptly. I turn. Jasmine has moved the elastic of her strapless dress down over one breast. The baby is latched on, making suckling noises.

I point at a chair by the table. "Please sit down."

She takes a seat, smiling down at her baby.

"Can I get you anything?"

She lifts her dark eyes to me. "Water, please. If it's not too much trouble."

"No, I mean, yes, of course not." I fill a glass with water. "Ice?"

"No, thank you."

I place the glass next to her on the table. My heart is beating so hard I'm sure she must be able to hear it. "I'm going to see where Jake is. I'll be right back."

Escaping to the lounge, I stop in the doorframe. Jake is leaning through the open window of the taxi, handing the driver a bill from his wallet. Nancy stands next to him with Noah's hand clasped in hers. Noah is holding his rugby ball under one arm. How vulnerable he looks. How easily his little heart can be broken if a father he barely got to know is ripped from his life.

When Jake turns, our gazes clash. For a moment, neither of us moves. His expression is veiled. The only sign of emotion is the stormy darkness in his eyes. A hundred words must be passing between us, but their meaning is lost in the air. I can't get enough of a grip on myself to make sense of anything.

"Come on, big man," Nancy says, shooting me a meaningful look. "Let's go push you on the swing." She ushers Noah toward the giant oak tree where Jake has fixed a swing to a branch.

Jake holds my eyes as the heels of his shoes fall hard on the concrete path. He walks with purpose, strong and sure, climbing the three steps that put us on eye level. How can he be so unruffled? Stopping short of me, he stares at me for another moment with that hard, unreadable look. I'm plastered to the spot, my brain strangely shutting down. It's only when he advances and I'm forced to make way for him that I move. Our shoulders bump when he passes, a small point of contact that feels like a violent eruption.

"Where is she?" he asks without looking back at me.

"In the kitchen."

He pauses in the hallway door. "Please give us a minute."

I nod, even if he can't see it. Tears blur my vision as he steps through the frame and vanishes from sight. I'm not sure why I'm crying, if it's the shock, hurt, or fear of the consequences, but squeezing my eyes shut doesn't turn off the valve. The tears keep on leaking through my closed eyelids. I can't let Noah see me like this.

Rushing outside, I escape to the backyard. Blindly, I walk to the garden table under the apricot tree and lean with my palms on the top. I'm gulping in air as if I've run a marathon, my whole body shaking. On the table stands Nancy's abandoned wine glass, a lipstick stain on the rim and condensation beading on the outside.

How out of place the glass seems here in the empty backyard.

Jake

THE WOMAN in the kitchen is cuddling a baby at her chest. The edges of a blanket fall open like wrapping paper around a gift. A blue blanket. A boy. He's the length of the forearm he rests on, his head so small it'll fit in my palm. His cheeks hollow as his mouth works greedily, sucking on his mother's breast, while his tiny fingers are folded around her forefinger. Looking away from her naked breast, I catch her tentative smile and gaze on me.

"Hello, Jake."

Her voice is husky and slightly familiar. It rings a bell in the back of my mind. I can't put my finger on it. I take a good look at her face—almond-shaped eyes, wide mouth, straight nose, sharp lines—but I can't place her.

"Do I know you?"

Her smile broadens, turning into a gesture that seems both sensual and forgiving. "Don't you recognize me?"

"I'm afraid not. Enlighten me."

"Dubai. The Princess Club."

I look harder. She's dressed in a strapless dress that falls to her ankles with a slit on the side. My gaze trails over her body for a clue. Slender, long legs. Toned arms. A little red birthmark on her shoulder. Fuck me. The wig. I didn't recognize her without the Cleopatra hair and make-up.

"I don't know your name."

"You don't remember?"

"I never asked."

Her tone is patient, musical. Too familiar. "I told you many times."

"Remind me."

"Jasmine."

"What are you doing here?"

She looks at the baby who's fallen asleep on her breast. "His name is Ulis. He's yours."

"He's not."

"You fucked me, didn't you?"

"I used a condom." Always. I learned my lesson the first time round with Kristi. Only a dumb bastard would make the same mistake twice.

"Condoms break."

"I think I would've noticed."

"You were wasted."

"Never enough to not know what I was doing." I never lose that much control. Not even when I was fucked or drunk.

She looks away.

I shove my hands in my pockets. "Where did you get my address?"

"Ahmed."

"Ahmed gave it to you?" I doubt that very much. I sent him my new address to ship my personal belongings, but that play-it-by-the-rules, over-cautious dandy would never have given my address to anyone without my permission. "I don't believe you."

"Fine. I stole it."

"You stole it? How?"

"From the database at the club."

The owner, Izak has never been good at putting passwords on his computers. "How did you get here?"

"I told Ahmed about the baby. He gave me the money for the flight ticket."

Bull-fucking-shit. Ahmed would've called me. Taking my phone from my pocket, I swipe the screen. "Fine. Let's call him to let him know you arrived safely."

"No," she cries, startling the baby. "Look, I didn't know what else to do. You know the club rules. I can't work there if I have a child. Your child."

"Stop bullshitting, Jasmine. You and I both know I never had a broken condom."

Biting her lip, she averts her eyes.

I take a step closer. "What aren't you telling me?"

Slowly, she meets my gaze again. "I punched holes in it."

318

"What?" The word is cold, measured.

"I took it out of your wallet when you came in and asked for me, while you were at the bar, and stuck a needle through it. Several times."

Rage threatens to smother me. "Why the fuck would you do that?"

She keeps on looking at me with her doe eyes and her lip caught between her teeth.

I'm seething. "You tried to catch me."

"I love you."

"No, you don't."

"I do! I always did. We have something, me and you, something no one else can give you."

She's referring to the strangling, to the rough way I got off, until that last day. For Christ sake, I couldn't even get it up. "You're wrong."

Tears shimmer in her eyes. "Don't say that."

"If you love me like you claim, you'd never have done something like that."

"Please, Jake. I have nowhere else to go."

I'm shaking inside. My future, the one I worked so hard for with Kristi, is falling apart at the seams. I feel it slip through my fingers as sure as regret for my past actions eats me alive.

"I don't know what else to do," she whimpers.

"Jake?"

I fling around at the sound of Kristi's voice. She's standing in the door with her arms folded over her stomach, wearing that pretty sundress and the telltale signs of crying.

Her gaze moves between Jasmine and me. "I don't want to interrupt, but I have to grab some things for Noah."

I inhale deeply and exhale through my nostrils. Helplessly caught in this shit storm, I stand immobile as she takes Noah's jungle cooler box from the cupboard. My heart jams into my ribs when she packs his water bottle and favorite spoon inside. Fuck. I know how much this must hurt for her. It's one thing to know about my past, but another to have a prostitute I fucked in her house. In her home. With a baby. Kristi drops an apple and a mini packet of wholegrain cereal into the cooler box. Is she leaving me? Is she taking Noah away from me? My breathing speeds up like a train about to run off the tracks.

"Wait here," I say to Jasmine as Kristi leaves the room.

I come to a dead stop in the corridor. She's taking a pillow and stack of linen from the closet at the end of the hall. When she carries the pile through the door on the opposite side, I charge after her into the spare bedroom. If she thinks she's sleeping here, she's got another thing coming.

Every breath I drag in hurts. "What are you doing?"

She barely glances at me from pulling a fitted sheet over the mattress. "Making the bed."

"I can see that. Why?"

She straightens. The pain in her eyes makes me want to howl. "For Jasmine, of course."

It takes a moment before the meaning sinks in. My relief is so great, my body sags. I have to brace a shoulder on the wall. "I was going to drive her to the hotel."

"With a newborn? With no money?"

"I would've paid for the room."

"That baby is fragile, Jake. Do you have any idea how susceptible their undeveloped immune systems are to viruses and germs? A breeze outside and he'll catch a cold, or worse, pneumonia."

"You're right." It floors me to say because Kristi's hurt is my destruction. "It's best if she sleeps over."

She grabs a flat sheet and shakes it out over the bed. "We can give her Noah's crib for the baby."

"Why can't the baby sleep with her in the bed?"

"Too many risks. He can slip under the pillows or covers and suffocate. She can roll onto him in her sleep."

"What about Noah?"

"He's sleeping at Nancy's place tonight." Straightening again, she rests her hands on her hips. Her voice cracks a little on the last word as she says, "It's better like this."

She's not going to Nancy's place, sleeping in the spare room, or banishing me to the couch, but it doesn't mean she'll be here tomorrow. Kristi will take care of everyone like the night Gina took care of us after my father hit Kristi with his belt. She'll cook dinner, make sure we're all fed, put Noah's needs first, and then she'll leave. After everything I've subjected her to and now this, how can I blame her? My insides twist. Pain punches into my gut as sure as a physical blow. I thought I'd saved us, but my mistakes may still destroy everything I care about.

"If you want to give Noah a kiss," she says quietly, "you better catch Nancy before she leaves."

Dismissed. She may not say it in so many words, but she doesn't want to look at my face. Pushing away from the wall, I grant her what she wants.

Seeing Noah in his car seat in the back of Nancy's car nearly kills me. I kiss him and give in to the urge to ruffle his hair.

"You sure it's not too much effort?" I ask.

"Not at all. You go and deal with whatever you have to."

"I appreciate this."

"I'm not his godmother for nothing."

When I get back to the house, Kristi is frying steaks. Ulis lies in Noah's old stroller in the kitchen, fast asleep.

"Where's Jasmine?"

"Taking a shower."

My heart swells, aches, and then breaks for the woman who'll take care of the baby of a woman I fucked several times, cooking for that very woman, so that said woman can have a shower.

If I could, I'd chop off my arms and legs to take this away, but all I can offer are my hands. "What can I do to help?"

Her voice is raw, like a chafed wound. "You can set the table."

We work in silence, pain drifting around us like toxic air, the innocent baby sleeping under a blue blanket a tangible reminder of the hurt that won't lift. When I place a third place setting, Kristi stops me.

"Jasmine is tired. I'll take a tray to her room."

She dishes up steak, egg, and French fries, and loads the plate with a pitcher of ice tea on the tray. I would've offered to carry it, but how will Kristi feel about me being alone with an ex-lover in her bedroom? How does my wife feel about anything right now?

Kristi comes back for the stroller, and then we're alone. We eat in silence, both of us as stiff and upright as cardboard cutouts. I don't taste the food I swallow. Eating is mechanical. The only reason I'm chomping down my dinner is not to insult Kristi's efforts. I load the dishwasher while she leaves a note for Gina and Eddie, for now only letting them know we have a guest so they don't get a fright running into her in the morning.

When we finally go to our bedroom, I'm both relieved and filled with the worst kind of anticipation. I can't wait to get the talk we need to have out of the way while simultaneously wanting to put it off for longer.

Kristi kicks off her shoes and sits down on the edge of the bed, her hands clasped between her knees. I click the door shut and lean against it.

Her gaze searches mine over the distance. Only a few strides separate us, but it feels like continents apart. Too far. I want to touch her, but I don't dare. I want to confess, but she deserves to speak first.

There's a tremor to her voice when she finally asks, "Who is she?"

This is going to hurt, but she also deserves the truth. "She used to work at The Princess Club in Dubai."

"Can the baby be yours?"

"I never fucked anyone without a condom except for you. I didn't lie about that."

"Is *she* lying then?"

"She says she stole the rubber from my wallet and pierced it with a needle."

"Why?" she cries on a gasp. "No, don't answer that. I know why."

"She meant to catch me."

"So, there *is* a good chance you're the father."

"I'm not taking anything at face value. I want a paternity test."

"And if you are?"

Walking over slowly, I stop in front of her. "That's a question for you to answer."

She frowns. "What do you mean?"

I swallow and push the words from my throat. "Would you leave me?" Correction. She'd keep the house. "Would you want me to leave?"

"Jake." Her hand reaches for mine, her fingertips playing over the limb that hangs like dead weight at my side. "I love you. I made a commitment when I made my choice. If the baby is yours, we'll handle it. Together. You can't be a father to Noah and not to another child of yours. It won't be easy. We'll have to be honest with both children when they get older, but you'll be a good daddy to him, just as you are to Noah, and no matter how hard it is or what history you have with Jasmine, she'll be the mother of your child just as I am. She'll need our support. I have no idea how we're going to work out the logistics or what Jasmine's plans are, if she wants to stay in town or go back to Dubai, but we'll just have to take it day by day and handle each hurdle at its comes. If we all work hard, we can make it."

Her words knock my heart sideways in my chest. They are pure, angelic. Her sacrifice redefines beauty, and she's the personification of it.

Falling down on my knees, I brace my hands on either side of her body on the bed. "I don't deserve you."

She cups my face. "You deserve love, just like everyone."

Not everyone. Some people act with selfish intentions. Not everyone acts in the other's best interest. She's giving me unconditional love. If I've ever doubted her love, she just gave me a declaration that, like her inner beauty, redefines the whole meaning of love. She's one in a million. The only one. Mine.

A possessive rush heats my gut. An obsessive need pulses in my lower region. I came too close to losing her. Again. Volatile emotions and a primitive compulsion to prove my claim on her fuse together into raw passion. Uncontrollable. My hands shake not only from the intensity of my desire but also from the force of controlling it as I flatten my palms on her knees.

Holding her gaze, I push up her dress while spreading her legs. She's wearing white cotton panties underneath the floral fabric. The innocence of that simple fabric is hotter than any silk or lace. Her breath catches on a hitch when I trace the seam of her pussy through the fabric. Contrary to the urgency clawing through me, I'm slow in hooking my fingers into the elastic and pulling those good girl panties down her thighs. I want to drag out the moment. I want to make it last. Though, it's hard when she's posed on the side of the bed like a naughty picture with her dress bunched up and her underwear pulled down. Gripping her ankles, I bend her knees and place her feet on the edge of the mattress. She falls back, catching her weight on her arms. With her panties constraining her legs, she can't spread, but the simple idea of having her bound, even in this minute way, is more erotic than the widest split.

The first time I tasted her made me dizzy. I've never eaten another woman's pussy. Somehow, it feels more personal than fucking. Like kissing. Throwing her thighs over my shoulder, I lower my head to that spot that gives me goosebumps. The first lick is a tease, more for me than her. She cries out when I nip the soft flesh where her ass meets her thigh. I kiss my way back up to her clit, clamping the nub between my teeth while flicking it with my tongue. She hollows her back, trying to pull away from the touch, but a soft bite has her surrender quickly. Her pants drive me crazy. The sounds tell me she's close, and I'm not going to spare her.

Gathering her arousal, I push two fingers inside. Her channel tightens when I start to pump, but I'm beyond giving her a reprieve. The only objective is making her come as quickly and as hard as possible, which she does when I curl my fingers and find her G-spot. Her back hits the mattress as her arms collapse. My cock is so thick it aches. It's not the explorative lust from those first couple of times, but a dark desire that has grown into a dangerous need as my fixation with her has fully matured.

I French kiss her folds like an inexperienced, overeager teenager, all tongue and teeth, and suck hard on her clit one last time before abandoning my favorite foreplay for something far more darker, far more intense. I'm not suppressing it any longer. I embrace it. This is who we are, who we've always been.

We were made for each other.

"Get rid of the dress," I order in a hoarse voice as I peel out of my clothes.

She opens her eyes to stare at me with that hazy light she gets with the afterglow of her orgasm, her gaze dropping south when I reach for my pants.

"Now, Kristi."

I'm naked before she's pushed the straps of her dress over her arms. Too late. The darkness that drives my need outweighs my patience. I crawl over her, trapping her hands between our bodies. For a glorious moment, she's pinned under me, the weight of my body keeping her where I want her, on her back with her bent legs turned to the side. I lift just enough to grab the root of my cock and position the head at her slit. A small forward roll of my hips, and the tip parts her pussy lips. Her head tips back, all efforts of undressing forgotten. She moans as I rock my hips until I've worked the head inside. I finish the task of pulling her dress over her head, and she arches her back obediently to make my work easier. Lying naked in front of me except for those panties around her thighs, she's the most beautiful sight of ruined innocence. Perfect beauty. My pure angel.

I brush a thumb over her bottom lip, smearing her lipstick in an erotic way, a way that makes me twitch to plunge deeper inside her. "Do you want it rough?"

Her inner walls contract, gripping me harder. Her eyes widen a fraction.

"Do you, ginger?"

"Yes," she whispers.

A whisper isn't going to do it. I need certainty. "Beg."

"Please. Please, Jake."

My inner demon roars. Lust makes my ears ring. Sliding my palms over the smooth skin of her stomach, I drag them up over her ribs. I fasten one on her soft breast, and the other around her slender neck. Tightening my grip marginally, I push her into the mattress and drive home. The scream she almost utters as I take all of her in one go is cut short by the squeeze of my fingers. I'm not cutting off her airflow, but the simple act of controlling her sounds sends a rush straight to my groin. I pin her down as I start to move, hammering a rhythm into her that is going to leave bruises. Her lips part in soundless cries, her eyes rolling back in her head. I can fuck her like this all night.

I seek her lips, my kiss gentle, both a reward for being a good girl and encouragement for what's still to come. When she's soaked up the kiss, I give it to her harder, because this is what my girl needs. I sink deep and pull back only to sink deeper with strokes that makes my body break out into a sweat. She grabs my upper arms, her nails biting into my skin as our groins slap together with a relentless pace. With her legs bent to the side, the angle of penetration is intense, and it only takes another few minutes before her grip on my cock tightens and her inner walls flutter. I let her ride out the orgasm, keeping her body pinned in the same position before pulling out and flipping her over. Boneless, she lies flat on her stomach. I spear through her folds from behind, letting the curve of her ass cushion my balls. She hums her appreciation when my hands fold around her neck once more, holding her in place with a tight grip as I fuck her senseless.

There's one more thing that's due, a part of her she promised me. Pulling out, I grab her hips and pull her onto her knees so that her ass is up in the air. For this, I need her wide open. I wiggle her panties, which have fallen to her knees, over her calves and free her feet. Then I gather her arousal and lubricate her asshole.

"Jake," she cries on a little shocked whisper, straining her neck to look back at me.

"You promised, remember?"

I want all of her. I need everything.

"I don't know—"

"I'll go slow. We'll stop if you can't handle it."

She whimpers when I sink a finger into her tight hole. I give her time to adjust before pumping slowly. Her tremulous exhale tells me she feels a bit of pain. Using my free hand, I play with her pussy, building her need again. She moans when I part her folds and dip two fingers inside. I work her up until her inner walls start tightening around my fingers and then add another one to her ass.

Seeing her body accepting me, both her holes stretched and filled with my fingers, is almost too much. I push down the lust that demands I pummel her ass right away. I focus on her. If she's going to take my cock in her virgin hole, she'll have to get used to three fingers first. I gather more of her slickness and ease a third into her tightness. She squirms, pushing her ass back as I start to finger fuck her in all earnest. Sweat runs over my temple. My body is a furnace, about to burst into flames.

"Still good?" I somehow manage to get out. My voice is guttural, more animal than man.

"Yes," she whispers, looking at me with her cheek pressed flat to the mattress.

"You'd maybe want to stuff some of the sheets into your

327

mouth." This is private. I don't care to broadcast what we're doing to Jasmine or anyone else for that matter.

Her fingers clench on the comforter, bunching it in her fists. "I'm ready."

It's all I need. I pull my fingers from her body. Spitting in my palm, I lubricate the head of my cock and place it at her dark hole, so prettily stretched and ready for my cock. Even if I ease in gently, her body already tries to expel me.

I rub a hand over her back, up her spine. "Relax."

She takes a few deep breaths, and I sink deeper. Fuck, she's tight. Her virgin channel grips me so hard I'm already close to coming. Pinching my eyes closed, I shut out the alluring visual. I focus on her breathing, going deeper every time she exhales. It takes a long time, but I don't want to hurt her. When I'm lodged inside up to my balls, she doesn't ask me to stop. She's still on her knees, offering her ass. We're both shuddering, me from holding back and her from the strain of taking all of me. I start moving slowly. She pushes her fist against her mouth, her eyes scrunched up.

"Must I stop, ginger?"

She utters a muffled, "No."

Placing one hand on her nape and the other on her hip, I keep her upper body down while holding up her ass for support. When I really start moving, her legs are going to cave.

"Ready?"

She opens her eyes and gives a small nod.

I lengthen my strokes until I glide in an out at an easy pace. Her asshole clenches every time I leave it empty before my cock head stretches the ring of muscles again to take my length. She does beautifully, grinding back against me and biting on her knuckles to stifle her moans. When she's fully with me, her body adapted to the new kind of invasion and her need as high as mine, I go for the last stretch with all I've got. I'm beating into her, letting her tightness squeeze me closer to climax. It builds like an electric storm, lashing over my body and erupting in hot jets of cum that fill up her ass. My cry is savage, barely contained. Jerking out, I lean over her to grab a rubber from the nightstand. While I tear open the foil with my teeth, I unabashedly watch my cum dribble from her ass. The sight is erotic and satisfactory. It spells only one thing. Mine. I quickly roll on the condom and sink my still hard cock into her soaked pussy. I can go another round. I can go several with her. She never fails to excite me.

I work her hard, not that I need to. She's close. I can hear it in the high pitch of her moans. Our pants fill the room. I hammer into her while my cum leaks from her asshole. That sight alone triggers the start of another ejaculation. Fuck. I'm going to come dry. I flatten the heel of my palm on her clit and rub in circles. Her lower body contracts. Her channel closes like a vice on my cock. My climax hits just as she comes with a soundless cry, her whole body pulling tight. As predicted, my cock doesn't spit up cum. I grimace as my dick spasms painfully, futilely trying to produce some relief. I'll need another few minutes before I have juice again. Maybe I can keep my cock inside her, make us both come again.

The sound of her whimper is her surrender. I may be holding her down, but she's the one controlling the game. When she gives a meek shake of her head and says, "No more," I stop moving. Catching my weight on my arms, I lean over her body to kiss the corner of her mouth. I slowly kiss my way down her spine, worshipping every vertebra.

Emptying myself inside her body fills me with primal satisfaction. I don't only want my cum in her ass, I also want it in her pussy. I've always wanted her like this. Getting her pregnant was always a given. It happened sooner than either of us planned, but it would've happened regardless. The knowledge is a deep-seated certainty, a truth that comes to the surface when time has finally eroded all pretenses and masks.

Folding my arms around her waist, I bring us to our sides. I brush her hair aside and kiss her neck. "I'll always love you, Kristi, no matter what happens now or in the future."

THE MINUTE the sun is up, I make coffee and take a cup to Kristi, who's still asleep. I kiss her lips. "Wake up, ginger."

She moans and stretches, then winces.

I brush a thumb over her scar. "Sore?"

"A little." She smiles and yawns. "In a good way."

"Tired?"

I hate to disturb her sleep, especially since we've all had a rough night with Ulis's non-stop fussing, but Nancy will be here shortly to drop off Noah before going to work. I hate to think this is how nights were with Noah, and that I wasn't here to help Kristi. It was wrong. It'll feel even wronger if I get to be there for Jasmine.

Kristi rests her back against the headboard and takes the cup from me. "Mm. Coffee in bed. Thank you."

"You're welcome."

"What are you going to do?"

"Speak to Ahmed. According to Jasmine, he gave her the money for the flight. Then I'm booking a paternity test."

"I better speak to my mom before she runs into Jasmine and hears it from her."

"What will you tell her?"

"The truth."

"All of it?" I don't even want to think what my mother-in-law's opinion of me will be.

"What happened is in the past. You made mistakes. Who doesn't? I'm not ashamed of you, Jake."

There are mistakes, and then there are *mistakes*. Right now, my gratitude is too big to contradict my sweet, generous wife.

WHILE KRISTI IS HAVING A SHOWER, I call Ahmed.

"Hello, old friend," he says. "To what do I owe the pleasure?"

"Jasmine is here."

"Jasmine?"

"The girl from The Princess who dressed up as Cleopatra."

"I know who she is. My response wasn't a question. It was an expression of surprise."

"She has a kid."

"I know."

"She says he's mine."

"Is he?"

"If he is, she tricked me. She said you gave her the money for the flight."

"Why would I do that?"

"My question exactly."

"That's quite a mess you find yourself in."

"You have no idea."

"How's your lady taking it?"

"I don't deserve her."

"No, you don't."

"Do you have any idea how Jasmine got her hands on enough money for a one-way ticket to South Africa?" I know how much the club pays. There's no way she earned enough for airfare.

"You know I don't hang out at the club. I'll have to ask around."

"I'll appreciate that. How's the business?"

"Growing."

"Then you're not missing me."

"Didn't even notice you were gone."

I chuckle. "Take care, asshole."

The line goes dead.

Kristi steps out of the bathroom, a towel draped around her body. "What did he say?"

"He doesn't know where she got the money from, but he's going to ask around."

"Does it really matter how she got here?"

"I have a funny feeling about this, and I don't like it." If she stole the money, she may be in some serious shit, and the minute she stepped foot into this house, she dragged my family into it. Walking to Kristi, I cup her face and steal a quick kiss. "Don't worry about it. We're going to sort it out. I promise."

Her smile is faint as she goes on tiptoes and kisses me back. My lips still tingle with her touch when the doorbell rings.

"Damn," she says, hopping on one foot while fitting the other into a pair of shorts. "That'll be Nancy."

"I'll get it."

Noah jumps into my arms when I open the door. Laughing, I kiss the top of his head. "Hey, bud. Did you have a good time?"

"Super," Nancy says. "Don't tell Kristi, but we watched Spiderman and ate French fries until past his bedtime. Definitely don't tell her I let him have ketchup with those fries."

Yeah. I grin. Kristi insists on a healthy diet for Noah, and according to her, there's too much sugar in ketchup.

Peering over my shoulder, Nancy clears her throat. "I better get going. Tell Kristi I say hi."

When I look back, Jasmine is standing in the door.

I can't stop my voice from sounding a little hostile. "Where's Ulis?"

"Sleeping." She pulls her hair into a ponytail. "Finally."

Lowering Noah to the floor, I take his hand and start making my way to the kitchen. "I'll make breakfast."

"He's cute," she says, staring at Noah while sawing her bottom lip between her teeth.

"Yeah, he is."

I don't offer more. Not for now.

GINA DOESN'T FREAK out when I explain about Jasmine. Of course, I don't go into the gritty details of fifty times. Kristi told her and Eddie what's going on, but I still feel they should hear it from me. I book a paternity test in Johannesburg. It's quicker to get an appointment and more discreet. Jasmine resists until I give her an ultimatum. It's the test, or I'm sending her back on the next flight.

Ahmed calls back a short time later.

"Did you find out anything?" I ask.

"Jasmine stole the money from the club when she came in for her last paycheque. Izak's been looking for her."

I go cold. Theft isn't something Izak will simply let slide. "How the hell did she manage that?"

"The profits from the gambling room was lying on Izak's desk when she came in for her cheque. He said he answered the phone, got a drink, and after she'd left he noticed the money was gone."

"Idiot."

"He never thought one of the girls would try something so stupid."

Dragging a hand over my unshaven jaw, I sigh. "I'll deal with it."

"Let me know if Izak gives you any trouble."

"I appreciate that."

I hang up and dial the club. It takes me a long time to strike a deal with Izak, offering to pay him back double the money Jasmine has stolen. A transfer later, and the deal is sealed.

I take it up with Jasmine in the car on the way to take the test. "Are you fucking crazy?"

She fiddles with the strap of the safety belt. "I was desperate."

"Izak could've had you killed. Damn you, Jasmine. He could've hurt my family."

"I didn't mean anyone harm."

"Next time, think your actions through and don't put your hands on things that aren't yours."

"What now?" She trembles visibly. "Did you tell him I'm here?"

"I paid your debt. If it happens again, you're on your own. Got it?"

"Yes, Jake."

"Good." She puts her hand on my leg, but I move it away.

"There's one thing you've got to understand. Whatever the outcome of that test, I'm with Kristi. That's the way it's going to stay."

"I made you feel good once. I can do it again."

"I was a different man back then, and I don't like that man."

She lifts her chin. "Yes? What made you change?"

"A letter." A woman.

She snorts. "Men don't change. Do you think I don't know you? Knowing people is my business. You'll grow tired of your small town. You need more. You love a challenge. You'll get bored with your white picket fence life. When that day comes, you'll grab the first carrot someone dangles in front of your nose. You'll leave her, just like before."

CHAPTER 22

Kristi

*W*hen the test results become available online the next day, Jake and I sit on the bed in our room, our hands clasped together as we wait for his laptop to boot up. Too nervous for conversation, I stare at the screen with a hollowness spreading in my stomach. I meant it when I said we'd deal with whatever comes our way, but it will be a bumpy road. Jake used the opportunity of taking the paternity test to also run tests for STDs. Thankfully, both his and Jasmine's came back clean.

It takes forever for the document to load. Black letters blur on the white background. My eyes skim over figures, words, and numbers, but the only thing I can focus on is the word that reads negative.

I glance at Jake, my breath trapped in my lungs. "Is it…?"

"Negative." He closes his eyes and presses a kiss to my hand. "He's not mine."

I let out the breath I was holding on a long exhale. The multiple complications I envisioned are no longer a factor.

His voice is thick. "I'm sorry I put you through this."

"She lied."

Dragging a hand over the stubble on his jaw, he puts the laptop aside. "I'm going to speak to her."

"Would you like a moment?"

He holds a hand out at me. "I'd like you to come with me."

We find Jasmine in the kitchen, breastfeeding Ulis. Her face pales when we sit down at the table. Something tells me she already knows the answer.

"It's not me," Jake says, his face grim. "You made up the story about the condom, didn't you?"

She stares at him levelly but says nothing.

"Why did you lie, Jasmine?"

"I love you."

I cringe inwardly at the declaration.

"Do you know who the father is?" Jake asks.

She shakes her head.

"Where is home?"

Her voice is small. "Turkey."

"Do you have family there?"

A nod.

"I'm buying you a ticket to Turkey then. You're leaving on the next flight."

"Jake," she exclaims. "Please."

"I'll give you enough money to set you up and take care of your son. The rest is up to you."

"Just like that? You pay me as you used to, and I become nothing but a part of your past?"

"You are a part of my past," he says regretfully. "I hope one day you'll find your own love."

"Mark my words," she says through thin lips, turning to me,

"one day, *you'll* be the one who's nothing but a part of his past. That's how men like him work."

Fists clenched, Jake pushes to his feet. "Pack your bag. We're leaving as soon as I have a booking confirmed."

Jake

THE ATMOSPHERE in the house is considerably lighter when I get back from dropping Jasmine and Ulis at the airport. The change in ambience isn't due to their departure, but to the certainty of knowing Kristi is there even before I walk through the door, knowing she'd always be there. She proved her commitment when a tough hurdle was dumped in our path. There's no doubt in my heart she'd stay by my side through thick and thin. She's the kind of woman any man can only dream of wearing his ring. I'm glad Noah happened. I love that kid more than life. It's more than that, though. When Kristi told me she wanted an abortion, a part of me was disappointed, but I understood the implications of having a baby so young. I respected her wishes and the future she had in front of her. I would've never denied her that decision, but I'm thankful my father did. I can't, don't want to, imagine a life without Noah, but even without him, as sure as I'm breathing, I would've always found a way back to Kristi. She was mine from the start. She'll always be.

Following the smell of chocolate, I find her and Noah baking brownies in the kitchen. She smiles up at me brightly. Relieved. I take her in my arms and kiss her until my head swims and there's a pluck at the leg of my pants.

I look down. Noah's little hand is fisted in the fabric, his eyes hopeful as he glances toward the backdoor.

"Want to play a game before dinner?" He loves when I let him score a try. "Just let me make a quick phone call."

I walk out on the front porch and dial Ahmed to give him an update, telling him about the deal I made with Izak, the test results, and that Jasmine is on her way to her family.

He listens in silence until I've finished before he says, "My father has been asking about you."

That comes as a surprise. Yousef never asks about anyone or anything without good reason. "Why?"

"He wanted to know how you're doing."

"I'm sure my welfare isn't on the top of his list of concerns."

"You know he's always liked you."

I pace to the rail, looking out over the front lawn that needs mowing. "Can't fathom why."

"I told him you took over your father's business and turned your life around. He's impressed."

"Hardly an accomplishment."

"Here's the thing." There's a short pause. "He wants to give you another chance."

I still. Sinking down in the chair beside me, I ponder the statement and all the ways the answer could change our lives. "How?"

"He's willing to let you come back and make the money you lost."

"Come back to the company or to Dubai?"

"He can't be your mentor if you're in … what's that place called again?"

"Rensburg."

"I know this is a tough decision, but I owed it to you to run it past you."

A chance at redemption, to clear not only my conscience but also my reputation and name. "How long?"

"However long it will take to finish your degree and get the franchise business off the ground. It could be a good few years. I'd say six, at least."

"Can't say he's not being fair."

"More than generous."

I'm quiet for a moment, trying to process the information.

"I would've said you could bring your family," Ahmed continues, "but you know how it is."

Long hours. Constant traveling. I'd never be home.

"She'll probably be happier there with her family," he says, "than here all alone."

A mountain of strain shifts onto my shoulders. "By when does he want an answer?"

"Next month."

I rub a hand over my jaw. "I'll get back to him."

"Get back to who?" a soft voice asks behind me as I cut the call.

I turn in my seat. Kristi stands in the door, a glass of iced tea in her hand.

I pat my leg. "Come here."

Her slow steps and the way her brows pinch together tell me she heard more of the conversation than she should've. When she stops in front of me, I take the tea and leave it on the table before pulling her into my lap.

"That was Ahmed," I say, nuzzling her neck.

"I gathered."

"His father wants to give me another chance."

Her body stiffens. "What does that mean?"

"However many years are necessary to complete my studies and give the franchise project another go. I can't see it be less than six years. Seven maybe."

"It's a chance to make amends," she concludes accurately.

"Yes."

"Will you have to go back to Dubai?"

"Yes."

"You say it like there's a but."

"Dubai will just be a base. The project requires traveling to many countries."

"How much traveling?"

I rub her back. "A lot."

"Define a lot."

"I won't be home for more than a couple of days a month."

"That's…" She catches her lip between her teeth. "Quite a lot."

"I'm not leaving you and Noah." I kiss her shoulder. "Not for months on end."

Despite the declaration, the tension doesn't leave her body. She climbs from my lap, strain evident in every clenched muscle as she walks back to the door and pauses in the frame. "You say it like your decision is made."

"It is."

"You said we'd make the decisions together."

"I'm not leaving you. End of discussion."

She turns back to face me. "Running the factory isn't what you want."

I don't like where this is going. "It pays the bills."

"Do you think I don't know how unhappy you are?"

"I love you, Kristi. You and Noah are my life."

"A life consists of more than just family."

"Nothing is more important than family."

"Working is part of your life, a very big part of it."

"You don't work, and I don't see it getting in the way of your happiness."

"We're not the same, Jake. We've never been. I'm happy to be at home. The factory will slowly but surely kill you. It's already taking its toll."

"We're doing fine," I grit out.

"Do you wake up ecstatic every morning when you think about going to your late father's office?"

"I wake up ecstatic thinking about you."

"Exactly my point."

"I'm staying for you. For us. Isn't that enough?"

She hugs herself. "I'm afraid it won't be. Not in the long run."

"I can't believe we're having this conversation." It's too much like a flashback into the past. This same issue once tore us apart. I'm not allowing that again. "What's the problem with wanting to stay?"

"The problem is you can have more, and I'm holding you back. Don't you see? We're back to square one, right where we started when you first left."

"What do you want me to do?" I exclaim, rubbing my breastbone to relieve the knot that ties painfully in my chest.

"Tell me honestly. Does manufacturing bricks make you happy?"

I grit my teeth because I can't lie to her.

"There," she says, tears glistening in her eyes. "There's your answer."

I'm on my feet and in her face. The thought of letting her go again makes me lose my grip on sanity. "Is this what you call making decisions together?"

"I'm calling your bluff, Jake, because your decision isn't made, not really. I want you to think about it carefully. I want you to be brave enough to face the truth, and then tell me again."

Kristi

MY HEART IS BREAKING. I can't eat or sleep. I can't think about anything but the decision Jake faces. I don't want him to go, but if there's one thing I've learned, it's the truth has a way of catching up with lies. Jake can lie to himself and me for only so long. He's bought us a house and given us a home, one with walls and a roof and a proper bathroom. No more trailer. No more showering in the ablution building. He's working hard at building us a new life, but the price is killing him a little every day. Every morning, more of the spark in his eyes is lost, his lust for life burning out right in front of me. What happened in Dubai left a terrible mark on him, terrible enough for him to have gone onto a self-destructive path of drugs, alcohol, and women. Terrible enough for giving up on his child and me. How can he not want a chance at redemption? How can I deny him such an opportunity?

My thoughts heavy, I leave Noah with Jake after he comes home from the office and drive to town to meet Nancy at the bakery. She sits at a table in the coffee corner when I arrive.

"Am I glad you're here." She pushes a catalogue over the table. "There are so many to choose from."

Draping my jacket over the chair back, I sit down and pull the catalogue closer. There are photos of cakes in themes varying from flowers to fruit.

"The berry one is beautiful," I offer. "Stylish. It'll go with your lilac color scheme."

She scrunches up her nose. "Mm. Too much cream, I think."

"Do you want something simpler?"

She makes a face. "I just don't know." She scoots closer and flips the pages. "The one with the gold and black is quite dramatic. Maybe a little too over the top? The square one with the sunflowers has a simple beauty to it. Very classy. It's what my mom would've told me to choose."

"But?"

"The flowers won't go with our theme."

She pauses on the page with the most traditional of all the cakes, a three-tier creation with white marzipan icing and sugar roses weaving around the layers. It comes complete with the happy groom and bride on the top. The plastic couple stands proudly on the summit as if they've earned their place by climbing their way from the bottom. Will Jake and I ever reach such a happy place, a place of certainty and belonging? The way forward was never going to be easy. If I'm honest, I knew it would one day come back to a choice.

"Hey." Nancy touches my arm. "Are you all right?"

"Yes." I smile for her benefit. "Of course."

"Don't lie. I know that look on your face."

"What look?"

"What did Jake do? If he hurt you, I swear I'll—"

"He didn't do anything. Not directly, at least."

She leans back and crosses her arms. "It's that woman. Jasmine, right? Is she still giving you trouble? You don't have to put up with it. You don't owe her anything. Neither does Jake. He's done more than enough for her."

"It's not that."

"What then?"

"We're here to choose your wedding cake. It's not the moment."

"Like hell." She kicks my foot. "I'm not looking at another cake until you tell me why you look like your life is falling apart."

I sigh. "Nothing is falling apart. Jake has a difficult decision to make, that's all."

"What decision?"

I stare at my hands. "He had a job proposition."

"What proposition?"

"To finish what he started in Dubai."

I'm not looking away from my hands, but I can feel her stare on me.

"You mean going back there?"

"Yes."

"God, Kristi. For how long?"

"However long it takes to finish his degree and get the business off the ground. Six years minimum."

"Wait." She grabs my hand. "You're not saying you're moving to Dubai, are you?"

"Not a feasible option." I finally dare to meet her gaze. "Jake will be traveling for most of the time."

Her perceptive gaze narrows. "How much time?"

"He won't be home for more than a couple of days a month."

"Shit." She drops my hand and falls back in her chair. "Shit, shit. This is terrible."

"It depends on how you look at it."

"You'll be separated. There's no other way of looking at it."

"It will be great for Jake's career, not to mention his self-image."

"How can you even think of his self-image when your heart is at stake?"

"He still hates himself for failing and disappointing his mentor. It's a golden opportunity to fix his mistakes, a chance not many people get in life."

She places a hand on her forehead. "Is he going?"

"He says he doesn't want to leave us, but I think it will be a mistake. I told him to think about his career and what this opportunity means to him, and to give me an answer after he's been honest with himself."

"No, no, no." She grips my hand again. "No, Kristi. You're not going to make the same mistake as the first time. You're not going to give him your blessing to go."

"I don't have a choice."

"How can you not have a choice?" she exclaims. "After everything he put you through? He fucking owes you."

"He hates working at the factory. You've seen how he's changed during the last few weeks. He's tense all the time. He's living more in his head than with us, and he barely sleeps at night."

"It sounds as if you already know what his decision is going to be."

"I have no doubt he'd stay if I ask, but I love him too much to make such a selfish demand."

"Selfish? What's selfish about wanting to keep your family together?"

"I love him, Nancy. The thing about love is that the other person's happiness becomes more important than your own. Jake's happiness means everything to me. I'm not going to take this chance away from him." Softly, I add, "Wouldn't you have done the same for Steve?"

Her lips part, no doubt on a protest, but then she clamps them shut. She stares at her lap for a moment before asking, "Are you going to wait for him?"

I swallow twice before I can speak. "Not this time. This time, I'm going to live my life."

"So, you're setting him free."

"I suppose you can put it like that."

"Oh, Kristi." She drapes an arm around my shoulder. "I'm so sorry."

If we don't stop talking about this, I'm going to cry. I inhale deeply and give her my brightest smile. "I'll deal with it when the day comes, but today is not that day. Today, you're choosing your wedding cake." I push the catalogue toward her. "Indecisive time is over. Pick one."

"It seems cruel now, after what you told me. We should do this another day."

"Nonsense. The wedding is in a month. You're not putting off your decision any longer."

She bites her lip, scanning over the pages again.

"Know what I think?" I turn the page to the three-tier cake with all the toppings. "I think you should go for this one."

Her eyes light up. "Really?" She gives me a dorkish smile. "It's kind of old-fashioned, isn't it?"

"It's the one you want. You shouldn't worry about other people's opinions."

"How did you guess?"

"You looked at this one longer than the others, and you had this dreamy expression on your face. Plus, this was the cake you described whenever we played getting married since the age of ten."

Her smile turns into a grin. "You're right. I really like the traditional cake."

"Done. That means you don't even have to pick a flavor."

"Fruitcake it is," she says. "Is it weird that I hate fruitcake?"

"This is your day. If you want a cake just for the looks of it, that's your business."

"Right." She elbows me. "That wedding game was my favorite." Her gaze softens. "You, on the other hand, only wanted to play house."

Closing the catalogue, I drop it in her bag that hangs over the back of the chair. "I guess I grew up."

~

Kristi

THE NEXT FEW days are the most stressful of my life. The wait is even worse than for the paternity test results. In a far corner of my mind, I have already accepted Jake's answer, but he still has to deal the blow, and then will come the hardest part. Until then, I try to live in the present. When Jake doesn't work, we play with Noah in the garden and have long, happy dinners with Gina and Eddie. They're the kind of dinners I always admired in magazine pictures, the kind where a long table is set with pretty crockery and colorful dishes, and a big family with cheerful faces clink their glasses together. This is my dream. My ambition. It doesn't matter that it's not a fancy job or a clever degree, or that most of it sprouts from my dreams of living in a proper house with a big family. It's a real desire, a valid one, and it's mine.

Noah is in his own bedroom, adjoining to ours, sleeping in his new bed. Our new sofas arrive. Day after day, our house is turning into more of a home. The only shadow over our happiness is the decision Jake has to make. We take Noah to a speech therapist in Johannesburg. On her recommendation, we spend hours reading to him and singing songs. Jake is nothing if not dedicated, making sure he gets home early enough to read Noah's bedtime story and tuck him in.

When we're not having leisurely family lunches on weekends,

we spend time with Nancy and Steve or hang out at all the regular town events. We go to the weekend picnics at the lake, the charity ball, and the annual lamb on the spit. No matter how much fun these get-togethers are, I often drift into a moment of quiet observation. The more we're integrating as a family, the deeper my roots grow in this town, and while I'm making a place here for myself, I can't help but wonder if Jake is already cutting himself lose, preparing for the inevitable.

October is upon us. The effortless glide from one season into another only adds as a reminder of the swift passing of time when all I want to do is catch the hours in my fist and keep my fingers tightly wrapped around the minutes. We can't push back the decision for much longer.

As the hourglass empties, our need for each other grows. We're like starving animals, Jake becoming more dominant and me blossoming at the way he orders me to my knees and defiles my body, only to pick me up off the floor and treat me like a princess afterward. The way he increasingly lavishes attention on me is both amazing and disconcerting. He's already making up for lost time. In a subtle way, he's preparing me for his decision. Much sooner than I want, I'm going to lose him, this time forever.

The knowledge makes me desperate, desperate enough to push Jake to his limits. We're having drinks at the Bluebell Bar with Nancy and Steve and a few of Jake's colleagues from the factory on Saturday evening. Gina and Eddie are staying in, keeping an eye on Noah. It's spring, but the weather is still cold. I snuggle closer to Jake on the bench we share, absorbing his heat.

I'm doing my best to focus on a conversation with Nancy while Jake is listening to something Steve is saying over the noise of the music. It doesn't stop Jake's hands from wandering under the table to cup my jean-clad sex. My reaction is instantaneous. Heat gathers in my core. A little pressure from his forefinger on my clit sets me ablaze. I open my knees a bit, giving him better access. He drags his thumb along the seam of my jeans, up and down my slit.

I'm squirming in my seat, my body humming with need, which invites a knowing smile from him.

Upping the game, I rest a hand on the hard muscles of his thigh. All that physical power and strength flexing underneath my palm as his body tenses sends a rush of desire to my head. Mimicking his action, I slip my hand between his legs and cup the hardness under his zipper. He stills. His chest doesn't rise with a single breath as I trace the outline of his length and the shape of his head with a fingertip. He visibly shudders before catching my hand, but instead of moving it away, he presses it down harder, letting me feel my effect on him. I'm dizzy from his touch and hot from teasing him. When he scrapes a nail over the seam of my jeans, causing a jagged, erotic vibration as his nail catches on every stitch, a soft moan tumbles over my lips before I can stop it. Thankfully, the sound is lost in the noise.

He turns his head to study me. The heat in his eyes makes me falter.

Without breaking our stare, he says, "I'm afraid we have to go. We have to be up early for Noah."

There are protests from around the table, but Jake ignores everyone as he drapes his jacket over his arm and uses it to hide his erection. At the entrance, behind the protection of a pillar, he helps me into my coat before getting the door. A cold wind hits me when we exit into the parking lot and make our way to his truck. While he fishes his keys from the front pocket of his jeans, I wrap my arms around him from behind and lean my cheek against his broad back. He smells so good. My hands travel down, finding his erection, and I moan when he rolls his hips and presses harder against my palms.

"Kristi." His breathing is labored, his voice hoarse. "Let me get you home."

Home is nice. He'd take me to bed and make love to me gently so we don't disturb Noah or wake my mom and Eddie, but tonight I don't want nice. I want Roxy's Bar. I want to go back to that moment in the past. I want dirty. I want everything I can get before the clock strikes an hour I don't have to think about with two beers buzzing in my veins and my hands full of his hardness. I squeeze. He hisses. I stroke him through his jeans while grinding my groin against his ass. In a flash, he spins us around so my back is pressed against the truck.

"Not here," he growls. "Behave."

I bat my eyelashes. "What's wrong with here?"

"It's cold."

"Are you scared?"

In the bright light shining from the lamppost, the russet color of his eyes shimmers like a winter sunset. "Are you trying to provoke me into fucking you on the hood?" He shakes his head in a slow gesture of disapproval. "By now you should know all you have to do is ask."

My breath catches at the dare. Jake won't deny me, but he prefers straightforward honesty, so I give it to him. "Please."

His reaction is a simple, unquestionable command. "Pull down your pants."

My hands tremble with anticipation as I undo the button and pull down the zipper. Cold air hits me between the legs when I shove my jeans and underwear down to my thighs.

His gaze caresses me where I'm naked. "Perfect."

Taking a wide stance in front of me, he lifts his eyes to mine while dipping the tip of his finger between my folds.

"Soaking," he declares. "Is this for me?"

I nod and moan as he rubs two fingers over my clit. I arch my hips forward, trying to take more, but he withdraws his touch.

"Naughty girl. You're not getting off this easily. I'm going to take you hard. Are you sure you're up for it?"

All I can do is nod again, my eyes drifting closed as he palms my bare ass.

He grips my chin, forcing me to look at him. "Say it, ginger."

There's a new wildness in his eyes, a feral light, but I need this too badly to let him go easy on me. "Yes. Please."

He unfastens his jeans and frees his cock with impatient yanking, stroking it almost violently. Oh, shit. I'm so out of my depth. Thinking I could tease Jake and handle the consequences was a joke. His movements are urgent as he shoves his jeans and briefs over his hips. They're no less rough when he flips me around and bends me over the hood of the truck. One hand folds around my nape, holding me down, while the other fastens on my hip. With my jeans around my legs, I can't move, not even widen my stance. I barely have time to register the head of his cock at my entrance before he slams in, taking me in one go. I choke back a cry. I can only hope no one heard, because we're exposed in the well-lit parking lot. The fear of being caught adds to my arousal, slicking his entry when he pulls back and takes me with another harsh stroke. He pivots his hips faster, not giving me time to adjust, but this is how I want it. I cry out again when he hits a barrier. It hurts in a good way, in a way I don't want to end.

My pants form white puffs in the misty air. "More."

He picks up the pace, driving into me with a force that shifts my upper body over the hood. It feels as if he's going to break me, but I'll crumble if he stops. When he changes the angle of his penetration, driving up with sharp stabs of his hips, I go on tiptoes to escape the bite of pain that mixes with the pleasure. A sharp slap falls on my ass. It stings as much as it rings out in the quiet lot. I still momentarily, my body tensing, and then I'm over-conscious of the sound of our bodies slapping together with a rhythm that reverberates harshly. It makes me turn even wetter. I strain my neck to look back at Jake. Seeing him punching his hips with sharp jabs against my ass is almost enough to send me over the edge. I'm so close. I try to wiggle a hand between the hood and my body to touch my clit.

Jake abandons my hip to grab my arm, pushing my wrist onto my lower back. "Naughty girl. You come when I decide."

"Jake."

"Shh." He bends over to plant a kiss in my neck. "It'll be worth the wait. I promise."

I'm used to Jake's stamina, but he usually lets me come at least once to take off the edge. This is torture. I ache with need, trying to rub my clit against the cold metal, but with every thrust he drives into my core, my back hollows, pushing my ass out. With his big hands around my neck and wrist, I'm as good as tied up. I'm helpless, forced to take what he's willing to give. Male grunts punctuate every stroke as he hammers the breath out of my lungs. Pleasure starts building in the spot he repeatedly rubs with the big head of his cock, but it coils through my lower body too slowly.

"Can't," I utter on a moan that turns into a muffled scream as he impales me with a deep thrust that feels as if it's splitting my body in two.

"You love this," he says, the edge in his voice telling me he's close.

He's right. I do. I love everything about this. I love the hard. I love the dirty. I love him.

"Are you ready to come?"

"Yes, please." I can't take another minute. My insides feel raw.

"Don't make a sound."

I brace myself, barely swallowing the sounds as he goes for the final stretch. It's savage, raw, and more desperate than any of the times we've been together. I watch him with my cheek pressed to the hood, drinking in the beautiful beast who is my husband. He releases my wrist and sucks his thumb into his mouth, all the while holding my gaze. That point of connection, the intangible that flows between our eyes, is as much a warning as reassurance. He wants me to know exactly what he's going to do. Even if I expect it, I still gasp as his thumb penetrates my dark entrance, stretching the tight ring of muscle. The pressure climbs, adding to my fullness, adding to my need.

Another cryptic command. "Stay."

He lets go of my nape and slides a hand around my body to roll my clit between his fingers. I bite down on my lip not to scream.

His voice is even. He's in control. "Condom?"

"No." I don't want anything between us. I want him to come inside me.

He bends over me, his lips teasing my ear. "Ass or pussy?"

"Pussy."

"You sure?"

"Yes."

I'm not going to fall pregnant. I've just finished my period. I need this. I want this. Like a parting gift.

He steps up the game, filling both my holes with a severity that has me on the verge of passing out. His fingers on my clit never falter. When warm jets fill me inside, I come with such a force, my vision goes hazy. He grinds and thrusts, milking every last aftershock from my body until I sag over the hood like a ragdoll. Depleted. Boneless. Ecstatic.

A rustle of clothes followed by the pull of a zipper sound at my back. He pulls up my jeans and turns me around so he can fasten them. The minute we're covered, his lips slant over mine in a kiss that's both lazy and greedy. He parts my lips with his tongue, coaxing me to meet the urgency of his demand.

I'm not sure if I'm trembling from the cold or the hard way in which he took me, but I don't care when he folds his strong arms around me and pulls me to his chest. I lean against him, soaking in the comfort of his warmth, letting him pet and stroke me, and tell me how good I've been. Lifting me in his arms, he unlocks the door with one hand and lowers me into the passenger seat before fitting my safety belt. He takes off his jacket and drapes it over me, tugging it around my body. Then he gets behind the wheel, starts the engine, and turns up the heat. Thankful for his consideration, I shift as close to him as the safety belt allows and rest my head on his strong shoulder, glad there isn't a console putting space between us. He puts an arm around me, effortlessly steering the automatic with one hand. I nuzzle his neck, inhaling his scent and submitting it to memory.

He twists a lock of hair around his finger, the gentle pull soothing and lulling me to a deeply relaxed state. He plays with my hair until we pull into our driveway. I'm warm and safe, close to drifting off.

He kisses the top of my head. "We're home."

"Mm. Already?" I want to stay like this forever.

"Let's have dinner tomorrow night, just the two of us."

Just like that, I'm wide awake. My heart turns over. Dinner, just the two of us. That's code for *we need to talk*. I freeze as if an absence of movement would preserve our beautiful equilibrium. I close my eyes against the sting of tears.

It's happening. Tomorrow. Finally. Too soon.

CHAPTER 23

Jake

The best restaurant in Rensburg is the steakhouse, which is why I drive Kristi to Johannesburg for dinner. When she walks ahead of me to our table at a popular seafood restaurant, I swallow. She's wearing a pink dress that hugs her breasts and hips. With her curvy body and that innocent dress, she turns all the heads in the room, male and female. The waiter serves water before leaving us to go over the menu. From the way Kristi bites her lip as she studies the options, I know she's nervous. It took me long enough to tell her what she's been waiting to hear, but I didn't want to break the news to her before I had all the details sorted out.

She drums her nails on the table as she continues to frown at the menu as if it's written in Latin. Reaching over the table, I cup her hand. I touch her not only because I can't resist, but also because she needs the comfort. At the contact, her fingers still.

"Shall I order for us?" I ask.

"Yes, please."

To look at the menu, I have to tear my gaze away from the woman who has given me everything—love, a child, acceptance, absolution, and most of all freedom. When the waiter returns, I order a bottle of their best wine and a seafood platter for two.

Alone again, I turn my attention to our surroundings. We're in a private booth in the corner with a magnificent view over Sandton. She stares through the window at the city lights, her pretty face illuminated by the single candle on our table. The strawberry color of her hair, dried straight tonight, glows around her face. With the natural blush of her cheeks and the dusting of freckles on her pale skin, she's all peaches and cream, all the sugar I'll ever need. Her attention is slipping again, probably dwelling on the reason we're here. I'm not going to make her wait longer.

Reaching inside my jacket pocket, I take out the velvet box and slide it over the table toward her. The action catches her attention.

Eyes widening, she glances from the box to me. "What's this?"

"Open it."

"I'm not sure—"

"I said open it."

The stern order works. She reaches for the box slowly, then gives me another uncertain glance before flipping back the lid. The rose gold ring sits on a bed of black velvet, the diamond catching the light and throwing it back over the table. She gasps softly. When she looks back at me, her brows pinch together and her mouth puckers around a soundless question.

"I never got you a ring." I brush my fingers over her knuckles. "Couldn't afford it the first time round."

Her voice drifts down like a feather, a frightened whisper. "I don't understand. What does this mean?"

"What do you think?"

She wets her lips, weighing her answer as if there isn't only one option. "You're staying?"

I tighten my grip on her fingers. "I'm not leaving you again. Ever."

"But… But what about the offer? It's the chance of a lifetime."

"We're a family. Families stay together."

"This is your dream."

"My dream is right here."

"Here?"

"In Rensburg."

"You always said you wanted to leave."

"I was running away. I have no more reason to run, only reasons to stay. You gave me something I never had. You gave me a family. No job or selfish absolution is more important."

She pulls her hand away. "I'm scared, Jake. I'm scared this isn't you. I'm scared you'll wake up one day, realize what a mistake you've made, and run away."

"I know you're scared. I know I'm to blame for all that insecurity, but I'm not going anywhere."

"You hate the factory. I don't want you to be unhappy."

"You were right about everything you said about that job, which is why I've put the business in the market."

"You're selling it?"

"I already have a buyer. My lawyer is drawing up the contract as we speak. It's just a question of formalities."

"What about Yousef? I know you, Jake. I know how much you hate yourself for disappointing him."

"When the sale of the factories goes through, I'm reimbursing him for his losses, with interest. There will be enough money left to start a new business. I've put a lot of thought into it, and I think the restaurant franchise idea is feasible, but instead of starting it abroad, I want to start it here, in Rensburg."

"You think that can work?"

"The figures add up." I also have a damn good gut feel, and I've learned to listen more to my heart. It seems my pretty little wife gave me back my mojo. "I'm not the only one with faith in the concept. Yousef has committed to invest in the project. When it pulls off, he'll make quite a bit of money, more than he would've made if I went back to Dubai to work for him."

"And he'll be compensated," she muses.

"Exactly. A win-win for everyone. You see, ginger, where there's a will, there's always a way. I choose you. Every time."

Her blue eyes mist over as she stares at me, her feelings written all over her beautiful face, but instead of making her vulnerable, it makes her strong. Her love and compassion are what attracted me to her from the start. She taught me how to be strong in turn, how to lay down my demons and fight for love. She showed me all of herself and taught me who I am.

It's sadly belated, but I get up, move to her side of the table, and go down on one knee. I want to give her what I didn't the first time, what she deserves. "Kristi Pretorius, will you wear my ring?"

Her smile is tremulous. "Forever."

"Then give me your hand."

She holds out her left hand that's been naked for far too long. Taking the ring from its encasing, I slip it onto her finger, where it belongs. It sparkles with a pretty shine that says *mine*.

"I love you, Jake Basson."

I take in her face, imprinting every detail. "I know."

I know everything that matters.

I know she loves to play house, and I love to come home to her.

I know she loves roses, and I like pancakes.

CHAPTER 24

Kristi

$\mathcal{I}$'m putting the last touches on the Christmas tree in what used to be the lounge of Jake's childhood home. With a quick glance around, I check the tables to make sure everything is ready. They're set with crisp, white tablecloths, silver cutlery, and crystal glasses. Heavy roses, their petals wide-open and their perfume ripe, tumble from cut-glass vases on the side tables. Classical music plays softly in the background. Soon, the room will be alive with the sounds of conversations, the clinking of glasses, and the voices of children. It's like one, long, never-ending, happy lunch, only better than the ones in magazine pictures because these ones are real.

My mom bustles through the door with Eddie on her heels. Her face is glowing with enthusiasm, her steps no-nonsense, even in her new heels. As our events manager, she's in her element, taking care of anything from group bookings to assisting with travel arrangements for our guest performers. Eddie is our procurement manager, and he's doing a damn fine job. His tight fist serves a purpose after all. We have zero wastage. Our chef has received several awards for his innovative African fusion cooking. Pared with the best of South African wines and top-performing artists, we're booked up months in advance. Jake has already published a recipe book and has a television show lined up in the new year. He sold several franchises around the country, and this month his first international one in Italy.

"Why are you still on your feet?" my mom chides when she spots me by the tree.

"Get down." Eddie rushes over and waves me down from the chair I'm balancing on. "Get down from there now."

He takes my hand and helps me down while I suppress the urge to sigh.

Eddie clicks his tongue. "Silly woman." He grabs the star from my hand. Taking my place on the chair, he attaches the silver star to the top. "There." He rests his hands on his hips, looking happy with himself. "Like that?"

It catches the light from the chandelier, shining happiness into the room.

"Perfect," I whisper.

My mom takes my shoulders and steers me to the futon against the wall. "You should sit down. Rest while you can."

A can pops.

"Here." Eddie hands me a ginger ale. "Drink it all."

"Yes, sir," I mumble.

"Did I hear my name?"

I look toward the sound of the voice and pause. Jake stands just outside the door with Noah on his shoulders. He's wearing a white shirt and black slacks with the kind of casual ease that doesn't make the tailored fit look formal. His chest is broad under the shirt, the hollow in his throat an enticing dip that makes me recall the sculptured hardness of his body under my fingertips. The tickle of his happy trail on my tongue is a memory that makes me shiver.

Ducking low so he doesn't bump Noah's head on the frame, he prowls to me. "You shouldn't be on your feet."

"That's what I've been trying to tell her," my mom says.

"You should listen to your mother," Eddie adds. "Mothers know best."

When Jake smiles, it's meant only for me. It's one of those private gestures that heats me from the inside out, that makes me feel like I'm the last woman left in his world.

He lowers Noah and places a palm on my big belly. The act is tender, possessive. "How's my princess doing?"

"Kicking." I move his hand to the right spot. "There. Can you feel it?"

Grinning, he addresses my stomach. "Go easy on your mama, Bella. She still has to carry you for three months."

"You done playing?" I ask Noah. "Let's go wash up. It's almost time for lunch."

"Actually," Jake says, "Noah and I came to tell you something."

"Yes?" I look between the two men in my life. "I'm all ears."

"Tell her, Noah," Jake says, crossing his arms in a proud father stance.

"Dadda," Noah says.

My heart misses two whole beats. I'm so overcome with emotion I hardly focus on the word. Breathless, I place a hand over my heart. "Say that again."

He looks up at Jake. "Dadda."

Jake beams. "I think he said daddy."

"Yes." I don't even try to fight my tears. It's futile with my hormones. "I believe he did."

My mom crouches down and hugs Noah. "This is the best Christmas present ever."

"We need to celebrate," Eddie says. "I'll get champagne and more ginger ale."

Jake glances at the can in my hand. "Still nauseous?"

"Just a little."

He kisses me tenderly as Eddie goes off in search of drinks and my mom takes Noah to the bathroom to wash up.

"Now do as everyone's been telling you," he says, pulling me down next to him on the futon, "and sit down."

I roll my eyes. "Yes, sir."

He lifts my feet onto his lap. "That's what I like to hear."

"I'll say it more often then."

He takes off first one then the other shoe, somehow making the simple act seem sensual, as if he's undressing me for his private pleasure.

"I love you, you know," he says as he starts massaging my feet.

"Yes." I smile. "I know."

He looks around the room. "We've come a long way."

I don't have to follow his gaze to know what he sees, because he's looking at the past.

He abandons my feet to cup my jaw, his thumb brushing over the scar on my cheek. "I'm glad it worked out."

"It was a good idea."

Knowing a house of this proportion in Rensburg wouldn't sell, Jake turned it into a boutique hotel and restaurant. Like his father, he provides many of Rensburg's inhabitants with a means of living, but he achieved so much more. When the restaurant became popular, Jake put Rensburg on the map like the brick factory never could. Tourism is booming. The influx of visitors resulted in the revival of many shops, as well as a new arts and crafts market.

"Turning something morbid into something happy is always a good idea," he says, "but that wasn't what I was referring to."

I know exactly what he was referring to, but I say, "Tell me," just to hear it again.

"I'm glad I caught you a second time." He trails his fingertips over the swell of my belly. "I might have to do it again."

That makes me ecstatically happy. I've always wanted a big family, and Jake is a great daddy. "I'd like a few practice runs before you catch me again. I don't want to miss the trip to Rome."

"As many as you like." He kisses my lips. "And I'm not going anywhere without you."

I nestle in the crook of his arm, enjoying the warm protection of his body and the beauty of his choices.

Some choices take you back to square one. Jake's choice brought us full circle.

~ THE END ~

Midnight Days

The Loan Shark Duet

(Dark Mafia Romance)

Dubious

Consent

Box Set

The Age Between Us Duet

(Older Woman Younger Man Romance)

Old Enough

Young Enough

Box Set

Standalone Novels

(Enemies-to-Lovers Dark Romance)

Darker Than Love

(Second Chance Romance)

Catch Me Twice

Krinar World Novels

(Futuristic Romance)

The Krinar Experiment

The Krinar's Informant

7 Forbidden Arts Series

(Fated Mates Paranormal Romance)

Pyromancist (Fire)

Aeromancist, The Beginning (Prequel)

Aeromancist (Air)

Hydromancist (Water)

Geomancist (Earth)

Necromancist (Spirit)

ABOUT THE AUTHOR

Charmaine Pauls was born in Bloemfontein, South Africa. She obtained a degree in Communication at the University of Potchefstroom and followed a diverse career path in journalism, public relations, advertising, communication, and brand marketing. Her writing has always been an integral part of her professions.

When she moved to Chile with her French husband, she started writing full-time. She has been publishing novels and short stories since 2011. Charmaine currently lives in Montpellier, France with her family. Their household is a lively mix of Afrikaans, English, French, and Spanish.

Join Charmaine's mailing list
https://charmainepauls.com/subscribe/

Join Charmaine's readers' group on Facebook
http://bit.ly/CPaulsFBGroup

Read more about Charmaine's novels and short stories on
https://charmainepauls.com

Connect with Charmaine

Facebook

http://bit.ly/Charmaine-Pauls-Facebook

Amazon
http://bit.ly/Charmaine-Pauls-Amazon

Goodreads
http://bit.ly/Charmaine-Pauls-Goodreads

Twitter
https://twitter.com/CharmainePauls

Instagram
https://instagram.com/charmainepaulsbooks

BookBub
http://bit.ly/CPaulsBB

TikTok
https://www.tiktok.com/@charmainepauls

80080235R00210